A Twisted Love Story

Also by Samantha Downing

My Lovely Wife
He Started It
For Your Own Good

Novellas

Sleeping Dogs Lie

A Twisted Love Story

SAMANTHA DOWNING

MICHAEL JOSEPH

PENGUIN MICHAEL JOSEPH

UK | USA | Canada | Ireland | Australia
India | New Zealand | South Africa

Penguin Michael Joseph is part of the Penguin Random House group of companies
whose addresses can be found at global.penguinrandomhouse.com

First published in the United States of America by Berkley,
an imprint of Penguin Random House LLC 2023
First published in Great Britain by Penguin Michael Joseph 2023

001

Set in 13.5/16pt Garamond MT Std
Typeset by Jouve (UK), Milton Keynes
Printed and bound in Great Britain by Clays Ltd, Elcograf S.p.A.

The authorized representative in the EEA is Penguin Random House Ireland,
Morrison Chambers, 32 Nassau Street, Dublin D02 YH68

A CIP catalogue record for this book is available from the British Library

HARDBACK ISBN: 978–0–241–44690–4
TRADE PAPERBACK ISBN: 978–0–241–44691–1

www.greenpenguin.co.uk

For the man who inspired this book
You're damn right I wrote about you

I

Wes can't get the song out of his head. It plays on a loop, over and over, until he finds himself humming it out loud. So addictive, and he doesn't have a clue who sings it.

The music doesn't stop until an alert pops up on his phone. His famous-quotes app sends daily words of wisdom.

> Love is a serious mental disease.
> – Plato

Wes swipes it away. Love is the last thing on his mind, especially today. The only thing that matters is time.

His calendar is a wall of meetings, back-to-back-to-back, without a single break. Wes has to leave the office by five thirty, drive home, shower, shave, dress, and get back out of the house by six forty-five. Assuming he wants to be on time for his date. Which he does.

They met at a bar called Liver. Her name is Annabeth, and she had been very specific about that.

'Not Anna, and not Beth,' she had said. 'I don't answer to either of those. It's *Annabeth*.' He said, 'I got it,' and she said, 'Are you sure? Because you wouldn't believe how many people forget.' And right then, he almost blew it, because he wanted to say, 'Jesus Christ, what kind of idiots do you date?' But he stopped himself. Wes told her, 'I promise. I got it.' Finally, they were able to move on.

The conversation improved after that. Her name had been the only problem. Otherwise, she was smart and interesting and fun to be with. Pretty, too. Not stunning, not the girl every guy wanted, and that was a good thing. Gorgeous girls are always – *always* – high-maintenance, and who the hell has that kind of time.

Annabeth is pretty in the wholesome way, the kind of girl who can dress up and be sexy if she wants but doesn't do it all the time. Dark hair, big eyes, and real curves. Not the implanted or injected kind. Good voice, too. A little husky, not too nasal or annoying.

In other words, he doesn't want to be late for Annabeth. And it has nothing to do with love.

But work has other ideas.

His three o'clock meeting runs over by fifteen minutes, making him late for the three thirty call. That pushes back his four thirty, which means he is screwed. Almost. An imaginary 'call from a client' comes in handy, because no one gets mad when you have to leave a meeting to talk with someone who pays the bills.

On the way back to his office, Wes stops in the break room to get an energy bar from the vending machine and check the time. Twenty minutes to go. Enough time to send a few emails and stay on schedule.

Bianca waves to him when he gets to his office. Wes holds up his phone and points at it, indicating that he is busy. Still pretending to be on the line with his pretend client.

In truth, if he had explained to her that he really wanted to be on time because he has a date, Bianca probably would have cleared his schedule for him. But it wouldn't be professional to involve her in his life like that. She isn't his personal assistant.

These days, not everyone has their own admin. The sales department has one who works for everybody, and that's Bianca. She is ridiculously young, he can tell, though he has never asked her age. That would be inappropriate.

Once he is back in his office with the door shut, he sits at his desk and puts down the phone. His fingers fly over the keyboard as he bangs out the last few emails of the day, and so far, so good. A few more minutes and he'll be gone.

The knock on his door is unexpected.

Bianca. He waves her in. She keeps her head down, almost like she is embarrassed to interrupt him.

'Mr Harmon,' she says.

That gets his attention. She never calls him Mr anything unless a client is around.

A woman steps into his office. Wes races through his mind, trying to figure out if she is someone he knows but can't remember or someone he should know but hasn't met yet.

'This is Detective Karen Colglazier. She's been waiting to talk to you,' Bianca says. She leaves and closes the door behind her.

Detective. Wes has to repeat that in his head a few times.

She is about forty-five years old, give or take, with olive skin and short, choppy hair. Dark eyes, sort of brown, sort of grey. He doesn't like them. Those eyes are full of shadows. They move around the room, taking in everything at once, before landing on him.

He gestures to the chairs in front of his desk. It's a test – he gives it to everyone, to see which one they'll pick. The one on the right is directly across from his own; anyone confident will choose it. The one on the left is off-center, seating his guest at an angle, forcing them to keep their head turned to maintain eye contact.

The detective picks the one on the right. She is quick to reassure him that nothing horrible has happened, that no one has been in an accident or been shot.

Wes is left wondering why she *is* here. She is not as quick to reveal that.

'Thank you for taking the time to talk to me,' she says.

'Of course. What can I help you with?'

'Well, this is more of a courtesy call, so to speak.'

Wes has no idea what that means. His brain is still scrambling, trying to figure out if this has something to do with work. It's possible. Siphon, Inc. is a company that links investors with startups. In other words, they're the middlemen. With access to a lot of money.

'May I ask what kind of detective you are?' Wes says.

'I'm with the Sex Crimes Unit.'

Didn't see that coming.

Something pings in the back of his mind. No, not a ping. An alarm. 'I'm not sure I understand,' he says.

'Yesterday, a young woman came into the station looking for help, because someone has been stalking her.'

'That's horrible.'

'Horrible enough to make her terrified. And angry.'

She lets that description hang in the air. Wes isn't about to grab it.

'What makes this situation particularly difficult is that her stalker technically hasn't broken the law,' Karen Colglazier says. 'So there isn't much the police can do.'

Wes feels his heart ramp up again, thumping so hard against his chest that it must be visible. 'May I ask what this has to do with me?'

For him, a rhetorical question. He knows the answer. Maybe he knew it as soon as Karen walked into his office, but he had shoved it aside, thinking it couldn't be true. Still, he manages to look surprised when she says it.

'The woman's name is Ivy Banks.'

The Plato quote pops into his mind. An hour ago, it was irrelevant. Not now.

His plans for the night dissolve, vanishing like they never existed. It doesn't matter when Wes leaves the office, whether it's at five thirty or ten o'clock at night. He will not be going out with Annabeth.

Because Ivy is back.

2

UC Davis, 2012, a Theta Rho frat party.

That's where he met Ivy, though he didn't belong to the fraternity. A friend of his roommate's brother did. Not that it mattered – it's not like they were checking credentials at the door. Theta Rho parties were known across campus, always huge bashes of the highest magnitude. The house was packed tight and hot as hell, exactly what the students wanted.

Wes was no exception. He was more than buzzed, less than drunk, and very, very horny.

Girls were everywhere. All kinds of girls, each one better looking than the last. Or they seemed that way. Might've been the beer. He maneuvered around them, smiling at one, then another, and then a third. Their eyes scanned him up and down, the same way his did to them. Everybody was looking for something, and on that hot spring night, it felt like they would all find what they wanted. Including Wes.

He was a junior, so he was used to these parties. At first, not so much. Going from tiny Holman, Michigan, to Davis, California, went beyond culture shock. Wes felt like he had stepped out of a barren, snowy field right into an MTV show.

It took a minute.

Over the course of two years, he morphed from a skinny, pale Midwestern boy to a Californian with a bit of muscle and a tan. His new normal. By his junior year, he had fully immersed himself in this big, wild world, where the rules changed stunningly fast.

Wes made his way outside, behind the big house, to get some air. The yard was almost as packed as the house, and that's where he found his roommate. They stood around talking, mostly about the girls, when someone stepped on Wes's foot.

Ivy had been walking by, and she stopped, turning back and throwing out a quick 'Sorry.'

She wasn't bad, but kind of plain. All covered up in a UCD sweatshirt and khaki shorts, hair in a ponytail, and no makeup. Not what he was looking for that night.

She kept walking, and he continued with his conversation. That was the end of it until he ran into her again inside the house, when he passed by her in a hallway. She was in line for the bathroom.

Now that he was closer to her, he noticed that she wasn't so plain after all. It was her lips: They were pink and full with a hint of shine. Like she had just licked them.

He stepped on her foot.

'I owe you that,' he said.

She looked at him, a little shocked. A little angry.

'Because you stepped on *my* foot,' he said. 'Outside, in the back –'

'Oh, right. Okay, fair.'

'I'm Wes,' he said.

'Ivy.'

He forced himself to look away from her, glancing down the hall at the line to the bathroom. 'You're going to be waiting awhile.'

'Looks that way.'

'You want another option?'

She gave him a half smile, like she was skeptical. He was back to looking at her lips. 'What is it?' she said.

Wes nodded toward the stairs. 'There's a bathroom in the basement. Maybe the line is shorter.'

'Thanks for the tip.'

She walked away from him like they were done. They were not.

Eight o'clock at night, Wes is at home by himself. The date with Annabeth had been canceled hours ago, easily broken with a call about work he couldn't get away from. She's a memory now. Vague, too, like she was someone he'd known years ago.

Wes replays the conversation with the detective a few times. A few hundred times.

'When was the last time you saw Ivy Banks?' Karen had asked.

He pretended like he had to think about this for a minute. 'Probably four months ago.'

'Where was that?'

'An engagement party for one of our college friends.'

'Did you talk to her?' Karen asked.

'Briefly. Hello, how are you . . . that kind of thing.' Maybe a little more than that, but he was not about to repeat every single word. Also no reason to mention how Ivy had looked.

That dress.

'So, no problems?' Karen said. 'No animosity, no anger?'

'Absolutely not.'

The detective didn't react at all to what he was saying, so it was hard to know how much she believed. But it was the truth: That engagement party was the last time he had seen Ivy.

'As I said, I'm here more as a courtesy than anything else,' Karen said. 'Someone has been bothering Ivy, leaving her notes and presents, along with pictures of her. They're letting her know someone is watching.'

'That's so disturbing,' he said.

'When I asked her who she thought was doing it, she gave me your name.'

'Ivy and I haven't been involved in a long time,' Wes said.

'Then why would she think it was you?'

'I have no idea,' he said. 'I can only think it's because we had a relationship that was . . . intense.'

'Intense?'

He sighed. On purpose, like this was a tiresome subject. 'We met in college. It was a first love kind of thing.'

'What does that mean?'

'Like I said, it was intense.'

'She said you dated for years.'

'On and off, yes.' Wes had never figured out if it was more on than off or the other way around, and he had spent a lot of time thinking about it.

'As I said, I'm here as a courtesy.' Karen didn't move when she spoke, didn't use her hands at all. As someone who used his all the time, Wes found this fascinating.

'If you're the one doing this to her, you need to stop,' Karen said. 'Get over it, move on, find someone else, do whatever you have to do. But leave Ivy alone.'

Not so courteous. More like a threat. 'I'm not the one doing this,' he said. 'I haven't gone near Ivy, and I certainly haven't left her any presents or notes.' Another sigh, followed by a glance at his computer screen. 'If I'm your suspect, you're wasting your time.'

Karen stared at him like she was waiting for him to say more.

Not a chance.

She stood up, the movement so sharp and quick it surprised him. 'Thank you for your time, Mr Harmon.'

'Of course.'

He also stood up, as he always did when a meeting ended. Wes waited until she was gone and the door was closed to sit back down. He swiveled his chair around, toward the window, though it wasn't to look at the view.

All he could see was Ivy. And he smiled.

3

Ivy clicks the ballpoint pen over and over, until it becomes a rhythm instead of noise. The repetitive sound keeps her focused.

She sits at her desk, where one computer screen displays her emails, the other a spreadsheet. Earbuds firmly stuck in place. To anyone walking by, it appears as if she's listening to music while working. She would be – if there was any to do.

That's the thing about working for a bloated corporation with bad management: No one realizes there isn't enough work to go around. Or they don't care.

She was done with her required tasks by lunch, and since then she's been listening to *Mandarin Chinese for Beginners*. This is her new thing, learning languages. Spending all day on social media got old forever ago.

The pen jams, breaking her concentration. She hurls it into the trash can and picks up another. Someone interrupts her before the first click.

'How're you doing?'

Lucia stands in the doorway to Ivy's tiny office. It's barely big enough for two people, nothing more than a cubicle with walls. Or a cage, because that's how it feels. Lucia fits because she is small; her near-Lilliputian frame squeezes right into the space.

'Oh, you know,' Ivy says, pausing the language lesson. 'Hanging in there.'

Lucia nods, patting her on the shoulder. Her eyes are big and can't hide anything – every emotion is visible. They're screaming sympathy. 'I'm glad you went to the police,' she says.

'Me too.'

'Well, like I said, you can always stay with me. I mean, there's not much room at my place, but if you don't want to stay at home, the offer stands.' She smiles a little but not enough to show her teeth, like that would be rude.

'Thanks,' Ivy says. 'I'll be okay.'

More sympathy eyes from Lucia.

She is one of the few who know about the stalking. Ivy only told a few people about it. None of them knows the whole story.

First, the notes left on the windshield of her car. Next, the pictures. Real photos, printed out and also left on her car. Someone had photographed Ivy walking to her car, going into her house, shopping at the grocery store.

Then came the chocolates.

The brand was everything. Läderach, the Swiss company. Wes used to give her a box of those truffles for Christmas and her birthday. Two days ago, she found them on her doorstep. Same-size box, same brand. Twelve truffles, lined up in two rows, except these weren't like the others. Every truffle had a bite taken out of it.

The note:

Just because.

She told the detective all of this. Damn near word for word.

Karen Colglazier had said she didn't have a lot of hope they would get DNA from the truffles, especially because it wasn't a crime to leave someone a half-eaten box of candy. The crime lab wouldn't prioritize it. Nor would the police budget. Ivy had assumed that. Had counted on it, in fact.

Doesn't matter, Ivy had said. *It had to be Wes. I can't think of anyone else it could be.*

Lucia doesn't know that part.

When she finally leaves, Ivy checks on her online order. Still due to arrive today. Just in time.

Back to the Chinese. Today's lesson is about the home, teaching her the words for *bedroom*, *kitchen*, *chair*, and *sofa*. The mundane words bore her, and she finds herself searching for others, like the word for *stalker*.

Gēnzōng kuáng.

Ivy memorizes it, mouthing the word over and over until she's positive she won't forget it.

Ivy lives on the first floor of the Breezy Village. The manager had called it a garden apartment, which meant it had a little walled-off patio in the back, with just enough room for a table, two chairs, and a tiny plot of land for planting. Ivy does not plant. A green thumb is not something she has.

Still, it's not a bad place. She's lived in worse.

The weather is beautiful, a spring night that isn't too warm, and she sits on her patio, smoking a joint. She doesn't indulge often, mostly because she grew up surrounded by it. Ivy is from Humboldt County, ground zero for pot farmers in California. Including her parents. They had a small plot of land where they grew and sold marijuana since before Ivy was born. Now they're in prison.

Turns out that even when marijuana became legal in the state, that didn't mean everyone could grow and sell it. There were fees, licenses, and environmental restrictions. Her parents didn't pay attention to any of that, nor did most of the others from her old neighborhood. Five years ago, a big sweep caught a lot of them. Drug laws still apply when you don't play by the rules.

Nowadays, weed is more than acceptable in Fair Valley, California, though cigarettes are not. Judging by the smell in the air, she isn't the only one outside smoking tonight.

The sliding glass door to her apartment is open; she can see right through the living room to the front door. It's locked and bolted. Her phone is right next to her, on the table, and it lights up with every message. The ones who know what's going on ask how she is, if she's okay, and they all hope she isn't alone.

She is.

It's after eleven when she finally goes inside, thinking maybe she is wrong. Maybe she has miscalculated. A rarity for her, after all these years, but there's a first time for everything. The idea that she could be wrong isn't upsetting, in part because she's high. In part because the unexpected is a chance for something new, something exciting. Something to make her life a little better than it was yesterday or last week or last year.

She locks the sliding door behind her, pulling the curtains closed, making sure every edge is covered. She turns off the lights in the kitchen and living room, then the outside lights. Front and back.

Knock.

Knock.

Two knocks, hard and slow. The sound doesn't scare her, doesn't make her jump. Ivy bites back a smile as she unlocks the front door and flings it open.

Wes.

About time.

4

Ivy wears her new nightgown, the one she ordered online. White silk, thin straps, it hugs her curves and hangs down to her ankles. Wes stands in the shadows, illuminated only by the streetlight behind him. Ivy can't see the expression on his face. She doesn't need to.

'You called the police,' he says.

'I did.'

He steps forward, into her apartment. 'A detective showed up at my office. My *work*.'

Ivy shuts the door behind him and follows him down the hallway. Wes turns abruptly, almost running into her. He places a hand against her chest; she steps backward until she hits the wall. His face is so close to hers she can see his pupils. Watches them dilate.

'It worked,' she says. 'Didn't it?'

Wes doesn't argue. He knows it's true. Once you start crossing lines, the road back is too crooked, too difficult to follow. Easier to keep going forward.

He presses her against the wall. She feels the heat from his fingertips as he leans in close, his lips almost touching hers. His hand slides down, across the front of her nightgown, between her breasts, and stops at her waist.

She holds her breath.

He pulls his hand away.

Wes steps back and turns from her. She exhales hard.

'No,' he says, shaking his head.

No.

Wes uses that word like it's a weapon. He also said it the last time she saw him.

Four months ago, at an engagement party in Sacramento. Ivy knew Wes would be there, so she brought a date. James was a guy she had met online. He wasn't very bright but he looked good. Very good.

The party was fancy; the bride and groom both worked in tech and had money to burn. Open bar, fresh flowers everywhere, two different bands, and a never-ending flow of champagne. And this was just the warm-up to the real thing: the wedding.

Wes brought a date of his own, a blonde with huge breasts and a too-small dress. Vanessa or Veronica, or who the hell cares what her name was – she looked fantastic, and everyone knew it. But Wes seemed more concerned with the guy Ivy brought.

They spoke once, near the buffet table, when he came up behind her.

'Ivy.'

'Wes.' She said it before turning around, taking her time filling up a small plate with finger foods.

'How are you?' he said.

She finally turned. As always, he stunned her. It was the way he looked, or maybe the way he looked at her. She struggled to respond quickly. 'I'm well,' she said. 'You?'

'Living the dream.'

'Good for you.'

Behind him, at a table, she could see his date. The blonde was talking to someone beside her, paying no attention to Wes.

'Did you find her on Tinder?' Ivy said.

Wes nodded toward another table, where Ivy's date sat quietly, waiting for her to return. Not the most outgoing guy, but James didn't have to be. He looked like he was posing for a magazine.

'And him?' Wes said.

'What about him?'

Wes smiled. 'No.'

He turned around and walked away.

Now here he is in her apartment, saying no again but for a different reason. Not that it matters. This time, he doesn't mean it.

Ivy walks up behind him, pushes up on her tiptoes, and whispers in his ear.

'Liar.'

The thing is . . .

The thing is . . .

Wes doesn't know what the thing is, not when Ivy is right up in his ear. When he needs rational thought the most, that definitely isn't the thing.

She has always done this to him. Starting way back in college, when they first went out. Dates weren't really dates back then, because they were both broke, so creativity was in order. Coffee was affordable enough. Hiking was free. So they did both – her suggestion.

Frog Pond Trail wasn't far, and it wasn't a long hike. Not difficult, either. At least not according to the internet. But it was full of picturesque views of the water and the ridge and everything nature had to offer. Wes suggested they try it on their first date. She agreed.

The sun was shining – not a cloud in the sky – and it all went well for the first hour and a half. They chatted about their backgrounds, stopping to take pictures every twenty feet or so. The internet wasn't wrong about the views.

Ivy suddenly stopped. 'I've had all the beautiful scenery I can take for one day,' she said.

He had been thinking the same thing.

The trail ahead sloped down and then up. In the distance, a giant tree stood out among the rest. He nodded toward it. 'Wanna race?'

Instead of answering, she took off running.

He was already a few steps behind, so he went off-trail, cutting across the hill on the left. The path was rougher, and he had to jump over a log or two, but it was the only way to get ahead.

He had almost done it when she fell.

They were less than twenty feet away from the tree when it happened, and he had been moving back toward the trail. As soon as she went down, he stopped.

She blocked the fall with her hands, ended up on her knees, and turned over to sit in the dirt. He sat down beside her.

'I guess you won,' she said.

Her hands were scratched up, covered in dirt and tiny pebbles. He wiped them clean, one by one, and then moved on to her knee. Scraped, but it wasn't too bad. He poured water over it.

'You okay?' he said.

She didn't answer. She kissed him.

To this day, he can't describe that kiss, can't capture it with words. But when he closes his eyes, he can feel it.

It's the reason he turns around to face Ivy now.

She was right. He was lying when he said no.

5

'We need to stop doing this,' he says.

Ivy rolls over in the bed to face Wes. The room is dark but not pitch-black; a bit of light comes in through the window. He is lying on his back, staring up at the ceiling.

'We always say that,' she says.

'I know.'

He still doesn't look at her. They've been down this road before, around and through and across, and they can't seem to find the exit. She isn't sure there is one.

But if there is, she probably wouldn't take it. Maybe because of the squirrel.

Years ago, not long before they graduated from college, they went to Lake Shasta for a weekend. Her roommate knew someone whose parents had a cabin, and a bunch of friends were headed up there. Wes and Ivy went in his car, an ancient Ford truck he had driven out from Michigan.

She never saw the squirrel. Ivy had been looking in her bag, trying to find something. Lip balm, a hairbrush, a piece of gum . . . She can't remember what it was, but she does remember the car jerking to the side. Wes had seen a squirrel and tried to avoid it.

Ivy does remember the thump when it went under the tire.

'What was that?' She turned, watching out the back. Wes pulled over to the side of the road.

'A squirrel,' he said.

Now a brown-and-red blob on the cement. 'Oh God.'

'Stay here.'

Wes got out and grabbed something from behind the driver's seat. Looked like a tire iron. They were on a side road, not the highway, so there weren't many cars. She tried to watch him push the dead squirrel over to the side of the road but had to look away.

He got back into the car and started driving. Didn't say a word for at least ten miles.

And then: 'Do you think that squirrel had a family?'

'I don't know,' she said.

Silence.

'I think squirrels are loners, aren't they?' she said.

'Google it.'

She didn't want to, but he pestered her until she did. Gray squirrels, as it turned out, lived mostly alone. The one he'd hit had been brown, and brown squirrels lived in colonies.

Wes didn't say anything for a long time. She thought about suggesting that he donate to a save-the-squirrels nonprofit, if such a thing existed, but she didn't want to sound stupid. Or insensitive. Neither of them had extra money for donations.

After another forty miles or so, he said, 'Hopefully, his colony finds him so they know he's dead. So they aren't out searching or anything.'

She wanted to say they would, and that it was a good thing he moved the squirrel's body to the side of the road so his family could find him, but she couldn't make those assurances. He knew that. He would see right through it.

When they arrived at the lake, he didn't mention the squirrel to their friends. She didn't bring it up, either.

But even now, years later, she would bet every penny she has that Wes still thinks about that squirrel. And he still feels bad about it.

*

'I didn't know the police would go to your office,' she says. And she hadn't. Karen told her she would speak to Wes but never said where or when. Ivy had assumed it would be at his home. 'Sorry about that.'

'Seriously, that was a little extreme,' Wes says. He still doesn't look at her.

'But it worked.'

'Yeah. It did.'

She reaches over, placing her finger on the side of his neck, an inch below his jaw. Right where he's the most ticklish.

He grabs her hand before she can do it. Then he dives under the covers, reaching for her feet. She squirms and tries to kick, but he's too fast.

'Don't!'

'Or what?' he says. His voice is muffled.

'Or I'll call the police on you again.'

'You would, too.'

His hand slips away from her foot, never tickling the bottom of it. He emerges from under the comforter and settles down on the pillow. Eyes back on the ceiling.

'Maybe we should get back together,' she says.

She watches him, trying to gauge his response. He doesn't move an inch.

'For real?' he says.

'Yes.'

Wes turns his head to look at her. In the dark, his eyes are shiny. 'Are you serious?'

'I am.'

'So . . . we're together again. Just like that.'

Ivy reaches out and touches his shoulder with her finger. She traces his little scar, the one he got when he fell out of a tree as a kid and there was a sharp rock on the ground and . . . She could tell the story verbatim, as if it were her own.

'It can't be any worse than having the police visit you at work,' she says.

He props himself up on his elbow. 'Are you screwing around right now?'

'No.'

'I can't believe you're saying this.'

'Why?' she asks.

'You said never. "Never, never, never again."'

Yes, she had. The last breakup had been particularly nasty, even for them.

'Before that, I said forever.' She pauses, bites her lip. 'So did you.'

A dozen times, at least. Maybe a hundred. Usually right before they broke up. Almost like they were trying to reassure each other that it wasn't going to happen. Again.

'We need rules,' he said. 'No games, no messing around.'

'Agreed. And no drama.'

'None. Zero. Zip.'

'I can do that,' she says.

'You sure?'

'Yes.'

He lies back down and closes his eyes. She loves that he has to think about it. Or pretends to.

But the fact that he makes her wait, not so much.

'No lying,' he finally says. 'Not even once.'

'Deal.'

'Done.'

6

Wes Harmon is late for work.

It's weird.

Bianca has worked at Siphon for almost fourteen months. After starting as an assistant in human resources, she was moved over to the sales department to be the admin for the whole team. Wes Harmon is part of it.

She keeps a close eye on him.

He slides right by her desk, coffee in one hand, computer bag in the other, and sunglasses covering his eyes. Wes smiles and holds up the cup, nodding to Bianca as he disappears into his office.

Hungover, perhaps, though she's never known Wes to be a big drinker. Then again, it's not every day the police visit him at work. Maybe he needed to drink more last night.

Bianca gets up from her chair and knocks once on his office door. She opens it to find him getting settled at his desk.

'Your call with the bank is in ten minutes,' she says.

'Got it. Anything else?'

Bianca doesn't move. She is halfway between the door and his desk, trying to decide if she should sit down and ask him more about what happened yesterday.

But he's busy. And he is late.

'No,' she says. 'Nothing else.'

She returns to her desk, still thinking about it. Not really her place to ask him anything unless it's work-related. She doesn't know if this thing with the detective is or not, because that little story he gave her yesterday isn't adding up.

'How's my favorite assistant?'

Tanner Duncan. A man so attractive he makes suspenders look good. He's intelligent with charisma to spare – everything a sales director has to be. Tanner is the one who brings in the money, the investors looking for somewhere to put their millions. No one is better than Tanner at matching up the money and the startups.

He's also a prick. Bianca has heard that from a few people but never seen it. Tanner has never been anything but polite and professional to her.

'Good morning, Tanner,' she says.

'What's happening?'

'The team from Porterhouse confirmed for eleven. Your lunch with James is at Trattorio, and your three o'clock pushed to three thirty.'

'And the team?' Tanner asks.

Bianca clicks to the schedule screen, listing off all the reps who are out of the office today on sales calls. 'We're still waiting on two reports for Thursday's monthly meeting. The rest have been distributed.'

Tanner leans over her shoulder to stare at the screen. 'What else?'

'Dana has that meeting today with Infinite Investments, and Marcus is still following up with Bio-Reality.' Bianca looks at him. Tanner is checking his phone and nodding.

His head snaps up. 'Good. Anything else?'

Yes, she wants to say. *A detective came to see Wes yesterday, late in the afternoon, when everyone else was in meetings. And today Wes was late.*

'No,' she says. 'That's it.'

Tanner walks away, toward his corner office.

Bianca checks her email and her phone. Still nothing interesting. But over the past eighteen hours, she has learned a few things about Detective Karen Colglazier. She has worked for the Fair Valley Police Department for over twenty years. Her husband had been a cop, as well, but he died in the line of duty. Bianca found an old picture from the funeral. Back then, it had been front-page news.

One more thing she learned about Karen: The detective is currently assigned to the Sex Crimes Unit.

Sex crimes.

Bianca isn't a genius. She has known that since grade school. Some kids were just smarter, quicker, they could grasp information and turn it around, flipping it into something innovative, while Bianca was still trying to figure out the basics.

But she isn't stupid, either. If there's one thing she's good at, it's figuring out people. She does it all day long, on the phone and in person, translating what people say into what they mean. The two are rarely the same. Being able to read people is what makes her such a good assistant. Maybe a great one.

It came in handy when she worked in human resources. She could weed out bad candidates before they went any further up the chain. Though she wasn't in the preliminary interviews, she had plenty of time to assess the applicants while they waited to be called into the back. She knew if they were early, on time, or if they were late, and she knew how they acted while they waited. Did they fidget, were they obsessed with their phone, or did they stare at themselves on a mirror app? If anyone didn't seem like a good fit, Bianca deleted them off the final callback list.

She considered it part of her job. If the HR managers didn't want her doing it, they wouldn't have given her that kind of access.

Yesterday, after the detective left, Wes came out of his

office and volunteered an explanation for the visit. 'There's been a few break-ins on my block,' he said. 'She just wanted to know if I've seen anything unusual.'

Bianca doesn't know a lot about police work other than what she has seen on TV, but it seems unlikely that Detective Karen Colglazier would be working on a neighborhood break-in. Sex Crimes focuses on things like harassment, stalking, assault, and rape.

She opens her desk drawer and takes out her Russian nesting dolls. She opens each one, seven in total, and works her way down to the second smallest. The eighth one is long gone, replaced with a key.

It isn't something she should have. Assistants aren't allowed to have a master key to all the offices.

7

Wes ends the conference call, tossing his headphones on the desk. He checks his schedule, hoping to see a cancellation, but his whole afternoon is still booked. Bianca always sends the agenda for the meetings, and he pulls up the next one. Hard to concentrate when all he can see is Ivy.

And if, God forbid, he forgets what she looks like, he can look at the picture on his phone. She doesn't know he took that picture of her lying in bed, asleep, with a tiny smile on her face.

It isn't recent. The picture is from the last night they spent together, almost a year ago, right before they broke up. When she had said, *Never, never, never again.* He had kept the picture as the wallpaper on his phone for a week after that, until finally forcing himself to remove it.

Now it's back. Along with Ivy.

This morning, he woke up to the smell of breakfast. Ivy, in the kitchen, cooking for him.

Never happened before. He doesn't count the Hot Pockets or the leftovers she microwaved back when they were broke. This morning, she made mushroom-and-cheese omelets with toast and fresh coffee. Ivy handed him a cup when he walked into the kitchen.

'This is amazing,' he said.

'Thank you.' She leaned over and kissed him, holding it longer than a peck but not as long as he wanted. 'You're welcome.'

While eating, they talked about their work, the day ahead,

and their future plans. All normal things, like they did this every morning. Ivy is going out tonight with her coworkers, and he is watching the Warriors game at a sports bar with his friends.

'Should we get together after?' she asked.

Yes. A billion times yes. 'If you want,' he said. 'I'll text you when the game is over.'

'Sounds good.' She shrugged a little, taking a bite of her omelet.

His most difficult task of the day was waiting to see her again.

Being late was the second. He hadn't meant for it to happen, but by the time he'd left her place and went home to shower and change, he was already behind schedule. And he had to pick up his regular large coffee because the stuff Ivy made was a little weak. He wasn't about to tell her that, though.

Ivy tries to concentrate on her Chinese lessons. Yesterday, she had no problem learning ten new words – her daily goal – but this afternoon is different. She keeps thinking about what happened last night. About Wes.

He's always been the one. Even when they're apart, even when they hate each other, she still knows that.

She has known it since college, when they went out one night to a cheap midnight movie. He had parked next to a puddle, and when she got out of the car, she stepped right in it, soaking the one nice pair of shoes she had. He stayed up that night blow-drying them.

To this day, he checks to make sure he isn't parking next to a puddle. He drives around for blocks if that's what it takes.

Contrary to what her best friend might say, getting back together with him isn't stupid or naïve. She knows what she's doing. Mostly.

Like last night, she hadn't planned on saying they should get back together. It just popped out. Her mouth had been working faster than her brain. That doesn't happen often anymore. She is no longer that impulsive girl who acts on every whim. These days, she deliberately thinks before she acts. Mostly.

But not last night. Not with Wes.

Sometimes it feels like her subconscious is ten steps ahead, leading her exactly in the direction she should go. Or the direction *it* wants her to go. She has never figured out if that buried part of her brain has good intentions or bad. No doubt Wes would have a few thoughts about that if she asked. She hasn't.

Her work chat pops up on the screen. It's Lucia and Brooke, the two colleagues she actually socializes with outside of the office.

Brooke: Just checking in!

Lucia: How are you doing?

Ivy: Doing well, thanks.

Brooke: Nothing from the stalker?

Ivy: Nope. Or the police.

Brooke: In this case, no news has to be good.

Lucia: We still good for tonight?

Ivy: Absolutely.

Drinks tonight, followed by food and more drinks. Brooke has become a pretty good friend over the past year. Lucia is a little newer to the group. All three have bonded in their collective corporate boredom, and they all have extracurricular activities. Ivy has her language lessons, and Brooke has a growing influencer account under a fake name. Lucia works a part-time job online while she's in the office.

Ivy closes the chat and picks up the phone, again, to call Detective Karen Colglazier. All she has to do is say she spoke to Wes, they made up, and everything is fine now. Sure, it would make her sound dysfunctional, not to mention a little crazy, but at least the police wouldn't show up at Wes's job again.

She just hasn't called yet.

When Ivy first met Karen, she was surprised at how seriously the detective took her complaint. She hadn't expected that. And when Ivy gave her the name of her ex-boyfriend, Karen was positive she could end this quickly.

'You'd be surprised how many stalkers disappear after a visit from the police,' she said.

'Really?' Ivy said. 'You're going to go talk to him?'

'We'll just have a little chat. Usually that's all it takes.'

Ivy replays this conversation in her mind, recalling how confident Karen had sounded. She would take care of this: That was her attitude. Just leave it to the professionals.

Maybe she doesn't have to call the detective. In fact, maybe it's better if she doesn't. Karen will think she worked her police magic, scared off Wes, and the whole thing went away.

Ivy puts down the phone.

8

Bianca opens her pocket mirror, reapplies her neutral lipstick, and checks her eyeliner, dabbing at the corner to erase
a smudge. She's careful about her makeup – not too much,
not too little – because she's the first one people see. One
time, a sales rep said she looked exotic, presumably because
she's biracial. Half-Mexican, half-white. Apparently, he didn't
know the word *exotic* is not okay. That put him on her radar.

Not tonight, though. Tonight is about Wes.

Again.

Six thirty on a Friday evening, and almost everyone is
gone. The only one left is Tanner. Though she's heard others
say that he sometimes acts like an overgrown frat boy, he is
actually a very hard worker. One of the last to leave the office,
even right before the weekend.

Bianca stays, cleaning out her inbox and writing up meeting notes, until Tanner finally comes out of his office.

'Go home,' he says to her. 'It's Friday.'

'I'm just about done.'

Tanner smiles. 'No big plans tonight? I can't believe that.'

She waves goodbye, doesn't answer.

He walks down the hall and gets on the elevator, but she
still doesn't move. Bianca waits another fifteen minutes, just
in case Tanner forgot something and returns. When he
doesn't, she takes out the nesting dolls to get the key. It's just
after seven, which gives her several hours before the over-
night cleaning crew starts to arrive. Plenty of time.

Wes doesn't have a corner office, because he isn't a

manager or director, but it's respectable enough. Decent size, plenty of seating for clients, including a small couch in the far corner. His desk is neat — no papers, no sticky notes — clear of all clutter. The Siphon employee handbook specifically states that any personal items are to be 'tasteful and limited.' Wes has only one that's visible: a picture of himself, his sister, and his parents.

In his top drawer, he has a few things pushed into the far corner. A brass key chain, tarnished and scratched and engraved with a heart, along with a deflated HAPPY BIRTHDAY balloon, and an old parking sticker for a downtown garage. She found all of those a long time ago.

Bianca sits down in front of his computer. Some of the reps have given her their passwords; they often ask her to check their emails when they're on vacation or out of the office. Those are the reps who keep their personal business on their phone or a different email. Wes is one of them.

One glance at his inbox tells her nothing has changed. All work-related, nothing of interest. But that's not why she's here, because if she wanted to see his emails, she could access them through her own computer. What Bianca wants to see is his calendar. On her side, she has a limited view. Business hours only. His entire calendar is only accessible through his computer or his phone.

She pulls up yesterday, which shows his day is blocked off for the evening, starting at five thirty. The only explanation is two letters:

AB

No idea what that means, but Wes didn't leave the office at five thirty last night. After the detective left, he stayed in his office for a long time. Didn't leave until after six.

Tonight, the first part of the evening is blocked off for the basketball game. He's the kind of guy who always has his schedule planned out, even for social activities. Bianca knew about the game – the reps have been talking about it all day, and right now they're all watching it at Scooter's. Wes's calendar is marked off until ten thirty.

Another engagement starts then, and it's marked with a different letter:

I

AB one night, *I* the next. Her first thought is women. Maybe one of them is the reason why that detective showed up.

Or maybe the letters have nothing to do with that. It could be something about a project or a deal. Impossible to know without more information.

Bianca looks ahead on the calendar, to next week, but sees only business dinners and another night marked off for a basketball game. Nothing of note for the rest of the month, no further letters or strange plans.

She checks his internet browser history, skimming through the news and sports sites, looking for anything unusual. Not tonight.

After locking up Wes's office, she takes a glance through a few others. Might as well, since her key is out and no one is around. She learns one of the guys is still cheating on his wife, Dana has started seeing a guy in accounting, and a sticky note on Tanner's desk makes Bianca think he has a new woman in his life. He doesn't send flowers to just anyone, but someone named Julia will be getting a delivery tomorrow.

Bianca double-checks that she leaves the offices exactly as she found them and that the doors are all locked. When everything is in order, she puts her key back and leaves. Her knowledge about people comes from intuition. Snooping just fills in the blanks.

If she didn't snoop, she wouldn't know about Wes. Wouldn't be watching him so closely.

About a month ago, she was making her rounds. She doesn't do it too often, because she doesn't want to get caught, but enough to know what's going on with everybody. When Bianca checked Wes's internet history, a donation site popped up in his browser: the Joseph A. Fisher Memorial Fund.

Joey Fisher.

Of all the things she has discovered at Siphon – the affairs, the interoffice politics, the gossip – this one shocked her the most.

9

I'll text you when the game is over, Wes had said.

The game is over. Ivy knows who won. She even knows the score. What she doesn't know is why there's no text from Wes. It would be fine if she texted him first. They are back together, after all. Not dating – in a relationship. She can text anytime she wants.

In theory.

In reality, she won't. Because she shouldn't have to.

Brooke smiles at her, holding up her almost-empty glass. She is a true California blonde, right down to the blue eyes, the beachy hair, and the tan. Though that's fake, because real tans cause wrinkles, and nobody wants those, especially not Brooke. Not aging badly is one of her prime goals.

'I just have to say you're handling this stalker thing so much better than I would,' she says. 'I swear, I'd be at home curled up in a ball or something.'

'I would've gone to my parents' house,' Lucia says.

Ivy would've done a lot of things if she had a real stalker. 'I'm not going to let some loser psycho decide where I go,' she says.

'Good for you,' Brooke says. Her eyes are glassy, and she slurs a bit. One too many gin martinis. 'Just be safe.'

'Always.'

Lucia slips between them and tries to get the bartender's attention. A few months ago, she started working in Ivy's department. It didn't take Ivy long to realize Lucia's the type that men want to take care of, including pouring her drinks, and she knows it.

Ivy checks her phone again. She should put it in her pocket, on vibrate, but it feels like she'll miss something. Holding it in her hand is far more comforting, though it doesn't go unnoticed by Brooke. Drunk doesn't mean stupid.

'You keep looking at your phone,' Brooke says.

Ivy rolls her eyes. 'I know, right? Bad habit.'

Lucia hands the drinks back, another round of gin martinis. They're at Salt, where everyone prefers clear drinks. No fruity mixed cocktails here, though scotch or bourbon is acceptable.

Brooke launches into a story about someone who did something that may or may not be interesting, but Ivy isn't listening. She wonders how bad it would really be if she texted first. She could ask Brooke and Lucia their opinion, but she already knows what they would say: bad. It would be bad to text first because if a guy wants to see you, he'll text. Or call. One way or another, he will make it happen. If anyone asked Ivy the same question, that's exactly what she would say.

It's not that she's angry he hasn't texted; it's the disappointment. The honeymoon period is so short.

Ivy takes a sip of her martini and continues to tune out Brooke's story. She curses herself in all the languages she sort of knows – English, Chinese, Russian, French – as she looks at her phone again. It shouldn't be like this. Her boyfriend, since Wes is her boyfriend again, should text when he says he's going to. He should keep his word. He should be as excited to see her as she is to see him.

The moments when they're on the same page are always the best.

A few years ago, after one of their increasingly ugly fights, they stayed apart for six months. At the time, their longest separation. She had started dating again, making profiles on the usual sites, meeting guys for coffee or a drink. Nothing had stuck. Nothing felt right.

Then an FBI agent showed up at her office.

Both tall and broad, he filled out his black suit and then some. Buzz-cut hair, square jaw, a nose that had been broken one too many times.

'Ivy Banks?' he said.

She nodded. Couldn't speak.

He used his index finger to beckon her, making her walk out of her office and into the hallway. The agent pulled out a pair of handcuffs, and just when it seemed like he was about to arrest her, he belted out 'Happy Birthday.'

It was not her birthday. Just a singing telegram from Wes.

When the performer-slash-agent was done, he handed her a card. The kind that comes with flowers.

I couldn't wait until your real birthday. Too far away.

No name. Ivy didn't need one.

When she left work, she went straight to his place. Wes was already there.

Waiting.

She blew past him at the door, walking right in. 'I can't believe you did that,' she said. 'You embarrassed me at work.'

'Did I?'

No, not really. It wasn't that bad – it wasn't like he had sent a stripper-gram, but still. 'You know you did,' she said. For dramatic effect, she even sulked.

Wes touched the bottom of her chin with one finger and lifted her head. 'But did I really?' he said. And he smiled. 'Or did you kinda like it?'

She kinda loved it. The telegram *and* Wes and his smile.

That's the thing. Ivy has seen him smile a thousand times over the years. At friends, at coworkers, even at his parents. But when he smiles at her, the *way* he smiles at her . . . well, that really is the thing.

Sometimes – no, always – she smiles when thinking about that moment.

'Are you okay?' Lucia says.

Ivy snaps back, realizing she missed more than one story from Brooke. It's Friday night, the bar is packed, and she is with her friends. She should be enjoying herself. Instead, she's obsessing over Wes. Again.

'I'm good, I'm good,' she says, holding up her drink. 'Let's make a toast.'

They clink glasses, attracting the attention of a group of guys at the bar. Brooke reels them in, and Lucia keeps them talking. Ivy finds herself in a conversation with a guy who isn't half-bad. Polite, interesting, good-looking: all the things that usually interest her. But tonight, this guy is nothing special. He doesn't say a single word that makes her forget about Wes. Not even when he talks about travel. This should make her ask if he's ever been to China or Russia or any of the other places where people speak the languages she has studied, but she can't fake enough enthusiasm to do it.

Halfway through their conversation, her phone lights up.

Sorry, ran into a client and he wouldn't shut up. I'm leaving now, want to meet at my place?

Adrenaline straight to the heart. Ivy smiles as she reads it a second time, forgetting all about the guy in front of her.

'Good news?' he says.

'It was nice talking to you,' she says, 'but I have to go.'

The honeymoon isn't over yet.

10

The morning sun lights up the bedroom, and Wes rolls over to see Ivy lying in his bed. She is still asleep, her brown hair half covering her face. He isn't surprised to see her there. Not once did he think she would disappear in the middle of the night. She never has before.

Wes goes to the kitchen, leaving her to sleep. Last night, she arrived in an Uber instead of her car, and she was in a good mood, too. Jumped right into his arms when he opened the door.

'How was the game?' she said.

'Good. How are the girls?'

'Good.'

'Are you drunk?' he asked.

'Buzzed. Are you drunk?'

'No.'

'Anything else?' she said.

'Nope.'

'Then we should go to bed.'

It was a good night.

Wes is taking his first sip of coffee when Ivy walks into the kitchen wearing one of his T-shirts. Her favorite, the one she has stolen a few times over the years. He always gets it back.

He pours her a cup of coffee and sets it down in front of her. 'I don't have any cream.'

'That's okay.'

It isn't, because she hates black coffee, but this morning

she is being agreeable. Not going to argue about that. He pops a couple of bagels in the toaster oven.

'Still eating bagels,' she says.

'Always.'

They smile. Bagels are an old inside joke. She loves them but hates all the carbs; he loves them and refuses to think about the carbs. Some things are better left ignored.

Wes opens the refrigerator and takes out the cream cheese. Plain, which she'll eat, but she'd prefer one of the flavored kinds. He makes a mental note to pick some up, along with cream, later today. He does have Fresca, though. Always.

'So how's your friend doing?' he says. 'What's his name? Hershey?'

'You know his name.'

'I know he's named after a candy bar.'

'Heath,' she says. 'His name is Heath.'

Yes. Heath. 'So how's he doing?'

'I haven't seen him in a while. He's working up in Oregon for a few months.'

Good. Heath is Ivy's best friend, and he's not on #Team-Wes. Or #TeamWesandIvy, for that matter. If Heath is on anyone's team, it's his own.

The toaster oven dings, saving Wes from saying any-thing else. The last thing he wants to do is screw everything up now.

He and Ivy slip into a familiar rhythm, eating breakfast while discussing plans for the weekend and exchanging gos-sip about mutual friends. Together, they clean up. Ivy pours a second cup of coffee, and Wes checks his phone, scrolling through whatever he missed.

It's a normal Saturday morning if you ignore all the time that passed between the last time and today. He does.

*

Ivy leaves around ten, because Wes has plans to play disc golf with his friends today. Unlike her, he doesn't live in an apartment. Wes owns a house, a small '70s ranch-style that he's had for two years, but she has never lived there with him. Last time, she came close, but then they started fighting a lot. Little things at first, as always. Like when she was half-asleep and turned off his alarm without thinking. Or when he conveniently forgot to buy more cream for her coffee.

They picked at each other, letting all those little annoyances blow up into something bigger. Sometimes it was for the sex afterward, always intense. But other times it was for the fight. The downhill spiral picked up speed, and the fighting became worse. No sex afterward, leaving them with all that anger.

One night, they went to a party and he caught her flirting with a guy she had gone out with a few times. She had done it on purpose, to make Wes jealous, as she had done many times before. But flirting with someone she had actually dated was a step too far for Wes. He left the party without her.

Ivy went to his house, ready for a blowout of a fight. He didn't want one. He didn't even want to talk to her. Everything she had left at his place was waiting for her on the front lawn. She couldn't get into the house, because she never got a key.

Since this was only a year ago, and she was no longer the impulsive girl she used to be, Ivy did not knock. She did not bang on his door. Instead, she stood outside his house, surveyed her options, and headed right for the garden.

She pulled up every plant, every flower, everything that made it one of the best in the neighborhood. Wes didn't take care of it – he paid a neighborhood kid to handle the gardening – but that didn't make him any less proud of it.

Wes never said a word about what she had done. Not directly. But two days later, she woke up to find her back patio filled with trash. He had thrown it over the wall. It wasn't random trash from the dumpster; she could tell by the junk-food wrappers. His favorites.

That was the last communication they had until four months ago, at the engagement party. Now here they are, together again.

When Ivy leaves his house, Wes walks her out to the Uber. Before she gets in, he wraps his arms around her. He hasn't shaved yet, and she rubs her hand over the stubble.

'You should grow a beard,' she says.

'I should?'

'Beards are sexy.'

He tilts his head, looking confused. 'You've never said you think beards are sexy.'

'I'm sure I have.'

'Not to me.'

She shrugs, kissing him lightly to avoid the burn. 'Well, I'm saying it to you now.' She turns away and gets into the waiting car. He leans down, and she lowers the window.

'Have a good day,' he says.

'You too. See you later.'

On the way to pick up her own car, Ivy thinks about that beard comment. She didn't intend to imply he *wasn't* sexy, but it seemed like he took it that way. Maybe she should've said she didn't mean it like that.

And she certainly wasn't trying to test him. Like trying to see if he would grow a beard just because she told him to.

Not consciously, anyway.

Tonight, she'll clarify that point. They're supposed to get

together around eight, after the disc golf and chicken wings with his friends. Maybe watch a movie. She'll have to find a way to bring it up again without sounding like she's obsessed with beards.

Unless he hasn't shaved. If he does decide to grow a beard, she isn't saying a word.

11

Saturday night, Wes didn't expect to be hanging out with his college friends, but when he got a call about a surprise birthday party, Ivy wanted to go.

'Why wouldn't I?' she had said.

He didn't have a good answer, or a good reason to argue.

The party is one town over, in a house three times the size of Wes's. Brand-new, shiny from floor to ceiling, the great room overflowing into the backyard. Beautiful, but no personality anywhere.

Ivy, standing beside him, wears a dress the color of red wine. Her lipstick matches. She leans in close and says, 'Airbnb?'

'Definitely.'

They smile.

She walks away, toward a group of friends, and he congratulates Luke. The man of the hour. His fiancée is the one who organized the party. She didn't go to college with them, but he's been with her for a few years.

'Thirty-one,' Wes says.

'I know, right?'

They talk about work and sports, the two standard topics, until Luke's fiancée pops in to whisper something in his ear. As she walks away, he watches her. Shakes his head.

'Can't decide if I'm ready to get married or if she's convinced me I am,' Luke says.

'Both, probably.'

'Maybe, yeah.' Luke shrugs. 'So ... Ivy. You're back together?'

Wes knew this would happen. Not everyone at the party knows how often he and Ivy have broken up and gotten back together, but Luke does.

'We are,' Wes says. 'I guess she can't live without me.'

'I heard that,' someone behind him said.

Ivy.

She's smiling, a drink in one hand and a small plate of finger food in the other.

Luke holds up his hand. 'Whoa, hold on. Don't start your drama at my party, please.'

Ivy laughs, handing the food to Wes. No sign of anger in her eyes. 'You have to watch him,' she says to Luke. 'He doesn't always get it right.'

'Once in a great while, I might be wrong,' Wes says.

'Obviously, you meant that *you* can't live without *me*.'

'That's exactly what I meant.'

She plucks a shrimp roll off the plate and blows a kiss at Wes before walking away. Luke doesn't get a chance to say anything else, because a few people walk over and wish him a happy birthday. Wes turns a little to the left so he has a view of the whole party. And Ivy.

She is talking to a group of women, most of whom he recognizes. He watches her smile and laugh, and at one point, she looks surprised.

Not a college girl anymore. She's a woman, and a sophisticated one. Being in sales, Wes knows how to work a room. Ivy is right up there with the best of them. The way she talks, the gestures she makes. Or doesn't make. The way she looks, too. Not as athletic as she used to be – her body has filled out a bit. More curves. Softer. His body is softer, as well, but it looks a lot better on her.

Ivy feels him watching, looks over at him. Winks.

They come together on the back patio, exchanging a bit of

gossip and a kiss on the cheek before separating again. Each on opposite sides of the saltwater pool. She starts talking to one of her old roommates from Davis.

'Hi there,' someone says.

Her voice is silky, her dress is lacy, and it's impossible to miss everything in between. Wes has no idea who she is, but she is talking to him.

'I'm Lisa Bates.'

'Bates? Are you related to . . .' He gestures to Luke's fiancée.

'We're sisters.'

'Well, it's nice to meet you. I'm Wes Harmon. No relation to anyone here,' he says. 'At least that I know of.'

She smiles, takes a sip of her drink. Takes a not-so-subtle look at his empty ring finger.

Wes isn't the best-looking guy in the room. He knows that. He also knows he isn't the worst. Women don't flock to him, but they don't avoid him, either. And he can be charming. Sometimes obscenely charming if he's in the mood, and that's an advantage. Getting a date isn't a problem, like with the woman in front of him.

If he wanted to.

He glances over at Ivy. She sees it all from a distance and holds up her drink like she's toasting him. He nods back.

They have passed go.

Lisa asks Wes how he knows the birthday boy, and their conversation continues. What they do for a living, where they went to school, who they know. He tries not to look at Ivy again, an attempt that lasts only a few minutes. Three, maybe. At best. When he does glance over, she is talking to a guy.

Of course she is.

Wes is quick to size him up. Clothes, hair, shoes – and, most importantly, the way he is looking at Ivy.

Back to Lisa. They've moved on to restaurants now: which ones they like, hate, haven't been to and want to try. But his mind is on the other side of the patio.

Lisa is still talking, maneuvering around the restaurant conversation, now adding in bars, as well. Waiting for him to suggest they try one together. Wes shifts his position so he can see Ivy out of the corner of his eye.

He continues to dodge Lisa's advances, evading any direct invitations so he isn't forced to say no. It's a dance, really. The whole party is filled with dances.

After not getting anywhere with the restaurant talk, Lisa pivots.

'What about sports?' she says. 'Are you a Niners fan?'

It's a nice move. She landed on a topic he can really talk about. And he does, starting with the Warriors. A few minutes go by before he looks over at Ivy again.

That guy is touching her.

Nothing overt, nothing sexual, but he has put his hand on Ivy's arm. Holding it, almost. He barreled right through the touch barrier as if it didn't exist.

Wes doesn't like the way Ivy is laughing. It looks too real.

'Everything okay?' Lisa says.

'Everything's great.' He gives her his best smile. 'How did you get so into sports?'

She starts talking about her dad and what a big fan he is. Wes tries to pay attention, but it isn't easy. Especially when that guy keeps touching Ivy. Three times now, by his count.

Even worse, Ivy has stopped looking over at Wes.

Lisa waves her hand in front of his face. 'Hello?'

'I'm here,' he says.

'You look like you're a million miles away.'

More like fifty feet, but who's counting. He doesn't want to go over there. Wait, no – he *does* want to go over there, except that's exactly what Ivy is trying to get him to do. She is practically begging him to walk over and interrupt her conversation with that guy.

And it works.

'Sorry, I'm not trying to be rude,' he says, 'but my girlfriend is trying to get my attention.'

'Oh, it's no problem.' If Lisa is disappointed, she does a good job hiding it. Big smile, no shock in her eyes. 'You better get going. Nice to meet you, Wes.'

He walks right over to Ivy and introduces himself to her friend. Oliver. Wes shakes his hand, gripping it hard. Ivy has a big smile on her face, though not because of Oliver. It's because Wes went to her before she came to him.

Later tonight, Ivy will tease him for that. He's looking forward to it.

I2

On Monday morning, Bianca arrives for work before anyone else in the department. Typical. And expected.

Today, she is wearing a new outfit. Or new to her, since it came from a consignment shop. But it's a high-end designer, the same kind worn by women at the office who can afford to buy it firsthand. The outfit makes Bianca feel like she fits in.

Nobody comes in late on Mondays. At eight thirty, all the reps have to attend what they call the pregame. No alcohol, just a lot of espresso, and they map out their goals for the week. Bianca notes that Wes is in the office by eight, second only to Tanner. It looks like Wes is wearing a new tie, as well.

'Morning,' he says.

'Good morning. How was your weekend?'

'Not bad. How was yours?'

'Very good, thank you.'

Wes nods and goes into his office, giving her no clue what *AB* or *I* means. Sales is the only department where there are very few cubicles. Most have an office with a door so they can speak to clients in private. For Bianca, it's a little annoying. It would be so much easier if Wes left his door open, but he never does.

During a midmorning break, she talks to Tanner, waiting for him to say something about the new woman he's dating. He gives her nothing. Next, she checks in with Dana, who doesn't drop a single hint about the guy in accounting she's seeing. Or sleeping with. Both, probably.

The lack of trust at Siphon is the only thing Bianca hates

about this job. She had hoped this would be more like a family, or at least closer to one. The same thing she had hoped about her sorority in college. But those girls had withheld more than they said, and several had outright lied. If they had just been honest, Bianca wouldn't have had to snoop through all their rooms.

Her family was no different. Three sisters, all older, none of whom would tell Bianca about their boyfriends or their dates or even their plans for the weekend. She found out anyway, because her sisters weren't that good about hiding things. Still . . . it was a lot of work.

But Wes: He wins the award for the most work she has ever put into someone. No friend, family member, or co-worker has even come close.

After seeing Joey Fisher's memorial fund on his browser, she tried to find out if he had actually donated. No luck getting into his bank account. She knew where he kept his money – Foundation Bank & Trust, also in his internet history – but couldn't access it. Wes wasn't stupid enough to save his password on a work computer.

She went through his entire social media history, all the way back to MySpace. Even back then, he didn't post much. Even less now. Not a single connection to Joey Fisher or his family.

His friends came next. Bianca checked everyone who followed him, along with their history. It took a couple weeks to get through it all. Nothing. Again.

She ponders this in the late morning, wondering what more she can do while trying not to think about how hungry she is or that lunch is an hour and a half away.

The elevator dings, and a woman walks toward her, someone Bianca has never seen before. The woman stops in front of Bianca's desk. Her style: designer corporate. Navy blue skirt, modest blouse, three-inch heels. Neutral makeup, manicured nails, and hair one inch above the shoulders.

'I'm here to see Wes Harmon,' she says. 'My name is Ivy Banks.' Her voice is bright and cheery, as if she wants Bianca to like her.

'Do you have an appointment?'

'No, I'm just dropping something off. He knows I'm –'

Wes's door opens, and he walks out smiling. Ivy smiles, too. So many smiles.

He motions for her to follow him back to his office. As she does, Ivy reaches out to hand him a phone.

His phone.

The door shuts, closing Bianca off from the rest of the conversation. Fine with her, because now she has part of the code to Wes's schedule.

I for Ivy.

Wes's phone rings as soon as Ivy is gone. The desk phone. On the caller ID: Tanner.

He takes a deep breath and picks up.

'Was that *Ivy*?' Tanner says.

'It was.'

Big sigh. 'Jesus Christ, man.'

'Don't worry. We're in a good place,' Wes says. '*She's* in a good place.'

'"In a good place"? Did you really just say that?'

This is why Wes didn't want Ivy coming into the office. He was supposed to meet her outside to get his phone, but his conference call ran over. He also couldn't get mad at her for coming in. She has a job and had to get back to it.

During the five minutes she was in the office, Tanner saw her.

There wasn't anything Wes could have done differently. He couldn't order Ivy out of the office.

And this is Tanner. Not only his boss, but the man who hired him seven years ago. The first person who ever told Wes he could be great at sales. Tanner may not be a perfect man, but he taught Wes everything he knows about Siphon's business.

He was also the one who got Wes into famous quotes. Tanner was always using them, starting on Wes's first day on the job.

'"The problem human beings face is not that we aim too high and fail,"' he had said, '"but that we aim too low and succeed."'

Michelangelo.

Wes downloaded his first quotes app that day. He has gone through several of them since, right up until he deleted the latest one. The quote about love being a serious mental disease was enough to break the habit. Maybe it was true, maybe it wasn't, but he didn't want that kind of thing popping up on his phone.

Of course Tanner knew who Ivy was; they'd met on several occasions. Over the years, she has been in the office a few times. One of which was tragically memorable.

Tanner will not let him forget it. Tanner is his mentor, his friend, his boss. He's looking out for Wes, as he has said on many occasions.

As your mentor and de facto big brother, I feel obligated to tell you that your girlfriend is insane.

'Nothing's going to happen,' Wes says now. He hopes this is true. He intends for it to be, he wants it to be, but how can anyone predict what someone will do. Sometimes he doesn't know what he'll do the minute before he does it. It's called being human.

Tanner isn't having it.

'Keep your relationship under control,' he says, 'or I'll ban her from the building.'

'You have my word.'

'How comforting. And in case I forget to say this, you're an idiot,' Tanner adds. 'You can quote me on that.'

What Tanner doesn't know is why Ivy had come to Siphon and damn near destroyed Wes's office.

No reason to tell him.

13

Ivy drives back to her office, thinking about this morning. Wes had spent the night, and when he left, he forgot his phone but not his electric razor. Ever since she mentioned the beard thing, he has shaved every single day.

Good.

She would never tell him, but it would've been so disappointing if he had started growing a beard. Someone who does everything you say is too boring. Tedious. No backbone, no opinion – just following orders like a robot programmed to obey.

Not Wes. He never budged. Not once, not even when he was trying to make up for something else he had done.

She liked that. Until it annoyed her.

Like when they first moved in together after college and the bathroom became a problem. She needed more room, because she had more stuff. After all, he didn't wear makeup and she did; therefore, she needed the space. A common argument, according to what Ivy had heard from her friends, but in her relationship, this was a battle. Wes even started referring to it as the Bathroom Wars.

When her products spread out too far, he swept them into a drawer to clear the counter. The second time, he hid the makeup all over the apartment, stuck in every nook and cranny he could find. She collected them and put every single thing back on top of the counter.

'I need this stuff,' she told him. 'Just be happy you don't.'

Wes was not happy. In fact, he was so unhappy that he

swept the makeup onto the floor, breaking all of it. Well, not *all*, but a lot. Enough to make her freak out, because in an entry-level job that paid close to nothing, she didn't have the money to replace what had been broken.

Guilt kicked in, and he bought her a gift certificate and a stacked organizer that fit on the corner of the counter.

Too late.

She was broke all the time, and buying new makeup was the last straw. Ivy had already gone out and secured a second job. Two nights a week, she would work at a strip club.

That started a whole new problem.

Amalgamated Services, Inc., is more than a building, it's a campus. Ivy has to be checked in at the gate just to park her car at work. Despite the bad management, her job isn't terrible. Good salary, decent benefits, and she has plenty of time to learn languages or, if she wanted, to work another job online. Hard to complain about that.

But the corporate life took some adjustment. All of life did, in a way, or at least any part of it with a rigid structure. College wasn't as bad; at least she could skip a class without being kicked out. At work, that would get her fired.

Growing up, she was used to having a lot more freedom to be impulsive. Spontaneous. Her parents even encouraged it, celebrating her wild ideas. No one does now. Not at Amalgamated Services. The corporate world is like another planet.

When she was a kid, marijuana was illegal to grow and sell, but her parents did it anyway. Raids weren't uncommon, nor were the planes flying overhead, seeking out the farms. Local police mostly looked the other way at the farmers, but the DEA did not.

When one of her parents' friends was arrested, everybody chipped in to help. Sometimes by taking care of their kids or pets, other times by donating for bail money. Small farmers weren't rich – not even close. Her parents certainly weren't.

And they weren't always there when she got home from school.

Her mom and dad were arrested twice when she was a kid: the first time, when she was eight, then again when she was fourteen. Both times they were out on bail in less than a week. A long legal battle followed, and as Ivy figured out later, it included a bribe or two. The marijuana business was an open secret, and a lot of people ignored it.

The latest arrest, the one that has put them in prison for years, came long after Ivy had moved away from home. She wasn't even there when it happened.

But when she was young, sometimes her parents were gone for other reasons. A delivery hadn't been made, and the driver had gotten into trouble. Maybe arrested. Her parents would have to make it right. Or it was to help one of the other farmers, someone in a similar situation who needed help. There was always a neighbor around to take care of Ivy when her parents were gone. They never watched her as closely as her mom and dad did.

The first time it happened, when she was only six, she cried every day until they were back. By the time she was twelve, she didn't cry at all. Her parents usually returned within days; the longest was a week. The idea of them disappearing was no longer scary. In fact, she started to look forward to going home just to find out what had happened while she was at school. It made the days a little more exciting.

And she knew they would always come back. Just like Wes does.

Ivy enters Amalgamated Services through the front, walking into an absurdly large atrium with a glass ceiling. The front desk has not one but two receptionists, both poised to greet whomever walks in the door. They wave at Ivy in unison.

She takes the elevator to the fifth floor, and as soon as the door opens, Ivy finds her manager standing in front of her. Helena is a typical fortysomething woman in California. In shape, in style, Botox and hair in place.

'Ivy,' she says. Her voice is almost a whisper. 'Please come with me.'

Ivy follows her down the hall, past the cubicles, to a conference room in the far corner. She keeps her eyes on Helena's slate grey shoes. Helena stops in front of the closed door.

'Someone is here to see you,' Helena says. 'I thought you might need some privacy.'

Ivy nods, still not asking any questions. Whatever is happening, it's best not to act confused.

It's a little surprising to walk in the room and see Detective Karen Colglazier. She is sitting with her back to the large windows, a notepad and pen on the table. Next to Helena, Karen looks her age. The wrinkles at the corners of her eyes are deeper, her skin doesn't have the same glow, and those tiny lines around her lips aren't going to get better. Also, Karen needs to stop furrowing her brow. That crease.

She is in shape, though. Maybe better shape than Helena, because it's natural instead of surgically enhanced.

Helena nods to both of them and closes the door, leaving Ivy and Karen alone.

'I apologize for showing up at your work,' Karen says. 'I just have a few more questions.' She is smiling, but not really. It's the same smile Ivy uses when talking to someone she hates.

'Of course,' Ivy says. She takes a seat across from Karen, folding her hands together on top of the table. 'I appreciate you taking this so seriously.'

'Stalking can get out of hand very quickly. I always take it seriously.'

Ivy nods, keeping her face blank.

'I spoke to Wes Harmon last week,' Karen says. 'He denied leaving you any gifts or notes. But I assume, since I haven't heard from you, that you haven't received anything new?'

'No, I haven't.'

'And have you heard from Wes?' Karen looks at her hard, like she's daring Ivy to lie.

'I did,' Ivy says. 'Wes contacted me after you spoke to him. He wanted to make it clear that he wasn't stalking me.'

'Do you believe him?'

Ivy pauses for a beat, like she has to think about it. Which she does. 'I'm just glad it's stopped. And I can get back to living my life without being afraid all the time.'

She smiles. Karen does not.

14

Bianca hovers by the break room on the fourth floor, one above where she should be. This is the second time today she's been up here but, so far, still no sign of Abigail Wright.

In theory, Bianca could just call her. They work at the same company, and Abigail had Bianca's job before being promoted to the CEO's executive assistant, so Bianca could come up with a good reason to contact her.

Amateur move.

That is not how you get information. That's how you get caught trying to snoop.

Today she spends all of her breaks up on the fourth floor, hoping to spontaneously bump into Abigail. When it doesn't work, again, she goes back down to her desk. There's always another way.

After work, Bianca moves her car as close to the front door as she can get. Easier now that the day is over. She sits in the driver's seat, scrolling through her phone while she waits. It gives her a chance to review what she's learned.

Ivy Banks, thirty years old, lives at 2212 Parkhaven, Apt. 1F. She's a graduate of UC Davis and employed at Amalgamated Services, Inc.

That isn't all she knows about Ivy Banks. She knows who Ivy's friends are, what kind of car she drives, who she follows online, and whose posts she likes. Social media makes this too easy.

A few things stand out. First, not a single connection to Joey Fisher.

Second, Ivy is fairly active on Instagram, posting at least once a week and sometimes twice. Wes follows her. But even though he spent the night at her place and forgot his phone in the morning, Ivy doesn't follow him.

Curious. Bordering on weird. Especially considering they're a couple. Or were a couple. Hard to tell, actually. Ivy's posts aren't exactly clear about their status these days, but they've known each other a long time. At least seven years.

Information. To make sense of all this, Bianca needs a lot more of it.

She glances up at her rearview mirror. Abigail Wright is a hard woman to miss. Very tall, very thin, with red hair and a perfectly symmetrical face. A lot of men tell her she should be a model. She responds by walking away from them.

When Abigail exits the building, Bianca gets out of her car, goes around to the back, and opens the trunk. She waves to Abigail while pretending to look for something.

Abigail, always polite, calls out to her. 'How are you these days?'

'Doing well, thanks. How's life on the executive floor?'

'Busy.' Abigail stops beside her. 'Is your car okay?'

'Oh, it's fine. I thought I threw my gym bag in here this morning, but it looks like I forgot.' Bianca turns away from the trunk and faces Abigail. She has to look up, that's how tall Abigail is. Especially in heels, which she always wears. 'Hey, I'm glad I ran into you. I have a question.'

Abigail pauses before answering. 'About Tanner?'

'No, one of the reps. Wes Harmon.'

'Wes? What about him?'

'I'm just wondering if there's anything I should be aware of.' Bianca leaves her question as open as possible, giving Abigail an opportunity to say just about anything.

'Hard worker, handles his business,' she says. 'He was one of the easier reps when I was there.'

Bianca keeps quiet, waiting to see if Abigail will say more. She does not.

'Why?' Abigail says. She stands perfectly still, like she's posing for a picture. 'Did something happen?'

'Not really.' Bianca shrugs, like it's nothing. 'Well, his personal life – not that I know anything about it – but it sort of came up in the office. Seemed a little . . . odd, I suppose.'

'Ah.' Abigail glances back at the office, smiling at someone walking to their car. 'Wes never said too much about it. He was always very professional.' Her lips contract, pursing into a tight bow. 'The only thing I remember is Ivy.'

'Ivy?'

'She's a problem.'

I've got a client thing tonight, but I'm free tomorrow. Dinner?

Maxwell's?

Perfect.

Ivy smiles as she makes a reservation online. Maxwell's has always been one of their favorites, a place that holds a lot of good memories and not a single bad one.

It also distracts her from thinking about the detective for a minute. Fair Valley obviously doesn't have enough crime, because Karen is spending entirely too much time on Ivy and Wes. Ridiculous, because Ivy hears about crime every day in the news. Karen has no business looking into a situation that's already over.

And the longer their conversation at the office had continued, the more Ivy realized she had made a huge mistake by going to the police.

'After meeting with Wes,' Karen had said, 'I did a little digging into your relationship.'

'Digging?' Ivy said.

'Eight years ago, Wes called 911. He accused you of vandalizing his car.' Karen scrolled through her phone, reading the details out loud. 'Broken windshield, slashed tires, and the rearview mirror was destroyed.'

'Then you also must have seen that no charges were ever filed. A number of cars were vandalized in our neighborhood,' Ivy said.

'I did see that. I just thought it was odd Wes immediately named you as the one who did it. He believed you were capable of that kind of violence.'

'*Wrongly* believed,' Ivy said. 'We had been fighting at the time. I guess that's why he thought it was me.'

Or maybe because he had watched her do it.

Ivy had thought of this possibility – that Karen would find that report. Ivy knew there was a record of it somewhere in their system. But she also knew it would be easy to dismiss it as a mistake.

'Wes recanted his statement,' Ivy said. 'He was angry at me for something else, and he made a mistake.'

'Yes, I saw that, as well,' Karen said.

Ivy assumed this would be the end of their conversation about the past. It was not.

Ivy heads into the dressing room with at least a dozen outfits. She has to split them up – only six allowed at a time! – but
she is a firm believer in trying things on. Even if you don't
love it on the hanger, you might love it on your body. Fact.

Not that she needs a new dress for dinner at Maxwell's.
She has a least a dozen that Wes hasn't seen, all bought over
the past year, but there's nothing like a new dress to make a
date special.

Plus, it stops her from obsessing about that detective.

Ivy and Wes have finally come to a point where everything
is good. Better than good. It's fantastic. No lies, no games –
they've returned to something real. Or rediscovered it.

She takes off the black dress, which is too boring, and puts
on the emerald green one.

Better, but not perfect.

Yes, she and Wes got back together in a screwed-up way,
and it probably never would've happened if she hadn't called
the police. But it didn't have to turn into all this. Karen didn't
have to dig so deep into the past. It's a little rude, to be
honest.

The blue dress is next. Sky blue, though not so light it's
transparent. Snug without being too tight, sexy but not vul-
gar, and it doesn't make her look like she's trying too hard.
It's also the most expensive.

She can almost afford it. Close enough.

On her way back to her car, she imagines being at Maxwell's tomorrow night. The little candle on the table, piano

music in the background – not so loud that you have to shout, not so soft that you can hear the other customers. Ivy is wearing her new outfit, Wes sits across from her, and they're smiling.

Until she tells him about her visit from the detective. She should tell him, because being open and honest is the only way to make a relationship work. Everybody knows that, and Ivy knows it from experience. Secrets can ruin everything.

She imagines how that conversation would go, especially when she tells him Karen has been digging into their relationship. More than anything else, she tries to picture the look on Wes's face when Ivy tells him the worst part.

It's not good. The only upside is how hot he is when he's angry.

Marcus walks into Wes's office without knocking. He is another sales rep, one of the most successful at Siphon, and he always looks like he just walked out of a magazine. Marcus is what they're all supposed to look like, but he is the only one who manages to pull it off. Other than Tanner, of course. The original. Everyone else is a copy-and-paste.

Marcus smiles and pulls two tickets out of his pocket. 'Tonight.'

'No way.'

'You doubt me?' Marcus throws the tickets on Wes's desk. The Warriors game, not floor seats but close enough.

Wes will be at Maxwell's with Ivy. If he cancels now . . . well, he doesn't want to think about what she would do. And it's a long drive to and from San Francisco. If he goes, he probably won't see her at all tonight. Yes, he would like to go to the game. No, he doesn't want to deal with the fallout of making that decision.

'I can't go,' Wes says.

'Excuse me?'

'I just . . . I have a date. No way I can miss it.'

'It's Tuesday,' Marcus says. 'Who dates on Tuesdays?'

'Seriously, I can't go.'

'Jesus, who is this girl?'

'My girlfriend.'

'First, when did you get a girlfriend?' Marcus says.

Wes shrugs.

'Second,' Marcus says, 'isn't that a benefit of being in a relationship? The freedom to cancel on her without repercussions?'

'Next time,' Wes says.

It's difficult to say those words and turn down Marcus's offer. Of course he would rather go to the game than out to dinner – especially tonight, because Wes isn't sure if he should tell her about Tanner. That he remembered Ivy, recognized her when she came into the office. And threatened to ban her from the building.

But should he tell her? Wes has been wrestling with that question all day.

No one wants to be told something like that. It might hurt her feelings, and that's the last thing Wes wants to do. Everything has been going so well, so amazing, that he doesn't want to ruin it.

He also doesn't want to hide anything from her. Been down that road a thousand times, and it never led anywhere good.

Lists have been made. The good reasons, the bad reasons, the horrible reasons, plus all the possible outcomes – good, bad, tragic. Including the end of their relationship. Again. And that's the problem. The last one. He can't decide if it's worse to tell her something hurtful or not tell her at all.

What he needs is a rule. A guideline. Something easy to apply so he can make a decision.

He flips the situation around. Ivy used to do that a lot, usually when they were arguing. She would say, 'Imagine if the situation was reversed. If I did to you what you did to me. How would you feel?'

Bad. The answer was always bad.

From now on, this is what he should do. When Wes isn't sure if he should tell Ivy something, he should ask himself if he would want to know. If he would want Ivy to tell him.

And if her boss was threatening to ban him from her workplace, he would want to know.

Probably.

Bianca stares at the door to Wes's office, wondering about him. She does that a lot.

She also wonders why he is turning down Warriors tickets. He loves basketball. He can't possibly love this Ivy woman more than he loves the Warriors.

Honestly, Bianca doesn't see what the big deal is about her. She has looked at every one of her posts, going back years. First, Ivy is not very original. The pictures are copies of copies of influencers'. Not well-done, either, if she is being honest. And Bianca is always honest, at least in her own head.

Ivy is cute. Bianca will give her that. Ivy looks like a woman you'd see on commercials selling tampons. More sweet than sexy. Not a woman who could set the world on fire. Except, apparently, for the world Wes lives in.

She's a problem.

Too bad Abigail hadn't expanded on that and given Bianca some details, but that was all she said.

Bianca has given her next step a lot of thought. She has to be careful before talking to any other coworkers, or else she runs the risk of word getting around that she's been asking

66

about Wes. Once is acceptable. Two or more times, and people start to notice.

Which brings her back, again and again, to Tanner. No other choice. Her boss asks for the gossip but rarely offers any in return. He wants to know what's happening but doesn't spread it. Tanner's ego is big enough that he doesn't need the boost.

Bianca does have to be clever in her approach. If she tries to be subtle, he will see right through it. Anyone that good at sales knows how to read between the lines and hear what isn't being said.

The next time Tanner comes around to ask what's happening – something he does three or four times a day – Bianca gives him the usual work updates. Where everyone is, who's meeting who, and what's coming up for the rest of the day.

'Good,' he says. 'What else?'

Bianca has never flirted with anyone at the office before. In fact, she makes it a point not to engage in behavior that falls anywhere on the flirtation spectrum. She has never done it with a coworker or a client, and certainly not with her boss.

Until now.

She has no choice. Her rule has to be broken, because this is about Wes. He's been driving her crazy since she found that memorial fund in his browser history.

And flirting will work, because it's Tanner. Assuming what she's heard is true.

Bianca leans in toward him. Tanner doesn't look surprised or put off at all. Instead, he responds by leaning right back into her.

'Wes turned down a ticket to the Warriors game tonight,' she whispers. 'He told Marcus he had a date with Ivy.'

'Ivy?' Tanner says.

'He told Marcus she's his girlfriend.'

Bianca watches his face. A roll of his eyes, followed by a quick shake of his head.

'That's not good,' he whispers.

'No?'

'No.'

He smiles.

She smiles back. And she winks.

16

Ivy wipes the steam off her bathroom mirror. She had left work a little early to shower and get ready for dinner, which is a good thing. Choosing the right products always takes a bit of time, because Wes has a thing about smell. Not a big fan of perfume. One time she wore Poison – a heavy, spicy scent – and he almost gagged.

'You don't need to smell like a bouquet,' he once said. 'Just fresh and clean and . . . like you.'

He never understood that smelling like that takes work. Natural doesn't mean product-free.

The name of her lotion is Pure; the scent is so light it almost doesn't exist. Next, the makeup – all neutral, all the time – and finally, her hair. He doesn't have a preference about either of those, though once when she had her makeup done for a fancy party, her eyelashes scared him a little. He got over it.

She would never tell Wes this, but getting ready for the date is sometimes the best part. That's when the whole night is open to every possibility, both good and bad. Which way the night goes and how it gets there is still unknown. It feels like a tingle, a faint hum that runs through her veins, right alongside her blood.

The anticipation never gets old. She hopes it never does.

The sky blue dress hangs outside her closet, her beige shoes on the floor beneath it. As she slips into both, the hum grows a little stronger.

Tonight will be a good one. That's her feeling about it. If

it's true you can manifest your reality just by picturing it and sending it out into the universe, then it might even be better than good. It might be spectacular.

Although she still hasn't decided if she should tell him about the detective. She will eventually, but tonight may not be the right time.

Maxwell's is located downtown, right between an old Hallmark shop and an upscale bakery for dogs. Fair Valley in a nutshell. A sleepy, out-of-the-way town that has exploded because tech industry money has spread across the state.

Wes's car is parked right out front, which makes Ivy smile. She drives past it and grabs the first open space.

One last check in the mirror before getting out. She isn't gorgeous. Regardless of whether they admit it or not, women know when they're exceptionally good-looking. And they know when they're not.

But she doesn't have to be gorgeous. Just pretty enough for Wes.

Maxwell's is considered fine dining, or as close as any restaurant in Fair Valley gets, so the lighting is low and a fancy hostess is standing at the door. Ivy smooths her dress as she walks to the table.

Wes is waiting, the wine list open in front of him. She is still ten feet away when he senses her. Or maybe she's wrong about that. Maybe he senses *someone* is walking toward him.

He looks up and smiles at her. Until he doesn't.

The smile disappears from his face, replaced by shock. Then anger. There is no look she knows better.

She has no idea why.

'Here you are,' the hostess says. She gestures like they're on a game show. Here he is, your prize: one angry man.

Wes snaps out of it long enough to get up and hold her

70

chair. Once Ivy is seated, the hostess hands her a menu and walks away.

'Hi,' Ivy says.

'Hi.'

She gives him the biggest, realest smile she can manage. 'Good to see you.'

Wes sits across from her, elbows on the table, hands folded, wine list forgotten. He looks at her, his eyes shifting from her face to her dress and back again. 'Nice dress.'

'Thank you.'

'Did you get that for tonight?' he says. 'Just for me?'

The edge to his voice makes her pause. He isn't asking what he really wants to know. He's asking something else.

'It's new, yes.'

'Thought so.' Even sharper this time.

'Is there a problem with it?'

'Oh no,' he says. The sarcasm is thick. 'No problem at all.'

A waiter arrives to take their drink order. While Wes chooses a wine, she looks at the menu. Salmon is what she always orders – it's one of her favorite dishes – but tonight it won't be enough. Something is brewing. All her senses are on high alert, preparing for whatever is coming, though she has no idea what it is. Feels like a puzzle wrapped in an electric fence.

She scans down the entrée choices, finally landing on prime rib. The kind of thing you eat before heading into battle.

17

Tanner recognized you in the office yesterday,' Wes says. The words spit out of his mouth, flying across the table and landing on Ivy.

Yes, he had decided. *This is a perfect time to tell her about Tanner.*

'Really?' she says. 'I didn't see him.'

'He saw you.'

She shrugs a little, like she couldn't care less. Wes watches the sleeve of her dress rise and fall back into place.

Only a few hours ago, he thought things would be different this time. That they wouldn't go down this road again: playing games, trying to hurt each other. They've had a great week together, and not going to the basketball game tonight had been a no-brainer.

Until she showed up.

'Tanner remembered you,' Wes says, 'from when you were in the office before.' He lets that hang there, allowing her a chance to see where this is going. It doesn't take long for her to remember when she nearly destroyed his office.

'I see,' she finally says.

'If you do anything like that again,' he says, 'you'll be banned from the building.' He could've said it better, nicer, but he didn't want to.

'Is that what Tanner said? That *he* would ban me?'

'Yes.'

'I won't do that again,' she says. 'Unless I have a reason to.'

Ivy looks at him, her eyes not wavering. Neither moves until the waiter arrives to take their order.

She has a lot of nerve – he'll give her that. But this is what she does. Ivy pokes and prods, nudging him until he has no choice but to respond.

A few years ago, she'd done it with a guy named Patrick. They were dating, or maybe in a relationship, which she broadcast all over social media. Ivy and Patrick at a restaurant, Ivy and Patrick in the park, Ivy and Patrick at the movies. All big smiles and heart emojis.

Patrick was not the guy for her. He was the guy who would make Wes react.

One night, she posted a selfie with the caption Date night at Pearl! Convenient, letting Wes know exactly where she and Patrick were going to be. He almost didn't show up. In fact, he made a huge effort not to. He went out to a sports bar after work with some coworkers, had a beer, watched a bit of the football game. No, he wouldn't give her the satisfaction of showing up at Pearl. He wouldn't give her what she wanted.

While he was at the sports bar, he saw a woman who vaguely, from a distance, reminded him of Ivy. She walked in with a man who vaguely, from a distance, reminded him of Patrick. They made him think about the real Ivy and Patrick, who were having dinner just a few blocks away.

Ivy was definitely trying to get his attention. But another thought had taken root, whispering in the back of his mind, making Wes start to wonder if this was something more. If she had really found someone else.

When he walked into Pearl, they were already seated. Ivy and Patrick smiling, laughing, drinking a glass of wine. Wes didn't hesitate. He blew right past the hostess to their table, where he stood over them. And he lied.

'Well, if it isn't Ivy,' he said. 'How funny to see you here, since you told me you were going out of town.'

Patrick looked at him, then at Ivy, and then back to Wes. He blinked.

Ivy did not. She kept her face still, not appearing surprised at all. She turned to Patrick and patted him on the hand. Wes almost felt bad for the guy. He was the only one who had no idea what was happening.

'I told you,' she said to Wes, 'that I never wanted to see you again. It doesn't matter if I'm in town or not.'

Wes laughed. Sounded more like a bark. He was attracting attention, and it didn't bother him a bit. 'Oh, okay. If that's how you want to play this, fine with me.' Then he turned to Patrick. 'Good luck with her. But let me give you some advice from someone who's been there,' he said. '*Run.*'

Wes walked out of the restaurant, betting that he would never see Patrick online again.

And he didn't. Instead, he saw Ivy when she came into his office the next day. Did Wes deserve it? Maybe. But only because she pushed him. Provoked him.

Like she is doing right now, wearing that dress.

Sky blue.

Wes can hardly stand the smell of Ivy's steak. He doesn't eat red meat, hasn't in years, yet she ordered it anyway. Another poke. She is full of them tonight.

'That detective came by my office,' she says, slicing off a bite of her steak. Medium rare, pink inside, and the juice oozing out.

'Karen Colglazier?' he says.

'That's her.'

'You told her it wasn't me?'

She nods. Vaguely.

'Ivy?' he says.

'She knows we spoke, yes.'

Not an answer. Not one he likes, anyway.

'She's been looking into both of us,' Ivy says.

Wes glances up from his plate, for the first time not seeing her dress. 'Looking into us?'

'Apparently, there isn't enough crime around here to keep her busy. She dug back far enough to find that 911 call about your car.'

The old Subaru. Ivy had really messed it up that night. He'd had no choice but to call the police. Once he calmed down, he decided a police record was a little extreme just for a damaged car. They had fixed it, though. Vandalized a few other cars to make it look like it wasn't personal. It's not like the police care about property damage.

'But the charges were dropped,' he said.

'She knows that.'

He goes back to his meal. The salmon. 'So then what's the problem?'

'I'm just telling you,' she says, 'because that's what couples do. They tell each other about their day. You told me about Tanner, and I'm telling you about the detective.'

He feels like he's being scolded. She's good at that, too.

The frustrating part is that somehow she makes it sexy.

18

Every time. Every damn time.

Wes is sweet, he's funny, he's attentive. Wes is the greatest boyfriend in the world . . . until his mood changes. Like the time they had gone down to Monterey for the weekend. On the way back, his switch flipped. He ended up leaving her at a rest stop.

She hadn't done anything. Not. A. Single. Thing. The only – *only* – thing she could come up with is that she had teased him for flirting with a waitress when they stopped for lunch. Some girl who looked nineteen, barely old enough for college, and Wes couldn't take his eyes off her. Didn't try to hide it, either. He wanted Ivy to see it.

Ivy showed a lot of restraint, given how she could've reacted. A bit of light teasing, not the seriously jealous kind, just to let him know she had seen it. Couldn't have missed it if she tried, actually. The next thing she knew, Ivy was alone on the side of the road. Wes can be so dramatic.

At least tonight she has her own car. This time, he was perfect for almost a week.

A *week*.

She can't think of that word in Chinese.

Maybe this is all because of what his boss said. Tanner hates her; she knows that. Or maybe Wes has that dissociative disorder. Multiple personalities. Ivy has never figured it out – not in ten years – and it doesn't help when that vein on his temple throbs. It kind of turns her on.

But one thing she does know, after all these years, is what to do when he turns into a dick.

Hurt him back.

She cuts another bite of her steak, knowing how much it bothers him. He doesn't say anything, not directly, but he wrinkles his nose at the smell. Good. If she has to sit across the table from him, she is going to enjoy her meal. And she does love a good steak.

'That was all she asked about?' Wes asks. 'The 911 call?'

Ivy takes her time chewing her steak, drawing out an extra minute. Not yet. She isn't ready to tell him Karen looked into the car. The old one.

She can imagine what kind of reaction he would have, the range of emotions that would pass through him in just a few seconds. Shock at first, followed by confusion, and then fear. Well, fear mixed with anger. But those emotions are so intertwined it's hard to tell them apart.

Ivy and Wes don't talk about that night. Not ever. Their relationship has a lot of black holes, a lot of places they won't venture down, but the night she started working at the Fine Line is by far the deepest.

It's too painful to think about, much less discuss.

'Yes,' Ivy finally says. 'That's all Karen asked about.'

Wes shakes his head, picking up his wineglass and inhaling deeply. Trying to get the smell of red meat out of his nose. 'But you definitely told her I wasn't stalking you? That she has no reason to look into us?'

'I told her we spoke and everything had stopped, and that I wasn't receiving any more weird gifts or notes.'

Not exactly the same thing.

Wes pushes back from the table, away from the smell and away from her. No scenes. Not tonight.

77

'I have to use the restroom,' he says. It's a lie, and despite all the promises about honesty, he doesn't feel bad about it. Maybe he will later, or maybe he'll forget all about it.

Once he's alone, in the men's bathroom, a flood of stronger emotions hit.

Every time. Every damn time.

He curses himself out far worse than he does her, because he should know better. Never should've agreed to get back together so quickly. Never, never, never. He had promised himself he wouldn't do this, vowed that no matter what she said or did, or how she looked, he would never put himself in this position again.

Yet when they were lying in bed and she said they should be together again, he didn't hesitate. Maybe it had sounded like he did at first, but in his mind the decision was already made. Another chance, another shot to get it right. The lure of the dream stronger than the fear.

It has been a fantastic week, though. Best he's had since the last time.

By the time he returns to the table, their entrée plates have been cleared. Ivy drinks the last of her wine, looking at him over the rim of the glass.

'I ordered two cappuccinos. I wasn't sure if you wanted dessert,' she says.

'No, coffee is fine.' He pauses, almost makes a joke but decides against it. 'I don't need any dessert. I'm pretty full.'

'Me too.'

'I'm not surprised.'

She doesn't react to that. Not even a raised eyebrow. Honestly, the woman should play poker, because she would make a fortune. But that isn't the game she likes.

The cappuccinos arrive, and Ivy talks about learning

Chinese. This is her third new language, but she doesn't speak any of them fluently because she can't practice speaking out loud at work. Though she has cursed him out in Russian and French before.

In the past, he has told her there are so many other things she could do with that kind of time at work. So many other things she could study. Tonight, he keeps his mouth shut.

There is no bantering. No innuendo. None of the usual talk they have during coffee. Wes had really been looking forward to this night. Now all he feels is disappointment. And anger.

When they leave, she stops and faces him in front of the restaurant.

'You seem like you're in a bad mood,' she says. 'Maybe I should just go home tonight.'

A war erupts inside Wes's head. It's all on him now. Either he apologizes for his mood and she comes to his place, or he doesn't and he goes home alone.

Sex or no sex. That is the question.

If only she hadn't worn that dress. Which, as it happens, looks fantastic on her. Especially out here, under the night sky.

If only she hadn't made it worse by ordering that prime rib, knowing how it makes him sick. If not for her behavior, he wouldn't be in this mood, and he wouldn't have to make this decision. The worst part: She knows all of this.

His internal war doesn't last long.

'I'm sorry I've been in such a bad mood tonight,' he says. 'It's work. A lot of problems at the office today.'

Sex with Ivy always wins.

19

Wes knows exactly when he realized Ivy was the one. Getting there was a process, and it started a few weeks after they met. Since he and Ivy didn't have a lot of money, they ate a lot of junk food. The first time they bought it together, they were at a gas station convenience store.

He picked up his favorites: Crunch bar, Flamin' Hot Cheetos, and Diet Coke. Everyone in California drinks water, but his Midwestern roots were too strong. Soda was the only option. The diet part was his only concession.

Her choices were completely different: Butterfinger, Harvest Cheddar SunChips, and Fresca.

Fresca.

When she grabbed a bottle of it, he assumed it was because they were sold out of Sprite and 7Up. But then she did it again at another store. Even when a cooler filled with 7Up was *right there*.

'Grapefruit soda? Not lemon-line?' he said. 'Who does that?'

'I do.'

'It feels weird,' he said.

'Not to me.'

She gripped that bottle like she would fight to the death if anyone tried to snatch it. And she continued to buy Fresca, which confounded him to no end. It was one of the strangest things about her, and he had noticed a few of them. Like the fact that she squeezed the tube of toothpaste in the middle. Not the end, not the front, but the middle. That was weird enough. The Fresca was even weirder.

But he stopped mentioning it because she wasn't going to budge. Plus, she never commented on his choices. Not once.

The topic of their favorite junk food didn't come up again until a couple months later, after a party. Wes had gotten a little drunk. No, a lot drunk. And he had . . . well, he had screwed up. According to her. He couldn't remember a whole lot about the night.

What he did remember, sort of, was that they had their first fight. At the time, he was living off campus with three other guys. After the party, he and Ivy ended up back at his place. To this day, the details aren't clear. He has flashes of what happened, of sitting on his bed while Ivy screamed at him. Vague recollections of Ivy accusing him of flirting with a girl (he hadn't, or at least not seriously). She demanded to know how long he had known the girl (not at all) and if he liked her (he couldn't even remember who she was). All he had wanted to do was lie down and pass out.

The last thing he remembered was the sound of his bedroom door slamming when she left.

In the morning, he woke up with a headache, along with the feeling that he had messed up. Wes didn't think he had, not really, but between the alcohol and the accusations, the truth had been lost.

He staggered to the kitchen, which was empty. If his roommates were home, they were still asleep. Or maybe avoiding the mess.

A bowl sat in the middle of the scratched secondhand table. The biggest bowl they had – a porcelain thing with yellow stripes on the side. It took Wes a few minutes to realize what was inside it.

Crunch bars. Flamin' Hot Cheetos. Both had been crushed into tiny bits, as if Ivy had smashed everything with a hammer. The chocolate crumbs and orange flecks were drenched in Fresca.

Wes tried to imagine Ivy as she did this, tried to imagine how she had ever come up with this idea. He knew for a fact there was no Fresca in the apartment; neither he nor any of his roommates drank it. Which meant she had gone out, bought it, and returned to put together this horrible concoction.

The fact that she had chosen his favorite snacks. The commitment to destroying every Cheeto, every square of chocolate. The amount of thought that had gone into this particular revenge. The fact that it was done out of anger didn't matter. Wes couldn't remember the last time someone had gone to so much trouble for him.

He wasn't about to let a woman like that go.

Wes went straight to her dorm and knocked on the door to her room. Lightly at first, harder when she didn't answer. He could no longer feel the hangover, only the fear. Fear that something had gone too far, that she would never forgive him for the things he couldn't remember. That she was gone for good.

Finally, she did open the door. Ivy looked as bad as he did, like she hadn't slept at all. Her room was filled with clothes. They were on the bed and on chairs and covering her desk. She had taken all her anger out on her closet.

They stared at each other, each waiting for the other to speak first.

He wanted to tell her that he didn't remember, that he wasn't trying to pick up another girl and he never would, because she was the only one he wanted. But she wouldn't have believed it. She would have thought he was saying it because that's the thing you're supposed to say after a drunken night of stupid choices. So he said something that he hoped would cover everything.

'I'm sorry,' he said. 'I screwed up.'

She slammed the door in his face. He knocked, called out her name. She ignored him.

Wes waited a day, hoping she would calm down, and tried to call her. Straight to voicemail. He sent a long-winded apology over eight text messages, and she left every one of them on Delivered. Never read them.

Three days went by, then four. More calls, more texts, all ignored. He stopped contacting her and decided he had to try another way. The kind of thing she couldn't ignore. Desperate? Yes. But did he care? No. If she wanted something bigger than calls or texts, that's exactly what he would give her.

The plan was expensive, at least for him. Didn't matter. He scraped up the money any way he could.

It began with a bribe to her roommate. A nice-enough girl, but she drove a hard bargain when it came to money. She gave him a key and agreed to be gone for the night. Wes went in as soon as Ivy left for her part-time waitressing job.

When she returned, Ivy walked in and stopped dead. Wes was sitting on her bed, eating a Butterfinger, with a bag of Harvest Cheddar SunChips in his lap, and he had opened a two-liter bottle of Fresca. The whole room was packed with her favorites. On her desk, on the bed, on the dresser.

'I was wrong,' he said. 'You always picked the best junk food.'

For a second, Wes thought she was going to scream at him about boundaries and invading her privacy. She didn't.

'See,' she said. 'I knew we were meant for each other.'

20

Ivy is a little bit offended Wes falls asleep so easily. After leaving Maxwell's, his anger was simmering right beneath the surface. So close, but he managed to keep it in check. Ivy never doubted she would be in his bed tonight.

Angry sex, even rough. The real argument never happened, and all that tension had to go somewhere.

He talked to her, too.

Wes thinks she falls asleep even quicker than he does. That's when he talks. Not always, but enough. Sometimes he says she's beautiful or he loves her. Sometimes he says she's crazy. Her favorite was when he called her a sorceress.

Tonight he asked a question:

'Why?'

Why what? she'd wanted to ask. But if she had, he would never believe she was asleep again.

She turns over, toward the window. Light from a streetlamp sneaks in through a break in the curtains. Her new dress is crumpled on the floor, one sleeve now torn. Ripped right out of the seam.

The way Wes talked about it at dinner comes back to her.

Nice dress.

Did you get that for tonight? Just for me?

The words had been thrown at her like daggers. She had no idea why. And she never thought it was about the dress itself; it was about his mood. Now she realizes she was wrong. The dress *was* the why.

Sky blue.

Maybe her subconscious was ahead of her again.

Seven years ago, Ivy wasn't sure if she could go through with it. She walked inside anyway. Even during the day, the neon sign of the Fine Line gentlemen's club was turned on.

The interior was dark, not a window in sight. Like a casino, where it was impossible to know what time it was. Not too many customers on a Wednesday afternoon. Not too many dancers, either, but the ones Ivy saw made her self-conscious about her body. She had no reason to be. She had just turned twenty-three and was in good shape, lived a healthy, out-doorsy life. But she didn't look like the women on the stage.

'Looking for someone?' the bartender said. Another gor-geous woman, albeit one wearing a small amount of clothes. 'Boyfriend?'

'Job.'

She looked Ivy up and down, slowly, not trying to hide it. 'Hang on.'

A man showed up a few minutes later. Clean-cut, wearing a suit exactly like the men Ivy worked with every day. No garish jewelry, no visible tattoos, no sleazy smile. A businessman who looked Ivy up and down the same way the bartender had.

'Have you ever danced before?' he asked.

'Oh no,' she said. 'I'm here to apply for the waitress job.'

'Have you waitressed before?'

'Yes.' In college, at a restaurant. But never in a bar, much less a strip club. She didn't tell him all that.

He pointed to the one waitress who was on duty. She was at the end of the bar and appeared to be bored. She was dressed like the bartender, wearing something similar to a bikini. Bright yellow and a lot more revealing than anything Ivy had seen in public.

'That's what you'd have to wear,' he said.

Ivy almost left. No way she could walk around with her butt and boobs hanging out like that. No way she could stand the way men would look at her. Like a frat party times a billion.

That final thought is what made her stay. The only thing she hated more than fear was allowing men to dictate her choices.

'I can wear that,' she said.

They talked about the schedule. She needed something part-time, a couple nights a week, just enough to supplement her income. The man brought her backstage, into a cramped dressing room filled with racks and boxes, and a long counter packed with makeup. The music was a tad muffled, making it easier to talk. Ivy was introduced to the woman who both managed and mothered the girls.

Coral was in her thirties, at least ten years older than all the dancers and waitresses. She had dark skin, red hair to match her name, and her breasts were twice the size of Ivy's. She looked Ivy up and down much faster than the others.

'You need a name,' she said. 'Customers are going to ask, and you can't give them your real one.'

A list of names ran through Ivy's mind. 'Crystal?'

'Already used.'

'Ummm . . . Brittany?'

'Nope.' Coral shifted her weight, turning toward Ivy with a sigh. 'It's good to have a hook. A theme. Something that'll make the guys remember you.' She winked, and somehow her fake lashes didn't get stuck together.

'A theme,' Ivy repeated. Now her mind was blank.

Again Coral looked her up and down, a little slower this time. 'Nice tan. You spend a lot of time outdoors?'

'Yes.' She and Wes were always out hiking or riding

bikes – even more so since they'd started working. Being stuck in an office all day made her want to run out and get some fresh air as soon as she could. Even her hair was lighter from all the sun.

'Summer,' Coral said. 'You look like a bright summer day.'

'Okay.' Summer wasn't a bad name. Ivy could think of worse.

'What are you? 34C?'

'Um. Sure.'

Sort of. Ivy was more like a 34B most of the month, a 34C when she was bloated.

It was one of the weirdest conversations she ever had. The weirdest thing she had ever done, too. The question on her mind was: *Could* she do it?

Apparently, yes.

Coral dug through a box, pulling out two packages and handing them to Ivy. 'Your uniform. You get two free. If they get lost or damaged, you pay for the replacement.'

Ivy took the cellophane-wrapped bags. A small picture of a woman appeared at the top, in the corner, and she was wearing an almost-bikini like the one worn by the waitress on duty.

Hers had been yellow. Ivy's was sky blue.

Bianca gives her computer screen the finger. It doesn't react, doesn't give her what she wants, but it makes her feel a tiny bit better. Information isn't always easy to get, but it shouldn't be this hard.

Bianca is at work early again, and she's already found everything she can on the internet. Searched through every post made by Ivy and Wes, read every comment, looked at all the tagged photos on other accounts, and all the free public records. What she can't get are police reports. For those, she is required to go down to the station and pay a five-dollar fee. Cheap, but she'd have to fill out a form and give them her name.

The only other option is paying for it online through one of the background-check sites. By comparison, not cheap. At least not for the reputable sites.

Human resources uses one to investigate potential employees, but Bianca doesn't have access to it anymore. Obtaining a single record isn't expensive, but it's not like she has any extra money to throw around. She is an assistant, not a sales rep.

What she does have is access to a company credit card. Bianca makes travel arrangements for the reps, orders their business cards, and restocks supplies for the sales department. Using it for police reports for an employee and his girlfriend would be against the rules. So is having a master key, but the credit card would create a record. A paper trail, as the detective might say. One that could get her fired.

Bianca searches the internet for another option, like a free trial. She finds a site called Who's Done What, which allows her to see if any police records exist, though not the reports themselves. Starting with Wes, she enters his name and birth date.

The site spits out the results: three records.

Three.

She does the same with Ivy. Her birthday is easy enough to find on social media, and Bianca enters the same year Wes was born.

Same result: three records.

Bianca doesn't believe in coincidences. In her experience, they don't exist.

She wants to see the reports, wants to know why Ivy is a problem and why a detective came to see Wes. Bianca starts to enter the credit card number, which she has memorized, but stops halfway through, closes the browser, and returns to her work.

Not worth it. There has to be another way. She thinks about it all morning while searching through her contact list, looking for anyone who works for the police department or down at city hall.

Just before lunch, Tanner stops by to ask about the latest. Bianca gives him the usual rundown, he listens and nods, and when she's done, he leans in close. Like she did the other day.

'And Wes?' he whispers. 'Anything new?'

'Not today. He's been very quiet.'

'He's in a bad mood?'

'I don't know,' she says, eyes wide. 'He's been in his office all morning.'

Tanner sighs and glances over at Wes's closed door. 'Good to know.'

'Does that mean something?' she says. She doesn't normally ask Tanner questions like that, but today she can't help herself.

'It might.' He smiles at her and winks before walking away.

Something is happening with Wes, something Tanner is aware of. But he isn't talking. What she wants to do is ask him about Joey Fisher. Specifically about Wes and Joey. But she doesn't dare.

As soon as Tanner is back in his office, she orders those police reports and charges them to the company card.

Wes doesn't really see his computer screen. Nothing registers. While he doesn't feel as angry as he did last night, he also doesn't feel good. Or even okay. All his emotions are muted, buried under the one that dominates.

Frustration.

Not the sexual kind, either. That would be easier to deal with. No, this is the kind of frustration that makes him feel like punching the wall to get rid of it. Or at least bring the feeling down a few notches.

Ivy didn't say a word about the dress before work. They went through the usual motions like robots, talking but not saying anything that wasn't necessary. *Is the coffee done? Where's my other shoe? Have you seen my keys?* At one point, Ivy launched into a story about a coworker that seemed like it was supposed to be funny, but neither one laughed.

The morning ended with a perfunctory kiss at the door before they went their separate ways. This fresh new day hasn't erased anything; it has only brought more questions:

Why would Ivy wear that dress? Why would she ever want to remind him about the Fine Line? And of that night.

Thinking about it upsets him. Visibly so, apparently,

because when Tanner walks into his office, the first thing he says is 'What's wrong with you?'

'Nothing. What's up?'

Tanner takes the seat across from Wes. 'Calvin called and wants to push the meeting back.'

'I know, Bianca messaged me about that.' It wasn't a good sign, either. It was supposed to be a closing meeting.

'You sure you're okay?' Tanner says.

'I'm fine. Just a little headache.'

Tanner raises his eyebrows. 'Trouble with the missus?'

Yes. 'No.'

'Sure, sure. Okay, I want to get the team together this evening to talk strategy. Since we've got some extra time, I want to make sure everything is on point. If they're waffling, we have to pull them back in.'

Wes makes a note on his schedule. 'Got it. I'll be there.'

'Bianca's going to set us up in a private room at White Rabbit, so there will be drinks.'

'Naturally.'

Tanner stands up, like he's about to leave, but then he snaps his fingers. 'Just to be clear, this isn't a plus-one event,' he says. 'Don't bring Ivy.'

Wes sighs.

'Just trying to help you out. Ivy is . . .' Tanner stops. He leans over Wes's desk, placing both hands on top of it. 'Ivy isn't good for you.'

He isn't joking around. Tanner looks at Wes like a disappointed dad.

At least, that's how it feels. Tanner makes Wes feel like a teenager all over again, sitting in front of his parents. Mom, a stern woman with a long list of draconian rules. The opposite of Ivy, who didn't have any.

And Dad, always by his mother's side, supporting her in

silence. Together, they were an unyielding force. Wes could never make them understand why a party or a football game was so important, that his entire social life might collapse if he didn't show up. Eventually, he stopped trying.

Easier to keep his mouth shut and sneak out of the house instead.

He does the same thing now. Doesn't try to explain anything to Tanner, doesn't try to make him understand his relationship. Wes stays quiet until Tanner leaves his office, knowing he is still going to see Ivy. Even if it means lying to his boss.

22

One of the best parts of being an assistant is that no one pays attention to you. As long as Bianca gets her work done, Tanner and the others have no interest in what she's typing or reading, or how many times a day she looks at her phone. No one cares. That lack of interest gives her plenty of time to read the police reports.

Ivy is indeed trouble.

Now Bianca knows why the detective came to the office. The report was filed just last week: Ivy had said she was being stalked and named Wes as a potential suspect. A week ago, Bianca wouldn't have thought that was possible, but today is different. She isn't sure she knows Wes at all.

That never happens.

And it's not going to happen now, either. She isn't going to be the type who finds out her coworker is some crazy psycho/stalker/murderer and says, 'He was the nicest guy. I never had a clue.'

She's going to find that clue. If it exists.

Bianca flips through the reports, going through them a second time. The newest one is about Ivy's stalker, someone who had been leaving her presents. The earliest one is from eight years ago, when Wes had accused Ivy of vandalizing his car. He changed his statement later – instead, blaming it on a series of crimes in the neighborhood – and the charges were dropped.

The third report was again from Ivy: She had reported her car stolen. An old Toyota 4Runner that had been parked in front of her apartment building. One morning, it was gone. Wes had also been interviewed, because they lived together.

At first, nothing in it stands out. Not until she sees the date the car was stolen.

Bianca swipes her key card, opening the side door of the Siphon building. The parking lot is empty. She has hit the sweet spot, after the staff have left but before the cleaning crew arrives.

Normally, she would've stayed until everyone was gone, but tonight she had to leave before she was alone. Two reps were still in the office, plus Tanner, and she'd had a family dinner to attend. If it had been anything else, she would have blown it off and remained in the office. But pissing off her mom was something she avoided.

Yes, the company will have a record of her card swipe. Doesn't matter – no one ever checks. And if they do, she can say she forgot to do something, an important task that couldn't wait. As long as nothing is missing or vandalized, no one is going to care if an assistant works late.

The sales department is actually kind of nice at night. Quiet and dark, but the windows allow enough light for her to see where she's going. She sits down at her desk and takes out her Russian nesting dolls, opening them until reaching the master key.

Tonight, she has to look at more than just Wes's schedule. He's been working at Siphon for years and has a huge number of emails. God knows how many files. While she can access them through her own computer with his password, she doesn't want that kind of record on the server. Better to be safe than sorry, especially because she has the key.

She doesn't turn any lights on in Wes's office, only his computer. She begins by searching for the oldest emails first and organizing them chronologically.

Ten minutes later, she hears the elevator ding.

Too early for the cleaning crew, which means it's one of her coworkers. Has to be. She contemplates running out of Wes's office. Or she could hide under his desk.

'Bianca?'

Too late.

Tanner walks up and stands in the doorway. 'What are you doing here?' he says. 'And what are you doing in Wes's office?'

Bianca's hand shakes as she closes out the inbox and shuts down the screen. 'There was an issue with his schedule,' she says, fighting to keep her voice even. 'It was my fault. I came here to fix it.'

'But how did you get in here?'

'The door was unlocked.' It's darker now, without the light from the computer, and she can't see the expression on his face. 'I needed to make sure our calendars matched. He has a meeting in the morning, and I needed to double-check the entry.' She stands up, straightens her skirt, and starts to walk out. 'All done,' she says.

As she passes by him, she smells the alcohol.

'What are *you* doing here so late?' she says, talking over her shoulder as she heads back to her desk to get her bag.

'Bianca.'

She turns. Tanner is right behind her, a foot away. Scotch. He's been drinking scotch.

'Yes?' she says.

'You must be one of the best assistants we've ever had. No, you're *the* best assistant. Ever.'

'Thank you.'

'Not many people would come down here this late to fix a scheduling snafu.' Tanner steps toward her, closing the gap to a few inches. 'But you did.'

She moves back and bumps into the edge of her desk. 'It's no problem. I wanted to make sure it was right.'

'Don't take this the wrong way, because I don't mean anything . . . weird about it,' he says, 'but you are extremely attractive.'

She nods. Doesn't answer him, doesn't say a word when he gets even closer, pressing his chest against hers.

'Seriously,' he says. 'You are beautiful.'

This. Can't. Be. Happening.

Her brain gets stuck on those words, unable to process what's unfolding in front of her. Unable to process *who* is in front of her. Tanner is her boss. Her drunk boss.

This. Can't. Be. Happening.

'I really should get going,' she says, trying to reach over the desk to her chair, where her bag is sitting.

His hands are on her waist, pulling her closer. She tries to push him back, but he doesn't budge.

They always said he was a prick.

They were right.

'Tanner, stop.'

He doesn't. The smell of his breath is making her sick, and he pushes her harder against the desk. She tries to lift her knee to kick him away, but he's blocking her with his legs.

'Come on, Bianca,' he says, his voice right in her ear. 'You were flirting with me the other day. I know you were.'

She was. But it wasn't an invitation to grope her.

'Stop it. I'm serious.'

He licks her ear. 'Aren't you feisty.'

This. Can't. Be. Happening.

Time shifts, splits in half.

Tanner moves quick, his hands are everywhere at the same time, holding her against the desk while feeling her up.

She reaches behind her, grasping for something. Anything.

96

Something to hit him on the head with. Just enough to stun him for a second so she can run. But it feels like she is moving so slow. She can't find something fast enough.

Sticky notes. Mouse. Notepad.

His hand moves between her legs as she fumbles blindly around, trying to reach the pen holder.

Finally, something useful.

A pair of scissors.

23

'I screwed up.'

First words out of Ivy's mouth. Wes has just arrived at her place, is barely through the door, and already he takes a step back.

She called him today at work, but he was in a meeting, so she sent a text claiming she 'absolutely, positively' had to talk to him. So dramatic. He refused to deal with it at work, so here he is. Ten o'clock at night, after the meeting at White Rabbit. His brain is maxed out, but once again, Ivy has shocked him. She seems to have a never-ending supply of the ability to do that.

'You screwed up,' he says.

'Come inside already.' Ivy walks away from the front door, into the living room, leaving him to follow. He does. If only to see what this is about.

She sits down on the couch, half-sideways, waiting for him to take his place next to her. An open bottle of wine is on the coffee table, along with two glasses and a plate of cubed cheese and apple slices.

Wes gets a bad feeling about this. He sits down gently, like the couch might bite him.

'The dress,' she says. 'I'm sorry. When I bought it, I honestly didn't even think about . . . all that.'

He doesn't have to roll his eyes. Not after all this time.

'I know it sounds like I'm lying, but I swear,' she says. Ivy tilts her head down and looks up at him. 'If I wanted to remind you of that, would I really pick a sky blue dress?'

She has a point. Subtlety isn't in her DNA.

'You believe me, right?' she says. 'Tell me you believe me.'

'There's more, isn't there?'

Ivy pauses to pour the wine and eat a cheese cube. 'Have some,' she says.

'You're not still full from that steak?' He can't help it. Really, he can't.

'That was wrong,' she says. 'I'm sorry.'

Another apology. Curiouser and curiouser.

Something worse must be coming, something she is working up to. Ivy wouldn't go through all this for nothing. If all she wanted to do was apologize, she would show up at his house with a giant balloon bouquet. Or naked under a coat. She's done both before.

But this is weird.

'Is that why I'm here?' he says. 'To hear you apologize?'

'Yes.'

'Really?'

She shrugs and eats another cheese cube. 'There is one other thing,' she says.

'And what might that be?'

'It's the detective,' she says.

Karen Colglazier. He should have seen this coming. 'What about her?'

'I didn't tell you everything she said.'

Now he gets it. He has caught up to what's really happening. And he needs a second to prepare himself. Wes takes a big sip of wine, stretching the moment out for as long as he can.

Part of him wants to ask why she didn't tell him last night, because now he wants to know what kind of game she's playing. Why hold it back? What good does that do either one of them? Doesn't make any sense.

The other part of him knows that's the least important part of this situation. The fact that a detective has fixated on them is the only thing he should be concerned with.

But old habits never die; they just go dormant.

'Why are you telling me this now?' he asks.

'Because you deserve to know. I should've told you last night.' She reaches over and puts her hand on his knee. 'But you were such a dick at dinner. I didn't think it was the right time.'

Fair.

A lot of things go through his mind. They come so fast his brain is a jumble of words. Half of them say to believe her. The other half remembers the past.

Wes has spent years trying to figure out if Ivy gives off any signs – like a tell in poker – when she lies. He has tested her, asking questions he knew the answers to and studying the way her eyes moved, if anything twitched, whether or not she smiled.

No. She does not have a tell.

He is forced to go with his gut. Not the most reliable source, in his experience, but it's all he's got. And it's telling him she's being honest, but that there's more to this story. Always is.

To stall for time, he grabs an apple slice. He stretches that apple out for three bites when it should've been one.

'That night,' he finally says.

'Yes.'

He takes another sip of wine, even bigger this time. If they're going to talk about that night, he needs it.

24

Above the Siphon building, the night sky is dark. A thin slice of moon keeps it from looking black.

Along with the flashing lights from all the police cars.

Detective Karen Colglazier walks up to the front door, where she is greeted by two uniformed cops. She knows them, particularly the short one, who did a good job on one of her crime scenes. It gives her some hope this will be handled right.

'What floor?' she says.

'Third.'

'Thanks.'

Inside, the lobby is quiet. A crescent-shaped reception desk is clear of clutter, the computer dark. The floor is polished, the windows staggeringly clear, exactly how it looked when she was here before. It makes Karen want to press her hand up against the glass.

On the third floor, another cop stands guard. A young man who has been on the force less than a year. He nods to her, his face grim as he hands her plastic booties to cover her shoes.

'How's it look?' she says.

'Not good.'

The floor is lined with cubicles that run almost end to end. In the distance, she sees movement on the far right. The sales department.

She knew there was more to this. As soon as she heard the Siphon address on the scanner, she knew.

The closer she gets, the stronger the smell is. People always compare the smell of blood to copper, but it isn't really the same. Blood has a distinct odor to anyone who has been around enough of it. Cops get nonchalant about it, even dismissive.

Karen is the same. Blood doesn't bother her because she refuses to let it.

The endless grey cubicles block her view until she emerges on the other side, where everything looks a little familiar. But not. The plush grey carpet is now soaked in blood. So much blood.

A voice comes from down the hall, rising above the rest.

'Cameras? Yes, we have them over the front doors, and in the lobby. Not in the offices.'

Karen tilts her head to look toward the voice, recognizing the speaker immediately. The CEO of Siphon is Ian Kelley, who is also the face of the company. He is in the media quite a bit – often with his husband, a local artist, and their giant dog, a Newfoundland.

Ian is about forty and dressed in a designer shirt, khakis, and expensive shoes that aren't covered with booties. Because when the police call in the middle of the night, you can't forget the Italian loafers. Or maybe that's all he owns.

Karen's shoes cost $19.99 on clearance. They're also real leather.

She feels bad for the cops who have to interview him. Not easy to get information out of someone who isn't used to being questioned by anyone.

'Karen? What are you doing here?'

Louis Knox, another detective, is standing behind her. They've been working together for years. She pretended to be happy for Louis when he was promoted to detective before she was, and he pretended to believe it.

He calls her Karen, as everyone else does, because Colglazier is not the ideal surname for a detective. For a while, the other cops called her Cole but it didn't stick. Karen did. That was long before the name became popular on social media, before she was a meme instead of a human being. She uses it to her advantage, because people have a preconceived notion about who she is. Acting against type catches them off guard.

'I heard a woman was assaulted,' she says to Louis. 'It was on the scanner.'

'That's the story, yeah. But it's a murder investigation.'

'Lot of blood.'

'She was standing here.' Louis points to a desk. There's blood on top and on the floor in front of it. The only clean surface is the center of the desk. 'She grabbed the scissors and stabbed him in the neck.'

The jugular. Explains all the blood, along with the clear spot on the desk. That's where the blood hit the woman instead.

She must have been covered in it.

Louis is right: Karen has no reason to be here. When she first heard about the incident on the police scanner, she ignored it. Not her problem. But then she recognized the address, because she had been here to talk with Wes Harmon.

'Who was he?' she says.

'Tanner Duncan. Head of the sales department.' Louis checks his phone, where he always keeps his notes. 'The assistant did it. Bianca . . . Bianca Mercado.'

Karen remembers her. Pretty, young, and very professional. The buttoned-up-tight kind.

'Where is she now?' Karen says.

'Hospital.'

'She's hurt?'

'Physically, I don't think so.' Louis shrugs, his jacket rising a few inches, because his shoulders are that big. 'But she was hysterical.'

Louis is called away, giving Karen a chance to study the scene a little closer. Besides being covered in blood, the top of the desk looks nothing like the one in the lobby. The pen holder is knocked over, the sticky notes are all over the place, even the blotter is crooked. Bianca had been grasping for something to hit Tanner with.

The Russian nesting dolls are particularly odd. They're open, all of them, from large to small. She wouldn't have had time to do all that while being attacked – if that's what happened. But she had done it at some point.

Two theories come to mind. Either a nervous habit, or because something was hidden inside the last one. Something she needed at that moment, late at night, before the altercation with her boss.

A question she would ask Bianca, if she were a detective on the case. Too bad she isn't.

The door to Wes's office is open. The others are closed. Karen can see straight into it, all the way to the window and the dark sky behind it. The chair at the desk is pushed back a little.

He isn't here, though. Maybe he had been. Maybe he left in a rush. Maybe he saw what happened. The security card swipes could show that, or the cameras, depending on the angle in the parking lot.

Or maybe Wes had left his door open.

She walks back to the elevator, turning all of this around in her head, trying to put the picture together. The jigsaw needs more pieces.

However, she did learn what she wanted to know. Wes Harmon wasn't the victim.

Too bad. That would've made everything so easy.

25

The email arrives when Wes is still in Ivy's bed. It comes from the CEO's assistant, Abigail, and the whole staff is copied.

> The Siphon office will be closed today due to an emergency.
> Details to come.

He smiles. The fire alarm probably went off again, triggering the sprinklers. It happened once before, and they were out of the office for almost a week. Wes puts the phone down and rolls over, sliding an arm around Ivy.

His house is small, with only two bedrooms, and he picked out all the furniture, including the bed. But he still likes hers better. It's so much more comfortable. Could be the sheets or the pillow-top mattress. Or maybe it's because the bed smells like her. And if he's in it, so is she.

She wakes up and buries her head in his shoulder. 'Hey,' she says.

'Hey.'

'Time?'

'A little after seven.'

'Shouldn't you be in the shower by now?' she says. She always teases him about the military precision of his routine. Her mornings are far more chaotic.

'I don't have to go in today,' he says. 'Some problem at the building.'

'Really?'

'Really.'

She snuggles a little closer. 'I'd take the day off if I could.'

'You can't call in sick?'

'Our weekly meeting is this morning. It's the one thing I really shouldn't miss.'

'Too bad,' he says.

She does stay in bed a little bit longer, curled up to him. So easy, in these moments, to think only of the good things. The bad doesn't exist right now, and he's just fine with that.

A few minutes later, she gets up and heads into the bathroom. The shower turns on, and he closes his eyes. He could get up and make breakfast, which would be a nice thing to do, since he doesn't have to go into the office. Or he could join her in the shower. Another good option.

Wes closes his eyes, deciding more sleep is the right answer. He should dream of his girlfriend, or at least about some woman he has always wanted but never had. A celebrity, maybe.

But he doesn't dream about anything or anyone, because he never falls back asleep. The detective prevents it.

Karen is a problem. He doesn't have proof of that, and so far it doesn't sound like she knows anything, but he feels it anyway. She has no reason to look into their past, especially not at something that happened seven years ago. Yet she is. It makes him wonder what she's up to, why she even cares. No matter how many ways he twists it around in his mind, it doesn't make any sense.

He thinks about her until his phone dings. And dings.

Again.

Again.

Again.

*

Karen has two stacks of case files on her desk. No shortage of work to do – there's a never-ending stream of sexual assaults and related crimes that end up in her division. Most mornings start with a cup of bad coffee, a packaged pastry, and the latest tragedy.

The stack on the left has the cases she is still working on. The stack on the right, in the far corner, has the cases she no longer has to work on. If it were up to her, she would have just one stack. All the cases, each one receiving an equal amount of attention. The DA doesn't see it that way, and neither does Karen's boss. The stack on the right contains all the cases that will never be prosecuted.

The station is buzzing today; activity swirls around her. Fair Valley has its share of homicides, but not too many professional men are killed by women in fancy office buildings. Not even in self-defense.

Earlier this morning, Karen talked to Louis and his partner about the Tanner Duncan case, and she offered to speak to Bianca.

'It might help,' she said. 'If she can talk to someone familiar with assault.'

'You mean it might help if she talks to a woman,' Louis said.

Karen meant because she has experience talking to victims of assault. But yes. That, too.

'I think we can handle it,' Louis said. 'But we'll let you know if we need you.'

He walked away, ending the conversation.

She turns to the file she is supposed to be working on. A man has been taking lewd pictures of women on the bus. He sits on the aisle, angling his phone underneath the skirts of the women standing next to him, and snaps a photo. So far, the women who have noticed either moved places or cursed him out, but none of them wanted to make a scene or disrupt their ride to work. Nobody wanted to be late because of a photo.

Upskirting is against the law in California, though technically it's a misdemeanor. Makes no difference to Karen. Her job is to stop him.

She has a sketch of the man, who always appears during commute time, when the buses between Fair Valley and Sacramento are the most crowded. What she doesn't have is manpower. No, the police force could not afford to put anyone undercover to catch some guy taking pictures on the bus.

Karen has been riding the bus herself, hoping to find this guy. The downside was having less time to work the other cases, both the stack at the station and the one at her house.

The third stack. Wes and Ivy are in that one.

26

Ivy has one dress for funerals. Simple, black, hangs to just below the knee. The last time she wore it was when her grandfather died. Today she wears it again, for Tanner.

The funeral home is stuffy; the air feels as still as the corpse in the room. The casket is closed – not a surprise, given how he died. She only knows the details because of Wes. The police haven't released everything about how or why he was killed, but the Siphon employees know. The rumors are out there, which is why the funeral is small and private. Less than fifteen people are here: Tanner's family, some of the sales team, and the CEO of Siphon.

Zànglǐ.

The Chinese word for *funeral.* She learned it especially for today, along with the word for *corpse. Shītǐ.*

When Tanner's brother breaks down at the podium while telling a story about their childhood, Wes squeezes her hand. She squeezes back tighter. Ivy isn't sure if she is holding him up or he's holding her.

Until the other night, she had no intention of being here. She doesn't want to be. Not for Tanner Duncan, a man who hated her and was killed while assaulting a woman.

But then Wes asked.

They had been in bed – his bed – a place they've been spending a lot of time this week, like the only way he can work through his grief is with sex. Afterward, he would lie awake for a long time, ignoring his phone, not turning on the

TV, and staring at the ceiling, the wall, the window. Any-where but at her.

She had been patient, staggeringly so, until he mentioned the funeral.

'You're coming, aren't you?' he said.

She thought for a second, deciding to hedge. Telling him she didn't want to go to Tanner's funeral probably wasn't the best idea. 'I wasn't planning on it, no.'

It was too dark to see the expression on his face or in his eyes. Wes was quiet for so long she almost fell asleep.

'He was the one who hired me,' Wes finally said. 'And trained me. Without Tanner . . .' He paused. Ivy listened to him breathe as she waited. 'I don't know if I would've done as well at Siphon.'

Tanner may not have been a hundred percent evil; she understood that. Just evil enough to get himself killed.

'And the assistant?' she said. 'What about her?'

'I always liked Bianca. She did a great job. I feel terrible for her.'

'Did you have any idea?' she said.

'No,' he said. 'This whole situation is so screwed up.'

No argument there.

Wes and Ivy have had countless conversations in bed, in the dark. Their own private confessional. In the early days, they talked about childhood traumas, told stories about their families, their triumphs and failures. Relationships, too. People they had loved, or thought they did, going all the way back to middle school.

Later, the talks revolved only around them. Who did what wrong, and, more importantly, why. Who's sorry, and who claims to be but really isn't. They have broken up in the dark and gotten back together, sometimes within the same night.

They have talked about their mutual love and their mutual hate, sometimes in the same sentence.

On a few occasions, they've even talked about how lucky they are. Unlike Ivy's parents.

They're in separate prisons and aren't allowed to be in contact. At all. They tried sending letters to Ivy to remail, but even those were opened and stopped by the prison. Calling wasn't an option, either. The prisons have to approve the people they can call, and her parents aren't on each other's list, because they committed their crimes together.

Ivy can't imagine not being in contact with Wes.

The topic of her parents comes up on their most serious nights, when the conversation becomes too dark to continue. They stop just short of talking about their worst night.

If there's been one good thing about Tanner, it's that Wes has stopped mentioning the club, the dress, and that awful dinner date. Everything they argued about days ago has disappeared.

'Ivy?' Wes had said.

'Yeah?'

'I'd really like you to go to the funeral,' he said. 'For me.'

It felt like a test.

Still does, even as she stands by his side, holding his hand and listening to wonderful stories about Tanner. They all sound like lies.

This morning, she almost called Heath. Her best friend has been out of town for almost two months, which normally wouldn't be a problem. Heath is an architect who specializes in environmentally friendly houses, and he's been putting together a community of tiny homes up in the wilds of Oregon. It wouldn't be so bad if the community wasn't off the grid.

She has gotten through on his phone a couple of times,

but her texts go unanswered more than half the time. He doesn't even know she is back together with Wes. And right now, he's probably the only one she would tell.

She tried to get hold of him before the funeral. Called and texted, neither one successful.

At the last possible moment, she left the office, went home to put on the black dress, and showed up at the funeral. It felt like she was doing something bad and something good at the same time. One minute, she thinks she's done the right thing; the next, she hates herself.

The service isn't long, thank God, like his family knew they shouldn't say *too* much. Wes, ever the polite Midwestern boy, waits around afterward to offer his condolences to Tanner's family.

'I'm so sorry,' he says. 'I worked with Tanner for years. He taught me so much.'

Mom cries, Dad puts his arm around her, and Tanner's brother shakes Wes's hand. Everyone is too polite to mention how and why this happened. Only the brother concedes this has all been 'such a tragedy.'

Ivy says nothing, only nods, because the air in the funeral home, along with dead Tanner, is starting to make her feel sick. She pulls Wes toward the door before he can start another conversation with his coworkers.

Outside, she can breathe. For a second.

Across the street, Karen stands in front of her nondescript car, looking right at them. Ivy drops Wes's hand.

Today, Karen is wearing a dark suit, and her short hair is slicked back. Her lipstick is the color of terra-cotta, something Ivy notices only because of the expression on Karen's face.

She is smiling.

Karen walks toward them, her face morphing into something more appropriate for a funeral.

'Hello,' she says. 'I'd say "Good afternoon," but that seems inappropriate.'

Wes nods. 'Hello.'

'You two look like you're getting along these days,' Karen says.

Nobody responds to this, certainly not Ivy. 'Is this your case?' she asks.

'I've been assisting on it. Sometimes, you need just the right detective for a case.'

Silence.

'Wes.' Karen turns to him, looking quite serious in a fake kind of way. 'Thank you again for taking the time to talk with me on Friday. I appreciate it, given all that's been happening.'

Ivy remains calm, but inside she is screaming.

Friday.

Wes never mentioned it to her. They spent the whole weekend together and he never said a word.

27

Karen walks away from Ivy and Wes, forcing herself not to look back at them. But she wishes she could watch what happens next.

Ivy didn't know about the second interview. She tried to keep her expression neutral, but Karen saw it. A slight widening of her eyes, a side glance at Wes.

Karen had stopped by Siphon last Friday to talk with him. In just a few days, the company had completely overhauled the front room of the sales department. New carpet, new front desk, new chair, and new assistant. Or a temporary one. Tanner's name had even been removed from his office door. No way to tell someone had been stabbed within the company's pristine walls.

When Karen identified herself and asked to speak with Wes Harmon, she was ushered right into his office. He looked surprised to see her.

'I spoke to another detective about Tanner a couple days ago,' he said. 'Detective Knox, I believe.'

'Yes, he's the primary on the case. I'm just following up.' Karen sat right down and made herself comfortable. Not her first time at the rodeo with Wes. 'This won't take long.'

She began with questions about Tanner: how long they had worked together, and if Wes had ever seen him do anything questionable with a woman.

'I never saw him act inappropriately,' Wes said. 'When we were outside of the office, at a bar or a restaurant, I saw him talk to women. Flirt with them. But nothing inappropriate.'

'Did you ever see him become violent? With anyone?'

'No.'

'Let's talk about Bianca,' Karen says. 'How well did you know her?'

'She has been our administrative assistant for about a year. I always thought she was professional and good at her job.'

'What about her relationship with Tanner?'

Wes shrugged a little. 'As far as I know, there was no relationship. They were colleagues.'

'So they weren't involved.'

'I never saw anything to indicate that.'

Louis probably asked all the same questions, and a hundred more, but Wes didn't remind her of that. He answered like this was the first time he had heard them. A lot of other people she interviews get impatient and complain, but not Wes.

It wasn't normal. And when that happens, it means something. At least it does to an experienced detective.

'What about you?' she asked. 'Did you have a personal relationship with Bianca?'

'No. I think the only time I saw her outside of work was at the holiday party.'

'So,' Karen said, 'it was nothing like your relationship with Ivy.'

Wes broke eye contact. She could almost see the wheels grinding in his head as he caught up to what the interview was truly about.

He could've responded by asking why she was really here, or why she was asking about his girlfriend. He could've become angry and told her to get out. Or he could have picked up the phone and called Louis to ask him what the hell was going on.

Wes did none of that.

'I don't see how the two are similar,' he said.

'I didn't say they were.'

'Again, I don't understand how Ivy is relevant to Tanner and Bianca.' Wes sat back in his chair, his hands clasped together, and he looked relaxed. Cool.

It reminded Karen of her husband. He used to sit just like that, looking at her the same way.

'You sound defensive,' she said, although Wes didn't.

'I'm confused.'

He shouldn't have been. Wes must have known she had asked Ivy about her stolen car. Karen had no doubt Ivy was the type who would tell her partner everything. Unlike Wes.

'I'm thinking about the potential relationship part of this,' she said, taking her tone down a little. 'I've been trying to figure out if Tanner and Bianca had one, if perhaps they were arguing about it when this happened. I'm sure you can relate, given your relationship with Ivy. You described it as intense. Maybe Tanner and Bianca were the same.'

'Like I said, I never saw anything like that.'

'I understand. I just thought with your experience, you might have some insight.' Karen smiled. She knew more than Wes realized, because Ivy has been active on social media for years. She had posted about how they first met, and about their first fight. 'You and Ivy have clearly broken up and gotten back together a few times.'

'As far as I know,' Wes said, 'Tanner and Bianca weren't personally involved.'

Karen backed down then, not pressing the issue further. She was already too far out of bounds and well outside the scope of her job. This wasn't her case.

She shouldn't have been talking to Wes about Tanner, and she certainly shouldn't have been trying to connect Tanner with Wes and Ivy's relationship. If Wes *had* picked up the phone and called Louis, she would've been demoted at best. Fired at worst.

But she also would've bet every dime she had that Wes would not call anyone. The last thing he wanted was to draw attention to himself – especially attention from the police. She knew that.

She knew a lot of things.

Like the fact that Ivy once worked at the Fine Line gentlemen's club. Her name had popped up when Karen searched through the court records to see if Ivy had ever been sued or had sued someone. She had not. But six years ago, the Fine Line had declared bankruptcy. According to the club's court filing, Ivy had been an employee who worked for four hours. She was never paid and never worked there again.

The one night she worked at the club was the same night her car was stolen.

Ivy had called the police almost a full day *after* her car had gone missing. According to her statement, she thought Wes had borrowed it. She reported it stolen after realizing he hadn't.

That case isn't one of Karen's, either, and she has even less business asking about it. But after being a cop for so many years, there is one thing Karen knows to be a fact.

There are no coincidences.

28

Wes pretends not to watch Karen get in her car and drive away from the funeral home. He doesn't say a word about the bomb she just dropped.

'Want to grab a cup of coffee?' Ivy says. She has that *We need to talk* tone.

'Can't. I have to go back to work.'

Long pause.

'Okay,' she says. 'I guess I should do the same thing.'

Her voice is normal, even relaxed, and so is the expression on her face. She picks a piece of lint off the collar of his jacket. But he can feel her anger. It radiates off her like heat from the kitchen when she burns something.

No, he didn't tell her Karen had come to see him a few days ago. Damn right he didn't.

'I'll call you later.' He leans over to kiss her. Cheek, not lips.

Wes leaves her standing in front of the funeral home and heads to his car. Doesn't look back, either. She has her own car. Ivy can get herself to work, if that's where she's going. Maybe she is lying, maybe she isn't. Right now, he doesn't care.

He drives away, cranking the music up as he pulls out of the parking lot. Ivy came to the funeral, yes. Showed up and said, 'I'm here,' like she wanted a gold star.

Aggravating, to be sure. But not why he's angry.

Ivy has conveniently forgotten that this mess with Karen is because of her. He wouldn't have to answer questions about their past if Ivy hadn't lost her mind. Because even for them, this was way too far.

Faking a stalker was bad enough. Calling the police and offering up his name was on another level. Now he has a stalker of his own: Karen. Of all the women in the world, a detective. Wes's mistake was not being angrier about this in the first place.

For the past day, all he has done is think about that night. That car. Like he doesn't have a hundred other things he should be thinking about. The worst part is, it should've been nothing. A footnote to their story, not a chapter. And definitely not a whole section.

Wes is still thinking about it when he pulls into the Siphon parking lot. He turns down the music and sits in his car, taking a minute to calm down, clear his head.

He's not the only one back at work. Those who did go to the funeral are not heading to the bars to get drunk; they're at the office. Marcus pulls into the spot next to him. They nod and walk toward the door. No chatting about the Warriors today.

When they get up to the third floor, to the sales department, the first person he sees is Abigail Wright. Technically, she is Ian's assistant. But since she used to be in the sales department, she has been temporarily reassigned until they find a replacement for Bianca.

Abigail nods at him. *Stunning* is the only word to describe her. Born to be on the cover of magazines but ended up an executive assistant – something Wes and the rest of the team have never understood.

Wes takes a deep breath, trying to shove aside the pain in his head. He likes Abigail, has known her since he started at Siphon. She is brutally efficient, professional, and she never loses her cool.

Except for that day Ivy almost destroyed his office.

He sits down at his desk, feeling about ten years older than he did yesterday. Filled with aches and pains, mostly on the inside and completely self-inflicted. He picks up his phone and scrolls through the address book.

Stella.

They've exchanged a few texts, a couple of interactions on social media, but he hasn't spoken to her in a while. Hasn't seen her in forever. Wes takes a deep breath and calls before he loses his nerve. She answers on the second ring.

'A middle-of-the-day call? This can't be good,' she says.

'It isn't.'

Stella sighs. He hears a door close. 'You're lucky I have a few minutes. I'm a busy woman.'

'I know that, too.' He stalls a little, trying to decide how much to tell her. 'But maybe Ivy has gone too far this time.'

He can almost hear her eyebrows rise. 'You've got my attention. Speak.'

Wes tells her the story. The stalking Ivy faked, calling the police, the detective showing up at his office. All the result of trying to get his attention. He is careful to sidestep around the real reason Karen is still questioning him. Not even Stella knows about that.

'Most people would avoid a woman who calls the police on them,' she says, 'but what did you do?'

He doesn't answer.

She hits him with a barrage of curse words. No one is more creative than Stella when it comes to swearing. He can imagine her sitting at her desk, feet up, her brown hair swinging wildly as she becomes more and more animated. More and more wound up. The only thing he can do is wait it out.

Finally spent, Stella comes to the inevitable conclusion. 'But you, being you, went to Ivy. You had sex, blah blah blah. And where are you now with her?'

'Back together.'

No sigh. No fist banged on her desk. No more curse words. Her silence is filled with disappointment, and he feels it.

'Yeah,' he says.

Still nothing from Stella. Maybe she is staring out the window. Or looking at her computer screen, glancing through emails, because she's done with him. Perhaps she's burying her head in her hands, cursing the gods for putting her in this position. Because it must be terrible. He knows that, and it's why he doesn't call her very often. Today is a rare exception.

'I'm not an idiot,' Stella says.

'Of course you aren't. That's why I call you.'

'In fact, I'm a really smart person,' Stella says. 'I could join Mensa if I wanted to. Hell, I could probably run Mensa.'

'I know.'

'But what I still don't understand,' she says, 'is how I ended up with such a stupid brother.'

29

Karen walks into her house, drops her bag, and kicks off her shoes. Her mug from this morning is still on the table, dishes from last night in the sink. She grabs a Monster Energy drink and a plate of leftovers before heading into her office. Karen still has to remind herself to call it that.

Sometimes, she sees the room the way it used to be. Starting with the crib and moving all the way up to the messy, dark room of a teenager. Then, finally, the empty room of a child who no longer lives with his mother. Jack is all grown up now and living his life in Southern California, but signs of him are everywhere.

The closet doors are scratched on the edges, where he used to fling them open and slam them closed. There's a dark spot on the wall, vaguely in the shape of a shoe, which he claimed to know nothing about. Tiny droplets of paint form a ring around where his desk used to be, left over from painting model cars and airplanes.

She didn't get rid of any of it, only the furniture. His old bed, dresser, and nightstand are gone, replaced with a desk, a comfortable chair, filing cabinets, and, on the wall, a large corkboard, similar to the ones they used at the station. Photos are tacked to it, along with names.

Ivy is in the center.

The picture was printed from her social media. Ivy is outside, standing in front of a beautiful view of tree-covered mountains. Big smile, no makeup, hair blowing in the wind.

The photo is from a couple months ago, but she could be mistaken for a college student.

Karen sits down at her desk. The second shift, she calls it. She fires up the computer and pulls up Check This on her phone. One to-do list is never enough, and the organizational app helps her keep everything straight.

She gets to work on Ivy's case, first checking the social media accounts for both her and Wes. It's really too bad he doesn't post more often. He does make comments on other posts, though. Karen checks every account he follows and finds a new one from this morning. The official Siphon account posted a memorial for Tanner, and Wes commented on it.

RIP †

Dozens of employees posted similar comments, along with a few that said Justice for Bianca. A little early for that, given that Bianca hasn't been arrested.

Next she goes through the 911 call list from the night Ivy's car was supposedly stolen. Perhaps the night it was in an accident.

Karen is betting it was.

Call it her detective's intuition. Call it a sixth sense. Or maybe Karen just knows when something is off because she's seen it so many times before. In this case, it started the day she met Ivy.

Ivy had walked into the police station looking like she had just come from work. Navy slacks, ivory blouse, understated jewelry. She carried a small shopping bag from Ulta, but there was no makeup in it. Just the notes, photos, and the box of truffles.

'I've received these over the past few weeks,' Ivy said, taking out each item one by one. A few were in plastic bags. 'I didn't think to be careful with anything at first, not until it continued.'

'Where were these left?'

'On my car. Mostly when it was parked outside my apartment building, but once when it was at a shopping center,' she said. 'At first, I thought it was just some kind of . . . admirer, I guess? Because the notes aren't threatening. I mean, they just say, "You're beautiful," or "You're so amazing."' Ivy paused to pull out the Ziploc bag of photos. 'Then I got these.'

Karen put on gloves and took the pictures out. Three of them, all taken from a distance when Ivy was somewhere in public. Walking to her car, into a restaurant, and leaving a bar.

'And the following day, I got these.' When Ivy pointed to the box of truffles, her hand trembled.

Karen opened the bag and the truffle box. Each one had a bite taken out of it. 'They were already like this?'

'They were.'

Throughout the exchange, Karen studied Ivy. She spoke in a halting voice with frequent pauses. Not unusual for people speaking to the police. She also broke eye contact a lot. Again, nothing out of the ordinary.

'The thing is,' Ivy said, 'my ex-boyfriend used to give me these truffles.'

That's when the tears came. Erupted, actually.

Karen handed her a tissue and waited a moment before continuing. She pointed to the truffles. 'He gave you the same brand?'

'Yes. Same kind of box. Same everything.'

Karen took down his name and birth date, explaining to Ivy how this typically works: Stalkers usually stop after a visit from the police. He may be angry, he may even be a little over the edge of sanity, but the idea of being arrested could set him straight.

Ivy asked no questions. She nodded repeatedly, thanking

Karen more than once. By the time she left, Karen's internal alarm had reached maximum volume.

Ivy hadn't told her everything – that much was obvious – but Karen could fill in the blanks. She had seen enough abusive relationships in her life to have an idea of what Ivy was going through.

Karen continues searching through the 911 calls. The list contains the time each call came in, along with the address and a brief description of the emergency. Or what the caller claimed was an emergency, because sometimes they weren't. It's tedious work, because she has to look up each address online to see where the incident occurred. She doesn't find anything near or at the apartment building where Wes and Ivy lived.

But then she happens across a call that came in at 12:18 in the morning. The address was listed as 3127 Third Street. Google says that address is a family-style restaurant called Moe's. Also known as the former location of the Fine Line gentlemen's club.

Strange place for a domestic disturbance.

Karen sits back in her chair and stares at the photo of Ivy on the corkboard. At all the pictures. Then she turns to the right and looks at the other picture in the room. It hangs on the wall, the only photo in a frame.

Her husband.

Her *late* husband.

30

Ivy wasn't mad. Not one bit.

Wes had a horrible time yesterday, given that he had to attend the funeral of his boss. No doubt Wes and the team went out drinking after work, and he probably stumbled into an Uber and passed out as soon as he got home. She was perfectly fine with the fact that he never called, even though he said he would.

Pas grave.

French for *No big deal.* She doesn't know the phrase in Chinese.

They didn't have plans last night, anyway.

And today is a new day. She arrives at work with a positive attitude and not an ounce of anger. Actual work takes up at least two hours, making the morning fly by. At about eleven o'clock, her phone lights up.

Not Wes.

It's Heath. Still in Oregon, but finally responding to her messages trying to get hold of him.

Sorry for the delay, just picked up your messages. I'll be back in town next week.

Thank God. For the first time in two months, good news from Heath.

When she was ten years old, Heath and his family moved into her neighborhood. His parents didn't grow marijuana, but his father was an ex-cop who had changed sides, so to speak, because he and his wife started a security company for the farmers. They had moved to California from Kentucky and had funny accents, making Ivy giggle when she first heard Heath talk. He pulled her ponytail; she pinched his arm. They've been best friends ever since.

Heath's southern accent is long gone now, and he is no longer the gangly kid she used to know. Instead of going away to college, he went to a nearby school and studied both architecture and environmental science, eventually moving closer to Ivy to search for work.

His message gives Ivy hope that today is going to be a good one, even though Wes still hasn't contacted her.

They're supposed to go out tonight for drinks after work, a plan they made days ago, so she has no problem contacting him first. Ivy waits until after lunch, because that's a reasonable time to check in about the evening plans. Above all else, she wants to appear reasonable. Not pissed off. Because she isn't.

After ten years, Ivy has learned a few things about texting Wes. If she wants a response, the best way is to act like they're already in the middle of a conversation. Maybe because Wes doesn't remember if they are or aren't, so he thinks he missed something and usually responds.

Palmer's sounds good to me. 6:30?

She sends the text, puts the phone facedown on her desk, and starts her next Chinese lesson. A few minutes later, she flips the phone so it's faceup.

Late in the afternoon, the three dots appear. He's typing.

A second later, the dots disappear.

By the time she heads home to change before going back out to meet him, Wes still hasn't responded. He hasn't contacted her at all.

6:28 P.M.

Wes is not dead.

127

He is not in the hospital, not lying on the side of the road somewhere. Ivy knows this because after work she drove by Siphon and saw his car in the parking lot. Forty-five minutes ago, he was still at work.

Now she sits in her own car in the parking lot of Palmer's. Wes hasn't arrived and his car isn't in the lot, but she is willing to sit here and hedge her bets. Just in case.

6:29.

Ivy has been patient. Understanding. Willing to cut him slack because of Tanner and the funeral and how upset Wes has been about the whole situation. Fine. That's why she is here, waiting to see if he does show instead of blowing up his phone with angry texts asking why he's ignoring her.

6:30.

She's the one who should be mad that he didn't tell her about Karen's visit the other day. He never mentioned it. Still hasn't. He knows that was wrong.

Maybe he just doesn't want to hear it. Wouldn't be the first time he went out of his way to avoid hearing something he didn't want to. The same way he refused to believe she took a job at a strip club. When she told him, he waved her off and turned back to the TV. The Warriors were playing that night.

So perhaps he's just being a baby.

6:33.

Or maybe she has been wrong this whole time.

She had thought, had hoped, that they were trying to make this work. For real. Honest and open, and all the things that healthy, functional couples are supposed to be. She believed they were on the same page.

At least 99 percent of her did. She'd refused to acknowledge the other 1 percent, but now it's like a buzzing fly she can't kill.

Perhaps this has all been part of his game. Maybe he's the

one who is mad. If she hadn't called the police, Karen never would've visited his office. Never would've asked about the stolen car.

The decision to go to the police had been impulsive. She can admit that. The night before, she had been out late, and it wasn't a particularly good one. She woke up tired, slightly hungover, and the first thing she had done was check her phone. Wes had posted on IG, which in itself was a rarity. When he did post, it was always of scenery or nature, photos he took while hiking. An occasional photo of himself. But he never posted pics of other people – not friends or family or even Ivy. But on that day, he did.

It had been taken at a bar, a selfie with a large group of people, and the caption said Happy Hour. Ivy recognized a few of his coworkers, but others she had never seen. Including the woman standing next to him. She wasn't looking at the camera, either. She was looking at Wes.

After work, Ivy went home and gathered up everything she needed – the photos, notes, truffles – and brought them straight to the police station. Wes deserved it. More importantly, she knew he would respond. She just didn't think he would be this angry about it.

Wes is not above payback. In fact, he loves it.

So he reeled her in, made her feel comfortable, and then disappeared. The simplicity of it is almost admirable. But not quite. Not from where she's sitting.

And it's a little hard to believe he would be that cruel. That calculating. Even for him, that's a little far.

6:40.

Ivy checks her phone one last time, then starts her car and drives home. At a stoplight, she bangs her hands against the steering wheel.

Forget *pas grave*. Now she's *furieuse*.

Karen woke up early to ride the bus to Sacramento and back before going to the police station. Still no sign of the voyeur, despite the fact that another report about him came in this week. When she gets to work, two new cases are waiting. The endless flood of sex crimes is no longer shocking. The only surprise comes when someone is arrested, tried, and convicted.

She goes outside, taking a deep breath just as a semitruck passes by. The exhaust in her lungs makes her feel like she's choking.

Perfect.

She stands on the sidewalk for a minute, looking up and down the street. The station is downtown, near the business district, and people are out running errands, grabbing that midmorning coffee, talking on their phones. She doesn't see them as individuals. Not really. What she sees are potential victims and potential suspects. That's the difficult part. Either one could be anybody.

'Morning, Karen.'

Louis Knox stands before her, holding his own cup of coffee. No, tea. She remembers that detail from all the way back at the academy. Even then, she was taking notes.

'Louis. Just the person I wanted to see.' Karen looks up at him, shielding her eyes from the sun with one hand. He looks a little annoyed.

'What can I help you with today?' he asks.

'I wanted to ask about the Tanner Duncan case. Are you making an arrest?'

'Waiting on the DA's decision about prosecuting Bianca Mercado,' he says. 'We've also been talking to a few other women Tanner had . . . propositioned.'

'Propositioned? Really?'

'We didn't find anyone he actually assaulted – at least not anyone who would admit it. But there's a few where the line got blurry. He was pretty insistent with some women.'

Insistent. Is that what they're calling it these days?

Before she can say a word, her cell rings. Louis moves on when she holds up the phone, indicating that she has to take the call.

'Hello?'

'Um, hi. This is Sara? Sara Walker? You left a message for me the other day.' She sounds impossibly young, like a teenager, though she is at least thirty.

'Yes, Sara. Thank you so much for calling me back,' Karen says. 'I'm looking into something that happened a few years ago. It would've been when you were working at the Fine Line.'

'And who are you again?'

'A private investigator,' Karen says. 'I'm working for a family that's trying to find their daughter. She briefly worked at the Fine Line.'

'What's her name?'

'Ivy Banks.'

'Dancer?'

'Waitress.'

'Doesn't sound familiar.' Karen hears Sara inhale and exhale, like she's smoking. 'I haven't worked at a club in a long time,' she finally says.

'I know this is a long shot, but I wanted to talk to you any-way.' After discovering the domestic-dispute call from the Fine Line, Karen used the bankruptcy filing to compile a list of former employees who were owed money, and then she started calling them. Most didn't answer the phone, and the ones who did hung up on her. So far, anyway.

Sara is the first to call back.

'Seven years ago, a 911 call was made from the club to report a domestic disturbance,' Karen says. 'Do you know if that kind of thing happened a lot?'

'Sometimes, I guess,' Sara says. Karen could almost hear her shrug. 'A woman looking for her boyfriend, or someone looking for one of the dancers. It happened.'

'So it wasn't unusual.'

'Not really. But the 911 thing is a little weird. We had secur-ity there to take care of fights.' Another inhale and exhale. 'It's not like anyone wanted the police at the club.'

Of course not. 'I don't suppose there are any incidents you remember?' Karen asks. 'Something that was more serious?'

'Ummm . . . I remember when one of the girls fell off the stage and broke her ankle. Someone called for an ambulance. Oh, and there were definitely overdoses, Oxy and heroin and that kind of thing. This was before fentanyl was around as much as it is now, but we always had Narcan behind the bar, so the police didn't usually get called,' Sara says. 'We didn't have any shootings, though. Those were all at that other club. Leopard or Tiger something.'

'Kitty Kat,' Karen says.

'Yeah, that's it.'

Karen asks a few more questions, but Sara doesn't remem-ber enough – or claims not to remember enough – to give her anything useful. She ends the call, knowing she shouldn't feel so disappointed. The incident at the Fine Line didn't even warrant a report from the responding officers. Finding someone who remembers such a nonevent would be difficult, Karen knew. Still, she had hoped to get lucky.

With a sigh, she goes back into the station and turns her attention to a new file. Time to get back to her other job. The one she is paid to do, starting with trying to track down that camera footage of an attempted rape. The case takes priority over riding the bus to Sacramento.

Hours later, long after her day should've ended, her vision is blurry from watching all the footage. All she ends up with is a man who is *possibly* the attacker. He isn't even facing the camera.

Never easy. Even with all the technology available, it's never easy.

By the time she gets to class, she feels exhausted. Mentally, physically, even spiritually. Her students are the ones who reenergize her.

One night a week, Karen teaches a self-defense class. A free service provided by the Fair Valley Police Department. Karen's time is also free, because she doesn't get paid. She volunteered.

Women make up 90 percent of the students. A few of the men who attend are there solely to meet someone, or to satisfy some fetish of being surrounded by women in spandex. Karen weeds them out quick. The men who come to actually learn self-defense can stay.

Tonight, nine people have shown up. She smiles at all of them. 'To those who have been here before, welcome back,' she says. 'And if it's your first time, please don't be intimidated. Everyone is here to learn the same thing: the best way to protect yourself.'

Karen looks each one of them in the eye, trying to get an

early read on their motive. Their reason for being here. Most show up because they're afraid of being mugged, attacked, or raped.

But every once in a while, someone wants to learn how to protect themselves from a person at home. They think the answer is to become stronger, faster, tougher. To fight back.

They're wrong.

More than one has ended up with their photo on Karen's corkboard and a file in that third stack. No one at the department knows anything about it. None of their business.

32

Wes rolls over to the other side of the bed.

Empty.

For the third morning in a row, Wes wakes up without Ivy next to him. It's the worst moment of his day, and his weakest one. This is when he wants to call her. He even picks up the phone and pulls up her number, but he stops himself when he sees her name. Yesterday, he changed it:

Don't

He puts the phone back down, forcing himself to get out of the bed and into the shower. Instead of thinking about Ivy, he thinks about Karen. About how this current mess is all Ivy's fault. Reminding himself why he won't, and shouldn't, contact her.

She must know it, too. She isn't calling him, either.

Maybe Wes shouldn't have called his sister. Not that her advice is bad, but it isn't always the best thing for *him*.

'Normal people don't do this,' she had said. 'Normal people run away. Far, far away.'

He argued with her, demanding she define a *normal person*. Her answer was succinct.

'Someone who doesn't have sex with the person who called the police on them.'

Fair.

That's what he'd said, but he was thinking that all those so-called normal people have never felt the way he feels about Ivy. He has tried to explain it to Stella many times, in many ways, including today.

'Do you like the feeling of falling in love?' he asked her. 'Like, the beginning part. When you feel alive, and everything is better. The whole world is –'

'It's called the honeymoon phase,' she said. 'Everybody loves that part. It just doesn't last.'

'For you.'

'So you're telling me that you and Ivy defy the normal phases of a relationship?'

'Every time we get back together,' he said, 'we fall in love all over again.'

After Karen showed up at his office, heading straight to Ivy's place was the only option. There was never a second choice.

Stella did make an impact, though. She always does, which is why he doesn't call her unless he is desperate. This time he was, but it had more to do with Karen than Ivy.

Unlike Wes, his sister did all the things their parents wanted their children to do. Stay in Michigan, for one. The most important one. Next, settle down and have kids. She has also done that, Stella is married and had a baby two years ago. Sometimes the things she says remind him of their parents, only she wasn't born fifty years ago and is more reasonable about his choices. Usually.

And sometimes Stella is right. Especially when she told him that as an adult, he has to deal with the consequences of his actions. But right now, they're so much worse than he expected. It feels like he made a choice that can't be undone.

This breakup with Ivy is different. Remarkable due to the lack of drama, of yelling, of threats. None of that this time. Wes tries to trick himself into thinking they're too grown-up or too tired for all that, so they've both settled for a mutual ghosting.

More likely, the anger hasn't built up enough.

The thing that sucks – that always sucks – is that when he and Ivy are together, he wonders how long it'll take this time. How long before they implode.

Even worse, when he and Ivy are apart, he knows they're going to get back together. It's not something he says out loud, and it's not something they discuss. It's something he knows down to the pit of his soul.

But it won't be because he calls her.

Ivy types an email, replying to her manager, and calls him an idiot. Because he is, and the question he asked was stupid. She also calls him a jackass, because he is that, too.

Delete.

She begins again, starting with Why are you wasting my time with this?

Delete.

Third time is the charm. That's what they say, though it wasn't true for her and Wes. But it could be for her email. She begins with Thank you for your question.

Better. As boring as her job is, she can't afford to lose it. She has already lost Wes.

Three days. It's been three days since she has heard from him, and that was at Tanner's funeral. Since then, not a word. Once, late last night, Ivy thought about calling Karen to complain about him again, thinking it would make her feel better. But that would be regressing back to her former, impulsive self. The one that slipped through a few weeks ago, when she went to the police.

Another ten minutes go by before she sends an email to her manager. No profanity and not a single insult. An exhausting task. Before she screws up and really does send something stupid, she opens up the group chat and vents.

Ivy: So I started seeing this guy and everything was going great. Like, really great.

Brooke: Uh-oh.

Ivy: Yep. He ghosted me.

Brooke: What a dick.

Lucia: It probably had nothing to do with you. He's just a child.

Ivy: Seriously, who ghosts someone at our age? How big of a baby do you have to be?

Brooke: You have to be a loser. Literally, a loser in all of life.

Lucia: Totally.

Ivy: We didn't even have a fight!

Brooke: Is words of affirmation your love language?

Ivy: No. But some form of communication is necessary if we're ever going to see each other.

Lucia: I'm not sure love languages are relevant here.

Brooke: I'm just saying. For the next time, you know.

Ivy: For the record, my love language is definitely acts of service.

The bigger the better, as far as Ivy is concerned. But she doesn't feel a need to tell her coworkers that.

Lucia: Just throwing this out there . . . but is it possible he's married? Or has a girlfriend?

Brooke: I bet that's it.

That's not it. But if she and Wes didn't have the history they had, a girlfriend or a wife would be a real possibility.

Ivy: You're probably right.

Brooke: Obviously, we need a girls' night.

Lucia: I second that.

Brooke: Happy hour at Luna tonight.

Ivy: Done.

Luna is one of those pseudo-upscale places, the kind that looks expensive. Up close, the decor and furniture are actually pretty cheap. So are the drinks, which is what makes it so perfect. When they walk in, Ivy makes a quick sweep of the room, looking for Wes. That habit has never died – not in ten years – and, no, he is not at Luna.

Good. The last thing she wants is for this to play out in front of her coworkers. It's also bad, because he isn't here.

Brooke holds up her drink, a dirty martini, and offers a toast. 'We have to celebrate that the guy who ghosted you is gone,' she says. 'Because he's a dick.'

'I'll drink to that,' Ivy says, and she does. A lot.

Girls' night moves from Luna to Buckshot to Palmer's. All of them are Ivy's suggestions, and she looks for Wes at every one of them. Three hours later, she's buzzed. Maybe a little more than that, but still sober enough to see that Wes hasn't been at any of the bars tonight.

'Feel better?' Lucia says. She is wearing blue today, though not sky blue. Still, close enough.

'I feel nothing,' Ivy says.

'Good,' Brooke says. 'Mission accomplished.'

Ubers are called, one for each of them, and they stand

outside together waiting. Lucia pulls out her phone. Ivy does the same. Still nothing from Wes.

She really doesn't feel anything during the ride home in the Uber. Not about the lack of contact or about her night out. Her driver is chatty, and at any other time, she might've enjoyed talking to him.

The lack of emotion continues until she gets home, collapses on her bed, and realizes she is alone. Drunk and lonely is a lethal combination.

She picks up her phone. Puts it down. Picks it up again and reads through all the texts she and Wes exchanged during the week they were together.

Puts it down.

Picks it up.

Flings it across the room.

It lands on the carpet, near her dresser. Ivy rolls off the bed and crawls over to get the phone. She is such an idiot. Never should've gone to the police, never should've told Karen about Wes.

Maybe she should apologize.

The idea takes hold in her mind, planting roots and growing branches, until she writes the script, imagining not only what she would say but what he would say. The whole conversation plays out, and it ends with her not being alone anymore.

Yes. This is what she needs to do. And at 11:47 on a Thursday night, she has to do it right now, while she's still sitting on the floor. No hesitation.

One ring. Two rings. Three.

'Hello?'

Ivy pulls the phone away from her face, double-checking who she called.

Definitely Wes.

Definitely not his voice. It's a woman.

33

Ivy passed out thinking of that woman's voice on the phone, and she wakes up with it still in her head. If she hadn't been drunk, she probably would've hung up as soon as the woman said hello. But she had been just drunk enough.

'Who is this?' Ivy had said.

'Excuse me?'

'Who. Is. This.'

Rustling in the background, like the woman was moving. The call ended.

Ivy dialed right back. Straight to voicemail. She called again. Voicemail again.

Ever since, she has been hearing that woman's voice in her head, trying to figure out if she recognizes it. Maybe. Maybe not. Hard to tell, since the woman said so few words.

Yes, it's been four days since Ivy had any contact from Wes. Yes, they are – presumably – no longer together.

It's over, again, with silence instead of an explosion.

Of all the ways to break up – of all the ways *they've* broken up – this is by far the worst. No chance to vent, to scream, to throw anything, to hang up on each other. No way to get the anger, the frustration, the heartbreak out. And she was never good at keeping things all bottled up.

It's unhealthy to do that. Causes high blood pressure and heart disease and all the bad things. Nobody wants that. She wouldn't even wish it on Wes, not on their most horrible day. There is a difference between being mean and being cruel.

And until he cut her off, she believed there was a difference between being a dick and being hateful.

Now a woman was answering his phone. Late at night. Less than a week later.

This breakup might be the worst thing he's ever done to her.

Karen is up early, though not to ride the bus to Sacramento. She makes a big cup of coffee and heads straight to her home office.

So much to do. Her lists are absolutely overflowing.

The Wes and Ivy file is by far the thickest one on her desk. Today, she attacks it with a new urgency. Ivy was the one who reached out to her when she reported her stalker, naming Wes as the prime suspect. She had practically begged for Karen's help.

Not everyone would realize this, but Karen, who has investigated hundreds of cases – many of which involved abuse – knows more than the average person. She has the expertise and the experience to recognize when someone is in a relationship they can't get out of. Even when the abuse is psychological and the bruises are on the inside.

Ivy has been in one of these relationships for years.

She has been screaming for help, starting all the way back to when she vandalized his car. Wes had pushed her that far, and then he swooped in to save her. Changed his statement, blamed the damage on someone else. Became her hero. No doubt he has done this so often Ivy feels like she can't live without him.

Except she is still screaming for help.

She reminds Karen of Melissa, a young woman who had been in a similar situation. Melissa's boyfriend had accused her of abusing him, but that was just part of his game. Abusers always have a game. Karen is one of the few who know all the rules.

And now she has the list.

It took a while to get it. What she had needed was a complete list of all the crimes, attempted crimes, and accidents that occurred the night Ivy's car was stolen. Fair Valley isn't a huge city, but this includes everything from fender benders to a pack of gum stolen from a convenience store, and it's far more descriptive than the 911 call list she had.

Karen is anxious to get a jump on it this morning. Dani, one of the clerks, finally sent it. When Karen had explained to Dani what she needed, and that the data was located in multiple places, she could almost feel Dani rolling her eyes. Karen knew pressing her into doing something that was technically outside the scope of her job wasn't a good idea. She had to wait until Dani was bored enough to actually do it. Last night, she was. Dani sent it while Karen slept.

Now that she has the list, the first thing she does is scan through it to see if anything jumps out.

It does. Instantly.

The name. Like every other cop who was around seven years ago, Karen remembers it. She can even picture him. Brown hair, freckles, big smile.

Jocy Fisher.

Karen googles his name, skimming through the articles to refresh the details.

Joey had been eighteen years old, only about a month away from his freshman year at UC Berkeley. One night, he visited a friend who had his own apartment, and what began as a small gathering grew into a full-blown party. Joey drank quite a bit. Jäger shots and beer, according to his friends. Eventually, he stumbled out of the party and around the corner, where his car was parked. Instead of driving home drunk, he passed out in the back seat.

They said he didn't feel a thing when someone hit his parked car.

34

Wes sits behind his desk, staring at the closed door of his office. He's been locked away all morning, trying to concentrate on his work, yet he still managed to be late for a conference call.

And he jumps when someone knocks on the door.

'Come in.'

Abigail walks in. It's been a week since she started her temporary assignment as the department's admin. Before she was promoted to the CEO's assistant, Wes had worked with her for years.

'Good morning,' she says.

'Morning.'

'You've been so quiet I wasn't sure you were here.' Abigail sits down across from him. She's wearing a grey skirt, below the knees, but it inches up when she crosses her legs. Her long hair is pulled into a bun at the nape of her neck.

'Just a lot of work to get through. I didn't mean to be rude,' he says.

'Oh, you're not being rude. I just wanted to see how you're doing.'

'We should – Maybe we –'

Abigail smiles. 'Yes,' she says. 'We probably need to talk about last night.'

'Yes,' Wes says. Except he has no idea what else to say. Calling it a mistake might offend her, and Abigail is the last one he wants to piss off. But that's what it was. A big mistake.

'Everyone's upset around here,' she says. 'Including both

of us. The situation with Tanner and Bianca has been so difficult.'

'Absolutely.'

'And we had been drinking. Probably too much.'

'I know I did,' Wes says. He had passed out quick, too. When he woke up, she was gone.

'Wes, we've worked together for years,' Abigail says. 'I don't think either one of us wants this to turn into a big thing.'

'I agree.'

'And neither of us wants this to be a problem.'

No. A problem isn't what he needs or wants – not with Abigail and not at work. 'No. There's no reason for that,' he says.

'Good. Then let's just write this off as a moment of temporary insanity. Or a *night* of temporary insanity.'

She smiles, which makes him feel a hell of a lot better. Given that she's back in the sales department – technically, as the administrative assistant – this could've turned into the worst possible thing he had done in his career. He's lucky that she wants to forget about it as quickly as he does.

Can't blame her. Given the amount of alcohol he had, it's a miracle he could have sex at all. And it couldn't have been good. Well, not *bad*, but less than great. Slightly.

'Agreed,' he says.

'Good.' Abigail stands up, all six feet of her, and towers over him. 'Now both of us need to get back to work.'

Thank God one of them is mature about this. Wes is totally okay with it not being him.

Finally.

Finally.

Heath is back.

Red hair sticks out from under his baseball cap, freckles

cover every inch of his skin. Even his ears. He's wearing khakis, T-shirt, loafers. When they were young, he wore
black-rimmed glasses. Not long ago, he got Lasik. Still looks
like a teenager, though. Even at thirty. If that kind of magic
could be bottled, he'd be a billionaire.

'So what the hell?' he says, waving his arms around. Beer
sloshes out of his bottle and hits the concrete patio. They're
at Ivy's apartment, several drinks into the night, and he has
just finished telling her all about his work in Oregon. 'What
was up with all those messages last week?'

'What do you think they're about?' she says.

He rolls his eyes, takes a swig. No reason to say Wes's name.

Heath knows a lot about their relationship, has heard
about it over the past ten years, and Ivy has told him everything. Almost.

She gives Heath the abbreviated version of what happened this time, starting with when she first went to the
police. Heath listens without interrupting, nodding at times,
looking a bit shocked at others. She skips the real reason why
Karen is looking into them and finishes the story with Wes's
ghosting, followed by the woman who picked up the phone
two nights ago.

He waits a second before saying, 'That's it?'

'That's it.'

'You haven't done anything since?'

'Not a thing.'

Heath sits back a little and sets his beer down on the table.
Starts scratching at the label. Maybe thinking about what he's
going to say, which words to use. Unlike her, impulsiveness
has never been his style.

'Say it,' she says.

'Let's recap this, shall we? Before I left town, you ran into
Wes at that party.'

147

'The engagement party. Yes.'

'And you started talking about how much you missed him,' he says. 'Then Wes stalked you, even followed you, and took pictures, and you went to the police. Which, I have to admit, is one of the sanest things you've ever done.'

'Thank you.'

'Don't thank me. Because then you got back together with him, which is completely insane.'

Ivy says nothing.

Heath shakes his head at her. 'Unsurprisingly, he dumped you. Again.'

She glares at him.

'The truly shocking part about this story is that he ghosted you and you've done nothing since,' he says. 'Then a woman answered his phone, and you still haven't done anything?'

'Correct.'

He finishes off the beer and walks inside her place. He returns with two more and plunks them both down on the table. 'I don't know how to say this without calling you a liar,' he says. 'But I'm not sure I believe you.'

'I'm not lying. Every word is true.'

'Then there must be more to the story,' he says.

'Nope.'

'Nope? Seriously?'

'After giving it some thought . . . No, after giving it a lot of thought,' she says, 'I've come up with a theory.'

'Go ahead.'

'You know I always get a little . . . dramatic,' she says. 'And so does Wes.'

'Understatement. But continue.'

'So what if this ghosting thing Wes is doing, which is so weird and so out of character for him, what if this is a grand gesture?'

Heath stares at her.

'No, seriously,' she says.

'Ivy.'

'Yes?'

'Have you been watching rom-coms again?'

'I've seen them all,' she says. 'But this isn't about movies. The grand gesture is a real thing.'

'Every time Wes does something ridiculous, you call it a grand gesture.'

'Because it's true. You can have more than one. There's no limit on them.'

He gives her a look that almost makes her feel crazy. But not quite.

'Let me ask you something,' he says.

'Go ahead.'

'For one week with Wes, was it worth it?'

Yes. A billion times yes.

She has tried to explain this before, tried to make Heath understand what it's like when she's with Wes. A day, a week, a month. Maybe a minute. It's always worth it. She has tried so many times to find the best way, the best analogy, to explain how it feels. But it's never quite right.

She usually goes back to the night she met him in college, at a frat house, when Wes told her about the downstairs bathroom. That was the last she saw of him at the party.

Eventually, the night escalated to the point where everyone was too drunk, too high, too disconnected. Including most of her friends. She left alone, walking the few short blocks back to her dorm. Davis was a pretty safe place, all things considered, and she wasn't scared until a guy stepped out from behind a tree.

He wanted money. This guy was trying to mug her on a college campus. Not the brightest criminal, but he was the one standing in front of her. Ivy, who didn't have much money and wasn't about to give up twenty dollars, refused to hand it over. On principle. And alcohol. The guy moved forward, trying to grab her.

Out of nowhere, Wes appeared.

He flew out from the side, or so it seemed, and dive-tackled the mugger. It happened so fast Ivy didn't realize what had happened until the guy was on the pavement, face-down, Wes on top of him.

Wes said he had seen her walk out of the party alone and wanted to make sure she got home okay. Heath has never believed that.

'It's creepy he followed you,' he told her. Many times.

Not to Ivy. Nor did she ever think of Wes as her hero, because she doesn't need to be saved. What she needs is someone who has her back.

When it matters, Wes does.

'Yes,' she tells Heath, finally answering his question after pausing to take a sip of her beer. 'This week was worth it.'

'You're addicted to him,' he says. 'And just so we're clear, all the crazy things Wes does aren't grand gestures. Over in the mentally healthy world, we call that love bombing.'

'Ghosting is love bombing?'

'Not that,' he says. 'But a lot of the other things.'

Ivy sighs.

Heath reaches over and places his hand over hers. It feels cold from the icy bottle. 'Ivy, I love you, I support you, I will always be here for you,' he says, 'but I think you deserve so much better.'

'Thank you.'

'If I didn't say it, I wouldn't be doing my job as your best friend.'

'I know,' she says. 'And I appreciate it.'

End of lecture. Now they can move on.

'What are you going to do?' Heath asks.

'How do you know I'm going to do anything?'

'Because you don't let anything go.'

He's right, but she doesn't have to admit it out loud.

Heath leans forward, elbows on the table. 'Time to get serious.'

Ivy smiles. 'I'm ready.'

'Then let's figure out what you're going to do next.'

35

At exactly ten o'clock in the morning, Wes and the sales team gather around the big screen in the boardroom. Ian is here, as well, and his presence keeps everyone from saying what they're really thinking. CEOs have that effect.

Abigail is also in the room, poker face on. No emotion. No reaction to the press conference on TV. Wes glances over at her too much, something he has done ever since their night together. He shouldn't, but he does it anyway. Maybe because thinking about her keeps him from thinking about Ivy.

On the screen, the DA stands in front of a podium. He isn't a particularly attractive man, but he must be doing something right, because he has been the DA for as long as Wes can remember.

'For the past two weeks, we've worked with the Fair Valley Police Department to investigate the death of Tanner Duncan,' he says. 'After reviewing security footage, speaking to dozens of people, and interviewing the woman who was with him at the time, we have decided not to press charges. This was a clear-cut case of self-defense.'

Not a surprise. Everyone in the office assumed this was coming when Bianca hadn't been arrested after the first day or so. Still, Wes looks over at Ian. Like Abigail, his face shows nothing.

On the screen, reporters are shouting questions, all of which the DA ignores. He holds up his hand and says, 'That's all I have. Thank you.'

Bianca's name is never mentioned, nor was it ever. Not

publicly, because she was an assault victim. *Alleged* assault victim. The media has been reminding everyone of this on a daily basis.

Wes believes her. He wasn't sure at first, but now he is. A lot of stuff about Tanner has come out since he died, a lot of stories he hadn't heard are now circulating at the office and online.

Abigail turns off the screen at the same time Ian clears his throat.

'We all know this has been a difficult time for everyone, and for the company,' Ian says. 'Now that the case has been closed, so to speak, the media interest will end. I want to thank everyone for not speaking to reporters and letting our PR department handle it.' He looks like he's about to say more, but he stops himself, nods, and walks out of the room. Abigail isn't far behind.

Wes avoids her and heads straight to his office. It's still uncomfortable, at least for him, though she isn't treating him any differently than before. Part of him wants to blame his sister for this, since she's the one who told him the best way to get over an ex is to sleep with someone else.

Stella probably didn't mean someone from work. And she certainly didn't mean the CEO's assistant.

Still, she's his sister. And if he can't blame her, then he has to blame himself. Which he does. Wes knows he didn't have to sleep with Abigail; he didn't have to sleep with anyone. But if anyone ever asks, the idea came from Stella.

When he gets back to his desk, the first thing he sees is a missed call from Karen.

It couldn't be to talk about Tanner. Not after that press conference. He takes a moment to sit down, tries to get comfortable, and calls her back. She picks up on the second ring.

'Mr Harmon, thank you for returning my call,' she says.

'Wes. Please.'

'All right. I won't take up too much of your time, Wes. I just have a few follow-up questions about Ivy's car. The one that was stolen. Why did she think you borrowed it?'

The question comes so quick it makes his heart jump. Or maybe it's the topic. 'We shared the car,' he says. 'Technically, it was in her name, but we lived together. We both used it.'

'I see.'

'I'm not sure why you're asking about a car that was stolen years ago,' he says.

'You do know the car was found a couple of years later?'

'I do. The police called her about it.'

'So you saw the pictures?' she says.

'I did.'

'I think that's all the questions I have,' Karen says. 'Thank you for your time, Wes.'

She hangs up.

Wes stares at his phone, a chill running up the back of his neck. The only thing Karen wanted to ask about was the car. That can't be a coincidence.

Karen glances behind her. The parking lot behind the station is empty, but she checks anyway. While she tries her best not to work on side projects when she's supposed to be working on her assigned cases, sometimes it has to be done.

She would've preferred to ask Wes these questions in person – to see the look on his face when she asked about the car. Helpful to her, not so helpful to her job. If Louis or his partner happened to be at Siphon, perhaps to give them a heads-up about the press conference, her presence would've set off too many alarm bells. And probably a call to her sergeant.

But Wes wouldn't have made that call. No chance he's

154

going to tell anyone that a detective is calling him about his past. Or about his relationship.

Wes hadn't slipped once, hadn't offered any additional information. She had recorded the call anyway, just in case. It wasn't legal – not without his consent – but this isn't for court. It's for her own investigation.

Earlier, she finally had a chance to look at the Tanner Duncan file. Now that the case is closed, Louis put it in the corner of his desk, on top of a pile of cases waiting to go into storage. Easy enough to sneak a peek.

Karen hadn't forgotten that the door to Wes's office was open the night Tanner was killed.

But according to the report, he wasn't there. No sign of Wes or his car on the security footage from the parking lot, nor was his card swiped to get into the building. Bianca said in her statement that she had been in his office, fixing a mistake on Wes's schedule, when Tanner walked in. Louis didn't press her further on that, but he did check her phone for calls or messages from Wes. Just in case. Nothing there, nothing to indicate Wes had any part in what happened that night, so Louis left it alone. Karen couldn't blame him. If she hadn't been looking into Wes about something else, she wouldn't have investigated any further, either.

The other thing that interested her was the set of Russian dolls. They were taken into evidence, and Louis had asked Bianca about them. She said it held a flash drive, a backup of everyone's schedule in case something happened to the servers, and she always updated it.

That gave Karen something to work with.

She heads back into the station, typing into the Check This app as she walks, preparing her to-do list for tonight. She had been stuck before, unsure about which direction to go. Joey Fisher had shown her the way.

The more she thinks about it, the more items end up on her list. So many things to do, so many things to check. It motivates her to do more, to work harder.

No one was there for her when she needed it, but she's there for them.

Including Ivy.

36

Wes had planned for a smooth day at work. Fifteen minutes in between meetings – enough time to send a couple emails, grab a coffee, and prepare for the next.

Karen's phone call blew it all up.

Everything is off, in his mind and everywhere else. Thoughts zoom around in his head like a swarm of flies, the buzzing so loud he can't concentrate. Can't do anything right. Too much sugar in his coffee; he'd put it in twice. He writes the same email three times. Checks his schedule a dozen times and still doesn't remember what comes next.

He misses Bianca. She used to remind him about upcoming meetings or any changes in the schedule. Abigail is more hands-off. Probably a good thing, given what happened the other night, but still.

In the middle of an online meeting, a woman reminds him of Karen. The way she talks, firing off questions. The woman makes him think about the call again, along with the car.

Not to mention Ivy.

His mind is rotating in a dangerous loop, one that's left him not only confused but also making bad decisions. Starting with Abigail. That was the only night he hadn't ended up alone at his house, phone in hand, trying to convince himself not to call Ivy.

Ghosting Ivy is starting to feel like the worst choice he could've made. The healthier thing, the more mature thing, would've been to talk to her. Have a real conversation about what she had done, and about Karen. It doesn't make him feel stupid that he ran straight to Ivy after she called the police. It makes him feel stupid that he didn't react well when Karen kept showing up.

More than anything, he is surprised Ivy hasn't contacted him. Also, he's not surprised at all.

'Wes? Are you with us?'

And now he's being called out in a meeting. This day has gone to hell.

Somehow he muddles through the afternoon, making more mistakes than sales, though only one thing on his schedule is important. The afternoon client meeting. He is still trying to prepare, reading background info, when a message from Abigail pops up on his screen.

Abigail: They're in the conference room.

Wes: Already?

Abigail: It's 3:30.

Right. It certainly is. Only he thought the meeting started at four. He curses himself under his breath, ordering his brain to get it together.

During the meeting, the flies in his head are mercifully quiet. He forces them away every time the buzzing starts. It's a strain on what's left of his mental capacity. By the time the meeting is over, he's exhausted. Fighting his own brain can be more tiring than working out.

His original plan had been to go home and watch the game. Any game.

His reality is Liver, where Marcus is buying the first round of drinks. The whole sales team is already there when he arrives.

Wes heads to the far end of the bar, where Dana is

holding court. She is one of the few women on the sales team, and she's telling a story about someone she just started seeing. Some of the guys are gathered around her, thinking they'll learn something about women. Wes orders a scotch and joins in.

And he really, really tries not to think about the women in his own life. But the story Dana is telling reminds him, vaguely, of Ivy.

He glances over at Abigail, catches her looking back at him. Wes averts his eyes quickly, looks back at Dana, but something makes him glance toward the front door. Almost like he has a sixth sense about her.

Ivy. With Heath.

They maneuver through the maze of tables, walking toward the bar. Heath says something, and Ivy turns to him and laughs. It looks like they are heading right for Wes.

Ivy is about a foot away when she passes by. Doesn't look at him, doesn't say a word, doesn't acknowledge he exists.

Like he's a ghost.

Okay, fair. What Ivy is doing is perfectly, undeniably fair. Wes knows this.

That doesn't make it any less awkward. Or painful.

He turns around and acts like nothing happened. Marcus is saying something, Wes has no idea what. He's too busy imagining Ivy ordering a drink and laughing with Heath. And if he knows his colleagues, they're checking Ivy out.

Someone touches his sleeve.

Abigail.

'Hey,' she says.

'Hey, how are you?'

Without breaking eye contact with him, she says, 'Isn't that Ivy?'

For a second, he thinks about playing dumb, like he doesn't know Ivy is in the bar. But this is Abigail. She knows too much. Has seen too much.

'Yes,' he says.

Abigail looks like she's waiting for more, but he has nothing else to say. He turns to Marcus and asks him a question, something about the Warriors. The answer is irrelevant. Wes doesn't listen to Marcus cite player stats and make predictions. The energy coming from the other side of the bar is too strong. He can hear Ivy's voice, or at least he thinks he can.

Abigail takes a sip of her drink. Whiskey or scotch, like everyone else. Ivy hates it. Wes knows without looking that she is drinking a gin martini.

He gets distracted by a group of women who have just walked into the bar. Five of them. Dressed up in Instagram-worthy outfits, with high heels, a lot of skin showing, and long hair everywhere. They get the attention of everyone at Liver, which appears to be the goal.

A brunette catches his eye. She is wearing a black skirt and a flowy green blouse. Bare shoulders.

He watches as they sit down at a table and order drinks from the waitress. Their voices ring out across the bar, packed with giggles and not-so-sneaky looks toward Wes and his colleagues.

Marcus nudges him, nodding toward the women. 'Let's go.'

'Nah.'

'Come on. I need a wingman.'

Marcus always needs a wingman, and he usually asks Wes. The nice guy. That's the role of a wingman – to keep everyone happy and distracted while Marcus focuses on the girl he's interested in.

Tonight, that task is a little more difficult. Ivy on one side of the bar, Abigail on the other, new girls in the middle. Like the Bermuda Triangle of women. Wes analyzes the possible outcomes the way he analyzes sales numbers at Siphon.

Abigail is the type he usually avoids: too good-looking, too high-maintenance, the kind with her pick of men. He and Abigail may have hooked up, but she must have better options. A lot of them. Still, given her position, and given that she was in his bed only a few days ago, it wouldn't be the smartest decision to hit on another woman when she's around.

Ivy will be pissed – that's a given – and she would punish him for it. Eventually. But tonight, in this bar, in front of his colleagues . . . probably not. She is doing an excellent job of pretending he doesn't exist. Ignoring him is the least dramatic thing she's ever done. And it's unnerving. Like he's perched at the edge of a cliff, waiting for her to push.

It's so much worse this way.

Last but not least, he thinks about whether the brunette is worth all the trouble. Hard to tell. He doesn't even know her, but she is cute.

Marcus slips a fresh drink into his hand. 'Come on. Let's go.'

Wes is far from being in a good place. He has a detective diving deep into his past, an unpredictable girlfriend-slash-ex – who happens to be in this very bar – and he just slept with the CEO's assistant.

If there was ever a time to say *Screw it*, this must be it.

37

So predictable.

Ivy rolls her eyes as Wes and his coworker approach the girls, though it does help cover the sting of what she just did. Pretending Wes doesn't exist is a lot harder than she thought it would be. When she walked by him, her heart seized up.

Heath leans in and says, 'He's just trying to make you jealous.'

'Of course he is.'

'Don't you dare –'

'I'm not. I won't.'

She turns her back to Wes and the group of women, facing the bar. The bottles of liquor are lined up against a giant beveled mirror. Ivy can see herself, and, yes, she looks good. Dressed straight from work, albeit with fresh makeup and styled hair. Maybe not her best, but at least she doesn't look as bad as she feels.

It's a lie, what they say about time. Doesn't heal anything. Not love, anyway.

But she has taken a step back, assessed the situation from a distance. It helps having Heath in town, because she has someone else to call, someone who understands. Someone who is there when she feels like calling Wes.

Most of her free time has been spent with Heath, talking about Wes and refusing to answer his questions about how healthy or unhealthy that may be. Self-improvement can wait for another day. Especially after being ghosted by someone she has known, and loved, for ten years.

Unless she's right, and this *is* a grand gesture. Heath still thinks she is crazy for thinking that, yet she can't discount it. Not yet.

In the mirror over the bar, she sees what's happening behind her. Wes and Marcus sitting with those women.

'You knew he was going to do something,' Heath says.

'After the way I ignored him? Of course he was.'

'Still, he was so shocked. It was perfect.'

Yes, it was. No doubt Wes thought she was about to make a scene. Can't blame him, either – she has done it often enough. She wishes she could've seen his face when she passed right by like he wasn't even there, but she didn't dare look.

'We have to stay now,' she says. 'I can't walk out while he's talking to them. He'll think it's because of him.'

'And it would be,' Heath says.

She doesn't answer. She's too busy watching Wes talk to that girl, the one wearing a ridiculous green blouse. Like she's the grassy knoll or something.

Ivy looks around the bar, checking out who else is here. Specifically, the men.

Heath knows exactly what she's doing. He nods to a man who just walked in and sat down a few seats away.

She glances over.

Simpatichny.

Russian for *handsome*. The man Heath points out is definitely that. Beautiful eyes, strong nose, and the best part: He has a beard.

'Perfect,' Ivy says.

Karen picks up the phone and dials the next number.

'Hi, Daisy. It's Karen. Just checking in to see how everything is going. Call me back when you have a chance and let me know if you need anything.'

She hangs up, crosses Daisy off her list, and moves on to the next name.

Tonight, she came home straight after work, skipping her usual bus ride to look for the voyeur. It's check-in day. Once a month, Karen puts aside some time to call a few of the people she has helped. Daisy, Patrice, Michael, Darren, Liz, and Georgia had been stuck in abusive relationships. None are now.

After checking in with three of them, she returns to her stack of files. Ivy has been taking up a lot of time, but she is far from being the only one who needs help. Caitlin, Drew, and Anna also need her. With a gulp of her energy drink, she digs in.

Marathon, not a sprint.

She flips through the pictures on her phone. Earlier today, she visited the evidence room, and for the first time saw what they had gathered on the Tanner Duncan case. Not that she could take anything – that's never allowed, not even after the case is closed. Maybe that happens on TV, but not at the Fair Valley Police Department. Myrna keeps that evidence room on lock.

But Karen didn't need to take anything; she just needed pictures. Online, she orders what she needs.

At nine o'clock, she takes a break to call her son. They have a weekly phone call, always the same day and time, and she never misses it. Jack answers on the second ring.

'Hey, Mom.'

'Hi, honey.' The sound of his voice makes her tear up. Happy tears. Jack hates it, and she does her best to keep her voice even. 'How are you?'

Jack is a man now, a young one but still a man. Twenty-three years old, he's an engineer living in Los Angeles, sharing a house with three friends and struggling to pay the bills while still trying to have some fun. No serious relationship at the moment. Jack hasn't found the right man yet, but he will.

For the past couple of years, they've been able to see each other three times a year: Thanksgiving, Christmas, and her birthday – which is coming up soon. Less than a month away.

He doesn't ask about his father anymore, thank God. Jack was a toddler when his father died and doesn't remember anything about him. He knows what the rest of the world knows: His father had been a cop who was killed in the line of duty.

True story. Not the whole story.

Karen's husband had been called to the scene of a robbery in progress. He and his partner were the first to arrive, and they found themselves in the middle of a shoot-out between the robbers and the store owner.

When the call for backup came, Karen was sitting in her patrol car. The store wasn't far away. Three blocks, to be exact. She knew they were probably the closest and could get there faster than anyone else. But her partner had just gone into a deli to grab lunch for both of them.

Normally, she would be the first to rush to her husband's aid. To be his protector, his helper. His apologist.

Not that day.

Something in her shut down. Maybe because her son had just turned two and she didn't want him growing up with a father like that. Or maybe because, at that moment, Karen didn't want to answer the call. She did not radio her partner. Did not tell him to leave the deli immediately so they could get to the scene.

Karen waited in the car, listening to calls come over the radio, and for the first time in years, she felt nothing. Not good or bad, not anxious, not scared, not anything. Like her heart stopped beating for a few minutes.

By the time she and her partner made it to the scene, her husband was dead.

38

Karen picks up her Red Bull and takes a long sip. Eight o'clock at night, and she's still working, still trying to find a connection between Joey and Wes. Frustrating.

No. Infuriating.

Her phone rings, and when she sees the name, she hesitates. A long list of things to do is waiting for her. If she answers, she'll be lucky to get half of them done.

Darren. Always Darren.

He had not been one of the three she checked in with tonight. Karen picks up the phone because she has to.

'Hi,' she says. 'How are you?'

A deep, rumbling sigh.

'Darren? You okay?'

'I did it again,' he says. A tiny voice, like a child admitting he broke something. Darren is a thirty-six-year-old man who has obviously returned to Alaina, his girlfriend. For the third time. Staying out of an abusive relationship can be harder than getting out.

Her long to-do list goes out the proverbial window. She can't turn Darren down, can't ignore him. She has never been able to arrest Alaina. The woman hasn't come close to breaking the law. And Karen looked. Hard.

Alaina doesn't hit Darren. She is possessive, manipulative, degrading, and controlling – which is a problem, because most emotional abuse isn't illegal. Even when it crosses the line, it's hard to prove in criminal court. The DA won't even try those cases, because making a jury understand the difference between something said in anger and a real threat isn't easy. Alaina knows that.

Karen does, too. So did her husband.

It was subtle at first. Karen didn't even see it happening. If someone had told her she was being manipulated or abused, she never would've believed them.

Long before Karen married her husband, it started. The first time he asked her to cancel plans with her girlfriends, they were still in the dating phase. When he said he really wanted to see her and begged her to go out with him instead, Karen thought it was sweet. He brought her flowers, and they spent a romantic evening at a nice restaurant.

The first time he asked her to skip a weekend with her family, it was because he had something special planned. And he did. A rented Airbnb in the wilderness, two days without seeing anyone else – and without any clothes.

The first time he got jealous was right after they both graduated from the police academy. They had been in a relationship for over a year, and he asked about Karen's partner at work. A man who had been on the job for almost fifteen years. Her boyfriend wanted to know if her partner ever checked her out, ever hit on her. Always in a light tone, like he was teasing. She thought it was cute that he was jealous.

No red flags, as far as she was concerned. When he proposed, she said yes without hesitation. Karen was madly in love with this man who cared so much about her.

The first time she noticed how small her circle of friends had become was when she shopped for a wedding dress by herself. Still, she told herself this was normal. The natural result of spending most of your time with the person you're going to marry. You build a life together, replacing the one you had when you were single.

The first time he texted and asked where she was, they were already married. He wanted to know why she was late getting home from work. Her husband was worried, and rightly so, because they were cops. When he did it again – and again, and again – Karen started texting him first, letting him know exactly when she would be home. Always before he had a chance to text her. If she didn't, he would blow up her phone.

Completely understandable. Anything can happen when you're a cop. Her husband wasn't doing anything out of the ordinary.

The first time he made a suggestion about what she should wear, Karen had been impressed. Not many men paid that much attention to clothes. He started doing it more often, until he was choosing all her clothes for her. By then, she was convinced he knew more about fashion than she did. Karen let him dress her, because he was better at it.

Everything was so easy to explain. To herself, at least. She didn't share any of it with coworkers or the few friends she still had. This was relationship stuff, the private things you don't run around telling other people. She didn't want to, either. It would require too many words, too many questions.

Karen still didn't realize she was doubting her own behavior, because he had convinced her not to.

And his smile. That goddamn smile.

It was hard to think a man smiling at her like that didn't love her. Didn't want the best for her. Didn't want the best for their family.

So she kept making excuses for him. Kept telling herself all of this was normal. It was only after Jack was born that she started realizing how dangerous her husband was.

The knowledge came slowly, one drop at a time, each one more painful than the last. Like a special kind of torture designed for people who had married the wrong person.

The first time he accused her of cheating, she laughed, because it had to be a joke. It wasn't. And he kept on doing it. If she looked at a waiter for too long, laughed at a bartender's joke, or even thought about having a drink with her partner, it meant she must be cheating. Or that she wanted to.

The first time he threatened to kill himself if she left him, Karen assumed he was just being dramatic. She left anyway. He called her and claimed he was holding his service weapon, ready to blow off his head. Rather than call the police – and potentially make him lose his job – she went back home.

The first time he threatened to kill her if she left him, he also said he would find her. Wherever she went, whatever she did, he would be there. Karen woke up, took a hard look at her life, and realized she was exactly where he wanted her to be.

Trapped.

39

It takes Ivy less than a minute to learn that the man with the beard is named Milo.

Milo.

She hates the name, and hates the way it sounds with her own. Ivy and Milo. Doesn't work. It also doesn't matter, because she isn't looking for a new life partner tonight.

At least he is polite and asks all the right questions: what she does, who she knows, how she spends her free time. Heath fades into the background, burying himself in his phone, leaving Ivy alone with Milo. She doesn't dare look over at Wes, who is still talking to the group of girls in the middle of the bar. But he is paying attention. And she is paying attention to him.

Milo, oblivious, goes on and on about his podcast. 'My friends and I started it for fun, something to do because it didn't really cost anything. We recorded our conversations about pop culture and current events, stuff like that, and loaded them on YouTube. Then it kind of took off.'

'What's it called?'

He smiles, looking a bit sheepish. 'Promise you won't judge me by the name.'

'Promise.'

'It's called *Broken Men.*'

Good thing she isn't genuinely interested in Milo, because he is waving a big red flag right in her face.

She laughs. 'That's quite a name.'

'Like I said, it started as a joke. It wasn't like we planned it.'

'So is that what you are?' she says. 'A broken man?'

'My therapist doesn't think so.'

A nice save, mentioning his therapist, but she still doesn't care. Milo will have to be some other woman's problem. But she continues talking and flirting, and accepts the drink he offers to buy her.

'So if I say the wrong thing,' she says, 'am I going to end up a story on your podcast?'

'I wouldn't do that.'

She doesn't believe him, but the question does make him recount the stories he tells on the show. He keeps talking until a burst of laughter from the middle of the bar interrupts the conversation. Ivy knows it's coming from the table where Wes is sitting and forces herself not to look over there. She glances at Heath and gives him a tiny nod. He discreetly holds up his phone.

In the mirror, she sees that the group of girls is leaving. So is Wes. They all walk out of the bar together.

'It was really nice talking to you,' she says to Milo, 'but I've got to meet some friends for dinner.'

Milo asks for her number. She gives it to him, though she can't imagine dating a self-described broken man. It somehow seems preferable when a man is clueless about how damaged he is. Milo is the type who tells women in advance how screwed up he is so he can use it as an excuse later.

Heath walks out before she does, and they meet outside. He holds up his phone, showing her the pictures he took. Her and Milo, together at the bar. Talking. Laughing. Smiling.

Perfect.

Farrah unlocks the door to her place and holds it open. 'Come on in.'

Wes does as he's told.

She lives in a tiny apartment, basically a studio with a curtain walling off the bed. She has fabric on the walls, too, and a crystal-looking chandelier hanging from the ceiling. It feels like he has walked into a music box.

Not a bad thing.

'I have wine,' she says. 'Pinot grigio?'

'That's perfect.'

He sits down on the overstuffed couch, which feels as comfortable as it looks. It's still a little shocking he's here. When he and Marcus first approached that table full of girls, he never expected to end up at the brunette's house.

It didn't happen right away. They left Liver in a big group, and the night continued over several hours, multiple locations, and a lot of drinks and food. Wes and Farrah live relatively close together, and she had asked if he wanted to share an Uber. He did.

'That last bar was so loud, wasn't it?' Farrah says. She returns from her tiny kitchen – more like a kitchenette – with two glasses.

'It was loud.' He takes a sip. Cheap wine. Doesn't matter.

'So you were telling me about disc golf.'

Right. Disc golf. She's never played before, and he was trying to explain the game to her. He finishes describing it, watching the way she listens, nods, comments without interrupting. She really is cute, and not just because he's been drinking.

Eventually, he leans in to kiss her. She kisses him back, hard, and pulls him in closer.

Right before she pushes him away.

'Sorry,' she says. 'I mean . . . we just met.'

Ah. Okay. 'You're right. We did.'

'I didn't mean to give you the wrong impression by inviting you over. I was just having such a good time talking to you,' she says.

'I like talking to you, too.'

She smiles. He takes another sip of wine and wonders what time it is. Must be getting late, and he has to work in the morning. But if he leaves right now, he's the bad guy. Can't even risk a glance at his watch.

Farrah starts talking about hiking, a subject he is genuinely interested in, but right now he's counting down the minutes until he can leave. He isn't looking for someone to date, and he's definitely not looking for a new relationship. Just a hookup, someone to distract him from everything else.

Farrah is not it.

That doesn't stop him from getting her number on the way out, or from giving his number to her, only because he would be a dick if he didn't.

On the ride home, he plans the morning in his head. Every choice has consequences, including the ones he made tonight. Now he'll have to take an Uber to pick up his car and then drive to work. He thinks about seeing Abigail in the office. She certainly saw him and Marcus leave the bar with all those girls. Not that she would care, but still. Her opinion matters.

And he thinks of Ivy. Always Ivy.

He checks his phone for messages. Nothing from her. But she has posted a photo from Liver on IG. The guy with the beard.

40

Karen hesitates before knocking on the door. Her nerves flare up, along with the alarm bell in her head. The one that says you're doing something wrong. She pushes through it, forcing herself to raise her hand. Sometimes, the result is the most important thing. Not how you got there.

She knocks three times and waits, listening for movement from inside. A bit of shuffling, the creak of the floor. Thin doors and walls can be an occasional benefit of cheap construction.

When the door doesn't open, Karen knocks again.

'I don't have anything to say.' Bianca's voice comes through loud and clear.

Karen takes out her police ID and holds it up to the peephole. 'Miss Mercado, I'm a detective with the Fair Valley Police Department.'

Another creak from inside the apartment, followed by a sharp click. The door opens. Bianca stands before her, dressed in leggings and a T-shirt, no makeup, her hair in a messy ponytail. She looks about sixteen.

'I remember you,' Bianca says. 'You're the one who came to see Wes.'

'That's right,' Karen says, holding up her work tote bag. 'And I have something to return to you.'

'You have to contact my lawyer.'

'This isn't about Tanner Duncan. I'm here on another matter.'

Bianca stares at her for a moment before opening the door

a little wider, allowing Karen to enter. As she does, Karen gets a good look at Bianca's eyes. Dilated pupils. Valium, maybe. Can't blame her. She wouldn't be human if she didn't have nightmares about that blood.

Her living room isn't spic-and-span clean, but it's neat enough. Bianca had obviously been lying in front of the TV when Karen knocked. The position of the pillow, blanket, and remote tell her that.

Off to the left, there's a round table with two chairs, and a tiny kitchen next to it. A basic starter apartment with inexpensive furniture, mostly secondhand. Nothing unusual about it.

Karen perches herself on the edge of a chair that looks like a basket. Bianca plunks down on the couch.

'How are you doing?' Karen asks.

'Okay.'

'I imagine this has been very difficult.'

'I wasn't trying to kill him,' she says. 'I told the other detectives that. I just wanted him off of me. Away from me.'

'I know.'

'You know?' Bianca says.

'Sometimes you have to do things that are . . . inconceivable. To protect yourself.'

Bianca nods hard. Karen assumes she has been in therapy, which is good, and the medication must be helping. Despite the fact that she is lying around watching TV in the middle of the day, she is doing pretty well for someone who stabbed her boss in the throat.

'And Siphon?' Karen says. 'Are they helping?'

'They're still paying my salary, benefits, and everything. My lawyer says it's because they don't want me to sue.'

Her lawyer is right. She has a hell of a case against them after being attacked at work. But Karen isn't here to talk

176

about that. She leans down and removes a Ziploc bag from her work tote.

'This was taken as evidence,' she says. 'Now that the case is closed, I thought you might want it back.'

Bianca snatches it out of her hand. She removes the Russian doll set from the bag and, one by one, opens them up.

Mentally, Karen keeps her fingers crossed. These are not Bianca's Russian dolls, though they look the same and cost only $12.99 on Etsy. Karen had checked out the original set quite thoroughly, and removed the smallest one to make sure the sets matched. The only thing she didn't do was add the blood splatter.

She watches Bianca put them all back together and place the large doll on the coffee table.

'Thank you,' Bianca says.

'You're welcome. It seemed like something that was personal. A gift, maybe?'

'I collect them.'

'They're beautiful. I had one when I was a kid and used to hide pieces of candy in it. My brother never figured it out.' Karen smiles, like this false memory makes her happy.

'Yeah, they're pretty good for that,' Bianca says.

'If you get rid of the smallest ones.'

'Obviously.'

'You know, I noticed all the dolls were open that night. What did you put in there?'

'A flash drive,' Bianca says. 'I keep a backup of the schedules on it, just in case. I got it out to compare what I had with Wes's schedule on his computer. That's why I was in his office.' The same story she gave to Louis Knox. Bianca speaks robotically, like she's repeated those words a hundred times. Karen doesn't believe a word of it.

'Wes,' Karen says. 'He's an interesting one.'

Bianca sits up a little. 'That's why you're here? To talk about Wes?'

'I just wanted to get your thoughts about him, given that you worked together,' Karen says. 'I've been looking into him on another matter. Nothing to do with what happened to you.'

'I never had a problem with Wes,' Bianca says. 'But, then, I never had a problem with Tanner, either. Until I did.'

'Funny how that works.'

'Did Wes do something wrong?'

'That's what I'm trying to figure out.' Karen shifts in her seat, recrossing her legs, while trying to decide how much to tell Bianca. And how much she might repeat to someone else. But Bianca isn't about to contact the police – not after they decided against charging her. She won't invite more attention from them.

Karen is also so far outside the scope of her job that one more step doesn't mean much. As long as she doesn't fall over the edge.

'Do you remember Joey Fisher?' Karen asks.

Bianca blinks. 'Joey Fisher?'

'It was years ago, so you were probably very young. Joey was sleeping in the back of his car when someone crashed into it and killed him.'

Bianca stares at Karen, waiting for more. Maybe waiting for the point.

'I've discovered some information that possibly links Wes to the accident,' Karen says. 'Obviously, I want to chase down every lead. I don't have a complete picture yet, so I'm looking for anything that could help me sort this out.'

'I'll try to help,' Bianca says, picking at a thread on the couch. 'If I can.'

*

178

After Karen leaves, Bianca locks her door. She stands there for a minute, not moving, trying to process everything the detective said. She knew it. She *knew* there was something about Wes and Joey.

Her intuition hasn't been wrong yet.

Bianca picks up the Russian dolls and opens them, returning the Siphon master key to its original place. She still has it; the key had been in her pocket when Tanner attacked her. No one ever figured out that she had it. And she wasn't about to tell Karen or any other cop, so she made up the story about the flash drive.

Bianca puts the dolls on her bookshelf, where all her others are lined up. The collection started when she received one as a birthday gift. She has nine of them now. Eventually, she'll find her tenth.

She returns to her couch and pulls her laptop out from under it. Her work laptop. Siphon either forgot about it or doesn't have the courage to ask her to return it.

Online is where she spends most of her time these days, mostly on forums for assault survivors. Before getting started, she goes to the kitchen and opens the refrigerator for the twentieth time today. So much food inside.

She pulls out a chicken-and-black-bean casserole and nukes a giant slab of it. Her mom has been bringing food over every day since she returned to her own apartment, and Bianca has been eating it. Her new medication makes her want to shove all the food in her mouth.

It also relaxes her. Lets her sleep without waking up screaming. She spends a lot of time sleeping because it makes everything else disappear.

Bianca turns on the TV and skims through all the streaming networks, looking for something to watch. She's already seen everything that looks interesting or halfway entertaining. The inevitable result of not leaving her apartment.

Well, that's not completely true. She did go out once, for a walk, to try and get some sun. Her online therapist said it was important.

Everything was going fine until she started having flashbacks to the moment Tanner attacked her. She started becoming suspicious of everyone she saw, crossing the street to avoid them, finally hustling back to her place. She hasn't gone out since.

Her therapist told her this sometimes happens to people who have been assaulted.

'It's quite common to have flashbacks of the attack,' she had said. 'And to imagine it happening to you again.'

Luckily, Bianca lives in a world where she doesn't have to go out. Everything can be ordered online, from food to toilet paper, and her only moments of stress are when the delivery drivers come to the door.

Bianca doesn't miss going out. For now, she is content to sit down at her computer and check in on her coworkers. Former coworkers. Whatever. She can't log in to her own email; Siphon changed that password quick. Her files, her messages, they all belong to Abigail now.

But that was the only password that changed. She can still log in to all the others she had access to. Their passwords are the same.

She has been messing with Wes's schedule for the past week, at least the part of it she can access. Changing his meetings, making him a little late – nothing too bad, just enough to make her laugh. Something to do while she continues to read his new emails.

Underneath her benzo-induced haze, she is angry at Wes. Not just because of Joey, either. If it wasn't for Wes, she wouldn't have been at the office late at night. And she wouldn't have been attacked by Tanner.

Irrational anger? Yes. Real anger? Also yes.

She logs in to Wes's email and starts downloading all his files. It makes her feel a little more alive, makes her mind a little sharper. Snooping is an activity that feels comforting, like wrapping up in a cozy blanket or wearing her favorite sweatshirt.

And she's good at it. Karen confirmed it. There really is a connection between Joey and Wes, though it's far worse than Bianca imagined.

While waiting for the download to finish, she picks up her phone and goes straight to the cloud. All her pictures are there, dating back to when she was in high school. Bianca scrolls back through them until she finds the photos of Joey Fisher.

She even has one from her sixteenth birthday, when Joey gave her a set of Russian dolls. The first gift from her first boyfriend.

41

Hey, it's Farrah. Wanted to see if you're up for having a drink sometime this week?

Wes is a little surprised to hear from Farrah, given that he has ignored her. No texts, no calls, no follow-up after he left her apartment. Any interest he had evaporated when he realized she was looking for a relationship. He isn't. And he has no time to pretend otherwise.

He could answer Farrah's text. Could reasonably get away with claiming he has been swamped at work and will contact her next week, and then never do it. But why bother? No matter what he does now, he's going to end up being the bad guy, regardless of how it plays out. Either he ignores her today or he ignores her later.

Briefly, he considers telling her the semitruth. That he is involved with someone, sort of. It's complicated. He could say that while Farrah is very nice and very attractive, he just doesn't have the bandwidth to start something new right now.

As he mentally writes that text, he can see how bad it sounds. No way around it: He'll be the bad guy. Might as well ignore her, the same way he's been ignoring Ivy.

Except in Ivy's case, she lives full-time in his head.

Wes has been checking her IG nonstop for days, watching for another post of that guy from Liver. Waiting to see if she is going out with him.

Milo.

Yes, he knows all about Milo now, has listened to several

episodes of his podcast. *Broken Men* is the kind of thing guys create when they're trying to attract women. The type who want to fix men.

Objectively speaking, he gets it. Specifically, he hates this guy. Hates his name.

Hates his *beard*.

Ivy stares at the text, not understanding it at all.

Why did you tag me?

No name, just a number, and she doesn't recognize it. Ivy pauses her Chinese lesson and pulls up her IG account, checking over her recent posts. She looks at the phone number again and realizes it's in her address book. No name. But now she knows.

Milo.

They had exchanged phone numbers, but she'd never bothered to type in his name. Yes, she had tagged him when she posted the picture of them sitting at the bar. Milo wasn't hard to find, being a podcaster and all, though he did over-state the popularity of *Broken Men*. Hard to believe he can make a living off so few subscribers.

She doesn't mention that in her reply.

Just giving you some extra publicity ☺

Milo answers immediately: **We only had a drink together.**

Now she is confused again. He's acting like she called him her boyfriend or something, which seems rather dramatic.

I'm aware of that, she says.

Look, it caused a problem. You should've asked.

Ivy makes a face at her phone. Why does she always have to meet the psychos. **Tagging you in a post caused a problem?**

Yes. With my fiancée.

Jesus Christ. He never – not once, not even in passing – mentioned a girlfriend, much less a fiancée.

If you had bothered to mention that, I never would've posted the picture.

The dots appear, then disappear. Good. Maybe that shut him up. The last thing she needs right now is another problem with another guy.

She returns to her Chinese lesson, pausing only to look up how to say *lying pig*.

Dà piànzi.

It's the closest translation she can find, and it's a good one to know. She repeats it ten times to make sure she remembers, because you never know when it'll come in handy.

Nothing more comes from Milo. By the afternoon she isn't thinking about him anymore. She is thinking about Wes and that girl from Liver. The cute one. Ivy hates that he doesn't post on social media more often and that when he does it's something stupid, like the view from wherever he's hiking or a funny meme. He makes it so difficult for her to know what he's doing. On purpose.

Late in the afternoon, when her brain is tired and she can't learn any more new words, she gets a DM from a woman named Clarissa.

Look, I'm not trying to be a stalker, but that guy in your post is my fiancée. Can I ask what happened between you two?

How Ivy got pulled into this drama just by posting a photo is beyond her.

But if it were her, and she had reached out to someone for information about Wes, she would hope the woman would answer. If she was polite. So far, Clarissa hasn't done anything offensive.

Clarissa is quite active on IG. She has posted a lot of pictures of herself and Milo. Including the engagement ring.

184

We met at Liver, spent an hour or so talking and having a drink. He asked if we could exchange numbers, and I agreed. He didn't mention having a fiancée. He never called me, and I never called him.

Clarissa's response is instantaneous: Thank you.

With that, Ivy is done for the day. She logs out of her computer, puts her earbuds back in the case, and gathers her things. On the way to her car, she receives yet another DM from Clarissa.

Do you mind if I ask why you posted the picture? I'm just curious, since you barely know each other?

Because she wanted to make Wes jealous. That was it. Nothing deeper than that. And it's not something she is willing to tell Clarissa.

I thought his podcast sounded interesting, so I was just spreading the word about him.

It sounds lame, but it's all Ivy has. Now she is really done, because this relationship is not her problem. The only upside of this day is that she hasn't heard from Karen.

42

Karen's entire body aches as she crawls out of bed. Up early again, though not to search for the voyeur. Every extra minute is focused on Wes.

As much as she wants to sleep a little longer, thinking about her son makes her get up. She imagines what Jack would be like if he had grown up with his father in his life. How different he would be now.

And the likelihood that he would have also ended up in an abusive relationship. The statistics on that are astounding.

She thinks about all the children going through the same thing, stuck in abusive households, growing up watching their parents fight. Maybe they try to defend one parent against the other, or maybe they hide in the corner. No good options for a child stuck in that cycle.

Another reason risking her career is worth it. Another reason to get out of bed.

If Karen's car wasn't in such bad shape, she would drive to Sacramento. But she isn't sure it will make it. Back to the bus. This adds an additional thirty minutes to the trip, so it's almost lunchtime when she arrives at 327 Bluebell Court.

Nice little house with a well-kept lawn and a welcome mat in front of the door. It opens before she has a chance to knock.

Hugo Garrison is at least seventy, maybe older. Hard to tell. He has a little bit of hair left and a smile as big as his belly.

'Karen?' he says.

'Yes, I apologize for being a little late.'

He opens the door wide, motioning for her to enter. 'Not a problem. When you're retired, time is just a number.'

'I supposed that's true.'

Karen steps into the house, which immediately feels stuffy. Hugo leads her down a hall lined with boxes and into a living room, where there are more boxes and plastic containers. A space with two chairs and a table has been cleared off for them to sit. 'I'm not a hoarder, if that's what you're thinking,' he says.

She smiles. 'I wasn't thinking anything.'

Hugo offers no further explanation for all the stuff lying around. 'So you said you needed some help with a case?'

'Yes, my old partner gave me your name. He said you were the best he had ever seen at crash reconstruction.'

Hugo's smile gets even bigger. It fills up the only empty space in the room. 'Percy used to say a lot of things.'

He's right about that. Percy had been Karen's first partner after she made detective. He taught her a lot she needed to know and a lot she didn't. Now retired and living down near San Diego, he had been happy to keep her on the phone for an hour before giving her Hugo's name.

Karen takes out photographs of Joey Fisher's car. His case file had a lot of them, and she made copies of everything.

'This is the car that was hit,' she says.

The next photos she takes out of her bag are of Ivy's car. Two years after it was reported stolen, a child had gone missing near Oxhill Lake. When it was dredged, they didn't find the child but they did find Ivy's car. It's long gone now; all Karen has is the pictures from when they pulled it out of the lake.

'This car was found a couple years later,' she says. 'See the damage on the front end?'

'I do.'

Hugo puts on a pair of glasses and leans in close to examine both cars. Suddenly, he stands up and walks out of the room, muttering to himself as he goes. Karen hears a bit of banging as he opens and shuts a few drawers and cabinets.

When Hugo returns, he has a magnifying glass in his hand and he's smiling again. 'This is a real doozy you brought,' he says.

'I know it may not be possible to tell —'

'I didn't say that. I just need to see these in more detail.'

Karen waits in silence as he studies the photos. She glances around the room, noting that the wallpaper is the same kind that was in her house when she first moved in. Off-white, with dark red flowers and brown leaves. She'd removed it immediately.

Just as she starts theorizing about what he keeps in all the boxes, Hugo gets up again. He goes straight to a stack of containers in the corner and starts digging into one of them.

Files. The box is filled with files.

He returns to his seat with one of them and flips it open, thumbing through the pages with alarming speed. Hugo is muttering to himself again, and Karen does not interrupt.

'This reminds me of another case,' Hugo says. Out loud, like he's talking to her. 'Do you have pictures of the road?'

She pulls the file out of her bag. A copy of the original. 'I do.'

Hugo flips through the file, stopping to study each picture. Next he looks at Ivy's car. 'I can't tell for sure, but this looks like a Toyota 4Runner from the mid-2000s.'

Karen opens her Check This app and searches for the list about Ivy's stolen car. 'Two thousand six,' she says.

'Perfect,' Hugo says.

He gets up and disappears again, returning with an iPad.

He pulls up a large color picture of the car. Karen waits as he goes back and forth between looking at the screen and looking at the picture of Joey's car with the magnifying glass.

'Look here,' he finally says, holding out the photo. 'Right here.'

She takes the magnifying glass and looks where he points. She has no idea what she is supposed to see other than a dent.

'See it?' he says.

'No.'

'Right *here*.' He points again. 'It's faint, but it's there. The outline of this.' Hugo points to the 4Runner, which has square edges in the front. 'Those headlights are shaped like parallelograms,' he says. 'You can see one side of that shape.'

Now she sees it. A portion of the parallelogram has been imprinted onto the side of Joey's car, right against the back door. His head had been on the other side of it.

'Now look at the other car,' Hugo says, holding out the picture of Ivy's 4Runner. It was covered in algae and muck from the lake, sitting on the dirt after being removed. 'The front left side.'

Karen raises the magnifying glass and focuses on the front fender, which has been crushed. The headlight is smashed.

'If I had to guess,' Hugo says, 'the Toyota hit the other car at an angle, coming from the left. The force from the collision crushed the fender, and that headlight went right into the door.' He shakes his head at the photos. 'Strange no one caught this at the time.'

'They were a little busy with the LeBlanc murder. It was a few days later.' Karen says this with no small amount of disdain.

'Ah.' Hugo nods. No further explanation necessary. 'Well, it's impossible to be one hundred percent sure it was a 4Runner with just the photos. What I really need is the measurements.'

'Measurements?'

'Exactly how high up this dent on the car was made. Compare that to the height of the headlight on the 4Runner. At least then you can confirm it's the right make and model of car.'

She pulls the file out of her bag and hands it to him. 'I bet they're in here.'

'Perfect.' Hugo snaps his fingers and goes back to his iPad. 'With this much detail, I bet it can be re-created.'

'The accident?'

'It's a computer program,' he says. 'We had them when I was working, but they're a lot better now. Between the tire tracks on the street and the pictures of these cars, I bet someone can put it all together and get an accurate visual. Or as accurate as possible, given that you don't have the cars.'

A visual re-creation of the accident would be very helpful. Juries love them.

43

Marcus and some of the guys invite Wes to go out tonight. He says yes before he says no. Bad idea. The last thing he wants to do is run into Ivy at one of the bars. She could be out with Milo. Or another guy. And she would definitely ignore him.

No desire to experience that again.

But he doesn't want to go home, either. Being by himself, trying to work or watch TV, is another bad idea. His mind will wander, and he'll think about Ivy. Where she is, who she's with, and, worst of all, what she is doing. Once he reaches that point, his imagination can't be stopped.

This is the hardest part of their breakups. Just as he gets used to their life together, it's gone. Ripped away.

Like when he tore off her dress after that night at Maxwell's . . .

Damn. There he goes again.

The gym. That's where he should go. It's been a while since he kept to a regular schedule, and tonight is a great time to change that. Play some loud music, lift some weights, run on the treadmill until he drops.

Best of all, Ivy won't be there. She isn't a member and prefers to exercise outdoors. Perfect.

And it is. Right up until he walks into the gym.

She doesn't see him, but he sees her. Impossible to miss Abigail. She's on one of the weight machines, working out those long legs, her red hair pulled up in a high ponytail.

Granted, she's been as mature and cool as anyone could

be after a one-night stand with someone in the office. Wes, not so much. He still feels a little uncomfortable around her. And a bit ashamed.

Tonight, he wants an escape from everything, including her. The gym isn't it.

He spends ten minutes sitting in his car, wondering what to do with himself. Briefly, he considers going to the grocery store, buying a ridiculous amount of food, and spending the evening cooking. Maybe grilling on the barbecue.

But not being able to share it with anyone – with *Ivy* – eliminates that idea.

A bike ride or a hike are the only ideas he has left. But it's starting to get dark, so the hike is out unless it's a short one. And a bike ride . . .

He sighs. All the energy he had for working out is gone. He tries to get it back, tries to motivate himself into driving home, grabbing his bike, and riding until he collapses. He even starts his car and puts it into reverse, only to shut it off again.

Wes glances at the door to the gym, knowing he has to leave before Abigail does. As he starts his car again, a sign across the street catches his eye.

The movie theater.

He can't remember the last time he went to a movie. There always seems to be something better to do, but right now sitting in the dark and eating a lot of junk food sounds pretty good. And he doesn't need any energy to do it.

He walks over and studies the list of films and start times. Unfortunately, the action film started forty-five minutes ago. That leaves him with the documentary or the drama. Neither sound like the best escape, but he picks the documentary, because it's about animals instead of people. Wolves, to be exact.

Fifteen minutes into the movie, he learns that wolves mate for life. The documentary is an animal love story.

Ivy sits at Dominique's, not at all energized by the activity around her. It's her first night out since going to Liver and watching Wes leave with those girls. Tonight, she didn't want to go out at all. Heath insisted.

'Doesn't it feel good to be here?' he says.

No. 'Sure, it's okay.'

'You can't sit at home and wallow.'

'I haven't been *wallowing*. I'm in the mourning period. Which is a necessary and healthy thing.'

Heath gives her a look. She ignores it. And she hasn't been wallowing or mourning. She's been disappointed. Wes never reacted to that picture she posted online, didn't contact her at all. The only ones who did were Milo and his fiancée.

At least it gives her something to talk about with Heath.

'That guy never said he was engaged,' she tells him. 'Never mentioned a girlfriend or anything.'

'Did you like him, though?'

'Not at all. I'm just saying: If he had told me, I wouldn't have posted the picture.'

'Yes, you would have. That photo was for Wes.'

Heath has a point. She probably would've posted it, but she wouldn't have tagged Milo and he never would've seen it.

She looks around the bar, seeing only the couples and none of the groups or single people. This is why she didn't want to go out. Love is everywhere. Or lust. Something more than what she has right now. They all look so cute and so happy, and it makes her feel sick. Especially that couple right across from her, who are obviously in the falling-in-love phase and oblivious to everything else.

Ivy hates them.

She nurses her drink, limiting herself to one after that last drunken escapade. The last thing she wants to do is call Wes again. Mainly, because she's too scared. She'd rather not know who might answer his phone.

'Hey,' Heath says. He nods toward a guy who just walked in the door. 'I know him. Nice guy.'

'Not tonight, please.'

'Someone new is what you need.'

No, that's the last thing she wants or needs, along with being in this bar. Every time she looks around, she spots another couple. It's disturbing. And rude.

'Let's go to a movie,' she says.

'A movie? When was the last time we went to a movie?'

She puts down her drink and stands up. 'I can't sit in here any longer.'

They leave and stand around in the parking lot, looking up what's playing and the start times. Fair Valley only has two theaters. One is older and plays art house flicks; the other is a multiplex with six screens.

Heath rattles off the titles: a superhero movie, a thriller, an Oscar contender, a documentary. They go in one ear and out the other. Ivy doesn't pay attention, doesn't care. Which is how the night gets even worse.

It isn't until she's sitting in the theater with popcorn, soda, and candy, that she realizes which movie Heath picked.

'We're seeing a rom-com?'

'You love rom-coms,' he says.

Used to. Ivy doesn't say that out loud. She sinks down in the chair, thinking horrible thoughts about everyone and everything in the movie. The only part she likes is when they break up in the middle because of some misunderstanding.

The last few minutes, though. She won't watch that.

'I have to go to the restroom,' she tells Heath. 'Meet you in the lobby.'

'But you'll miss the –'

'They all end the same way.'

With a lie.

On her way back into the theater, she sees a guy in the distance. He's walking out the front door, into the parking lot, and he looks a lot like Wes.

No. Couldn't be. Wes never goes to the movies.

Her mind is playing tricks on her. That rom-com really messed with her head.

44

Bianca doesn't answer the call from her lawyer. Sends him straight to voicemail. It's not that he is a bad guy. She likes him – she really does. He's a friend of her father's, and he wants her to sue.

'Don't you want Siphon to be held accountable?' he keeps saying. 'Don't you want them to pay for employing someone like Tanner?'

The first thing she had wanted to do was not get arrested. Now that the police have said they won't be pressing charges, maybe she'll think about a lawsuit. Money doesn't seem like enough, though. Like they can just pay her off and everything will be okay.

But that decision can wait. Money isn't her concern right now, and it won't be, as long as Siphon keeps paying her. Her only focus is Wes Harmon.

Because of Joey.

In a roundabout kind of way, what happened to Joey was her fault. She has been to therapy for that, too. It helped a little, because now she doesn't believe his death is 100 percent on her. Maybe 50 percent.

She was supposed to be at the party that night. This guy Aiden had graduated a year earlier, and he was the only one they knew with his own place. A tiny little studio, cramped with video games and a futon, but still. Anyone with their own apartment was impressive. When Joey told her that Aiden was having a party on that Thursday night, she wanted to go, but she would have to be late.

One of her closest friends, Laurel, had organized a party for the same night, only hers was at Six Flags. A retro thing, as Laurel called it, given that they were sixteen and rarely went to amusement parks anymore. It was summer, no school the next day, and since she didn't have to be home early, Bianca thought she could split the evening. Half at Six Flags, the other half with Joey at Aiden's party. The perfect middle ground between her friends and her boyfriend.

The Ferris wheel screwed everything up.

Bianca was on the ride with Laurel, and they were near the top. A view of the whole park spread out before them, and they were talking about which ride to go on next. The abrupt halt of the wheel made their passenger car swing more than usual. Both grabbed the safety bar.

'Whoa,' Laurel said. 'That was weird.'

Bianca leaned over the side and looked down. 'Maybe someone fell.'

'That's horrifying.'

'Right?'

No one had fallen. The wheel was broken. Bianca and Laurel were stuck near the top for almost three hours. By the time she was finally back on the ground, thanks to the firefighter rescue, she had a good story to tell but was too late for the party. Joey had already texted to say he was leaving.

Going home. C U tomorrow.

The downside of autocorrect was that the text looked normal: no misspellings, no errors. She couldn't tell how drunk he was and had no idea he passed out in his car instead of driving.

The next day, she found out he was dead.

He wouldn't have been that drunk if she had made it to the party. First, because he knew she hated it when he drank too much. Second, because he would rather have had sex than pass out.

Logically, she has always understood it wasn't her fault the Ferris wheel broke down.

The problem was, logic didn't help when someone was dead. Not then and not seven years later.

Bianca settles down with a cup of coffee and her computer. Her wallpaper is now a picture of Joey. Reminding her why she's doing this, and reminding her the police had forgotten about him.

Strange that she is working with Karen now. But obviously they need the help. Her help.

Back to the emails.

It's a time-consuming task to go through seven years of emails. Wes has filed them into a slew of folders, archiving an extraordinary number of messages. But Bianca is thorough. Not everyone is. Years of snooping have taught her how to find things others miss. When people have something to hide, they try to be sneaky. Most suck at it.

Attachments, for example. They aren't always what they seem. An innocuous spreadsheet might not be a spreadsheet at all. In theory, it's a great way to hide things. Most people won't open every attachment to see what's there. Bianca does.

She started from the beginning, when Wes was first hired, and read through the emails in chronological order. Exactly what she was trying to do in the office when Tanner had interrupted her.

If you want to follow the story line of someone's career, and life, this is the way to do it. Starting in the middle doesn't make sense. It's like walking into a movie fifteen minutes after it starts. You miss the whole setup.

Same with Wes. The setup is in his earliest messages.

Back then, he had given the email address to friends and former coworkers, a number of whom sent their congratulations. Most came from professional email addresses; a few, from personal accounts. A lot of information to sift through.

She makes a list of the email addresses that look personal, noting the ones with actual names, for later research. Most of the messages are invitations to parties or dinners or disc golf games. She spends hours wading through them, finding nothing useful.

Until she finds the picture.

The email had come from Ivy's Gmail address, and the subject line said Pics? Wes had put it in a folder marked Miscellaneous. The date of the email was two days after Joey was killed.

I sent this to the police. It's the best picture I could find of the car. Let me know if you have any others.

In the photo, Wes is sitting behind the wheel of a dark blue Toyota 4Runner. The car is parked on the street, and Wes is smiling. No. Laughing. Maybe laughing at Ivy as she takes the picture.

Bianca does a quick search for any other messages from that email address but finds only two. In the first, Ivy congratulates him on his first day at work. The next asks him about plans for that evening. The last one was the picture. Wes answered it with one line.

No, I don't have any other pics.

Bianca enlarges the photo and examines everything: The houses behind the car, to figure out where it might have been taken. The clothes Wes is wearing, the way his hair is cut, even his fingernails. She zooms in on the inside of the car, the dashboard, the interior, even the steering wheel. But she doesn't see it until she starts looking at the windshield.

Her first thought is to send the photo to Karen right away.

Her second thought, as always, is to gather more information.

45

Karen bought her new suit because of the color: steel grey. It makes her feel strong, and today she needs that. It isn't often she meets with her sergeant, lieutenant, and captain all at once. In a cramped conference room at the central police station, all three men sit across from her. Highest-ranking in the center.

The suit doesn't keep her hands from shaking, though. She keeps them firmly clasped on her lap.

'The files you have include copies of all my reports, along with transcripts of the interviews I've conducted,' Karen says. 'There's also a signed, notarized statement from Hugo Garrison, retired crash investigator and consultant.' The wording of it took some negotiation, because Hugo didn't want to commit to too much information, but it's a convincing document for anyone who doesn't fully understand it. 'In addition, I've included the original photos from the traffic cam.

'As you know, we didn't have as many cameras seven years ago, which is part of what made the Joey Fisher case so difficult to solve. However, we did keep screen grabs of all the cars that passed by a security camera not far from where the accident occurred.' She lays the photos across the table, setting them down one by one. 'Since it was late, there weren't too many cars. Twelve, to be exact.

'Hugo Garrison examined these pictures and looked into each of the cars. This is the only one that matches the type of damage done to Joey's car.' She points to the 4Runner.

'Because the security camera was positioned in front of a building and not the street, the license plate isn't visible.'

The driver is, at least from a distance. And it's a man.

Karen always knew Wes was the problem. She knew from the first moment they met at Siphon, when he smiled at her as she walked into his office. It's always the goddamn smile.

'The police didn't track the cars caught on camera?' her captain says. 'Or the types of cars, at least?'

'The LeBlanc murder was three days later,' she says.

He purses his lips and nods.

'Ivy Banks owned a 4Runner that she and her boyfriend shared,' Karen says. 'It was reported stolen and subsequently found in Oxhill Lake. You'll find more details about that in Mr Garrison's statement, specifically regarding the damage on the recovered car.' She waits for a reaction. They don't give her one. 'I've also included everything I've found so far about an incident at the Fine Line gentlemen's club the same night. On the bankruptcy filing, you'll see Ivy worked at the club for one night – the same night Joey Fisher died. There was also a 911 call made from the club that night, reporting a domestic disturbance. So far, what I've uncovered points to someone I was investigating in connection with another crime.'

'Wes Harmon,' her lieutenant says.

'Yes. He and Ivy have been in a relationship on and off for years. In the most recent incident, Ivy accused him of stalking her.' Karen takes a deep breath, knowing this is where she needs to sell this story. The evidence isn't there – not yet – but all she needs is a chance to find it. 'I've worked hundreds of cases in the sex crimes division, many of which involved domestic abuse, and I believe Ivy Banks is in danger. I also believe that something happened between Ivy and Wes on that night seven years ago, and it led to the death of

Joey Fisher. What I'd like is to be officially assigned to the case. It's still open, as all of you know, but it's been inactive for years. This may be a chance for us to clear two cases, as well as help someone who needs us.'

Her captain speaks first. 'You've put a lot of work into this,' he says. 'Considering the case isn't yours.'

'Yes. Of course, I've done it all on my own time.' Karen stops there, not elaborating on her outside activities. 'I felt compelled to see if there was a connection.'

Her captain nods. William Doyle is the highest-ranking man in the room, the first Black captain in the history of Fair Valley. He had started as a uniformed cop and worked his way up, earning a degree in criminal justice along the way. Doyle is a fair man, with a firm belief that all victims are equal and should be treated as such. It isn't true – not in a department with limited resources and outside pressure – but he makes everyone wish it was.

Doyle is her most important ally. The fact that Joey's case was ignored because someone else was more important has to upset him.

'But you don't have enough to arrest the suspect,' her sergeant says. 'Or any connection between him and Joey Fisher.'

'Not directly, no,' Karen says. 'However, some of her former coworkers at the Fine Line might be more willing to talk if they know there's a connection to Joey Fisher. The case was a big one, at least for a few days, and some are bound to remember it. It's also been seven years. The club is closed, and many have moved on and no longer work in the industry, so they won't be putting themselves at any risk.'

Another nod from Doyle.

'So the point is,' her lieutenant says, 'you want to work on a case that you weren't assigned to and never worked on.'

Karen doesn't like her lieutenant, who has always been

more concerned about the politics of policing instead of the actual work. It makes sense that he zeroes in on this particular point. As if the only reason she's here is to get a promotion.

'I don't want this connection to be ignored,' she says. 'That sounds like a public relations nightmare to me.' She keeps her voice level, matter-of-fact. Not angry. Not emotional. Two things a woman can never be at work, especially in a room full of men.

'Are you threatening to go to the press?'

'I'm not threatening anything,' Karen says. 'I'm simply presenting what I found.'

Doyle holds up his hand, ending the back-and-forth. 'Enough. Karen, thank you for bringing this to our attention. Your work here is admirable,' he says. 'We'll discuss it and get back to you.'

Exactly what she expected. She had spent a lot of time thinking about whether she should present this case or not. The last thing she wanted to do was reveal she had been working on cases she had no business working on, but she had hit a concrete wall. There were only so many ways to get around the rules. To continue investigating, she needed police resources.

Right now, she doesn't have enough to get to Wes. And rescue Ivy.

'Thank you.' Karen closes her file and puts it into her briefcase. Brand-new and too expensive, but worth it because it matches her new suit. 'I appreciate your time.'

She walks out of the room and exhales, finally able to breathe. She did the best she could. And she has enough evidence to back it up.

They have no choice but to move ahead with this. She can feel it.

46

As soon as Karen drives away from the station, her phone rings.

Siphon.

She puts on her earpiece. 'Karen Colglazier.'

'My name is Abigail Wright,' a woman says. 'I work at Siphon. We spoke last week when you called for Wes Harmon.'

Karen pictures the tall, redheaded woman who sits where Bianca used to. Beautiful, poised, and icy.

'Yes, Abigail. I remember.'

'I understand you wanted to speak to Wes about Ivy. Because someone had been stalking her a while back?'

Interesting. Karen hadn't asked him any more questions about the stalking, only more questions about that stolen car. 'Do you know something about it?'

'I understand that Siphon and its employees have been under a great deal of scrutiny due to Tanner Duncan,' she says. 'But I can assure you, Mr Duncan and his behavior were not representative of anyone but himself. I personally have worked with Wes Harmon for years. I have also met Ivy Banks.'

'Is that right?' Karen says.

'Yes. I was here the day she came in and nearly destroyed Wes's office. She disrupted the office, smashed his computer screen, and broke a lamp.'

'Were the police called?'

'The incident was handled by our internal security.'

'I see,' Karen says.

'My point is that from what I've heard and experienced, Ivy is the one who is unbalanced,' Abigail says. 'Not Wes.'

'Thank you.'

Karen ends the call, making notes about it in her phone. Abigail certainly made her position clear, blaming everything on the woman being abused. A woman at the end of her rope.

Abigail is firmly on #TeamWes.

Karen thinks for a minute, considering her options. Her approach. When the script is written in her head, she calls Ivy.

The banging sound Wes hears isn't a dream. It's at the front door. One o'clock in the morning.

Only one person it could be.

He goes to the door, flinging it open. Ivy stands on his porch. Black leggings, a UC Davis sweatshirt, and sneakers. Like she threw on the first clothes she found and came straight to his house.

They haven't spoken in over a month, haven't seen each other since the night they were both at Liver.

'What the –'

'About time,' she says, walking past him to go inside.

Wes follows her into the living room. She stands in the middle of the room, showing no signs of relaxing or sitting down. Wes plops down on the couch and rubs his eyes. 'Why are you here?' he says.

'Didn't Karen call you?'

'Today?'

'Yes. Well, technically it was yesterday,' she says. 'Since it's already tomorrow.'

'No. I haven't heard from her recently.'

Ivy sits down, though not on the couch. She picks the chair across from him and leans forward, elbows on her knees. 'Then I'm doing you a favor,' she says. 'Which is pretty nice of me, considering you just vanished.'

Wes almost takes the bait. He wants to, since this fight has been coming for a while, but the call from Karen is more important. 'What did she say?' he asks.

'Karen is on the Joey Fisher case. They're "reactivating the investigation."' She uses air quotes for those last words.

'Are you joking?'

'At one in the morning? No, Wes. I'm not joking.'

If he wasn't fully awake, he is now. 'Well, damn.'

'Eloquent.'

'They have new evidence,' he says. 'They must.'

'Obviously. She has no reason to tell me about Joey unless she's found a connection.'

Wes feels the anger start to expand inside him, growing like a tumor. Again. Ivy could've done a lot of things to get his attention other than call the police. Showing up at his place in the middle of the night works pretty well.

But that would've been too boring for Ivy. For him, too, if he's being honest. He would've been disappointed at her lack of creativity. Although being bored and disappointed sounds pretty good right now.

'At some point,' Ivy says, 'we'll need to address the fact that you're dating someone new. But for now, let's make sure we're still telling the same story.'

Again, Wes almost takes the bait and says something about Milo, but he holds off. 'You start,' he says.

'It was a Thursday night. My shift at the Fine Line started at nine o'clock. I took a taxi to the club and arrived around eight thirty to get ready. I was in training, so I followed another girl around for a couple hours to learn how to log drinks into the computer and print out the checks. The club wasn't too crowded at that point – it was the lull between happy hour and the after-dinner crowd. Started to pick up about ten o'clock. After that, I was busy all night.'

'I showed up at the club around midnight,' Wes says. 'I had gone out with some friends and stopped by to say hello and have a drink.'

'I saw you but didn't want to get in trouble on my first night, so we didn't really talk.'

'Right,' Wes says. 'I hung around and had a drink, and then your shift ended. You decided to come home with me instead of calling another cab.'

Ivy nods. 'The next morning, when I woke up, you had already left for work and the car was gone. I assumed you had taken it.'

'But I got a ride with a coworker who picked me up, because I thought you needed the car that day.'

'Except I didn't know that until you came home from work without the car.'

'Which is when we both realized it had been stolen,' Wes says.

'So I called the police.'

'Eventually, they showed up to make a report,' Wes says. 'Took them about two hours to get –'

'Two and a half hours,' she says.

'Two and half hours to get to the apartment. We gave them the description, showed them where it had been parked, and that was it.'

'I gave a copy of the report to the insurance company,' Ivy says. 'And eventually, we bought another car.'

Wes rolls his eyes. A *Saab*. He hated that car, but it was what Ivy had wanted.

She does not acknowledge his disdain. 'We never heard

anything from the police about the 4Runner. Not until two years later, when it was pulled out of the lake.'

'Damaged. The car had been damaged, and it wasn't like that when it was stolen.'

'Right,' she says. 'What kind of questions do you think they'll ask?'

'Probably about that night, when we left the club. They'll ask who was driving, which route we took, the streets we used.' He rattles off the directions he memorized, which isn't exactly the way they went.

'What about the club?' Ivy says. 'What if Karen knows what happened there?'

'How? You barely worked there. No one is going to remember us seven years later.'

Ivy gives him a look.

'Okay, some people might remember what happened at the club,' he says. 'But there's no way to prove it was us. Even if the club had cameras all over the parking lot, no one will have the footage. The Fine Line doesn't even exist anymore.'

Ivy nods, conceding his point.

'I don't know if it'll get this far, but if they want to bring me in for questioning at the police station,' Wes says, 'I'm getting a lawyer.'

'You don't think that'll make you look guilty?'

'It'll make me look like I have a brain,' he says. 'And you need to get a lawyer, too.'

She looks down, playing with the strap of her bag. 'I thought we were in this together.'

'Ivy, we can't have the same lawyer. That's not how it works.'

She stands up, knocking a pillow off the chair. 'I guess that's it, then. Nothing more to talk about.'

'Don't be like that,' Wes says, getting up off the couch. 'Don't be mad. This is what we have to do.'

'You're the one who's mad. You're so . . .' Ivy waves her arms around, gesturing to nothing and everything. 'You're so *angry* with me.'

He is, because of that call she made to the police. She must know that, though *he's* not going to be the one to say it. Turns out, he doesn't have to.

'How was I supposed to know?' she says. 'We have no connection to Joey . . . None. At all. And it's been *seven years*. Why would I think anyone would dig it up now?'

Wes actually feels a little bad for her. No way she wanted to start all of this.

'Hey.' He walks over to her and puts his hands on her shoulders. 'We're going to be fine. Just stick to the story, and this will all blow over.'

'Promise?'

'Promise.'

'Okay,' she says. A smile. A small one, but it's enough.

'Stay here tonight,' he says.

'You're dating that girl.'

'I haven't seen her since the night at Liver,' he says. 'And you're dating that guy on your Insta.'

'I am not.'

'You posted his picture.'

'You ghosted me.'

'You ignored me.'

They stare at each other, neither one backing down. Like kids in a blinking contest.

Ivy never breaks first. She looks at him, jaw tilted up, hands on hips. Seriously, why is she so hot when she's angry? It's so annoying. So *distracting*.

He slides his hand down to hers, taking it into his own, and leads her to the bedroom. She doesn't argue with that.

Wes pushes her onto the bed. She turns over on her back and smiles at him. An invitation he accepts.

Until she rolls away from him and off the bed.

Now he's lying down, and she stands over him. A smirk on her face.

'You really think I'm that easy?' she says.

'You really want me to answer that?'

47

Ivy slams the phone down on her desk. Tired of checking it, tired of trying to decide what to do next. Tired of making the wrong decisions. Last night was a mistake; Ivy knew it before the sun came up.

She picks up her phone and texts Heath.

I saw Wes last night.

His reply: ???

She grips the phone tight for a second, then gives in to the urge to confess. I slept with him.

Minutes go by before he responds. Way to play it cool.

That had been his advice: Play it cool, act like you don't care. Don't get angry, don't blow up at him. It was good advice – she knew that – and she had sex with Wes anyway.

I tried, she says.

She waits, expecting him to answer. Maybe he'll bring up therapy again. Over the years, he has tried several times to get her to see someone. Once she did see a therapist he'd recommended, an older woman with deep bags under her eyes. Not even her glasses hid them, and her personality was even worse. She was like a mean girl who turned into a cruel therapist. Ivy lasted two sessions before quitting.

That hasn't stopped Heath from trying. Ivy isn't sure when he became such a convert to talk therapy, but he's convinced it's exactly what she needs.

Not today, though. He doesn't answer her last text.

Ivy puts down the phone and goes back to the list of lawyers she found online. Google seems like a terrible way to find a defense attorney, so she researches each one and checks all the rating sites.

Last night didn't go exactly how she'd expected. It all went sideways when he brought up the lawyers. Logically, she does know Wes is right. They're not married, they're not even officially together, so of course they have to do it. Separate lawyers, same story. A solid plan, and probably the correct one.

But he brought it up at the wrong time. Telling her like she didn't already know, and doing it when she preferred to talk about something else. Like the fact that they need to stick together right now. A united front.

Which is why it was stupid for her to leave as soon as Wes fell asleep.

Wes started at the top, with the two largest law firms in the area. Expensive, but every lawyer is expensive. Only a matter of degree.

The first one he contacted never responded to his call. The second cited a 'potential conflict' and said they would get back to him. It didn't make sense until he did a little research. Law firms rarely represent two defendants for the same crime, largely because one usually blames the other.

Ivy was already doing the same thing he was. She was way ahead of him, no doubt giving the firm his name in case he also called. That's something Ivy would do, and it made him a little nervous. Maybe a lot nervous.

Add in the fact that Karen had called Ivy about the Joey Fisher case but she hadn't called him. Wes didn't like that at all.

Worst of all, Ivy left in the middle of the night. Ten years into this relationship, and she has never done that.

Which makes him think of Heath.

He's back in town, saying God knows what to Ivy. Telling her to ignore him, to stay away. To leave in the middle of the

213

night. Heath tries to get into her head, and sometimes it works.

In the beginning, Wes got along with him. Heath seemed okay, like he just wanted the best for Ivy. That was when they were still in college and lived several hours away from each other, and neither Wes nor Ivy saw him very often. Things changed when Heath moved to Fair Valley.

The first thing Wes noticed was that they never did anything together. Not dinner or drinks or even a movie. Ivy saw Heath. Wes and Ivy did not.

It was weird, and it got weirder when Wes ran into him one night. At a bowling alley, of all places.

Wes and Ivy had broken up, again, and they had been apart for about a month. Wes wasn't bowling with a date, though. He was with his colleagues, attending what Tanner had called a team-building event.

Heath had been on a date. A gorgeous woman with long dark hair and the body of a swimsuit model. The kind of woman Wes normally went out of his way to avoid. Heath brought her over and introduced her. The three of them talked for a minute about the usual things – where they worked, who they knew – before Heath's date excused herself to go to the restroom.

Heath did not leave. He stayed right by Wes's side.

'So,' Heath said, 'Ivy told me you two broke up.'

'Yeah. We did.'

Heath nodded, pausing to watch someone bowl in front of them. Gutter ball. 'She said it's for good this time.'

Wes said nothing. Maybe Ivy did say that. But only out of anger, because it wasn't true. At least, he didn't believe it.

He also knew better than to argue with Ivy's best friend. One-way ticket to trouble.

Instead, he tried to change the subject, motioning in the

direction Heath's date had gone. 'And what about you? Are things getting serious with her?'

Heath ignored the question. 'Leave Ivy alone.'

Now Wes had to say something. No choice, not even a question. 'What happens between me and Ivy is our business,' he said. 'Not anyone else's. Including you.'

'I'm looking out for her,' Heath said. 'You aren't good for Ivy.'

'She can decide for herself who's good for her.' In Wes's mind, Heath was definitely not. 'She makes her own decisions.'

Heath's date returned, ending the conversation. Wes never told Ivy about it, because he wasn't about to get in the middle of their lifelong friendship. But he also never forgot it.

When Karen gets the call, she pinches herself. Literally.

She started doing it long ago, in the early days of her relationship, when it was so good it felt like a dream. A couple of years later, she did it again, trying to wake herself up from the nightmare.

Now she pinches herself as a reminder of how far she has come. That, yes, this is her life, she is doing the right thing, and she is helping others.

Because Karen has been assigned to the Fisher case. Officially.

She can finally spend her days doing what she has spent so many nights doing: solving a case that's crying for justice.

And getting Wes Harmon away from Ivy.

She starts by pulling up her lists, adding everything that needs to be done now that she's authorized to access police resources. She makes a flurry of calls. One of them is someone Karen has been targeting for a while: Coral St James.

She gets lucky when Coral picks up the phone. That's the kind of day Karen is having. A lucky one.

'I'm investigating a case from several years ago. Perhaps you remember Joey Fisher?' she says. 'The young man killed while sleeping in his –'

'I remember.' Coral's voice is softer than Karen expected. She almost sounds sad.

'I'm looking into a possible connection to the Fine Line gentlemen's club. Do you mind if I come by and ask you a few questions? Given your position at the club, I thought you might have a unique insight into some of the employees.' Karen is careful not to call them girls. Coral was the backstage manager, according to the bankruptcy filing. The Fine Line had owed her a good deal of money.

After a long pause, Coral agrees.

Another pinch. Karen can't help it.

48

Coral St James lives in a quiet neighborhood, the kind with basketball hoops above garage doors, well-kept lawns, and CAUTION: CHILD-AT-PLAY signs on the sidewalk. A Ring camera lets Coral know Karen has arrived.

She looks about forty, wearing leggings and a big T-shirt with a small stain on the front. No makeup, and her hair is no longer red, it's black and slicked into a tight bun at the nape of her neck. A small boy peeks out from behind her long legs. Coral looks exactly like what she is: a woman who has two young children and is married to a dentist.

But for five years, she worked as the backstage manager at the Fine Line. Before that, she had been a dancer at a club in Sacramento.

'Come on in,' Coral says, opening the door wider.

Karen follows her down a hallway and into the kitchen. The child, a boy of about four, stays by his mother's side but looks back at Karen as they walk.

'Have a seat.' Coral points to the table. 'I'm making coffee.'

Karen waits until Coral gets her son settled in the other room in front of the TV. Once the coffee is poured, Coral sits down and exhales.

'Your son is adorable. So well-behaved,' Karen says. As much as she wants to talk about her own son, she has a job to do. And if there's one thing today has proved, it's that Karen isn't half-bad at it.

'You said something about Joey Fisher?' Coral says.

'Yes. We've uncovered new information about his case.'

Coral drums her nails against the table. They're long, neutral in color, and perfect except for the chip on her left pinkie. Motherhood does take a toll on nails, along with everything else.

'Joey's case is what led me to you,' Karen says. The downside to officially being on the case is that she can no longer pretend to be a private investigator. Every witness and every piece of evidence will be part of a trial. Hopefully. 'We have reason to believe the person who hit him may have been at the Fine Line before the accident.'

'Reason to believe,' Coral says. Not a question.

'Obviously, I can't go into too many details of an active investigation.'

'Of course.' Coral stills her hand and glances back into the living room. Her son hasn't moved. She then looks around the kitchen, like she's making a mental list of things that need to be done. Karen can relate.

'I have to be honest,' Coral says. 'If this was about anyone else, I wouldn't be talking to you. Those days . . .' She waves her hand, like she's swatting a bug. 'They're long gone.'

'I understand. Thank you for talking to me.'

'Go ahead,' Coral says. 'Ask your questions.'

'Given your position at the club, you must have known all the women who worked there.' Karen takes a photo of Ivy out of her bag. It's an old picture, printed off Ivy's now-dormant Facebook account. As far as Karen can tell, it was taken around the time she worked at the Fine Line. 'Does this woman look familiar?'

Coral studies it, her face showing no expression. 'She looks really . . . wholesome.'

She did. The picture had been taken outside, in the sun, with her hair blowing in the wind. Ivy was wearing a sundress and a smile.

'Her name is Ivy Banks,' Karen says. 'She worked as a waitress at the Fine Line.'

Coral tilts her head to the side. 'Maybe? I'm not sure.'

'On the same night Joey was killed, someone called 911 from the club. They mentioned a domestic disturbance, and I believe it involved Ivy and her boyfriend.'

'We had a few problems with boyfriends over the years,' Coral says. 'That wasn't unusual.'

Karen takes out a picture of Wes. Another old photo, also from Ivy's Facebook page. 'This was her boyfriend. His name is Wes Harmon.'

Coral stares at it for a minute. 'No. I don't recognize him.' She picks up Ivy's picture again. 'But she does look a little familiar. With more makeup and fewer clothes . . . maybe.'

'After the night Joey died, there's no record she ever returned to the club.'

Coral's head snaps up. 'Really?'

'Yes.'

'Okay, that helps a little. I vaguely remember one story about a new girl and her boyfriend, but I don't remember the details.'

Karen's shoulders drop. She had been hoping Coral remembered something useful.

'Have you checked with our security guys?' Coral asks. 'One of them might remember more if there was some kind of trouble.'

'I've tried to reach a few of them. So far, none have called back.' Karen opens one of the lists on her phone and reads off the names of the bouncers who were working that night. Or at least the ones who were owed money in the bankruptcy.

Coral listens to all the names and then says, 'Uncle Bobby.'

'I'm sorry?'

'Robert Tubbs. Everyone called him Uncle Bobby,' she says. 'That's who you want to contact. He knew everybody.'

Karen pulls up the calls on her phone. She had tried to call him over a week ago. Left a message and never heard back.

'Coral,' she says, 'do you think you can get him to talk to me?'

She shrugs. 'I can try.'

49

Ivy turns down drinks with her coworkers to have dinner with Heath, who wants to show off his fancy electric car. He's been wanting one for a while, though it makes her feel even worse about her own financial situation. Her fault, not his, but that car makes her feel the weight of her own decisions.

'They must pay you a lot to build those communities,' she says.

'I can't complain.'

'How about the women? Do they like it?'

'They don't hate it.' He smiles in that dorky way guys do when they're proud of themselves.

She shouldn't be annoyed, but she is.

Not that it's personal to Heath. Everything is irritating her tonight and the alcohol hasn't helped. She puts on a smile, trying not to show her surly mood. This is Heath, someone she's been friends with forever, and he deserves better than how she really feels.

Heath hasn't had the most successful love life. Yes, there have been a lot of dates and a lot of women, each one more beautiful than the last. But no one 'special.' His word. Ivy isn't sure a fancy car will attract the right woman. At least by her definition.

'I'm so proud of you,' she says. 'Everything seems to be going so well.'

'Thank you. It really is.' He leans back in his chair, smiling. 'So tell me about this lawyer.'

'He's expensive.'

'And you're sure you need one?' he says. 'It's not like you're a suspect or anything.'

'I know.'

Back when Ivy first took the job at the Fine Line, Heath was a billion times more supportive than Wes. At least he had talked to her about it, asking if she was nervous and if she really wanted to work at a strip club. But Wes didn't even believe her.

Now, Heath doesn't understand why she needs a lawyer, because he still doesn't know the whole story.

'But you know how the police can be,' she says. 'You say anything, and they just twist it around.'

'And Wes?'

'I'm sure he has a lawyer, too. Haven't talked to him since I left his place.'

'In the middle of the night,' he says.

Another thing for her to regret. Not a good time to piss Wes off. 'Yeah, that was wrong,' she says.

'Really? Of all the things you've done to Wes and he's done to you, leaving in the middle of the night is the one that's wrong?'

'I didn't say it was the *only* thing I've done wrong,' she says. 'It's just the one I feel bad about today.'

'Okay, seriously,' Heath says. 'Please get into a relationship that isn't so dramatic. Come over from the dark side.'

'I've had other relationships. Wes isn't the only guy I've been with.'

'And?'

'And,' she says, 'I'd rather be with him. Not all of the time, but a lot of it. Most of it.'

'Yet you still left in the middle of the night.'

'Because I didn't want to be with him right that second,' she says.

'You do know how . . .' He stops and clears his throat. 'That sounds a bit contradictory.'

'Yes.' But also, no. Wes doesn't make her feel stupid. Sometimes Heath does, though. He has a way of acting like the smartest guy in the room. And a lot of times, he is. But not always. 'Are we done with the "shame Ivy for her relationship with Wes" part of the evening?' she asks.

'Sorry.' He places his hand over hers. 'I just think you could do so much better.'

'I appreciate that. Now change the subject.'

He does, and she makes a silent promise not to mention Wes again. Still, she knows Heath is counting the minutes until she breaks it.

It's rare, if not unheard-of, that Karen sits in her home office, puts her feet up on the desk, and thinks about how well things are going. Tonight, that's exactly what she does.

Everything is moving so much faster now.

Today, she walked away from Coral's house with a new contact. Since then, she has spent some time researching Uncle Bobby.

He's a former MMA fighter, now fifteen years past his prime, with an ex-wife – a former dancer – and a current wife, along with three children. He is built like a wall, most of it covered in tattoos, and Uncle Bobby also has committed a few crimes. Mostly small stuff, mostly beyond the statute of limitations, but there are a few things to work with. Enough for a little arm-twisting if it becomes necessary, though she hopes it won't. Anyone who is forced to give information doesn't make a great witness in a trial, and Karen fully expects there will be one. Wes isn't the kind of guy who will take a plea deal. His ego is too big for that.

It's uncanny how they're all so much alike. Sometimes she

feels like a profiler, only for abusers instead of serial killers. The FBI ought to look into creating a department for it. But until they do, she'll be right here in the trenches of Fair Valley, fighting on her own.

Karen updates her file on Uncle Bobby. It's a shame she didn't get more information from Coral, and she crosses her fingers that he can provide more. She needs a break in this case. Badly.

Her phone vibrates, and she grabs it, hoping it's Uncle Bobby.

No.

Her son. Seeing his name makes her heart jump, and not in a good way. Tonight is not their weekly call.

'Jack? What's wrong?'

'Nothing's wrong,' he says. The words come out in a rush, like he was expecting the question. 'Everything's fine.'

She takes a deep breath. It feels like she went from zero to a hundred and back again, all within seconds. 'Thank God.'

'But I have some not-great news,' he says. 'I'm not going to be able to come up there for your birthday this year.'

Disappointment hits, spreading faster than gossip at the station. Her birthday is two weeks away, and she hasn't seen Jack since Christmas.

'It's work,' he says. 'We're on this big project, and I'm the new guy, so . . .'

'So you have to stay there and work,' Karen says. 'Of course you do.'

'I'm so sorry, Mom.'

'I understand. Everybody has to pay their dues.' Something she has said many times over the years, both to herself and to Jack.

'I'm definitely doing that.'

'Maybe I can come down to LA for your birthday,' she says.

'Absolutely,' he says. 'We can celebrate both.'

After the call, Karen blinks back her tears. Tries to shake off the sadness.

Refocus all this emotion into her work: That's what she needs to do. It's the one good thing to come of this.

50

Wes closes his eyes and rubs his temples. After spending half the day trying to find a lawyer, he still has real work to do. Nine thirty at night in the office, his head is pounding, and there isn't an Advil in sight.

He wishes, not for the first time, that he had told his sister everything. She would wake him up from this nightmare.

But, as always, he's too ashamed to make that call. Imagining her disappointment when she hears about Joey Fisher is bad enough to keep him from picking up the phone.

He tries to focus back on his screen. The spreadsheet in front of him doesn't look good. Siphon has taken quite a hit because of Tanner. Clients are quick to jump ship from a company that can't get its internal business together. They aren't wrong. Wes would do the same thing if he were a client instead of an employee.

'Hey.'

He looks up and blinks. Abigail.

She stands in the doorway of his office, her bag in hand like she's on her way out. He thought he was here alone.

'You're working late,' she says, walking in. She sits down.

'So are you.'

'No choice. I'm basically doing two jobs,' she says. 'But that shouldn't last much longer. We've been interviewing for Tanner's position.'

'That's good to hear.' Wes clears his throat. He hasn't been alone with Abigail since that little talk about the night they spent together. It wasn't comfortable then, nor is it now.

Eventually, he hopes it will be. 'It's a tough time for every-one,' he says.

'Indeed. How are you doing?'

'Just trying to get through it, like everyone else.'

'We're also scheduling interviews for Bianca's job,' she says.

'Good. Then you can get back to yours instead of being stuck down here.'

'I hope so.' Abigail stands up, straightens her skirt. 'I was going to stop and have a drink on the way home, if you want to join me.'

No. Yes. Definitely not. The way she asks sounds so benign, so innocent. Not suggestive at all. But that's how it started last time.

'Probably not a good idea,' he says.

'I didn't mean it like *that*.' Her voice is sharp, like Wes is implying something would happen. Which he is.

'I just meant I'm so tired I'd probably fall asleep after one drink,' he says.

'You should know that I've started seeing someone.'

'That's great,' he says. 'Really, it is.'

'It's not serious yet,' she says. 'But I'm not interested in anything . . . else.'

'I'm really happy for you.'

'Thank you. Have a good night, Wes.'

As she walks away, he starts to relax. Until she stops at the door and turns back.

'There's something I should probably tell you,' she says. 'About that night. I meant to tell you before, but . . .' She glances down at the grey carpet, away from him.

A rarity. Abigail always looks him in the eye. He braces himself, his whole body tensing up for whatever is coming next.

'When you were asleep,' she says, 'your phone rang. I thought it was mine.'

'You answered my phone?'

'It was wrong, and I should've told you earlier. And I meant to. I just . . . never did. It was an accident, and I never would've done it on purpose. I'm so sorry I didn't tell you earlier. I was just . . . well, I was embarrassed.'

He already knows who called, or she wouldn't be telling him about it at all.

Heath nods to a man standing at the bar. 'What about him?'

Ivy sighs. Heath has dragged her out to make her forget about last night with Wes.

She side-eyes the guy, who is around her age, with black hair and brown skin. Quick smile, big eyes, and lashes visible from ten feet away.

'He's pretty hot,' she says, slurping up the rest of her drink. The night has gotten away from her, because Heath is obsessed with finding her a new man. Again. 'But I don't think I'm in any condition to –'

'Sure you are.'

Heath gets up before she can stop him. Sometimes, he's her best friend; other times, her pimp.

Sometimes, it's fun; other times, not.

Heath can talk to anyone – he's that kind of guy. No fear of strangers. It doesn't take him long to strike up a conversation with the guy at the bar and his friends.

Ivy digs in her bag for her lipstick, turning her back so they don't see her putting it on. Won't be long until Heath brings that guy over. She might as well look good.

It also gives her a chance to check her phone. She has kept it in her bag all evening, only taking occasional glances. Otherwise, Heath would lecture her about waiting for Wes.

Sometimes, she really is just checking it, but he never believes that. Probably for good reason.

Ivy doesn't expect to hear from Wes, especially after she left in the middle of the night, but that's always when it happens. He contacts her when she least expects it.

Like now. Not just a text. A double text.

I had no idea you called the other week. Things got really messed up that night.

I'm sorry.

She reads it once, twice, and then again, her heart beating faster each time. But in a good way. Followed by a bad way. Angry, happy, furious, elated. Each time she reads the texts, the wheel of emotions picks up speed.

'Ivy,' Heath says, 'this is Leo.'

The hot guy is in front of her now, standing next to Heath. They both take a seat at the table, and Heath hands her a fresh drink. Now that she's right next to Leo, she realizes he and Wes wear the same loafers. Not unusual. Their clothes are similar, as well: khakis and untucked dress shirt. The typical uniform for professionals in Fair Valley.

Still, the shoes are distracting.

'Heath says you work at Amalgamated,' Leo says. 'I know a few people over there.' He rattles off a few names, some of whom Ivy recognizes. She nods along until she hears the name Brooke.

'I know her,' Ivy says. 'We're in the same department.'

'We used to work at Indigo together,' Leo says.

Somewhere in the back of her mind, Ivy knows she should ask where he works now. Be polite, keep the conversation going like she's a normal person. But the front of her mind is dominated by Wes.

Maybe, just maybe, Wes is actually sorry. That idea makes her heart sing instead of thump.

She still doesn't know what happened when she called or who the woman was. It couldn't have been the one from Liver; they didn't meet until after that call. So he was with another woman that night, someone who picked up his phone without his knowing.

Maybe it doesn't matter who she was. They weren't even together at the time.

'Ivy?' Heath says. He's waving a hand in front of her face. 'You with us?'

'Sorry,' she says. 'I was thinking about something at work. One of those things that keeps you up at night, you know?'

'I do,' Leo says. He starts talking about something that kept him up all last week, and Ivy tunes out the details.

She shouldn't be thinking about Wes, given that he's the one who ghosted her. She also shouldn't have gone over to his place last night. And she definitely shouldn't have left the way she did. So maybe the reason he texted has nothing to do with his being sorry – it's because of the investigation. If for no other reason, they have to stick together because of that. Because if they turn on each other, it's over for both of them.

Mutually assured destruction.

'What about you?' Leo says.

Ivy realizes both he and Heath are staring at her. She not only missed the question; she missed the whole conversation.

'I'm sorry,' she says. 'I'm just not . . . feeling well.' Heath gives her a look. She ignores it and gathers up her things, stands up. 'Leo, it was really nice meeting you. I'm sorry I've been such terrible company, but I should go home.'

Ivy starts to walk out, but Heath follows and grabs her by the arm. 'Are you really going home?'

'I don't know yet.' It's the truth.

He sighs.

She looks up at Heath, almost feeling sorry for him. It's

not his fault. He is trying so hard to save her, but as she's always said: She doesn't need a hero.

She needs Wes.

'Are you really sorry?'

When Wes picked up the phone, he wasn't sure what to expect. Ivy could have cursed him out. She could have called him a liar. Neither would have been surprising.

But sounding sad is.

'I am,' he says. 'Nobody else should be answering my phone. It never should've happened.'

'And you waited until now to tell me this?' she says.

'I swear, I didn't know. I just found out tonight.'

She goes quiet. A car horn beeps in the background. His phone dings with a message, but he doesn't bother to look.

Wes can almost feel her thinking. Trying to decide.

'You better be alone,' she finally says.

51

Three thirty in the morning, and Ivy is alone. A little strange, because she is in Wes's bed.

She looks toward the bathroom. Door open, light off, no sound. She gets up and wraps a blanket around herself. His house is usually colder than her place. As she always explains to him, that's why she has to hog all the covers.

Ivy checks the other bedroom, then wanders into the kitchen. Still no Wes. Not in the family room, either. After searching the whole house, she finds him in the backyard, sitting on a lounge chair. Looking up the stars. She snuggles up next to him and shares half her blanket. Maybe a little less than half.

'You remember when I bought this house?' he says.

Two years ago, in the spring. It was all part of Wes's life plan. He has always been like that, the kind of guy who has a list of things to do before he's thirty, forty, fifty years old. Goals. Like buying a house before his thirtieth birthday, and he managed to do it a couple years early. Or getting married before he turned thirty-five. A few years left for that one.

He's always been a planner. Ivy, not so much.

'I remember the housewarming party you didn't invite me to,' she says.

'You came anyway.'

'You knew I would.'

'I would've been disappointed if you hadn't,' he says.

A horrible night, then a fantastic one. All within two hours. She curls up a little closer, burying her face in his T-shirt.

There's something about his smell. She read once that when you're attracted to someone, it's not all about the way they look or act; it's also their smell. Even if you're not consciously aware of it.

She likes that idea. That there's a reason beyond the drama. Maybe it all comes down to his scent.

'We could be screwed, you know,' he says. 'If the case really is active again, Karen has already found something.'

Anger starts to creep in. Of course this is why he texted, because of the case. She knew that from the start, knew it even as she stood in the parking lot of the bar and called him. As much as she wanted him to be sorry, hoping didn't make it true.

But he's not wrong. There's a reason why she's spending a fortune on a lawyer.

Ivy takes a deep breath, shoving the anger deep inside. Not a good time to fly off the handle. 'What do you think she has?'

'No idea. Could be a witness.'

'I don't think anyone saw –'

'That you know of.'

He's right about that.

Even if someone did see something, they wouldn't have said a word. At least not about what happened at the club. Fine Line employees had an unspoken rule about keeping your mouth shut, especially when the police were involved. But that was seven years ago. God only knows who would talk now. Someone might be looking for attention. Or a favor.

Wes strokes her hair, and she wishes it didn't feel so good.

'We have to stick together,' she says.

'Yes. We do.'

'No matter what.'

'There's another thing we can do,' he says. 'To protect both of us.'

'What's that?'

His chest rises as he inhales deep. He holds it for a second before answering.

'We can get married.'

Wes hadn't intended to bring that up so soon. It's been on his mind since she told him the case was being reopened. Somewhere along the way, he had heard spouses don't have to testify against each other. At work, he researched that random piece of information. Turns out, it's true.

Spouses *can* testify against each other, but they cannot be compelled to do it.

Ivy sits up and looks at him. He knows her almost as well as he knows himself, but right now he has no idea what she's going to say.

'*Married?*'

'Married.'

'Married,' she says again.

He can't tell if she likes the idea or hates it. And he doesn't know if that's good or bad.

'You're just saying this because of that rule. The legal thing,' she says. 'Not because you really want to marry me.'

'Why not both?'

He means that. It surprises him as much as it seems to surprise her.

Ivy looks fully awake now, all the grogginess gone. She tilts her head to the side, studying him like she's trying to see into his head. Under the blanket, she's naked. He wants to slide his hand down, feel her skin against his, but he doesn't want her to think this is about sex.

Ivy flops back down onto the chair, and onto him, putting her head on his shoulder.

'Wes,' she says.

'Yeah?'

'That was a horrible proposal.'

'First, it wasn't a proposal,' he says. 'But if I did propose, would you rather I take you to the beach and write it in the sand? Fly a banner through the sky? Or put a ring at the bottom of a champagne glass?'

She giggles. They've heard about all those proposals from their friends, along with some that are even more ridiculous.

'I'd hate that,' she says. 'It would make me say no.'

'Exactly. It's not us.'

She is quiet for a long time. He imagines the war in her head is like his own. The one that's already been fought.

His internal war is over. Maybe it was when he researched that spousal law. Maybe it was when she called a few hours ago, sounding like a lost puppy.

Or maybe it was the minute the words came out of his mouth.

52

The lawyer Ivy hired looks like the mild-mannered dad in an old TV show. Stan Mitchell has dark skin, close-cropped hair, and a ridiculously big smile. Supposedly, he is a nice guy, but behind the smile he's a shark. That's what they say online, anyway. Hopefully, the internet is right this time.

When she sees his name on her phone, her heart jumps a little. She hasn't had a lawyer long enough to know if calls from him are a good thing or a bad thing, but she does know it will cost her a chunk of money.

She pauses her Chinese lesson, closes her office door, and takes the call.

'Ivy Banks,' she says.

'Ms Banks, this is Stan Mitchell. How are you today?'

'I'm doing well, thank you. And, please, call me Ivy.'

'Yes. Thank you. I called because I received a request from Detective Karen Colglazier. She would like to interview you about an incident that occurred at the Fine Line gentlemen's club. It happened the same night Joey Fisher was killed.'

Bad. A call from the lawyer is definitely bad. 'Interview me,' Ivy repeats.

'That's correct.'

'What do you think?' she asks.

He responds with a whole paragraph of words she doesn't understand. Someone needs to make an app that translates lawyerspeak.

Stan doesn't know what really happened, nor does he want to know. The first thing he told her when they met: *Don't tell me anything unless I ask.* She has stuck to his rule and therefore doesn't say much of anything to him. But she does ask questions.

'What do you suggest?' Ivy asks.

'Well, she says this is just an informal conversation and she's trying to gather more information. You are not officially a person of interest in the case.'

'Do you believe her?'

'I'm afraid I don't know her well enough to answer that. This could just be a fishing expedition, or she might have something specific to ask you about,' Stan says. 'Difficult to say until we know what she has.'

Ivy wants to know what the evidence is. She doesn't want to be interviewed.

'My advice is to do the interview,' Stan says. 'Let's hear the questions and see if she really does have new evidence.'

'Do I have to answer all her questions?'

'You don't have to answer any of them,' he says. 'You don't have to do the interview at all.'

'I don't have to talk to the police?'

'No. The only time you have to show up is when you get a subpoena. This isn't one. It's a request.'

Ivy thinks about this. When Ivy told Karen she'd hired a lawyer, and all communication had to go through him, Karen didn't sound happy. In fact, she'd sounded pissed off.

Stan said that was normal. Police hate dealing with lawyers.

At the same time, Ivy wants to know what Karen has discovered. Not just for her, but also for Wes.

She weighs the pros and cons of both decisions as her lawyer's billable time continues to rack up. What she fears more than anything is being blindsided. If Karen asks something Ivy isn't prepared for, she might say exactly the wrong thing. Or worse, she might get angry.

'I want to decline the interview,' she finally says. 'I don't have anything to say.'

Wes puts the phone down on his desk, faceup. Still waiting for a text from Ivy. Always from Ivy. He knows better than to think she'll be consistent or reliable, but that doesn't stop him from hoping.

Self-awareness is such a double-edged sword.

For the past week, they've seen each other every night. Together again, just like they'd said. They just don't talk about the case – not one word – and now Karen wants to interview him. The call from his lawyer came in this morning, a voice-mail Wes hasn't answered yet. He wants to talk to Ivy first.

Finally, in the afternoon, she responds. A phone call, not a text.

'Karen requested an interview,' Ivy says.

'Same.'

'I declined. You?'

'Haven't answered yet,' he says. 'But I'll do the same.'

'Good. See you later?'

'Of course.'

As Wes ends the call, it occurs to him that he and Ivy are exactly on the same page. For once.

Abigail is perched at the edge of a shabby chair, wearing an outfit the color of a Creamsicle. She seems out of place in Bianca's apartment. Abigail looks like she should be sitting on a satin chaise. Which is weird, since they're both assistants. Or they both used to be.

At least Abigail is here. Bianca wasn't sure she would come at all.

'We've all been worried about you,' Abigail says. 'But I didn't know if you wanted to hear from anyone at Siphon.'

'I didn't expect anyone to come running.'

'Still. No one has any hard feelings,' Abigail says. 'Especially not the women.'

Bianca clears her throat, not wanting to discuss all that. 'Before I forget,' she says, 'there's something I have to give you.' She jumps up and goes to the shelf that holds her Russian dolls. The key is sitting on it, already taken out. 'This belongs to Siphon.'

'A key?'

'I never had a chance to return it.'

Abigail turns the key over in her hand, inspecting it. Her nails are a peachy color that match the suit, with pomegranate-colored tips. 'This is a master key.'

'Yes,' Bianca says. Like it's totally normal.

Abigail nods and slips the key into her bag.

'So, I wanted to ask you something,' Bianca says. 'Do you remember Joey Fisher?' Her voice almost catches on his name. She can't remember the last time she said it out loud. 'He was killed in a hit-and-run about seven years ago.'

'No. I probably wouldn't have heard about it, though. I grew up in San Francisco.'

'That makes sense. It wasn't a national case or anything,' Bianca says. She picks up her tablet and wakes up the screen. 'Anyway, there's something else I need to talk to you about. Starting with your Instagram account.'

Karen stands across the street, where she has a decent view. The bar called Crisis is one of those overpriced places she has never stepped foot in, but Ivy looks comfortable there.

She is with a group of women from work, and they all have martini glasses in their hands. Ivy smiles and laughs, giving no indication of how miserable she really is. But Karen knows. It's honestly difficult for her to watch. Between Wes and her new lawyer, Ivy is under so much pressure.

It's the only explanation for why she turned down the request for an interview. Ivy wants to talk; she just can't.

Karen can't stand out on the street all evening. She moves her car into a place that gives her a view of the front door. For the past couple of days, she has been trying to 'run into' Ivy in a public setting. Preferably in a place that doesn't make Karen look like she's following or waiting for her. Not as easy as it first sounded. Ivy doesn't go to the grocery store nearly enough.

She does go to Wes's house, though. That's where she went last night after work, and two nights ago they met at a restaurant before going back to her place. No surprise that they both declined to be interviewed. He is keeping her close. Abusers always do.

Karen checks her phone and finds a text from her son, a response to one she sent hours ago.

Everything's good, just working a lot. Call you this weekend.

He is such a good boy. No, he's a man. And her biggest

fear is for Jack to end up in a relationship like her own. Or like Ivy's.

She puts the phone down and stares at the entrance of Crisis. It's never easy to figure out the best way to help someone.

Sometimes, all it takes is a threat to the abuser. Other times, it's something more elaborate. A sting operation to catch them doing something wrong, like cheating, which tends to make them remorseful instead of angry. That makes it easier for their partner to leave. Or disappear, if necessary.

When Karen gets lucky, the abuser has broken the law and she can put them behind bars.

Like Wes.

One hour and twenty minutes after Ivy enters the bar, Karen watches her leave. Ivy's friends are with her; they laugh and talk while walking to their cars. No opportunity to get her alone on the street.

Karen shouldn't talk to Ivy at all. She knows this. Once someone has a lawyer, she can't talk to them without counsel present.

But sometimes you just run into a person. Unavoidable, really. Fair Valley isn't tiny, but it isn't a huge city, either. And it would be rude if Karen didn't say hello.

Ivy may not know it, but all she needs is an outlet. Someone to reach out to, someone to confide in. She obviously has no one. Girlfriends and coworkers, yes, but they're clearly not that close. Any decent friend would have helped her get away from Wes years ago.

When Ivy pulls into a shopping center and parks in front of a drugstore, Karen pinches herself.

Finally.

She parks on the other side of the lot and enters the store

after Ivy. After spending a couple of hours sitting in her dark car, Karen finds the light in the store almost blinding. It takes a second for her eyes to adjust. She makes her way to the center aisle and walks through it.

The pharmacy section. Ivy is standing in front of the painkillers, looking at the ibuprofen, aspirin, and Tylenol. All that pressure must be giving her one hell of a headache.

'Ivy?'

She turns. The more Karen sees her, the more she realizes Ivy is such a lovely young woman. Delicate features, flawless skin, and the most open, engaging smile. Although right now, she looks a little scared.

'I thought that was you,' Karen says.

Ivy takes a step back. 'Oh. Hi.'

'Hello. I guess it was inevitable we'd run into each other out here.' Karen gestures to the aisle. 'In the real world.'

'I guess.'

'How are you doing?'

'Fine, thanks.' She grabs a bottle off one of the shelves. 'I've got to get going. Have a good night.'

'Wait.'

Ivy turns back, the smile on her face now gone. No light in her eyes. Wes has really done a number on this woman.

'I was sorry to hear you turned down my request for an interview,' Karen says.

Ivy taps the bottle with her thumb, over and over. Like she's clicking a pen. 'I can't talk to you without my lawyer.'

Karen steps forward, closing the gap between them. 'Of course. I just wanted to say that the interview would've been a chance for you to discover things you might not realize. Not consciously. But they could be important.'

'Seriously, I can't talk to you without my lawyer.'

Karen holds up her hand, backing off. 'Understood.'

'Good night.' Ivy nods and starts to walk away. Karen lets her take one step.

'How's Abigail doing?' Karen says. She changes her voice, using the one she usually saves for abusers. Offer a suggestion, but make it sound like a threat. 'Have you talked to her yet?'

'Abigail?'

'The admin at Siphon,' Karen says. 'She took Bianca's place?'

Now Ivy is the one who steps forward. Karen thought that would get her attention, given that Abigail is so firmly on #TeamWes.

'What about her?' Ivy says.

'Oh,' Karen says, looking surprised. 'I just thought you would've spoken to her, given the whole thing with Wes.' She waves her hand, like it means nothing. 'Anyway, I don't mean to hold you up. Have a good night.'

Karen walks away, pausing outside the store to collect herself. What she did to Ivy, mentioning Abigail in that way, was so manipulative. Planting a seed of doubt and hoping it will grow.

Just like her husband used to.

Of course that's where she learned it. Who else would it have come from? Except he made Karen doubt herself, not him. She is trying to make Ivy doubt Wes.

It still makes her feel horrible. But when someone needs help, it has to be done.

54

Ivy sits in her car, replaying the conversation with Karen in her head, but remembering what her lawyer said.

The police lie.

Stan said they do it all the time. They do it to mess with people's heads, to confuse them, to get them to admit to something. That must be what Karen is doing.

Still, Ivy can't help but think about how beautiful Abigail is. She also thinks about the voice that answered Wes's phone, but she can't remember what Abigail sounds like. Ivy searches for her on social media, hoping she has posted a video of herself talking.

A knock on the window interrupts her scrolling.

Ivy is still sitting in the parking lot of the drugstore, so she expects to see Karen. But it's a man.

She doesn't recognize him at first. It's nighttime, she is alone in her car, and now there's a man just outside. This scenario has played out a dozen times in true-crime documentaries, and it never ends well for the woman.

But then she knows. It's the beard.

'Milo?' she says.

He can't hear her because her window is still up. He motions for her to lower it. She does, only a few inches.

'Ivy,' he says. 'I thought that was you.'

'Yes, hi. It's me.'

'How are you?' he says.

Everything comes back to her now, the whole story about the picture she posted online, and this starts to feel weird.

'I'm fine,' she says. 'And you? How's your fiancée?' Snarky, yes. Deserved, definitely yes.

'Not too well, actually,' he says.

'Sorry to hear that.'

'Clarissa thinks you and me are having a "thing."' Air quotes around *thing*.

'She messaged me. I told her we just had a drink together,' Ivy says.

'I know. She didn't believe you.'

Ivy restrains herself from rolling her eyes. 'Well, maybe you shouldn't have drinks with women in bars and ask for their numbers.'

'Maybe you shouldn't tag pictures of guys you aren't going out with.'

This is so not her problem.

'Goodbye, Milo.' Ivy rolls up her window and backs her car up.

Milo watches her leave, illuminated by her headlights. He looks a lot creepier than she remembers from Liver.

She forgets about Milo as soon as she drives away and heads home. Her mind is back on Abigail.

Ivy has met her a few times. Abigail had been the admin in Wes's office for years. Ivy saw her once when she stopped by to have lunch with Wes, and again at a Siphon holiday party.

Abigail had also been there the day Ivy had been in a rage, tearing apart Wes's office.

He deserved it. His coworkers may not have understood that, but Wes did. Abigail was the one who had walked in first, raising her voice above Ivy's. She grabbed Ivy's arm and told her security was on its way. Tanner rushed in behind her, yelling for her to get out. Ivy did, before the guards arrived.

She has a clear memory of the look on Abigail's face.

Disgust. Even though Ivy kept her head high, as always, she felt that look.

But it's hard to believe Wes would hook up with her. Work is too important to him, and the majority of his career has been at Siphon. Messing around with the admin in his department would be idiotic. Granted, he has done stupid things in the past – a lot of them – but something like this could be career suicide.

Still, that woman on the phone.

Ivy shakes her head, trying to erase the voice. Her mind is playing tricks on her, making connections where there may not be any. No, she is not going to ask him about it. Not going to call Heath, either. She already knows what he would say. Heath claims to be on #TeamIvy, but when she really thinks about it, he is #TeamAnyoneButWes. This would just add to Heath's pile of evidence, the one he throws at her whenever things aren't going right.

As Ivy enters her apartment, she gets a text from Wes.

I'll be done in about half an hour. Your place or mine?

She looks around at her disaster of a bedroom. Clothes are spread out everywhere, hanging on the door of the closet, stacked in a pile on the chair. Right next to the open suitcase.

I'll come to your place, she says. Text me when you're home.

She tosses her phone on the bed and looks around her room. So much to do. And now she is pissed off, and it's all Karen's fault.

But in a few days, none of that will matter.

After Wes suggested marriage in the middle of the night, the subject was dropped. They went back to bed. In the morning, they were both groggy, sleepwalking through the coffee and bagels, and neither one brought it up. Ivy went to work thinking the whole conversation had been a fever dream.

Until he invited her over for dinner that night.

It was a late meal, because she had to go home and take a nap to make it through dinner without falling asleep. Around nine o'clock, as she drove up to his house, he sent a text.

I'm in the backyard. Gate's open.

Not unusual. Wes likes to grill outside when the weather is nice, and that night it was. Clear sky, not much of a breeze. She walked down the side of the house, and it hit her just as she entered the yard.

Red meat. The smell was unmistakable.

She thought it was coming from next door, that a neighbor was outside grilling. Because Wes wouldn't even touch it, much less cook it.

The patio was lit up with strands of Christmas lights, the table set with candles and fresh flowers. Before she could speak, Wes took her hand and led her to the table, where a slab of steak was waiting.

He got down on one knee.

Over the years, she had imagined this moment a hundred times. A thousand. It never looked like this.

'I can't promise I'll never be an asshole,' he said. 'But if you want to eat that disgusting steak, I promise never to complain.'

'Never?' she said.

'Probably never.'

'Fair.'

'So, then, Ivy Noelle Banks, will you marry me?'

'You know I can't promise I'll never be an asshole,' she said.

'I wouldn't have it any other way.'

55

Karen orders dinner from her favorite restaurant, which makes her feel a little better about tonight. It's never easy when someone is as deeply entrenched as Ivy is.

Uber Eats drops off her chicken tetrazzini, and she brings it into her office. Now that the case is moving faster, she was forced to buy another corkboard for the Joey Fisher case. The new one is covered in sticky notes and stickers, all color-coded. Green on the right, indicating evidence she already has. Yellow in the middle, for things she's waiting on or that need follow-up. Red on the left, for the things she needs but can't find. The details are kept in the lists on her phone; the board gives her the big picture at a glance.

Tonight, she tackles all things red.

First, she makes her calls. The advantage of being a detective for so long is knowing a lot of people in a lot of different businesses. People she can count on when she needs information, always promising to help out on some future issue they may have. Amazing how many people will agree to it.

One of them is Vilma Naquil. Karen has to go through an operator and an assistant to get to her.

'Karen,' Vilma says. Her voice is deep and grainy. 'What do the police want now?'

'What I need happened seven years ago. I assume your records go back that far?'

'My records are impeccable.'

Once upon a time, Vilma Naquil was known as the taxi queen. Before Uber and Lyft, she owned the largest taxicab company operating in Fair Valley and a few of the surrounding towns. She also had a way of putting other companies out of business by buying them.

Times have been hard in the past few years, forcing Vilma to diversify her businesses, but the cab company is still hanging on. Barely.

Karen gives Vilma the address of the old Fine Line club and the address of where Wes and Ivy used to live. 'Any rides between those addresses, to or from, on the night of July sixteenth?'

'Seven years ago?' Vilma says.

'That's right.'

Vilma promises to get back to her within twenty-four hours. In Karen's experience, it will be less than that. One of the things that makes Vilma such a good businesswoman is underpromising and overdelivering.

Next, Karen pulls up the recording of her call with Uncle Bobby. She transcribes it, in preparation for a submission to her sergeant tomorrow.

Uncle Bobby had a lot of interesting things to say about the club. The stories spilled out like he had been itching to tell someone. Most were useless to Karen, having nothing to do with the night Ivy worked there.

But he did remember the new waitress who looked like apple pie and sunshine. Even better, he remembered Wes. Though Uncle Bobby claimed – strongly – that he wasn't the one who called 911. Must've been a customer, he said, because no one who worked there would've called about an irate boyfriend unless he'd had a gun. No one saw Wes with one.

What Uncle Bobby saw was a man who was not happy about his girlfriend working at a strip club.

'Happened all the time,' he said. 'Sometimes they stayed

anyway, sometimes not. Little Miss Sunshine left, though. Her alias was Summer.'

Oddly enough, he remembered all of this because of one thing: She had to come back the following day to get her bag. 'She left without it the night before,' he said. 'Then she showed up at lunchtime the next day, right after we opened, to pick it up. That was weird. Who leaves their phone, wallet, and keys behind? Who doesn't come back right away to get them?'

Good questions. And another piece of the puzzle. Karen adds it to her growing list of evidence, creating a picture that should be easy for the DA – or a jury – to see.

Just as she finishes transcribing the call, a new email pops up in her box.

From Bianca.

Ivy has spent two nights shopping for the perfect dress. Not a lot of time and not an easy thing to find, given that she's going to be married in Vegas this weekend at a place called the Hitching Post, and the wedding will be officiated by a Dolly Parton impersonator. Elvis is so overdone.

After trying on so many different dresses, starting with traditional and working her way all the way down, she finally decided to go ridiculous. Silver sequins, spaghetti straps, draped neckline. At least she didn't have to worry about jewelry. Just the ring.

She and Wes bought the bands last night. Plain platinum, no decoration, no diamond, just an engraving on the inside with their wedding date. She has already checked five times to make sure they're packed, along with her shoes, bag, and the fancy clip she bought for her hair.

All with money she doesn't have. All with money that has to be spent. They both know why they're getting married so quickly, though they don't talk about it.

In the back of her mind, it was always going to happen. Eventually. And if Karen is the woman who ended up pushing them over the edge and toward the altar, then so be it. But it's not the *reason* they're doing it. It's the reason why it's happening *now*.

The only person Ivy has told is her college roommate, Sabine, who lives in Arizona with her husband and two kids. They haven't seen each other for a while, but she's the only one Ivy knew would be happy for her. Sabine has been saying for years that Ivy and Wes need to separate for good or stop breaking up and get married. Preferably the latter, because she believed in fate.

'I knew there was a reason you two kept getting back together,' Sabine said when Ivy told her. 'You're soulmates.'

Heath would have a different reaction if she told him. Ivy has avoided talking to him for days. On purpose. Everyone else can wait until after they return.

She packs up her makeup and toiletries, pouring what she needs into those three-ounce bottles. She checks her list, which is actually on paper. Ivy stares at it, clicking her pen over and over. It always helps her think.

She has never really written out a list before – not like this – but she did for her wedding. And she takes great joy in checking off each item.

Maybe this will be the start of something new. Maybe she'll become the kind of wife who writes out lists and puts them on the refrigerator under a crafty little magnet.

But probably not.

56

On Friday, Ivy arrives in Sacramento at nine in the morning. She heads straight to Oblivion, the day spa, where they wrap her in a plush robe and make her a cappuccino. They also take care of her bags.

The sequined wedding dress is carefully wrapped, her suitcase double-checked no less than ten times. Everything on her list is accounted for, but that's exactly why she doesn't trust it. Not on the list, not in her bag.

She tries not to think about that. Just before she lies down for her facial, she texts Wes.

Made it to the spa, see you this afternoon ♥

She still hasn't answered Heath's texts, and she doesn't do it now. After the weekend, when she's a married woman, she will have a lot of time to tell him.

After the facial: the mani-pedi combo. Ballet pink nail polish on her toes and fingers.

Her hair doesn't take long – just a few highlights around her face and a blow-dry. Last but not least: a massage. It lulls her into a daze, and she floats up to the register to pay her bill. Doesn't pay attention to the final total.

Because it's her wedding, for God's sake. Skimping is not an option.

Neither are negative thoughts. Whenever Karen or the investigation enters her mind, she thinks of the Chinese word for *no*: *bù*. She repeats it as she leaves Oblivion and drives to the airport.

The flight is at two, and she pulls into the long-term

parking lot at twelve fifteen. Plenty of time. Compared to San Francisco, the airport in Sacramento is small. No need to rush through security. Even taking her time, she arrives at the gate by twelve forty-five. She sits down with a magazine and a bottle of water and checks her phone.

Again.

Still nothing from Wes. Over the past couple of hours, all thoughts of the wedding and the case have been slowly replaced by the fact that she hasn't heard from him at all. Not once today. A bad feeling creeps in, wondering if he is ghosting her again. Her future husband.

Ivy has been trying to make herself comfortable with the word *husband* for days, ever since they decided to go to Vegas. Doesn't quite feel comfortable yet, but it will.

She texts him again: I'm at the gate.

Fifteen minutes later: Are you at the airport yet?

And finally: They're starting to board.

She tries to call him: straight to voicemail. Calls again: same thing.

She redials, over and over, her messages alternating between panic and fury, right up until they close the plane door.

Bù.

Bù.

Bù.

This. Can't. Be. Happening.

Ivy bangs on the front door of Wes's house. Half crying, half full of rage, she flips back and forth by the second. Her throat hurts from screaming. Her head hurts from trying to figure it out. And her heart hurts because it's cracked in two, broken either because he chose not to show up or because something horrible has happened to him. No idea which one she prefers.

She gives up on the front door, opens the side gate, and

heads into the yard. The back door is also locked, and the curtains are drawn, giving her only a sliver of the view inside.

Nothing looks out of place. No body on the floor.

He isn't at the office – she has already checked – and his car is nowhere. Not at his home, not at Siphon, not in the long-term parking lot at the airport. She checked every row.

Now she walks around his house, searching for an unlocked window. Not a single one. The rock comes next. She breaks a single pane in his back door, not bothering to clear out all the glass before reaching in to unlock it. A sharp edge slices through her skin, on the side of her thumb, but she doesn't slow down.

Inside, his house looks like it always does. No sign of him, no sign of a struggle. She walks through it, looking for something – anything – that explains why he didn't show up.

His bed is made. The towel in the bathroom is almost dry, like he had woken up at his usual time and used it hours ago.

She checks his dresser and closet. A few empty hangers, no suitcase. He had definitely packed and taken his bag with him when he left the house. He had *planned* to meet her in Sacramento.

Knowing he hadn't been lying relaxes her a tiny bit.

Unless he went somewhere else.

Maybe with Abigail.

She shakes that idea away, refusing to consider it. After wrapping a towel around her hand, she checks the news for car accidents. Hospitals come next. She calls all of them.

'Wes Harmon's room, please.' She asks this way every time, making the assumption he is there instead of asking. It always makes them check, just like at a hotel.

No luck in Fair Valley, so she expands her search to all the hospitals between here and Sacramento.

Still nothing.

By now, her hand is starting to hurt. She washes out the cut and continues to make calls while searching for a first aid kit.

An idea in the back of her mind starts to grow: Call the police. A logical next step.

Then again, they would probably laugh at her. Left at the proverbial altar? Not their problem.

Maybe your boyfriend flew to the Caribbean with his other girlfriend.
Maybe you don't know him as well as you think you do.

Maybe they would be right.

The anger roars back, front and center, making her temples pound. Hard to think, impossible to make a plan. She sits down on Wes's couch and puts her head between her knees, resisting the urge to start destroying everything. That won't help find him.

His friends. The real ones, not his coworkers. He doesn't see them a lot these days, but she could try calling. The problem is, those guys are loyal to Wes, not her, and even if they know something, they aren't going to tell her.

Probably. But she won't know unless she tries.

Maybe if she cries enough, one of them will take pity on her. Tell her what's really happening. It's worth a shot, because right now it feels like she's punching in the dark.

Her phone is almost dead, and she races through the house, trying to find a charger. She locates one in the kitchen, in the junk drawer, and scrolls through her address book. Tries to figure out which numbers she has and whether any of them would be helpful.

A plan starts to form in her mind. A list. Try calling his friends first, and if nothing comes from that, she has to call the hospitals again. Maybe he hadn't been entered into the system yet. Maybe he had been unconscious and rushed into surgery.

She decides on someone Wes has known since college, a guy who also knows Ivy. She is about to call when her phone rings.

The number isn't familiar.

'Hello?'

'Hello,' a man says. His voice is pleasant, almost soft. 'May I speak with Ivy Banks?'

'Who's calling, please?'

'My name is Bryce Kendrick. I'm an attorney with Clarke, Greenburg, and Kendrick.'

'This is Ivy.'

'Miss Banks, I'm calling in regard to Wes Harmon,' he says. 'He asked me to call you.'

'Where is Wes? Is he okay?'

He pauses before answering, which makes her head feel like it's going to implode.

'This morning,' he says, 'Wes was arrested by the Fair Valley police.'

'Arrested? For what?' The question is automatic – it comes out before she can stop it. Because she already knows.

'Joey Fisher,' the lawyer says.

57

As soon as Wes was booked and in jail, Karen and two uniformed officers went straight to Siphon. The receptionist wasn't happy to see them; Abigail was even less so. She was the first person Karen saw when the elevator doors opened on the third floor.

Next to Abigail: a wiry man from their legal department. He looked over the search warrant, taking so much time he must have read it twice.

'This way,' he said.

They were led straight back to the sales department, where Abigail unlocked Wes's door. The warrant was limited to his office. Both Abigail and the wiry man stood in the corner while they searched. Every inch was inspected, from the family photo on his desk to the carpet under the furniture.

Karen didn't search the desk herself, but she did watch an officer do it. And she told him exactly what to bag, log, and take.

His computer was fair game, though the wiry man spouted off a bunch of legalese about work product and confidentiality. He didn't have to worry. The inner workings of Siphon, Inc., didn't matter to Karen. Her only concern was building a case against Wes Harmon.

She will never forget the look on his face when he was arrested. Shock, confusion, hate.

And guilt.

The same look her husband gave her the first time she

tried to leave him. Right before the threats came. At least Wes didn't try that.

As soon as they finish at Siphon, Karen heads to Wes's house. A much bigger place to search.

It's also a mess. She already had a heads-up about it from Wes's lawyer, who told her Ivy had been there looking for him. Karen just hopes Ivy didn't do anything stupid, like remove evidence. She makes a mental note to see about getting a warrant for Ivy's place, though that would be a long shot.

Karen begins with his most personal items. He has one photo album with pictures of his family but only a few of him and Ivy. By now, most of his pictures have to be in the cloud or on his personal laptop. It's password-protected, but they take it anyway, along with his tablet.

Other than the album, there isn't much in the way of items related to Ivy. A couple of birthday cards, one from Christmas, and some clothes that are probably hers. Ten years is a long time to be involved, yet most of their communication had to be electronic.

Soon enough, she'll know if they can get into his phone, the one taken when he was arrested. Otherwise, the DA's office will have to work with his provider to get copies of all his messages.

Karen didn't know what she'd expected to find, but she thought there would be more. The house is a bit of a disappointment. Not the office, though. That search was a lot more productive.

Thanks to Bianca.

Wes sits in jail by himself, on top of the hard cot, with his back against the wall, feet up on the metal edge. The facility is modern – no bars or cages, just a small room with a steel-reinforced door. A thick-paned window allows guards to look inside, and the door has a narrow slot for passing food.

One good thing, if there is a good thing, is that they didn't arrest him at work. He was stopped by a cop on his way to the office, and three more police cars showed up immediately. Karen had been in one of them.

She stepped forward and told him he was under arrest. She smiled when she said it, and reminded him of the Joker as she listed the charges against him.

Felony hit-and-run. Vehicular homicide.

Homicide.

Since being locked up, he has left the cell only once, and that was to talk with his lawyer. They sat in a room where the table and chairs were bolted to the floor and a guard stood outside. Wes had to keep his handcuffs on.

Bryce didn't seem surprised. At least one of them wasn't.

'Are you doing okay?' Bryce asked.

'Are you joking?'

'I mean, no one is mistreating you?'

Not in the way Bryce meant, no.

He was an older man with thick white hair and a beard. Santa Claus in a nice suit. Bryce had also been around this area a long time, which was one of the reasons Wes hired him. He knew everyone.

Bryce explained what would happen next: the arraignment, where the judge would set bail. Wes could enter a plea, and he would. Not guilty.

'I believe the judge will grant bail in this case. It doesn't always happen for a charge like yours, but this time the chances are good,' Bryce said. 'You don't have a record, and this happened seven years ago. There is no reason to think you would flee.'

Wes had to explain that he did have a suitcase in his car

when they pulled him over. 'My girlfriend and I were going to Vegas.'

'You were leaving town?'

'Just for the weekend. We were going to get married.'

Bryce raised his fluffy white eyebrows. For the first time, Wes saw that his eyes were brown.

'You can check the tickets, the reservations,' Wes said. 'We were coming back Sunday night. I was supposed to meet her at the airport today, but I got arrested.'

Bryce doesn't say anything.

'That's bad?' Wes said. 'I guess that's bad.'

'It might make your bail higher.'

Perfect.

Wes didn't want his parents called, and they couldn't help anyway – not with money. Same with his sister. He definitely didn't want Bryce calling her.

Wes does have a retirement account, though there isn't a lot of money in it. He also has his house. He could use it as collateral if necessary, and if Bryce could arrange it. Papers would have to be drawn up and signed, giving Bryce permission to secure the bond.

'Let's wait and see what the amount is,' Bryce said.

Now Wes is alone again, waiting for his arraignment. He tries to think about that and only that, but his brain doesn't cooperate. It keeps bringing him back to the same thought, the one he's had since being arrested:

Karen got it all wrong.

58

That night could have gone so many other ways.

Wes had been at home, watching a baseball game. It was a normal Thursday evening right up until Ivy walked into the living room, wearing shorts and a T-shirt. Her hair had been curled, and she was wearing a lot of makeup. Too much.

'Where are you –'

'I start work tonight,' she said. 'So I'll be home late.'

'You're taking the car?'

'I'll take a cab, in case you need it. I'll make more than enough to cover the fare.'

Wes laughed. She was carrying this whole strip-club thing way too far.

He figured she would give up this little act of hers and be home by eleven. When the baseball game ended, he opened another beer and took out his laptop to do a little work. Wes had just started at Siphon a few weeks earlier, and he had a lot of onboarding documents to fill out and research materials to learn.

Eleven o'clock came and went.

Close to midnight, he started to wonder if he was wrong.

Only one way to find out. Wes grabbed his keys and drove down to the Fine Line. He still didn't believe she was working there or that she would ever work at a strip club. She was probably out with her friends. But he felt a need to check.

While he had been to strip clubs before, he had never been inside the Fine Line. It was more expensive than the clubs he and his friends had gone to back in college. The parking lot was about half-full, even late on a Thursday. No cover charge, and the half-naked girl at the front barely glanced at his ID before waving him in the door.

The music was so loud he could feel the thump of the bass in his chest. More half-naked girls walked around in front of him. They seemed to be everywhere, all at once. Most of the customers were men, sitting at tables surrounding the stage. Wes watched a woman wrap her legs around a pole and hang upside down. The men cheered.

Wes snapped out of it and scanned the room, thinking this was stupid. No way Ivy was working here. No way she would put up with men like this, the kind who could barely control themselves in front of a mostly naked woman. No. Way.

He believed that right up until he saw her.

Saw *so much* of her.

Ivy was wearing – or barely wearing – something that was sky blue and resembled a bikini. Her whole body was bursting out of it. The shimmery material caught the light as she stood in front of a table filled with men, making her sparkle as she served the drinks on her tray.

And she was laughing.

'Ivy,' he said. It felt like he was yelling. Maybe he was.

She looked up and saw him, a smile still on her face. 'Wes.'

He looked down at the men who were salivating over his girlfriend. 'You can't work here,' he said to her.

'And yet I am.'

She walked away from him, toward the bar. He followed, heading her off before she reached it. 'We're going home,' he said.

'You go home. I have to work,' she said. 'And don't call me Ivy again. My name is Summer.'

'*Summer?*'

'Is there a problem here?'

The man who appeared in front of Wes was three times his size, he wore a jacket with SECURITY on the breast pocket, and he wasn't looking at Wes. The man was talking to Ivy, who now looked angry.

'He's my boyfriend,' she said. 'I'll take care of it.'

She put her tray down and led Wes toward the front door. Outside the club, in the parking lot, she ordered him to leave.

'I told you I was doing this,' she said. 'You didn't believe me, and that's your problem.'

Wes tried to calm down. He really did. He took a deep breath, telling himself to keep it together. This was not the time or the place for a screaming match with Ivy. But in his mind, all he could see were those men staring at his girl-friend's body.

One option. Truly. It was only idea he had, the only road forward he could see.

Wes grabbed Ivy around her hips, picked her up, and threw her over his shoulder.

As he walked to the car, she yelled and pounded on his back. Wes glanced back, expecting to see the club's security guys running after him. They weren't. Disturbances outside the club didn't seem to interest them at all – at least not between a couple. Not even when Ivy continued to yell at him.

'Put me down!

'Put. Me. Down.

'Wes, I swear to God, you better put me down.'

He did, eventually. He opened the hatchback of the 4Run-ner, put her inside, then closed and locked the doors. She immediately scrambled over the seat, but not fast enough to get out of the car before he got in and started driving away. That's when she climbed into the front passenger seat and started yelling in his ear.

'How could you *do* that?'

'Ivy –'

'You can't just pick me up and drag me out like some kind of caveman –'

'Stop pulling on my arm! I'm *driving*. Jesus Christ –'

'Turn around!'

'Calm *down*.'

'Don't you tell me to calm down!'

'Ivy, I swear to God –'

That's when she grabbed the steering wheel.

59

The 4Runner turned to the right, into the lane next to them. No one was there, thank God, because it was so late at night. They were away from downtown, in an area where the streets were quiet. Empty.

The car headed toward a storefront. Sprinkles, a frozen yogurt shop, and Wes can still picture the sign on the building. Curly pink font, next to a giant cup piled high with yogurt and multicolored sprinkles. The shop was closed and dark inside, along with everything else in the area.

Ivy was still yelling, cursing him out. He yanked the wheel back to the left.

Too hard. He lost control of the car.

They skidded across the road, almost in a circle, before coming to a stop on the curb. Ivy stopped screaming.

'We're okay,' she finally said. 'We're okay.'

'We're okay,' he said.

She turned to him, the glitter around her eyes catching the light. 'You've been drinking.'

'No, I —'

'I can smell the beer.'

'I'm not drunk,' he said. 'I had a couple beers while watching the game.'

'Get out. I'm driving.'

'You grabbed the wheel.'

'You lost control of the car.'

'We aren't going back to that strip club,' he said.

'Of course we aren't. You *humiliated* me back there.'

He got out of the car. She climbed over the center console, took off her stilettos and threw them in the back. Ivy drove toward their apartment. One left turn, two right. That was it, they were less than two miles from home. It was easy right up until it wasn't.

Ivy swerved. Hard.

They didn't get lucky a second time. Instead of hitting the curb, the 4Runner slammed into the side of a car.

'What the hell?' he said. 'Why did you do that?'

'There was something in the road!' she yelled. 'An animal, a squirrel or something. I swerved so I wouldn't hit it.'

Wes didn't see a squirrel or a cat or anything else, but he did see the car they hit. What he remembers most is the relief. It came after he realized the car was parked.

They didn't know anyone was in the car. It was on the street, no one was around, and no one screamed when they bashed right into it. Well, no one except Ivy.

They never called the police after the accident. Not after Ivy started having a meltdown. She was babbling about the animal in the road, going on and on about some squirrel from years ago and how upset Wes had been and how she didn't want it to happen again. She was also naked, or close enough. Ivy wasn't making sense, let alone in any condition to drive.

Wes did the only thing he could have. He drove away.

They switched places again, he started the car, and they went home. It was a miracle that was still possible, given the condition of the car and the weird scraping noise it was making, but they made it. He parked behind the apartment building instead of in the main lot. Only dumpsters and stray cats were in the back.

Not that anyone would mention or even notice the car. The only apartment they could afford was in a run-down

266

building filled with people who wanted to live somewhere else. Themselves included. No one asked a lot of questions.

Wes didn't find out someone had been in the parked car until the next day, when he was at work. During his first weeks at Siphon, his days were split between working and training. He was so busy the news alert didn't even get his attention:

One dead in hit-and-run.

He didn't bother clicking on it. First, because he didn't have the time. Also, because he didn't think it was about *their* accident. The car had been parked. No one had died.

An hour or two later, he got a text from Ivy.

Did you see the news?

The alert popped into his mind, so he went back to it and read the story. That's when he first heard about Joey Fisher.

He didn't know the name yet – it came out later – but he did learn someone had been in the car. Someone who was now dead.

Wes can still feel that moment. For a second, he couldn't breathe. Like his body had forgotten how to do it. When his body remembered, Wes gasped for air like he had been underwater.

He texted Ivy back: Call me.

She didn't, so he called her. Straight to voicemail. Wes didn't leave a message; he wasn't about to mention the accident on a voicemail. He texted again but didn't hear from her until he was getting ready to leave the office.

I got it.

He had no idea what that meant, and he didn't have time to try to figure it out. That day, they hadn't been able to use their damaged car, so he was getting a ride from a coworker who was anxious to leave the office. As soon as he got home, he checked behind the apartment building. The 4Runner was gone.

He called Ivy again. Straight to voicemail.

Another hour passed before he heard the key in the door. Ivy walked in, and the first thing he noticed was how puffy and red her face was, like she had been crying. She was also dripping wet. Hair, clothes, shoes. Everything.

'I took care of the car,' she said.

'Took care of it? What did you –'

She slipped out of her wet sneakers. 'It's at the bottom of Oxhill Lake.'

They discussed it only once. After she got rid of the 4Run-ner, after it was reported stolen, after the police had come and gone, Ivy sat down and cried. Wes didn't ask if it was from exhaustion, stress, or the fact that they had killed some-one. All three, he assumed.

Joey Fisher had been identified by that time. His name had been breaking news throughout the night.

'Eighteen,' she kept saying. 'He was *eighteen*.'

Wes sat next to her on the couch, an ugly thing she had found at a garage sale. Black with big yellow flowers. The cushion covers had been washed, and she had added some throw pillows, but it was still ugly.

'We can go to the police,' he said. 'Tell them everything.'

She nodded. Cried some more before answering. 'It's the right thing to do.'

'But you were the one driving,' he said.

'So I'll be the one arrested.'

'Absolutely. And given that we've already tried to cover it up, I will too. We both left the scene of the accident, and we filed a false police report.' He glanced at his watch. 'Less than an hour ago.'

'I don't want you to get in trouble,' she said. 'It should be me. I'm the one who did it.'

Back and forth they went, damn near all night, until Wes couldn't stand it anymore. 'We either have to do it, or we make the decision not to. Either way, I can't have this conversation a second time.'

Ivy was quiet for a long time.

'I don't know what to do,' she finally said. The tears were gone now. She was all out. And she looked broken.

He took both of her hands in his. 'Even if we confess, it won't bring him back.'

'I know.'

That was it. Their decision was based on the knowledge that it wouldn't fix anything, wouldn't undo the mistake. And because neither one of them wanted to go to jail.

'This has to be our secret,' Wes told her. 'You can't tell anyone. Not your family or your friends. Not even Heath.'

'I won't,' she said. 'I promise.'

He held up his hand, extending his little finger. She did the same, and they locked pinkies.

'Forever,' he said.

'Forever.'

60

Ivy is back at her own place, trying her best to sit still. According to Wes's lawyer, there isn't anything she can do.

No, she can't see Wes in jail.

No, she can't talk to him.

She'll have to see what happens at the bail hearing. Either Wes will be able to get out or he won't. If he has to stay in jail, he will be transferred to the county facility, where she would then be able to see and talk to him. But not now.

She also called her lawyer, trying to get a different answer, but was told the same thing: Wait.

Not her favorite activity.

Her lawyer had a lot more to say, as well, none of which Ivy liked.

'Let me ask you something.' Stan had said it in such an off-hand way she almost thought he was going to give her some good news. 'Is there any way Wes could implicate you in this?'

Foiled again.

'He wouldn't,' she said. The words came out automatically, as if she had always been ready for this. 'We're back together. We were supposed to get *married*.'

'Supposed to. So you aren't married?'

'No. We were going to Vegas this weekend to do it. We're supposed to be there right now.'

Stan was quiet for a long time. Too long, considering how much he charged per hour. 'Does Wes know anything that would tie you to this?' he finally said.

Tie her to it? Driving the car probably qualifies.

'Yes,' she said.

'Things look a lot different when you're in jail,' he said. His voice was still gentle. 'We don't know what Wes will say now that he's been arrested.'

Ivy understood what her lawyer was saying for once. But she doesn't believe Wes would tell the police what really happened. Not even to free himself.

He should, though. Wes should tell the police exactly how the accident happened, because he doesn't deserve to be in jail.

She wonders if he knew this was going to happen. Maybe he has been preparing for it. Maybe this is why he proposed, why he wanted to get married so quickly.

Though she had been the one to suggest Vegas. She was also the one who said they should go this weekend, not him. But he agreed. Quickly. He had even said their wedding had nothing to do with the case, and that if she was arrested, he would never testify against her. But he never said anything about telling the truth. Neither did she.

Because they didn't get married, she can be subpoenaed to testify against him. They'll ask about that night, and she will have to answer or plead the Fifth. The thought of either one makes her throat tighten, like even her body is afraid she'll say the wrong thing.

All these thoughts fly through her mind, bouncing off one another. Making noise. It's enough to drive someone crazy. If she thinks about it for one more minute, that might just happen.

A knock at the door saves her.

Must be Heath. By now, Wes has made the news. His picture from the Siphon website is everywhere. His reputation in Fair Valley has been shot to hell, probably forever. No matter what happens next, he'll always be the guy whose picture was in the news for all the wrong reasons.

She opens the door, expecting to see her best friend.

A woman is standing on her porch. Someone she doesn't know. She has blond hair, curly spirals that tumble down to her shoulders. Round face, pink cheeks, and blue eyes that remind Ivy of a chambray shirt.

'Ivy?' she says.

'Who are you?'

'Clarissa. I'm Milo's fiancée.'

Ivy takes a step back, physically trying to get away from Clarissa and whatever her problem is. 'What are you doing here?'

'I'm sorry to just show up like this. Your address was listed online, and I just . . . I have some questions. If you don't mind.'

She minds. A lot.

'Milo has cheated on me before,' Clarissa says. 'Once. And I know you said nothing happened between the two of you, but I keep thinking about how weird it is that you posted a picture of some random guy you met in a bar if you weren't . . . involved. Does that make sense?'

'I'm not involved with him. Never have been, never will be.'

Clarissa glances behind Ivy, like she thinks Milo is going to be standing right there. 'Seriously,' Clarissa says. Her voice is a little stronger. A little angry. 'If you are having a thing with him, just tell me. Because the last woman denied it, too. She was lying.'

'I'm not.'

'Please. I don't want a husband who's going to cheat on me.'

'Then don't marry Milo,' Ivy says.

She slams the door shut. Paces until Clarissa is gone.

When the coast is clear, Ivy leaves and gets in her car. She turns the music up to a deafening level, trying to drown out all the noise in her head, and drives without a destination. She makes random turns and goes in a circle without realizing it.

The circle becomes smaller and smaller until Ivy notices that she is at the police station, where Wes is being held.

61

Karen walks out of Wes's arraignment with Jocelyn Hughes, the assistant DA who has been assigned to the case. She's about thirty-five, with short black hair and the most incredible fingernails Karen has ever seen. Jocelyn is one of the more experienced lawyers they have. Sometimes the DA does know what he's doing.

It's late afternoon on Friday, and Wes is the last case for the judge. Karen wished it had been put off until Saturday morning so Wes could have spent the night sweating over whether or not he would be released. If he had been assigned a public defender, that's exactly what would have happened. But Wes's lawyer has all the right connections.

'That went better than I thought,' Jocelyn says. 'Considering this happened seven years ago.'

Karen nods, though she doesn't agree. She would prefer Wes had been denied bail. 'Thank you for all your work on this. I realize it all had to be done rather quickly.'

Jocelyn smiles. 'Doesn't it always?' She pats Karen on the shoulder, telling her to have a good weekend.

Karen will definitely do that. She's been riding a natural high since arresting Wes this morning. On TV, they talk about slapping the cuffs on the perp. Karen doesn't think of it exactly like that. For her, it's about getting a win.

A uniformed cop nods at her as she leaves. Perhaps a sign of respect, because he must have heard about this case. It's not every day an old case is solved, especially not one so many people remember. She thinks about this as she finally leaves for the day. Instead of going home, she stops at a cop bar. No paying for drinks tonight. Not after her success.

The Parkside Tavern used to be next to a park. Now it's a Costco, but the name of the bar never changed. Inside, the place is wall-to-wall police, and Karen recognizes most of them. She walks through until she comes across Louis Knox.

'Well, if it isn't the woman of the hour,' he says.

She smiles and nudges him over a little, making room for herself. He motions to the bartender, getting her a drink. Jack Daniel's, neat.

'I have to admit, when I heard you were looking into the Fisher case, I thought you were a little crazy,' he says.

Karen shrugs. 'It came up during another investigation. Sometimes, you get lucky.'

'That kind of luck might land you in the homicide division.'

She doesn't respond to that. Homicide is a double-edged sword for her. Yes, it would be a promotion and a bump in pay, but it wouldn't do anything for her real mission. By the time an abuse victim turns up dead, it's too late.

Louis points to the TV above their heads.

Wes.

His picture is front and center on the screen, and the chyron reads:

Local Businessman Arrested in Deadly Hit-and-Run.

It doesn't mention that the case is old. Not surprising, no news outlet is going to lead with that when they can lead with death.

Karen smiles a little. Wes may get out on bail, but he won't be back at work. Siphon isn't going to let him in the office now that he's all over the news. Not right on the heels of Tanner Duncan.

Tonight is a much bigger victory than her colleagues realize.

Ivy didn't intend to follow Karen; she wasn't even looking for her. She had been waiting in front of the police station, thinking – hoping – she would catch Wes walking out after paying his bail. Assuming he got bail. She still hadn't heard anything about that. Instead, Karen was the one who walked out of the building.

It was the smile. Ivy couldn't stand seeing that woman smile.

She followed Karen away from the police station and then to a bar. Ivy had never been to the Parkside Tavern and didn't plan to go, given how many cop cars were out front. She stays in her own car, down the street a little, and surfs through her phone, looking for information about how to post a bond. It surprises her that this can be done twenty-four hours a day, but first the bail amount has to be set.

She thinks about calling Wes's lawyer but doesn't, assuming he wouldn't answer her questions anyway. She then thinks about calling her own lawyer but doubts he would pick up the phone at eight o'clock on a Friday night.

Helpless. That's how she feels, and it isn't an emotion she is comfortable with. Or familiar with, for that matter, because there's always *something* you can do. Like sit in front of a bar waiting for Karen to come out. Somehow, this has to be useful.

When Karen finally does leave the bar, Ivy follows her again. All the way to her house on Nightingale Lane. Ivy passes by as Karen pulls into the carport, and she keeps going, wondering where to head next.

Not home. That will just make her mind spin again.

She could call Heath, but he would just try to get into her

head again about Wes. This would become another reason for him to try and convince her that Wes isn't worth it. Heath has no idea what Wes is doing for her right now, that he's in jail but it should be her. He probably wouldn't believe it if she told him.

Ivy turns up the music and keeps driving, circling her way back to the police station, because there's nowhere else she can think to go.

When her phone rings, she almost hits the curb trying to answer it.

Wes.

No hello. No greeting. She doesn't bother.

'Where are you?'

'Home,' he says. 'I just got home.'

62

Wes never hears Ivy knock, because she doesn't. She flies into his house and runs straight for the living room.

'Here,' he calls out from the kitchen. The first thing he did when he returned home was eat. He has just finished putting his dishes in the sink when she barrels through his door. The house is still a mess; he hasn't bothered putting it back in order yet.

Ivy appears in the doorway, her clothes disheveled, her hair wild. She runs to him, throwing her arms around his neck. He hugs her back, his shoulders relaxing for the first time since being arrested.

'I'm sorry about Vegas,' he says.

'Forget Vegas. How are you? What happened?'

He starts to tell her about the bail, which was high enough that he needed to put up his house as collateral to get out. Until he was arrested, he never realized how many things it would ruin. His career. His finances. His reputation.

And he wasn't even driving the damn car. She was.

'If not for the bail,' he says, 'I would've been out hours ago, but my lawyer had to arrange everything and get the bond and –'

'What's that?' Ivy is pointing at his ankle.

'That's the other part of my release,' he says. 'I have to wear an ankle monitor.'

'You're joking.'

'Clearly not.' Wes sighs and sits back down at the table. The number of problems that have piled up today is just starting to hit him. 'I can only go to work and home. Except I lost my job.'

'They *fired* you?'

'Technically, an unpaid leave of absence. For now. The message was waiting for me when I got out.'

'Bastards.' Ivy pulls a bottle of whiskey out of the cupboard. She pours two glasses, adds ice, and returns to the table. 'They're just cowards. You'll find a better job.'

Someday, maybe. But he won't be able to look for a job at all until the ankle monitor is off. And he can move out of this town.

Ivy wraps her arms around him again, except this time it feels more desperate. Even she can't spin his newfound fame as a murder suspect into anything good. Ivy leads him into the living room, and they get settled on the couch. More comfortable but not exactly comforting.

Ivy stands and picks up a bit, stacking things on the floor in the corner.

'My lawyer said reporters might show up here,' he says.

'Screw them.'

He tries to smile but fails. 'Seriously, you might want to go.'

'Come stay with me.'

'Can't.' He points to the ankle monitor. 'Not allowed.'

Ivy leans over and inspects it, touching his leg as she turns to see it from every angle. 'Doesn't look hard to remove.'

'It's not. But they would know. It has a tampering sensor.'

She flops back on the couch with a sigh. 'Tech really pisses me off sometimes. Our world is way too advanced.'

He can't even dig up an answer for that. It would take too much energy. But she seems to have enough for both of them.

'What did your lawyer say?' she says.

Bryce told him not much will happen until next week, when he'll meet with the assistant DA on the case.

Discovery on the case won't officially happen for a while, but he hopes to get some details about the evidence they have against Wes and find out if they're willing to make a deal. Nobody wants an expensive trial for a seven-year-old case.

'A deal?' Ivy says. 'You can't plead guilty to anything. You didn't *do* anything.'

He knew Ivy was going to say something like that. He also knows that she isn't thinking it through.

'We just have to wait and see what they have,' he says.

Wes leans his head back and closes his eyes. Every time he stops thinking about one problem, another pops up. Losing his job means losing his income, and he won't be able to work again until this is over. On top of everything else, he also has to worry about how he'll pay for everything while he waits for the trial. Or the plea deal.

He has to pay his lawyer. And for the ankle monitor. That bill is coming straight to him. Otherwise, he wouldn't be out of jail at all.

'I could tell them the truth,' Ivy says. 'They have no idea what really happened –'

'No.'

'I'm not going to let you go to prison for something you didn't even –'

'Please,' he says. 'Let's just wait until I talk to my lawyer.'

'No matter what, I'm not testifying against you.' She leans over and kisses him on the cheek. 'Never going to happen.'

He knows that she believes that. He also knows it's unlikely his case will ever get that far. Not if he can stop it.

Ivy does her best. Wes has to give her that. She does everything she can to distract him from his growing list of problems. She's staying with him over the weekend. She cleaned everything up from the search, stocked his house with groceries, and bought him another phone. Even did his laundry. She had never done that before.

He appreciates it. He really does. Because this would be a lot harder if she wasn't here. It's not like any of his friends are calling. Everyone from Siphon has abandoned him; they aren't checking on him and they certainly aren't stopping by. It's the same thing he did to Bianca after that whole tragedy. He had done nothing – never reached out to her, never offered support.

But on Saturday night, he's had enough.

All he wants to do is have a few beers and watch the Warriors game. A couple hours to forget everything. Ivy sits down next to him and works on a crossword puzzle, which is fine until she also starts one of her most annoying habits.

'Can you stop that?' he says.

'Stop what?'

'That.' He nods to the ballpoint pen in her hand. 'The clicking.'

'Oh. Sorry.'

Five minutes later, she's right back at it as she stares at the puzzle.

'Ivy,' he says. 'Please stop. It's right in my ear.'

'Sorry. I didn't even realize I was doing it.'

She gets up and moves to the far end of the couch. She sits sideways, facing him with her feet on the couch, elbow on the armrest, and her hand up holding the pen. It isn't long before the clicking restarts. Sounds even louder this time, too.

Wes picks up a throw pillow and tosses it at her hand. Knocks the pen right out of it.

Her jaw drops. 'I can't believe you just did that.'

'I can't believe you didn't stop clicking.'

She extends her leg, pushing it against his. Not hard, but it's enough to make him grab her ankles. To tickle her feet.

'Don't, don't, don't,' she squeals. 'Please, I'm serious – don't.'

'Do you promise to stop?'

'Promise. Cross my heart and hope to die.'

'Stick a needle in your eye?' he says.

'Definitely.'

He lets go of her feet. 'Use a pencil.'

'Never.' Ivy picks up the pen and settles back into her seat.

Wes goes back to watching the game, but he half listens for that pen. He knows she is going to do it again, probably on purpose. He keeps one hand on her ankle and one eye on her.

She repeatedly glances over at him, flashing him an innocent smile, holding up the pen.

'I'm not clicking,' she says.

'Good,' he says. 'I'm glad you have at least a bit of self-control.'

Soon, she is clicking.

He holds up her foot, threatening to tickle it.

She looks at him, head cocked to the side, and she stops clicking. Not only that, but she throws the pen across the room, followed by the crossword puzzle. The opposite of what he thought she'd do. Wes was sure she would continue clicking, continue annoying him, because that's what she always does. Instead, she had given up.

Ivy doesn't give up.

He spends the rest of the evening trying to decide if it made him happy that she was trying to be kind, or if it made him even more upset because she was acting different. Not in a good way, either.

63

Sunday morning, Ivy makes brunch. She goes overboard, as she does with everything. Eggs Benedict with turkey slices, and thick pieces of toast to mop up the hollandaise sauce. Freshly squeezed orange juice. Even her coffee is better, stronger – just the way he likes it.

She keeps the TV on ESPN, avoiding all the local stations. Still, Wes has seen the coverage. He checks it on his phone when she isn't looking.

Great. Everything she does is great. And it's getting a little disturbing.

'This is great,' he says, eating all the food he can, just short of making himself sick. 'Thank you.'

Ivy smiles, looking proud of herself, and pats his hand. It's supposed to be reassuring, but it feels patronizing.

She clears her throat, which reminds him of Siphon's CEO, the way he always did the same thing. Wes never thought he would miss that, but he does.

'I've been thinking,' she says. 'We may not be able to go to Vegas, but we can still get married.'

He laughs a little. 'How would we do that?'

'Right here,' she says, gesturing to his house. 'We can bring in someone to perform the ceremony.'

Standing in his living room, saying those sacred vows, sounds like the saddest, most pathetic wedding they could have. Ivy would try to make it nice, of course. She would decorate with flowers and all sorts of wedding stuff. It would still be horrible.

But the fact that she is willing to do it means something. He just isn't sure what.

'You'd really do that? Get married here?' he says.

'Of course I would. We can always do it again later, after all this is over.'

She puts her hand on his cheek. He hasn't shaved all weekend and the stubble is getting thick, so maybe he will grow that beard.

Or maybe not.

For once, Ivy couldn't wait to get to work on Monday morning. Couldn't wait to get out of Wes's house. Not because of him. Not exactly. He's depressed and upset and all the things he should be, given what's happening. She has tried to stay positive, keep his spirits up, help him do all the things he can't because of the ankle monitor. At the same time, she shoves aside her own worries, trying not to let them show. And she does it all while thinking about how to make a wedding at his house better than terrible.

Then there's the guilt. Wes is adamant about Ivy keeping her mouth shut, at least for now. Until they know what kind of evidence the police have. He keeps saying that if she confesses, it will make everything worse.

Ivy is not convinced he's right. He doesn't know how much worse it has already gotten.

After Joey died, she couldn't drive at night without thinking about him. Or without having a panic attack. Her heart pounded so hard it would make her dizzy. More than once, she had to pull over and calm down before she could get back on the road. Because of this, she was late a lot.

Wes blamed it on her lack of time management. She let him.

It was easier than admitting the real reason: Ivy thought they'd made a mistake. No. She *knew* they'd made a mistake not calling the police. She should've confessed what she'd done on the night it happened, but she's never been willing to say that out loud. Not with Wes, and definitely not with a therapist.

To this day, she hates driving at night. The panic attacks have subsided, but the memory of them lingers. Like her brain is constantly on alert, waiting for it to happen again.

Ivy sits back in her desk chair, covering her face with her hands. Everything about this is exhausting. As it should be. And she deserves it. She wasn't the one killed in that crash.

Unfortunately, punishing herself hasn't made anything better. Maybe confessing would, but Wes told her – *begged* her – not to do it.

Work was supposed to give her a break, a chance to decompress and think about something else. Hasn't worked out that way so far.

And she can't help but check the coverage about the case. Obsessively, in fact. She pulls up the website for the local newspaper, where they've reprinted the original story about Joey's death. Another article is about Wes's arrest, and it mostly sticks to the facts.

A 30-year-old Fair Valley man, Wes Michael Harmon, has been charged with vehicular homicide in connection with the death of Joey Fisher in a hit-and-run accident in 2015. Mr Harmon has worked in sales for Siphon, Inc., for seven years and has no history of criminal behavior.

Ivy couldn't argue with any of it. The facts were clear. She checks another local news site, and the headline is like a punch to her stomach.

EXCLUSIVE: Interview with the detective who may have solved a 7-year-old case

Karen Colglazier.

Her picture is right next to the article. Karen stands in front of the police station, the sign visible in the background, and she is smiling. Ivy's inner pettiness comes out before she can stop it.

That outfit is heinous and doesn't even fit well.

Needs to bleach those yellowing teeth.

Has she ever heard of YouTube? That makeup.

Once she is done mentally shredding the way Karen looks, Ivy settles down to read the interview. That's one good thing: The interview isn't on video. At least she doesn't have to watch Karen.

The article starts with Karen's background, how long she has been a detective, blah, blah, blah. Ivy skips past it.

Let's start at the beginning. How did you come to investigate a seven-year-old case?

I was working on another case, one that was quite recent, and it led me back to Joey Fisher. Wes Harmon ended up being the link between the two. He hasn't been charged in the second case, but we're still looking into it.

So there may be additional charges coming for Wes Harmon?

I can't comment on that.

When did you know he was the number one suspect?

Obviously, I can't talk about specific evidence in this case, as it remains ongoing. But in general, detectives have to be very careful not to speculate or make assumptions about who committed a crime. Our job is to follow the evidence, which is exactly what I did.

You said you can't talk about specific evidence, but can you tell us anything about why or how Wes Harmon became your leading suspect?

Joey Fisher died in his car, which was parked on a quiet street. There weren't many vehicles driving in the area, which we already knew. In general, the timeline of events is crucial to police work. What happened before and after. You never know what will be important. The smallest, most inconsequential thing might end up being the missing piece of the puzzle. That's where witnesses come in. Sometimes a person can see something and not even realize it was important.

Witnesses. There may have been someone from the club who saw their argument, but there weren't any witnesses to the accident. If there were, Ivy would've been the one arrested.

Karen has to be lying. Again.

64

Wes doesn't bother getting out of bed early in the morning anymore. No alarm set, and he doesn't budge when Ivy gets up. Not even if he is awake, which he has been, and he feels a little guilty about it. For the past five days, Wes hasn't seen anyone but her. All day, every day, except when she's at work.

It's been a lot.

When he is alone, he tries to remind himself he is lucky to have her. No one from his family lives nearby, and his friends and colleagues are nowhere. She's the only one by his side. And right now, it's not a bad idea to keep her extra-close.

But he still waits to get up until after she's gone. And he still thinks about the way she threw that pen across the room.

Today, he will finally get to see someone else. His lawyer. Bryce is coming to the house right after meeting with the assistant DA. Wes prepares for it like a real business meeting, making fresh coffee and putting out snacks, like they do at Siphon. He wears slacks, a dress shirt and tie, even shines his shoes. But he hesitates when it comes to shaving. The stubble looks better now, resembling something that was on purpose instead of the sparse two-or-three-day growth he had after the weekend. By the time the doorbell rings, he still hasn't done it. Not so much a decision to grow a beard as a decision not to shave. Which is different than doing it because Ivy said beards are sexy.

Petty, he knows. But pettiness is about all he has left.

He straightens his tie and opens the front door. Bryce stands on his porch, looking like Santa Claus in an expensive suit.

'Good to see there aren't any reporters out there,' he says, stepping inside. 'You haven't talked to any, have you?'

'Of course not.'

As they get settled in the living room, Wes thinks about the minutes ticking away, running up the next bill from Bryce. Almost worth it to see another human being.

'The meeting went about as well as can be expected,' Bryce says. 'Jocelyn Hughes is an excellent prosecutor, though it doesn't sound like they want a drawn-out trial for this. They're going to push for a plea deal.'

'And that would mean?'

'Prison time. The only question is how much. They don't want to give you probation for killing someone.'

Hearing his lawyer say that makes it feel more real. 'Did she tell you what kind of evidence they have?'

'She told me a few things,' Bryce says. He pauses to take a legal pad out of his briefcase. 'Right before the accident, you were seen at the Fine Line gentlemen's club.'

Wes nodded. He expected that.

'There's some evidence that you had a fight with Ivy in the parking lot of the club,' Bryce says.

'What evidence?'

'She didn't give me details. From what I gathered, they're going to allege that you and Ivy were arguing in the car, and that's when the accident happened.'

Yes. Except they had switched places.

'As for the accident itself,' Bryce says, 'they have pictures of all the cars that passed close by within that time frame.'

This is a surprise. After learning about Joey's death, Wes had checked for cameras in the area. There weren't any traffic cams that he could see, but who knows how many businesses had them.

'In addition,' Bryce says, 'they brought in an expert on car

289

crashes to analyze the damage and assess what kind of car could have caused it.'

'They can do that?'

'I haven't seen the analysis. This is just what Jocelyn said.'

'Anything else?' Wes asks.

Bryce nods, flipping to another page in his notebook. 'The 4Runner.'

'What about it?'

'Jocelyn claims they have evidence that can prove the car may not have been stolen.'

Wes works that sentence through his mind, turning it over a few times to make sure he understands what Bryce is saying. His first thought is someone from his old apartment building, someone claiming to see their damaged car after it supposedly disappeared. It seems incredibly unlikely that anyone would recall a thing like that from seven years ago.

Or maybe a camera caught Ivy driving the car when she was getting rid of it. Then again, who keeps footage for that long?

Wes covers his face with his hands, physically hiding from all that Bryce has told him. It sounds so much worse than he imagined.

'There's more,' Bryce says.

Jesus Christ.

'Go ahead,' Wes says. His voice sounds muffled through his hands.

'Jocelyn said there's a witness who heard you arguing with Ivy about the accident,' Bryce says.

Not possible. He and Ivy haven't talked about that night in years, much less fought about it.

'You aren't going to like this idea,' Bryce says, 'but given the incident at the club just before it happened, there's someone else who could've been behind the wheel.'

'Ivy.'

Wes knew this was coming. Of course Bryce wants to present an alternative, someone else who could have committed the crime. It's the most obvious defense strategy – a couple of true-crime documentaries are enough to teach anyone that – but Wes didn't expect it to come up this fast.

Also, it's the truth.

'Let's say, for example,' Wes says, 'Ivy goes to the police and says she was the one driving the car. What happens?'

'Two possibilities. First, they don't believe her, perhaps because they have some evidence to prove, or strongly suggest, that you were the driver.'

'And the second?'

'They do believe her. This case has gotten a lot of publicity, though. And if there's one thing the police hate, it's being embarrassed. You both would be charged for leaving the scene of the accident, and for covering it up. Most likely, she would be charged with vehicular homicide instead of you.'

Exactly what he thought. They would both end up in prison, but he would spend less time there.

65

Heath is in the far corner of the café, away from everyone else. Ivy waves and stops at the counter to grab a sandwich and a drink before joining him. It's the first time she has left the office for lunch in weeks, but it had to be done. No more drinks after work for her. She goes straight back to Wes.

Heath is wearing casual clothes today – a rugby shirt and khaki shorts – and he hasn't shaved. The stubble doesn't look as good on him as it does on Wes. As she sits down, she almost asks if he's growing a beard. She stops after seeing the look on his face.

He's angry.

'Thanks for finally calling me back,' he says.

Ivy unwraps her lunch and twists the cap off her flavored water. Heath has been blowing up her phone with calls and texts since Wes was arrested. She hasn't read half of them. 'I've been a little busy,' she says.

'I imagine trying to save Wes takes up a lot of time.'

'He didn't do this,' she says.

Heath takes a bite of his sandwich.

'Look,' Ivy says, 'I know you hate Wes.'

'I never said I hated him.'

'This isn't like we had a fight. This is something that could put him in prison for a long time. Maybe forever.' Her voice catches on that last word.

'I get that.' Heath's tone is softer now. He reaches over, touching her arm. 'After ten years, of course you're worried about him.'

'Yes, I am.'

'My focus is on you. I don't want to see you get destroyed alongside him.'

Heath wouldn't be saying that if he knew the real story. He would know Wes is protecting her, not the other way around.

Then again, this is Heath. Even if he did know, he wouldn't give Wes any credit for it.

'So what's it going to be today?' she says. 'I should break up with him, ignore him, not try to help? He's toxic, he's horrible, he's ruining my life, I should find someone nicer, calmer, not as volatile, so I can be in a healthy, functional relationship?' Ivy pauses to take a sip of water. 'Do I have that right?'

She has heard it all. Every insult, every judgment. There was a time they made it a game, when Heath would give her a reason why she should leave Wes – for good – and she would counter with a reason why she shouldn't. She always won.

That was all in fun, though. This is not.

Heath looks shocked at her outburst. He shouldn't be. After knowing her for so many years, he should know exactly what she's like. She can be more volatile than Wes.

'Ivy, I'm just trying to be a friend,' he says.

'Wes basically lost his job. He can't leave his house because he has an ankle monitor. He's spending every penny he has on a lawyer. His entire life is falling apart, and he hasn't been convicted of anything. So, please, if you asked me here to talk about how terrible he is, don't. Just don't.'

'I didn't,' he says. 'I invited you to lunch to see how *you're* doing.'

'I'm great. Compared to Wes, I'm perfect.'

She takes a big bite of her sandwich, though she isn't hungry at all. She just doesn't want to talk anymore.

*

Wes doesn't come up again during their short lunch. Ivy asks Heath about his life, to keep herself distracted. It doesn't help, though. When she walks out of the café, she takes a big gulp of fresh air like she's been underwater for the past half hour.

She knew this would be hard; she just didn't realize how hard. Her body aches, because she is tensed up all the time. Her head hurts from thinking about it, and from obsessively scrolling through the news, looking for the latest. Like she does right now.

Nothing new has been released – or leaked – by the DA's office, and Wes's lawyer isn't saying a word. This may be the only good thing that happens today. She'll take it.

When she gets back to her office, she texts Wes to see how the meeting with his lawyer went. It was supposed to start at eleven o'clock. Now it's after one, and he hasn't contacted her.

Hey, how did it go today?

His answer comes in a few minutes: **We'll talk about it later.**

Not encouraging.

When she leaves work and heads to his place, she tries to brace herself for whatever is coming. At least there aren't any reporters outside.

She unlocks the front door. After all this time, she finally has a key to his house and it doesn't feel like a victory.

The air inside feels heavy, weighted down with something she can't see. She finds Wes sitting on the couch. Nothing in his hands – no phone or book or anything else. The TV is off.

Wes is staring at the wall. She sits down next to him and takes his hand in hers. 'Tell me,' she says.

He shakes his head once and looks at the floor. Then he starts to cry.

66

Karen's sergeant is not happy. She can tell by the way his left eye twitches. He's upset about the interview she gave to the local paper, which isn't a surprise. Her sergeant has always been a surly little man with one hell of a mean streak. Borderline sadistic, in her opinion. She forces herself to look right at him, hoping her nerves don't show. He called her into his office specifically to talk about the interview.

Karen reminds herself that she's the one who figured out who killed Joey Fisher. He can't take that away from her, and he can't fire her without a public relations nightmare, because the media would speculate it's about the case. Everything would be thrown into chaos, tainting the potential jury pool, and he knows it. She repeats this in her mind, over and over, trying to stay calm.

'I'm so disappointed,' he says. 'You know better than to talk to the press.'

She nods. 'I won't do it again.'

He taps a pen against his desk, like he's thinking. Hopefully, about Joey Fisher.

'See that you don't,' he says. 'I'll be watching.'

Meeting over.

Karen holds her head high as she walks back to her desk, where a message from the ADA is waiting. She likes Jocelyn; she really does. Smart, determined, capable. She is someone Karen looks forward to working with more in the future.

She returns Jocelyn's call, answering a few questions about items found during the searches at Siphon and Wes's house.

No one had been able to get into his laptop yet, something that irritates everybody, and Jocelyn is still working on the phone provider. Wes has fingerprint security on his cell, and they haven't been able to access a thing there, either.

'Do you think you'll need the electronic records?' Karen says. 'It seems like there's *so much* evidence against him.'

'More is better,' Jocelyn says. 'The video from your crash expert will be compelling to a jury, but the witness may be what pushes Wes into taking a deal.'

The witness.

Pure luck. Even Karen couldn't deny that, because she never saw it coming.

'I gave you the taxi records,' Karen says. 'Ivy took a cab to work that night. Wes had the car.'

'Yes, I have that.'

'And the memorial fund?'

'I have someone looking into Wes's finances to confirm that,' Jocelyn says. 'We haven't found anything to indicate he actually donated.'

Bianca is the one who gave Karen that information. She had been in Wes's office one day and happened to see the Joey Fisher memorial fund pulled up on his computer. Looking up Joey's fund, or donating to it, doesn't mean Wes killed him. Still helpful, though. It was yet another link between the two, and combined with everything else, it's one more piece of the puzzle.

Karen isn't surprised, either. Wes works in finance. He's exactly the kind of guy who would try to buy his way out of guilt.

She knew from the start that connecting with Bianca was a good idea. Karen learned early in her career that assistants can be your best friend or your worst enemy. They know everything.

Bianca certainly does. The memorial fund wasn't the only thing she found.

Wes finally calms down enough to tell Ivy what his lawyer said. Every bad thing, because nothing Bryce said was good. Ivy is silent throughout, which means she knows it, too.

'This witness,' she says. 'When did we ever argue about the accident? And in public? We never even talked about it.'

'I know.'

He has been racking his brain, trying to figure it out. They have argued so many times and in so many places, but he can't think of a single time they fought about that night. Or who would have heard them.

'My lawyer said the police lie all the time,' Ivy says.

'But this isn't the police. Bryce met with someone from the DA's office. Wouldn't they get disbarred for that?'

'I have no idea.'

Wes makes a mental note to ask his lawyer about it. Bryce had said it would be difficult to get more information about the witness – at least until the full list is handed over, and that could be a while. The trial isn't scheduled for another three months.

His money won't last that long. Wes has avoided adding up the real numbers, but he knows he can't afford three months without a paycheck.

'If it's true,' he says, 'I may have to consider a deal.'

'No.'

'If Bryce can get something without prison time, probation, or community service.'

Wes is lying. Bryce had said the opposite. But he isn't going to tell Ivy how bad a deal would be.

'For killing a teenager? Not going to happen.' Ivy stands up and starts pacing around the living room. Her hands are balled up into fists, her movements sharp and fast. Wes can feel her anger.

Earlier in the day, he was angry like that. He wanted to punch something, kick his foot through the wall, or scream until he lost his voice. But he can't afford to lose it now.

'You can't take a deal,' she says.

'Ivy –'

'I'll confess before that happens.'

'You can't,' he says. 'Then we'll both go to prison.' He relays what Bryce said, watching her frown become more pronounced the longer he talks.

She says nothing. If there is a way out of this, he can't see it, either.

They talk it to death, arguing over the possibilities, throwing out legal theories that may or may not be based in reality. When his brain gets to the point where he can't even form sentences, they finally go to bed. Both collapse into it like they just ran a marathon.

He stays awake, waiting a few minutes before rolling over to whisper in her ear. 'I promise I'll take care of this. Just don't say anything.'

She doesn't move. But she is awake.

He knows that, has always known that, all the way back to the first time he whispered in her ear, so many years ago. She is not that good at playing possum.

But it gives him a chance to tell her exactly what she wants to hear. Or what he wants her to know.

67

Ivy sighs and picks up her phone.

Turns out, it's not easy to marry someone who is confined to his home. In California, both people have to appear in person at one of the county offices. There is an exception for those who are in the military in an active-service area, but no exception for people with ankle monitors.

Another call to her lawyer. Might as well. If Wes is going to go bankrupt, she will be right there with him.

Stan says a lot of things she doesn't understand, but she does get that he will check with the county and see if there's any way Wes can submit his paperwork with a notarized letter from his lawyer. Maybe that will work, Stan says.

Maybe.

The police know where Wes is every second of the day, thanks to technology, but a marriage license needs a lawyer negotiating with city hall.

Yúchǔn.

Stupid. Why everything is so stupid is beyond her.

She skips her Chinese lesson. It's been a waste of time this week anyway. Ivy can't concentrate on learning a language; she's too busy planning a wedding. Her entire afternoon is spent staring at pictures on the internet, trying to decide if all the inexpensive decorations look good or just cheap. She spends the rest of the day attempting to figure it out.

*

Ivy doesn't see the lights until she turns the corner. Red and blue, a blanket of police cars, and they're all in front of Wes's house.

She hits the gas, driving as close as she can before slamming on the brakes hard enough to make the tires squeal. Ivy gets out and bolts toward the house. Her heart thumps and she runs in sync with it right up until she is stopped by two uniformed cops.

'You can't go in there,' one says.

'I live here,' she says. An exaggeration, and a necessary one.

One of the cops is a pasty white man with a nose that's clearly been broken a few times. He looks at her and then at his partner, a woman with sleek hair and dark skin. While they exchange silent words, Ivy tries to see behind them. The front door is open, and a few people are standing on the porch.

Karen is one of them.

'What happened?' Ivy says. 'Can you at least tell me that?'

Again the cops look at each other. Ivy takes the opportunity to dart around them, toward Karen. A flood of possibilities run through her mind, and they're jumbled together in a horrific montage. Someone might have broken into the house and hurt Wes. Someone related to Joey. Or a psycho that read about his arrest and became a vigilante.

Or he might have hurt himself. She pictures him hanging from the curtain rod, lying in a bathtub, or with a gun. He doesn't even own a gun, but that doesn't stop her from picturing it.

A hand grabs her arm from behind. The cop with the broken nose. His partner grabs her other arm, and she tries to pull away but can't. There's no way to get out of the hold. She looks up at Karen.

'Ivy,' she says.

'Where is he?'

'I was just about to ask you the same question.'

Gone.

Wes is *gone*.

Karen says it three times, and Ivy still can't process the words. Finally, Karen leads her to the living room. The ankle monitor is on the floor, with a jagged edge where it was cut off.

'We knew immediately the monitor had been tampered with,' Karen says. 'But by the time we arrived, he was already gone.'

Ivy shakes her head, still not getting it. He never said a word to her about running. Never gave her a clue.

'As far as we can tell, he didn't take anything with him,' Karen says. 'He didn't take his car, either.'

Ivy's brain refuses to accept what is right in front of her. That Wes ran, jumped bail, and vanished. The mental wall eventually breaks down, brick by brick, and a flood of new questions come to mind: How long had he been planning this? Did he know from the start, or was it a last-minute decision? Why didn't he tell her?

Most importantly: Where did he go?

She doesn't have any idea.

'You didn't know.' Karen is staring at her, an intense look that makes Ivy feel like the detective can see right into her head.

'No.'

'We already sent a patrol car to your house,' she says. 'It's sitting out front in case Wes shows up.'

Ivy didn't even think of that. Wes wouldn't be stupid enough to go from his place to hers.

'Can you do us a favor?' Karen says.

'What?'

'Would you mind looking around?' she says. 'In case anything seems odd or if anything is missing?'

Like she would tell Karen if it was. Still, the task is welcome because it keeps her focused on small things. His clothes, toiletries, and earbuds. Everything is right where it usually is, as if he walked out the door with only the clothes on his back.

Or was forced out.

The more she thinks about that, the bigger the idea grows. Someone must have done this to him. He didn't really cut off the monitor and go on the run without telling her. That makes more sense to her. And, in a strange way, it hurts a little less.

Until she realizes it isn't true. A few of his things *are* missing. His backpack – the one he uses when they go hiking – is no longer on the hook in the closet. The prepaid phone she bought for him isn't on the nightstand, and neither is the charger.

The bathroom throws her off, because his toothbrush and deodorant are still there. But once she looks closer, she realizes his travel kit is gone. She doesn't mention any of this to the police.

'Ivy.'

Not Karen. Ivy turns to see a large man with white hair and a bushy beard. He introduces himself as Wes's lawyer, Bryce Kendrick.

'I'm sorry we had to meet under these circumstances,' he says.

She pushes back the feeling of being overwhelmed. What she wants to do is scream. Instead, she nods her head.

'If you happen to know anything, please let us know,' he says. 'The best thing for Wes is to come home now, before this goes any further.'

Ivy throws her hands up. Everybody expects she knows what the hell Wes is doing, but she doesn't.

Karen stands right behind Bryce – always hovering, always there. 'Our first priority is his safety,' she says. 'If you know anything that can help, please tell us.'

Ivy wants to slap her. She wants to hit those lies right out of her mouth, before she has a chance to spit out another. As strong as that urge is, the knowledge that it would be a very, very bad choice is stronger.

'There's nothing,' Ivy says. 'I don't know anything.'

She starts to walk past them and out of the house. They aren't going to help. Not the police, not Bryce, not her own lawyer. And certainly not Karen. Wherever Wes is, or whatever he is up to, he had better contact her. She's all he has.

'Ivy,' Karen says.

She sighs. What now.

'We need to get into your place,' Karen says. 'To check inside.'

68

Karen watches Ivy leave, resisting the urge to reach out and give her a hug. The poor thing must feel completely overwhelmed. With fear, mostly. Fear of where Wes has gone. Fear that he'll never show up again. Fear that he *will* show up again.

When Karen let her walk around Wes's house, she was almost breaking protocol. Technically, it's not a crime scene, because Wes ran. He wasn't abducted; that's clear even to a rookie. But typically, the police wouldn't ask a significant other to walk through the way Karen did.

She had hoped Ivy would finally talk to her, tell her the truth about Wes. But Ivy's not ready. Even after all he's done, she is still hooked on him. Probably protecting him, too.

In truth, Karen would've done the same thing. For a long time.

With nothing left to do at Wes's house, Karen heads out to her car. She pulls up the Check This app and tries to start a new to-do list, beginning with the most important thing: Get a warrant for Ivy's phone, if possible. And her email.

As soon as she gets back to the station, Karen calls Jocelyn about both. Halfway through leaving a message, a call comes in from the cop who followed Ivy to her apartment.

'No sign of him,' he says. 'Not inside or out.'

'She let you search her place?'

'Yes. Every single room. I even checked the closets. No indication the door or the locks have been tampered with or that anyone has been inside.'

'The toilet seat,' Karen says. 'Did you check that?'

'It's down.'

How disappointing. But even if Wes hasn't contacted Ivy yet, he will.

'One more thing,' the cop says. 'He has a new phone. A burner.'

'How do you —'

'Found the packaging in the trash outside his place.'

Karen sighs, wondering what else could go wrong today. Yes, it's possible to get a tap on a prepaid, but first they would need the phone number.

Once the cop leaves her place and she's alone, Ivy sits down. Her phone is blowing up again, with calls and texts from friends – including Heath – who have obviously heard about Wes. It must be on the news by now.

Her mind has been spinning since discovering Wes had gone AWOL.

She knows Wes. That's the best place to start: with the knowledge she has. Ivy knows his faults, knows his weaknesses, knows exactly how to get under his skin when she wants to. For Wes to do this, he must have had a plan. A reason. Something he wants to accomplish beyond just escaping. He wouldn't run just to run, at least not now, before the trial is even set to begin. There must be something he wants to do, because Wes always has a plan.

Unless he's angry. That's the one caveat. If he is mad, all bets are off and any plan can be ignored.

Which makes it even harder to know why he did this. He never said a word, didn't leave her a sign of any kind. Infuriating.

And a little bit disturbing. Because it makes Ivy wonder if he didn't say anything because he doesn't plan to contact her at all.

Gòule.

Enough.

That kind of thinking will only make it worse.

She has to focus on the case they have against him. The evidence. There must be more to it, something he didn't mention. Wes's lawyer isn't going to tell her anything. He probably couldn't even if he wanted to. Same with the ADA. The only other person she can think of is Karen.

Always back to Karen.

Karen isn't the first mutual enemy Ivy and Wes have had. There was a neighbor who was like a drill sergeant when it came to the garbage cans. Also an apartment manager who liked to check up on his tenants a bit too often. And the girl at the grocery store who hated them for no reason.

Then there was the lunch guy. He was the worst.

Ivy had been working at Amalgamated Services for about a month. This was a couple years after graduation. She was a step or two beyond entry-level but still pretty low on the corporate chain, and she didn't make enough money to buy lunch every day. She brought it from home and put it in the break room refrigerator.

Wes and Ivy were living together – for the second time – and one day, she came home from the grocery store with a bunch of packaged food. Energy bars, trail mix, and some candy. The only thing fresh was the fruit.

'What is happening here?' Wes asked.

'Someone's been stealing my lunch at work. I bought food I can keep at my desk.'

'Stealing your lunch? Like, everything? Even the containers?'

'Sometimes,' she said. 'Or they throw them in the trash.'

'What have you been eating?'

'Whatever I can get from the vending machine.'

She had reported it to HR, who put up a notice about not taking food that didn't belong to you. But the theft of Ivy's lunch continued, so she switched to the packaged food.

After a few days, she was grumpy. And hungry.

'I don't know what else to do,' she said. 'I can't sit in the break room all day to watch.'

But Wes could.

They prearranged a day she would bring her lunch and put it in the break room. Leftovers from the night before, like she used to bring and heat up in the microwave. Ivy wrote her name on the side, as she always did, and left it in the refrigerator.

Wes made an appointment to see someone at Amalgamated about investing through Siphon. Different department, not anyone Ivy knew, and not likely to be a successful call. But it got him in the building. He went to Ivy's break room and sat there with his laptop for two hours. That was all he had to do.

He texted her a picture of the person stealing her lunch. A man, about forty, with a bit of a paunch and sallow skin.

'Oh God,' she'd said. 'That's my manager.'

He had hired her. She reported to him. And he had been at his job for seven years. She hadn't even made it through her probationary period yet.

That evening, she came home to find Wes already there. He was sitting on the couch, wadding up scraps of paper and tossing them across the room, trying to hit the garbage can.

'I can't report him to HR,' she said, sitting down next to him. She picked up one of his paper basketballs and tossed it. Nothing but net.

'But you have proof,' he said. 'The picture.'

'I don't know how close he is to the HR manager. I can't risk it.'

Wes nodded. Tossed another ball of paper. It bounced off the edge and went into the can. 'Tomorrow, send me everything you know about him.'

'What are you going to do?'

'I'm going to take care of this.'

The next day, she texted Wes with the man's email, phone number, address, type of car, license plate, and social media accounts.

This is all I can get without asking too many questions.

Three days later, Wes told her to start bringing her lunch to work again.

'What did you –'

'I told you I'd take care of it. That's what I did.'

He refused to say more, wouldn't explain.

The next day, Ivy didn't see bruises on her manager, nor did he look injured. Wes wasn't the type to beat people up, though for a minute she was afraid that was exactly what he'd done. But the man seemed fine. Acted normal, even pleasant. And he stopped stealing her lunch.

Ivy still doesn't know how Wes did it. If he called or emailed her manager, maybe threatened him. Or maybe Wes blackmailed him with something. But he'd fixed it. Just like he said he would the other night, when he whispered in her ear.

She taps her nails against the coffee table. Stares at her phone. She should trust him, have faith that he knows what he's doing. But this isn't a stolen lunch.

And back then, Wes hadn't whispered in her ear the way he did last night.

I'll take care of this. Just don't say anything.

Not a comment or question, like he usually whispers. An order. One he gave when he thought she was asleep.

Unless he knew she wasn't.

Ivy jumps up, grabs her keys, and heads for the door. The last thing she's going to do is nothing.

69

Wes sits at the kitchen table, where he has a view of the driveway. The house is similar to his own, built in the '70s and about the same size. It's been updated throughout, the kitchen and bathrooms remodeled, and the hardwood floors have been refinished.

But the back door is the same. He broke one of the glass panes to get in.

Dusk comes, making everything outside look grey. Wes stands up and stretches a little. His entire body aches. It feels like all his muscles have been flexed since leaving his house.

He knows he shouldn't be here. He should be long gone by now.

The plan to run started the moment he was released from jail. In his mind, it was always an option. A backup, his press-in-case-of-emergency button. But he never thought it would come this soon.

Less than a week after being locked up in his house with no income, no job, and a lifetime of charges against him, he knew he wouldn't make it. By the time the trial came around, he would be living at Ivy's, his house in foreclosure, and probably with a public defender, because he wouldn't be able to pay Bryce.

He would never let that happen.

Even spending another night in his own house had become intolerable. His plan, if he could even call it that, was all he had to think about. And he had time to poke holes in it. A lot of them.

Fake ID, fake passport, new Social Security number.

No, no, and no. Wes didn't know anyone who can get them – not for any amount of money – and he wasn't about to blindly stumble around the dark web.

Cash. He has the money he had withdrawn to take to Vegas, which the police returned when he was released from jail. One thousand dollars. That, plus a ten, a five, and two ones.

Additional funds are the one part of this plan he knows something about. Finance. Banks. Money transfers. The problem was he didn't have much money to do anything with. Getting to his retirement account required paperwork and time, two things he didn't want to waste. His only option was cash withdrawals from his credit cards. The police would see it, probably right away, but then they'd have to find it.

He routed the money to a new bank account in the Cayman Islands. Easy enough to open online, but they would still be able to find it. Maybe even freeze it if the bank decided to be agreeable. So he transferred it again and again and again – as many times as he could, through a number of websites. PayPal. Online poker sites. Any place that would keep a cash account, all of them set up through his new phone. A pain, but it had to be done.

The police would find all of the transfers, but it would take a little time. That's all he needed. A few days to get out and get the cash. The current resting place for his money is an offshore account at an online casino, the kind of place that doesn't care who you are if you have money. No chance they're going to help police in the US. Not without a few interventions from the courts.

By then, it will be back in his hands. Hopefully.

Which left him with one last thing: getting out of town. No car, no way to get on a plane, bus, or train without being spotted on camera. What he does have is a mountain bike, which he used to get away from his house in the first place. He had no idea how quickly the police would be arriving after he cut off the ankle monitor. He jumped on it and rode across his backyard, then the one behind it, over to the next block. From there, it was a straight shot to the Bucket, a dive bar with lots of TVs and drinkers who mind their business.

Wes sat at a table, a baseball cap pulled down low, and ate a mediocre sandwich while nursing a beer. As soon as the news hit that he had disappeared, he left.

He was careful to avoid intersections with traffic cams, sticking to smaller side streets as he made his way across town to the one hiking trail in Fair Valley.

Chances are, they would search it. Eventually. But he was betting they would start with the people he knew. Ivy, his coworkers, and friends from college. He hasn't contacted any of them. Plus, he has been hiking for years. He knows how to hide.

The second stage of getting out was a rideshare app. He created a new account with a fake name and a blurry picture, along with an open request for anyone traveling east toward the Grand Canyon. A random location, because he had no idea where to go. He just needed to get out of this area and out of California.

Three responses came within a day. Wes chose a young guy who lived the van life and liked to 'smoke weed and vibe.' And, hopefully, not pay attention to the news.

The guy was leaving tonight on his trip. All he wanted was good company and help paying for gas along the way. They arranged to meet in the parking lot of the now-abandoned Rolling Hills Mall, where the guy had his van parked in a little community of road warriors.

That was it. His whole plan. Get out, get his money, figure out how to set himself up with a new life.

And then contact Ivy.

Of all the things he has to worry about, she is one of the biggest. Not because he really thinks Ivy will turn against him. He's had doubts, especially over the past few days. But when push comes to shove and everything gets real – which it is, very much so – Ivy has his back.

What she doesn't have is patience.

The decision to run came down to one thing: when. He had no doubt Ivy was going to confess at some point. Today, tomorrow, at his trial. It was inevitable. As much as she tries, Ivy can only control herself for so long.

Now that he's on the run, her confession would be useless. No one would believe it.

70

The escalation of Wes's plan came yesterday morning, when Bryce called with some additional news.

'My assistant knows a clerk in the DA's office,' he said. 'I have more information about that witness, though it sounds like rumors, so take it with a grain of salt.'

What Bryce had told him led to Wes sitting in this house.

He shouldn't be. Wes should be out on the hiking trail, avoiding detection until it's time to meet up with his ride-share, but he couldn't let this go. This isn't some random stranger. This is personal.

Darkness falls, which makes him tense up again. He watches the street and the driveway, not moving at all. Can't risk a trip to the bathroom now. He stays in the same place until he sees the headlights.

Wes gets up and goes into the family room, where he takes off his shoes and flattens himself against the wall. Behind him is the entryway. He listens to the front door open and close. The clink of keys as they hit the side table. No voices, which is the luckiest break he's had yet. He had been worried about guests.

Footsteps on the hardwood floor get louder as they move down the hall, toward him, and then they get softer.

The bedroom.

Perfect. No way out of that room without breaking the window.

He tiptoes down the hall, avoiding that one spot where the floor creaks. He had plenty of time today to discover anything that could give him away. Wes peeks around the corner, into the bedroom. The bathroom door is closed.

Wes moves over to the nightstand and picks up the cell phone. No landline in the house – he already checked.

He waits, standing in front of the doorway. A baseball bat leans against the doorframe next to him. He found it under the bed, hours ago, when he searched the whole place for weapons, and took it so it couldn't be used against him.

When Wes initially heard about the witness, his first instinct told him it was Heath. The obvious choice. Heath had never liked him, and he would definitely lie to put Wes in prison and away from Ivy. For years, it's pissed him off that Ivy can't see how toxic Heath is.

But the call from Bryce changed everything. The rumor, according to his assistant, was that they'd been overheard arguing about the accident, with Ivy blaming Wes for everything. And it all happened at Siphon, Inc.

Not Heath.

When she opens the bathroom door and sees him, she freezes. Not for long, though. And there's no surprise on that beautiful face.

They stare at each other, neither one moving, until he speaks. 'Abigail.'

Karen sits in yet another meeting with all of her superiors, along with the public information officer, Sierra. She's about thirty, a perpetually camera-ready woman that the reporters and viewers love. But she's tired of this.

'The police are still being blamed,' Sierra says. 'No matter how many times I say we have nothing to do with setting bail, or how easy it is to cut off that monitor, they're still blaming us.'

Captain William Doyle isn't happy with the coverage, either. 'I've spoken to the DA about issuing a statement.'

No one says anything, because no one believes the DA will ever issue a statement, much less make a comment. Why take the heat if you don't have to?

Doyle turns to Karen. Her sergeant wasn't the only one upset about the interview she gave to one of the local stations. Doyle had been, as well. Cart before the horse, he had said. Karen hadn't felt bad about making her sergeant angry, but she did feel bad about letting Doyle down.

'Are we *any* closer to finding Wes?' he asks.

No. Not at all. 'We have leads coming in from the tip line, and we're still chasing them down. But the reward has brought in a lot of false leads, as well.'

The money was a surprise to all of them. A local women's activist group is offering a $10,000 reward for anyone who provides information that leads to finding Wes Harmon. No one is happy about it. Money brings out the true-crimers, the opportunists, and the psychos. Rewards tend to clog up the tip line with nonsense.

'Where are we with the girlfriend?' Doyle asks.

Karen chooses her words carefully. 'I'm working on her. If Wes contacts anyone, it will be her.'

'Didn't they plan to get married last weekend?'

'They did. The DA is working on getting her phone records. Hopefully, it will –'

'He isn't going to call her,' Doyle says. 'He can't be that stupid.'

Probably not, but they have to go through the motions. Without stupid criminals, their arrest rate would be a lot lower.

'If he calls her, it'll probably be at work,' Karen says. 'There's no way for us to get access to those records quickly. But if I had to guess, he'll find another way. Maybe show up in person.'

'Or maybe they have prepaid phones,' Doyle says.

'We know he does. No confirmation about Ivy.'

Doyle flips through the pages in front of them. Wes's case file. Karen has been through it hundreds of times. 'What about his friends?' he asks.

'Most were colleagues. No one at Siphon is allowed to speak to us. The company directs everyone to their in-house counsel. He claims Wes hasn't contacted anyone there.'

'Of course he does.'

'What about other women?' the sergeant says. Back in his prime, he was a good-looking man. Now, not so much. But at one point, he probably had a lot of women. 'Was Wes seeing anyone on the side?'

Karen isn't ready to give a direct answer to that, in case it doesn't pan out. But maybe. 'I have one lead on that to track down,' she says. 'I'll let you know if I find anything.'

71

Abigail steps out of the bathroom. She wears yoga pants, a T-shirt, and sneakers, and her gym bag sits on the bed. It's the only thing between her and Wes. The irony doesn't escape him. Any other time, it might be funny.

'I tried calling you yesterday,' he says. 'A few times.'

She reaches up and casually adjusts her ponytail. 'That's weird. I didn't get any calls from you.'

'They weren't from my number.'

She waves her hand through the air, her long nails slicing through it. 'Then how would I have known?'

'You knew.'

She takes another step forward, and her eyes flick toward the door he's blocking. Her head turns a fraction of an inch as she looks toward the window.

'Not an option,' he says. 'You can't break it fast enough.'

Abigail shifts her weight, appearing to change her mind about trying to get out of the room. Her tone switches to something more friendly. 'Why don't you tell me why you're here?'

'Why don't you tell me why you talked to the police?'

Her eyes widen, becoming so large it reminds him of a cartoon. 'I had to.'

'You need to explain that.'

'They came to me,' she says.

Some truth in that, probably. Karen must have tracked her down; he had assumed as much. But she didn't have to talk. Didn't have to betray him.

Didn't have to lie.

Seven years of history between them. Seven years that included countless work problems, celebrations, holiday parties, a few personal conversations. And one night in bed.

Yes, they had told each other things, had confided in each other. He knew about a guy who broke her heart, and she knew about Ivy. Given their positions, the night they'd spent together was wrong. But if he put that aside, along with the uncomfortable days at the office afterward, they had been friends. Abigail wasn't a problem until she decided to become his biggest one.

'Let's go sit down and talk this through,' Abigail says. She gestures to the hall, toward the living room.

'You want to sit? Then sit.' He points to the bed. He grabs a chair from her vanity table, places it in front of the door, and takes a seat.

She perches herself on the edge of the bed, close to him, and crosses her legs.

'Before you were arrested, a detective came to see me,' Abigail says. 'She showed up late one night to talk about you. I played stupid, obviously. I didn't tell her anything about us.'

Wes narrows his eyes. He didn't mean to. It's a subconscious reaction to hearing her excuses.

'I'm not lying,' she says. 'After you were arrested, they came to Siphon with a warrant to search your office.'

He holds up a hand. 'Hold on. Didn't you skip a few steps? Maybe another conversation with the police?'

'Why would I do that?'

'Answering a question with a question is not inspiring my confidence.'

Her laugh sounds like a snort. 'Is that what they teach you in the sales training?'

Wes doesn't answer. She is still avoiding the question.

Abigail edges forward on the bed, getting a little closer to him. 'I don't understand what you think I did.'

'There's a witness who heard a fight between Ivy and me at Siphon. We had one argument at the office. Only you and Tanner were there,' he says. 'And Tanner's dead.'

'Sure, I told them about that. Karen asked if I'd ever seen you two argue, and I told her about the day Ivy lost her mind at the office.'

He winces a little at her description. Accurate, though. 'Except here's the problem,' he says, being careful not to admit or deny anything. 'Neither Ivy nor I ever brought up a car accident or Joey Fisher.'

Abigail doesn't react to that.

'But the witness claims we did,' he says.

'That wasn't me.'

'Here's the best part,' he says. 'The witness also said Ivy blamed me for the accident.'

She shrugs. 'And?'

'And it's wrong. Ivy wouldn't say that. Ever.'

Abigail looks confused, and he watches as she tries to work it through in her mind. It seems to take too long, like she's stalling for some other reason.

'So if it wasn't you that lied, who was it?' he says. 'You know everything that happens at Siphon.'

Before she can answer, the phone in his hand buzzes. Her phone. The name of the caller is surprising.

Bianca.

Abigail moves. She's so fast he doesn't realize what she's doing. By the time he lunges forward, trying to stop her, she has already reached into her gym bag and pulled something out.

A gun.

She stands up, pointing it at him, and she looks very pissed off.

Wes mentally kicks himself for coming to her house. He should have known better than to mess with Abigail. The gorgeous ones are always high-maintenance.

'Abigail, there's no need to –'

'You come into *my* house,' she says, 'and threaten *me*?'

'I never threatened –'

'You have a baseball bat.'

'That's yours,' he says. 'I took it so you couldn't use it on me. I didn't know you had a *gun*.'

'It's a dangerous world out there. A girl's got to protect herself.'

Wes takes a beat, then tries pleading with her. 'Abigail, I'm trying to figure out why you would lie to the police about me. I thought . . .' He lowers his hands a little, trying to appear nonthreatening. 'I thought we were cool. That we under-stood each other.'

She smiles. 'Did you, now?'

'If it wasn't you that lied to the police, then you must know who it was. You know everything that happens at Siphon.'

Her phone buzzes again. It's on the floor now, dropped when he moved toward her. Bianca has left a message.

'Is it her?' he says. 'Bianca?'

Abigail sighs. Her shoulders slump, and she looks exhausted. 'Oh, Wes. You are so stupid.'

Ivy sits in her car on Nightingale Lane, parked down the block from Karen's house. She wants to talk to Karen but isn't sure what to say. What she needs is a plan, but plans are Wes's thing, not hers. Ivy has other strengths, one of which stands out.

Shuōhuǎng.

Lying. She is exceptional at that.

While waiting for Karen to get home, Ivy invents a story in her head. She should've thought of this before. All Ivy needs to do is talk to her.

Not to confess, though. That may have been the right thing to do before, but now that Wes is gone all it would do is land her in jail. What Ivy needs to do now is tell Karen what she wants to hear. To pretend she is trying to help.

She'll say Wes contacted her. He called her at work on the main office line. That would make it impossible for the police to track down the number, since he has never called her office with his new phone. Ivy will say Wes refused to tell her where he is, only saying that he was far away from Fair Valley.

Wait, no. Ivy should give Karen a direction, a place she knows Wes won't go.

A list of possibilities runs through her mind until she realizes he could go anywhere except one place: Michigan.

Wes wouldn't go back home. He would shrivel up in shame if the police busted down his parents' door to look for him. He wouldn't go to his sister, either. Not yet, anyway. He knows the police will talk to her, the same way they talked to Ivy and everyone else he knows.

But she could say he's somewhere in the Upper Peninsula, a largely rural area he's familiar with, or at least she could claim he is, and he is hiding out in . . . a cabin. Yes. A hunting or fishing cabin – she isn't sure which. Not like he would give her the coordinates of it.

The questions will come next. Karen will ask why Ivy is coming to her with this information.

Ivy gets out of the car, stretching her legs and walking around the wooded green space next to where she'd parked. The pacing helps her think. It's dark, without many lights, so

Karen wouldn't be able to see her face if she drove down the street.

Ivy could pretend to be afraid. Fear is such a powerful, dangerous emotion. It would make her story more believable.

She loops around a tree, trying to work it out in her mind. Scared is good, but not scared of *Wes*, specifically. The fear of going to jail is better. She is giving Karen all this information because she doesn't want to be arrested for withholding it.

Also because Ivy has to think about herself.

Just in case.

In case Wes never contacts her. Because in reality she still hasn't heard anything from him. It's making her feel a little crazy.

A week ago, the idea that he would disappear forever was unfathomable. Now it's become a true possibility in her mind. The fact that he left so suddenly, so dramatically, has rattled her. The more time that passes without hearing from him has brought up a lot of doubts. About what he's doing, why he didn't say anything. Doubts about *him*. No matter how hard she tries to shove those thoughts aside, they keep popping up.

She can cover herself with this story, as well, by acting like she's on the fence about him and the fact that he ran. Which she is. And now that Wes has disappeared, there's no one else who really has her back. Not in the same way.

'Ivy?'

She whips around, startled at the voice. The male voice.

'I thought that was you,' he says. He takes a few steps forward, and his face becomes visible.

Milo.

72

Karen pulls over and parks but doesn't get out of the car. The radio blares out of her speakers, crackling a little, because one of them goes in and out. It's late for Sheldon Royce to be on the radio, but 'given all the local news lately,' he's added an after-hours version of his daily talk show, *The Loud Lounge*. It's a good description of his callers, because they all seem to shout.

What she wants to do is call in and explain how a case like this works, since none of the listeners seem to understand, but she restrains herself. The last thing she needs is another scolding from her sergeant and her captain. She is already on their radar and would prefer to get off it.

Karen stares at Abigail's house, wondering if she missed something. It was a little weird when Abigail called her a while back, claiming Ivy was the problem. Even weirder when she turned out to be a witness against Wes.

Had they been romantically involved? That's her first question. When Karen was with Ivy in the drugstore, Karen had implied that Wes and Abigail were involved. It didn't matter if it was true. Karen just wanted Ivy to think it was. But that was before Abigail came forward with evidence, and before Wes ran.

Does she know more? Her second question.

Wes's disappearance has changed everything. Can't put him in prison if he isn't here. The fact that he ran has made Karen rethink Abigail and what her part in this may be.

Has Wes contacted her? Or has she helped him?

The biggest questions, and the ones Abigail won't answer honestly. Not if she's involved.

Which is why Karen is still sitting in front of her house, trying to decide what to do next. Trying to figure out what Wes would do next.

So is everyone on the radio.

'Let's take predictions on how long it will take for the police to capture Wes Harmon. Call in with your guesses!'

Karen listens for a minute, hearing callers say everything from forty-eight hours to forty years.

She turns the radio off, but the silence makes things worse. Now all she can hear is her own thoughts.

After solving the Joey Fisher case – which should've been a highlight of her career – everything has imploded. Wes shouldn't have been out on bail, not even with an ankle monitor, and the judge is the one responsible for that disaster. Karen had no control over his decision about bail.

Which pisses Karen off even more. No matter how hard she works, there's always someone with more power, more influence, who can ruin everything. Sometimes it's the DA, when he decides not to prosecute. Other times it's her sergeant, when he takes her off one case to work on another. This time it's the judge.

After a minute of clenching and unclenching her fists, she starts her car. Talking to Abigail right now isn't a good idea. Not in this mood, not after this day. Questioning someone the wrong way can do more damage than not questioning them at all. And the last thing she wants to do is blow up the case against Wes by pissing off the most important witness they have.

Because Karen will find him and he'll go on trial. Eventually. He can't stay hidden forever.

Ivy stares at Milo, trying to understand what's happening.

'What are you doing here?' she says.

'Taking a walk.' He smiles. It looks more creepy than friendly. His eyes look wild, like he is on something. It isn't alcohol. 'I have a lot of time on my hands these days,' he says.

Ivy takes a step back, toward her car. 'Are you . . . are you following me?'

'As I was saying, I have a lot of time. *Why?* you might ask. Well, let me tell you. I have a lot of time because Clarissa moved out.'

'I'm sorry to hear that.'

'Are you? Do you even care what you've done?' It sounds like an accusation.

She tries not to show her anger at him for showing up in her life *again*. She also doesn't want to show how scared she is. She tells herself to act normal. Act like this isn't the most bizarre thing that's happened today. Because in truth, it isn't.

'Milo, I really am sorry about your relationship. If I had known posting a picture would lead to this, I wouldn't have done it. I told Clarissa we weren't involved, that nothing happened. And I never thought –'

'You never *thought*. That's the problem today. People don't think before they post on social media. They just take pictures and put them out there for the whole world to see, tagging whoever might give them some clout. Nobody stops to think about the ramifications. Nobody thinks about the people whose lives are affected by these posts.' Milo spits as he talks, practically foaming at the mouth. His rant sounds like it came from a think piece on the perils of the internet.

Ivy wants to tell him that if he hadn't cheated on Clarissa before, none of this would be happening. But her self-preservation instinct is stronger, keeping her mouth in check. Ivy wishes she had brought her phone with her. It's in the car.

She is only a couple feet away from it now.

'I agree – social media sucks,' she says.

'Yet you still use it.' Milo makes a face like he smells something horrible.

'I know, it's stupid. Anyway, I have to get going.'

She turns and reaches out for the door handle. Behind her, she hears Milo's footsteps moving closer.

73

Karen pulls up to her house and parks in the driveway. It's late, and this has been a long day. Unfortunately, not a productive one, because Wes is still missing. So frustrating to work countless hours on a case only to have it screwed up like this. Even if it isn't her fault.

She walks down to the mailbox, as she does every day, and retrieves the usual stack of bills. She still doesn't like to bank online. Something about it makes her uncomfortable. Maybe because she's seen too many people get in trouble due to their online activities. Karen has no social media presence at all. She won't even join LinkedIn. Another result of being a cop.

She also has to pick up the paper. Yes, the actual newspaper, which these days is no longer delivered first thing in the morning. It arrives at some random hour and rarely makes it to her doorstep. Sometimes, it's on the lawn; other times, on the sidewalk. Tonight, it's in the gutter. As she steps off the curb, her phone buzzes.

The lab.

It's late for them, though they've been working overtime like everyone else. She opens the email, expecting more bad news. Instead, a surprise.

The Läderach truffles.

When Ivy brought her those half-eaten truffles – the ones Wes had left when he was stalking her – Karen had sent them to the lab. She'd never expected them to do a DNA test. Those are expensive, reserved for the most serious crimes. Stalking usually doesn't apply.

She was wrong. They not only performed the test; they have the results. Karen opens the report and scrolls to the end to get to the point. She expects to see Wes's name.

Unknown.

Karen stands in the street, staring at the results, not under-standing this at all. They have Wes's DNA on file, and it should've shown as a match in the system. Must be a mis-take. Has to be.

She doesn't look up from her phone until she hears the car speeding down the street. It's coming right toward her.

By then, it's too late.

Ivy slams on the brakes.

An instinctual reaction, not one she thought about. It's something she did when she felt the impact. And saw some-one fly into the air after she hit them.

Ivy wasn't trying to hit anyone; she was trying to get away from that psycho, Milo. If he hadn't been out at a bar, talking to a woman who wasn't his fiancée and asking for her num-ber, this never would've happened. Milo thought he was going to get away with that, even after cheating before.

When he got caught, he did what men always do: blame the woman.

She looks back at the street.

A woman is lying in the middle of it. Despite the odd angle of her body, Ivy knows exactly who she is.

Karen.

Of all the people to hit, Ivy had to run right into the woman who arrested Wes.

Screwed. Ivy is completely screwed.

What she should do is call 911, just in case Karen is still

alive and can be saved. That would be the right thing to do. The human thing. As she picks up her phone, she remembers this is the same woman who tried to take Wes away from her. The one who ruined her wedding. Ruined her life.

Someone shouts. A neighbor rushes out of their house and runs toward Karen.

Ivy hits the gas, speeding away. The neighbors will call 911. Good thing, because she has to get the hell away from this accident.

And it *was* an accident. She never intended to hurt Karen or anyone else. It never would've happened if Milo hadn't shown up.

Why she ever thought beards were sexy is beyond her.

Ivy drives up to a house made of glass and concrete. Brand-new, in a subdivision called the Next Wave. She can't go home. Not after that accident. The police are probably still in front of her building in case Wes shows up. When they hear about Karen, they'll be waiting for her.

She pulls into a driveway alongside the house, hoping her car is obstructed by the huge trees, and runs up to the door. Ivy bangs on it once before it opens.

Heath.

'Ivy, what –'

'Are you here alone?' she says.

'Yes, I am.'

She pushes past him, into the house, down to his great room. The one with white furniture, and windows in place of walls. At least they all face the backyard.

Words explode out of her mouth, a jumbled version of what happened. What she has done. But she's not too rattled to edit out some of it, like the reason why she was going to talk to Karen.

'I just wanted to know what was happening. If they had any leads in finding –'

'Slow down,' Heath says.

'I can't slow down. They're going to be looking for me.' She paces around the room. Lots of space for that. 'I hit a cop. A *detective*.'

'But who were you trying to get away from?'

'This guy was harassing me, and I was trying to get away from *him*.' She doesn't go into the whole Milo thing. Doesn't matter now. 'I have to go. They're going to arrest me, and –'

'Stop. Just stop.' Heath takes her by the shoulders and leads her to the couch. She sits, and he's right beside her, holding her hand.

Deep breaths. After a couple of them, she nods at Heath. 'I'm okay.'

'So you hit Karen?' he says. 'The one that arrested Wes?'

'Yes.'

'And you left. Did anyone see you?'

'The neighbors were starting to come out, and I'm sure they saw my car. I don't know what happened to the guy I was running from. He was about a block away when I took off.'

'But as far as you know,' Heath says, 'this guy who was harassing you is the only one who knows you were driving that car.'

Heath's emphasis on the word *driving* gets her attention. 'That's true.'

'I think we have to consider the possibility that you didn't do this.'

'But I –'

'No. You didn't.'

He looks at her until she gets it. Heath is trying to give her an alternate story, one that doesn't include her.

'Who was driving?' she says.

'Isn't it obvious?' He smiles a little. 'Wes.'

'Wes? Why couldn't it be some random person who stole my car?'

'A random person who just happened to hit the detective that arrested him?'

Good point. The police won't believe anyone other than her or Wes was driving.

Ivy feels a bit dizzy, like her life is rotating in circles and this might be the biggest. Her *second* hit-and-run. Both were accidents, and the odds on this happening twice seem impossible, yet here she is.

Wes was arrested for the first one. Now, Heath is suggesting she blame the second on him, as well.

He's giving her a way out.

74

Bianca rushes to the kitchen, refills her glass with iced tea, nukes a slice of cake so it's gooey and soft, and runs back to the couch. She makes it just as the commercial break ends.

This running-around thing is new to her, but she's getting better at it. She usually watches streaming shows and can pause them at will, but she can't pause live breaking news. Nor does she want to. Bianca doesn't want to miss a single second of the manhunt for Wes Harmon.

It all started when Wes was arrested for Joey Fisher's death. Though Bianca knew there was a chance it could happen, it was still shocking. Now she can't get enough of the story.

But when Wes disappeared, she thought her head might implode.

Within a few hours, the local stations started covering it almost nonstop, and they still are. On one channel, a reporter is standing near Wes's house. Another has a helicopter in the air and is surveying his whole neighborhood.

Bianca rolls her eyes. Wes isn't stupid enough to stay in his own neighborhood.

But he may still be in town. If he tried to use a bus, train, or airplane, he would be caught on multiple cameras. On the other hand, he might have had help. No one on the news has mentioned Ivy, or any kind of girlfriend, but the police know about her. Karen certainly does. Ivy or one of his friends could have driven him out of town, to a bus or train station farther away. Or maybe just to hide somewhere.

So many possibilities. Bianca's head is spinning with them,

along with the caffeine and sugar she's been inhaling since yesterday.

She scans through the latest posts on Reddit. Manhunts are like an all-points bulletin for the true-crimers, and they don't disappoint. Someone is collecting a list of cameras in Fair Valley. Traffic cams mostly, since security cams aren't available to the general public, along with the public cameras from a nearby nature preserve. Just in case Wes happens to appear on one of them.

She flips back and forth between Reddit and watching the local news, constantly switching channels to keep up on all the stations. Each one has come up with their own name, starting with 'Hunt for a Killer.' Another calls it 'Search for Wes,' and a third has named it 'Fair Valley Manhunt.'

Still nothing interesting from the helicopter cam. No activity at Wes's house. A second helicopter flies over downtown Fair Valley. She takes a bite of her cake and goes back to Reddit. The site has actually been really helpful. Without it, she might not have found the date that picture of the 4Runner was taken.

Originally, she had gone to a photography subreddit to see if there was anything she was missing. Turns out there was. She learned about it after reading a conversation with someone named PhotoKid10.

Sucks that IG strips the data.

They all do, bro.

Bianca had no idea what they were talking about. She may be good at searching through emails, offices, and schedules, but she is not a techie. Unfortunately. It would've come in handy a number of times over the years.

She knew even less about photos or the data they were talking about, so she asked PhotoKid10. His answer came quick.

Exif data. IG strips it when you post a pic.

What about when you email a picture? she asked.

It's usually there, unless the photo has been edited.

That was all she needed. A quick Google search showed her how to find the data in a photo. So easy it was almost embarrassing. Good thing she didn't ask PhotoKid10 about that.

She looked up the data on the picture of Wes in the 4Runner. It had been taken on July 10, six days before Joey Fisher died. She also found the exact location of where the photo was taken, along with a bunch of technical data that didn't make any sense to her.

Bianca had included all of it in her email to Karen. It was the first time she had felt useful in a while.

Getting Abigail to help was the second time.

When she had been here, wearing that Creamsicle outfit, Bianca had opened her tablet and pulled up Abigail's IG page.

'You recently followed a new account. One that doesn't have any posts,' Bianca said.

Abigail's eyes widened.

'There isn't really a name on the account,' Bianca said. 'Just the initials "JTS."'

'What is this? What are you doing?'

Bianca didn't stop to answer the question, because that would've screwed her up. She had prepared exactly what she wanted to say to Abigail. A script. And she needed to follow it.

'The profile picture is a sunset,' Bianca said. 'So perfect it could almost be a stock photo. Like this person really doesn't want to be identified. But the thing is, when I did a search for that picture, it came up on another account as a post on their feed. Same picture, different account.' She held up her tablet for Abigail to see. 'Jeremy T. Scoggins. JTS.'

Abigail sat up a little straighter. 'I don't see why any of this is relevant.'

'And the thing about Jeremy T. Scoggins is . . .' Bianca said, scrolling through his public, real account. She stopped on a wedding picture and held it up. 'He's married.'

Abigail shrugged. 'So?'

'Would you mind if I contacted this guy's wife and asked about this other account?'

'Why would I mind?'

'On social media, these alternate accounts can be set up for a lot of reasons,' Bianca said. 'To spy on someone. To be incognito. Even celebrities have finstas. But this JTS account was set up by a married man. Sometimes they do that to communicate with someone through the DMs. Like when they're having an affair, they use DMs instead of texts so they can't be seen by the service provider for the phone.' Bianca pulled up the JTS account again and turned the tablet toward Abigail. 'This guy has one follower. And he only follows one account.'

Her heart was pounding, and she hoped Abigail couldn't tell. Bianca was experienced at snooping, but blackmail was new to her. She forced herself to do it for Joey.

Abigail looked from the tablet to Bianca, and she smiled. 'Nice work. And I get it. You want something, so you found something on me.' She paused, holding up one finger as she leaned forward. 'But here's the problem. That man, the one you discovered? He doesn't mean enough to me. I'm not going to protect him, and I don't care if you blow up his marriage.'

Of all the responses Bianca had prepared for, this wasn't one of them. She was sure – no, she was *positive* – that the man in Abigail's life was her weak spot. But not even close.

Her plan wasn't going to work. When Bianca realized this, she burst into tears.

Abigail touched her on the shoulder. 'Talk to me.'

Bianca did. She told her the whole story of Joey, from the time they met in high school to how he died. Including when the police stopped investigating his case.

'Wes,' Bianca said. 'That detective thinks Wes did it, but she doesn't have enough evidence to arrest him.'

'She's sure about this?'

Bianca nodded. It was Wes. Had to be.

Silence from Abigail. It went on for so long Bianca had no idea what to think. Maybe she was going to walk out. Maybe she would call the police and report her.

She didn't.

'Then let's get this bastard,' Abigail said.

75

Wes looks from the phone to Abigail, still not getting the connection with Bianca. The gun pointed at him is a little distracting. He isn't stupid, but his brain definitely isn't working at full capacity.

They stare at each other until Abigail sighs. 'You know, I stood up for you. At first, anyway. I called that detective and told her there was no way you would stalk anyone.'

'So what changed?'

Abigail nods toward the phone on the floor. 'Before you were arrested, Bianca called me.' She tilts her head to the side, looking at Wes. 'You didn't know her very well, did you?'

'If you're asking if I knew her the way I know you, no.'

'I'm not talking about sex.'

'No,' he says. 'I never really knew her.'

'She knew a lot about you,' Abigail says. 'Including that parking sticker in your desk.'

Parking sticker. He hasn't thought about that for a long time. Forgot he even had it.

He shouldn't have.

The sticker was for a garage downtown, the expensive kind that charged by the hour. Wes and Ivy didn't have the money for it, but Ivy had a friend who worked for the company. She gave Ivy a sticker, and they used it every time they needed a place to park downtown.

It was one of the only things Ivy kept from the 4Runner before pushing it into the lake.

Ivy didn't want to ask her friend for another sticker, so she kept the one they had and taped it onto their replacement car. The Saab. Eventually, it stopped sticking, which happened on a day Wes had the car. He put it in his pocket, then in his desk drawer, and never thought about it again.

Wes hears a click in his head as the pieces start to fall into place. The police have that sticker now. A hard thing to remove from a car that's been stolen.

But the picture isn't complete. Still a few blank spots.

'The sticker,' he says. 'How did she know it was important?'

'A picture of your car. The sticker was on it, and Bianca is the one who saw it.'

Of course. He hadn't even thought about the photos of their car. A perfect example of how and why criminals get caught. Very few can think of everything, himself included.

'That still doesn't explain why you lied,' he says.

'You thought I'd help you just because we've slept together?'

'You're answering a question with a question again.'

'Because of Joey,' she says. 'He was Bianca's boyfriend in high school.'

The news hits like a physical blow. Wes had no idea. This was all personal for Bianca, and she had brought Abigail into it.

The old saying is true: Hell hath no fury. Wes knows a little about that from Ivy.

'But why would you –'

'You think I'm going to help you get away with killing someone?' Abigail scoffs. 'I'm not your girlfriend, Wes. I'm just the one you slept with when you were waiting for Ivy to come back.'

'I didn't know about Joey and Bianca,' he says.

'I did. I also knew that parking sticker was in your desk. I even double-checked it was still there before the police arrived.'

'But why arc *you* helping her? That's what I don't under–'

'You don't need to understand,' Abigail says. 'Focus, Wes. Your concern should be the gun pointed at you.'

Wes has no idea what kind of deal Abigail and Bianca made, but she's right. He doesn't need the details. Whatever happened between them, it involved Abigail lying to the police.

'I may not know everything, but it's enough,' he finally says. 'I know you lied because of Bianca.'

She laughs at him. 'Like the police would believe you. Although you'll have plenty of time to try and convince them, because you won't be out on bail again.'

'You're going to turn me in?'

'Damn right I am.'

'Really? How are you going to call them?' Wes points down. Her phone is on the floor next to his foot.

'Kick it over to me,' she says. Her hand is still gripped around that gun, but it shakes a little.

It's his turn to smile. 'Come and get it.'

The more Heath talks, the more sense he makes. If Ivy wants to stay out of jail.

She does.

'Wes jumped bail,' he says. 'And if they do find him, he'll face more charges and he won't get bail a second time. You need to think about what's best for *you*.'

All true. Ivy knows this, and it's the only reason she's still sitting here. Still listening.

'Tell the police he came to you for help,' Heath says. 'And you refused.'

'I don't think they'll believe I turned him down.'

'You're right.' Heath squeezes her hand. 'Let me think for a second.'

Wes left without warning, not bothering to tell her what he was going to do or where he was going.

A betrayal.

Ivy has been avoiding that thought all day, hoping there was some other reason he did this. She wanted a sign from him, letting her know everything was okay. But there's been nothing. No note, no call, no text. Not even from his new number – the one the police don't have.

Heath is right. She doesn't have a lot of options now, and Wes is nowhere.

'Let's go through it in detail,' she says. 'I need to figure out exactly what I'm going to say.'

'Maybe Wes was acting crazy?' Heath says. 'Out of control, like he was on drugs. He scared you, so you wouldn't help and wouldn't give him any money.' Heath stands up, getting more and more into this story, gesturing wildly as he talks. 'He got angry, really angry, and he . . . maybe he restrained you? Tied you up, stole your money and your car?'

Ivy stares at Heath like he has lost his mind. 'Wes would never do that.'

'Doesn't matter. You have to sell this story.'

'I understand what you're saying about blaming Wes.' Ivy stands up, feeling a little shaky from the accident. And this conversation. 'But I can't tell the police he tied me up.'

'Ivy, are you forgetting that he *stalked* you? That you went to the police about it?'

Yes, she remembers. She also remembers that's what got them into this mess.

This is different. Heath is suggesting that she bury Wes in a hole so deep he'll never get out. 'I'm not saying he's on drugs or restrained me,' she says. 'He would never forgive me for that.'

'Who cares?' Heath rises up next to her, his body tight. 'Wake up, for God's sake. Wes is gone, and he *left you behind.*'

'Heath –'

'You owe him nothing.'

341

Yes. Yes, she does. Because he's already been arrested for something she did, and he kept his mouth shut. 'We have to think of something else.'

'But this will work.'

'Heath, I can't say these things –'

'No. I don't want to hear your excuses. I've heard enough of them.' He walks away from her. Now he's the one pacing. 'I can't believe you. I really can't. For *years*, he has screwed you over. Lied, manipulated, played games. Your relationship is so toxic you reek of it.'

'Stop yelling at me,' she says.

He comes over to her, placing his palm against her cheek. 'Ivy, this is your chance to get away from him once and for all.' His voice is softer, not a trace of anger. 'A fresh start.'

A fresh start sounds more than good. It sounds amazing. Ivy would love nothing more than to get away from what she's done in the past and what she did tonight. To live a life where none of it ever happened.

She can see it. Living in a different town, far away from Fair Valley, where everything is new. A place where she isn't haunted by Joey Fisher, doesn't think about him every time she drives at night. And nobody would know about Joey or Karen, or about Wes's arrest.

They could be happy. They could be free of their past. All of it. Maybe, just maybe, they would stop breaking up.

Ivy pictures building this life with new jobs and new friends. A new favorite restaurant, a better version of Maxwell's, to celebrate birthdays and anniversaries. She can even see what it looks like, what they would be eating. How much they would laugh.

As they sit in that imaginary restaurant, she smiles across the table at Wes.

He dissolves right in front of her.

Wes wouldn't be there.

If she does what Heath is telling her to do, she will destroy Wes's life. She will destroy *them*. No coming back from something like this.

That fresh start doesn't sound so good after all, because it would be without Wes.

Forever.

Bù kěnéng.

Impossible.

Which leaves her with one option: run.

She has to run the same way Wes did, because it won't be long before someone describes her car and the police will know she's the one who hit Karen.

Ivy rushes off – away from Heath and out of the room. She makes a last-minute decision as she goes. Instead of leaving out the front door, she grabs his car keys off the table in the foyer and heads into the garage. Behind her, Heath is yelling. Following.

'Don't do this,' he says. 'Please, Ivy. You're just going to make things worse.'

But he doesn't physically stop her. Doesn't put his hands on her. Heath watches her get into his car and back it out of the garage, maneuvering around her wrecked one. It hardly takes any work. She isn't used to such a smart vehicle.

Heath looks out from the garage, shaking his head at her. Visibly upset.

Visibly disappointed.

He doesn't understand. Never did.

Ivy heads straight home. The police will be looking for her car, not this one, and she only needs a few minutes to pick up anything she can sell for cash. Jewelry, mostly. She doesn't have a lot, but every little bit will help.

She drives behind the main building of her apartment complex, away from the main lot, and pulls up along the stucco walls separating the garden apartment patios. As she walks into the building, she notices the light in her living room is on.

It shouldn't be.

Maybe the police are already here. She almost leaves, but first she checks her door in the hallway. Closed and locked. Perhaps she left the light on.

Still, she opens the door slowly and looks straight down the hallway, into the living room. The sliding glass door to the patio is open. The metal frame on the wall is warped. She turns around to run when she hears him.

'Ivy.'

76

Wes.

His voice stops Ivy dead. Always.

She runs to the living room and finds him standing by the couch, his hand extended out to her.

'Hey, baby,' he says.

Ivy throws her arms around his neck. He slides an arm around her waist, pressing her body against his.

'You came to me,' she says.

'I always do.' He doesn't quite say the words; he breathes them. 'Even if the cops are after me.'

'What about wild horses? Could they drag you away?'

He smiles. She knows without seeing his face. 'Never,' he says.

Ivy feels her body relax for the first time since he disappeared. He is okay. *They* are okay.

Heath was wrong. So was she. Wes didn't betray her, and Ivy should've known that. Should've known better than to think it.

When they finally separate, she sees the blood.

It's all over the side of his shirt. There's so much she can't tell where it's coming from. Ivy reaches out to find the wound.

He nods to his arm, the one that isn't around her. A towel is tied around his bicep, the blood seeping through it. 'I got shot.'

'*Shot?*'

Wes nods. Grimaces a little as he sits down. Her first aid

kit is on the coffee table along with a bottle of Advil. 'It's not that bad.'

'We have to go to the hospital,' she says. 'Now. Let me help you up.'

'I'm fine. It looks worse than it is.'

'You need a doctor.'

'I'm not going,' he says. 'They'll put me back in jail, and I'll never get out.'

'But –'

'But nothing. I'm not going back.'

She slumps on the couch next to him, her mind in overdrive. She doesn't know anything about gunshot wounds, but this amount of blood can't be good.

Ivy removes the towel from his arm and pushes up his sleeve. It looks bad, but not as bad as she feared. The bullet ripped open the skin a couple inches below his shoulder, but there's no hole. No bullet inside him. She grabs the bottle of antiseptic and starts to clean it.

'Did the police shoot you?' she says.

'Abigail.'

She shakes her head, like she's trying to make the pieces fit. 'I don't understand.'

'Abigail is the witness. She said she heard us argue about the accident.'

'Why would she do that?'

'Long story.'

Now it clicks. Abigail really was the voice on his phone. Not that it matters right now.

'How did you get here?' she asks.

'I took her car.'

Ivy covers the wound in antibiotic cream, places a pad on it, and wraps the whole thing with gauze. As she finishes, his phone pings.

'They're going to come soon,' he says, using his left hand to open the screen. 'Only a matter of time before they find her. Someone must've heard the shot.'

'Find her? What did you –'

'I think she's alive, but I don't know. I hit her with a bat.'

'Jesus Christ.'

Wes furrows his brow, staring at the phone screen. He turns it toward her. A tweet from the Fair Valley Police Department.

Breaking:

Hit-and-run on Nightingale Lane. Police are searching for a dark blue or black two-door coupe. Partial license plate 157.

'Those numbers are on your license plate,' he says.

She nods. 'I had a little trouble tonight myself.'

'You thought we needed another hit-and-run?'

'It was an accident. I didn't mean for it to happen.' And she hadn't. Everything had unfolded so fast it was like she couldn't keep up. 'I went to Heath's, but he was talking crazy, and then I just left. I have his car.'

'Heath talking crazy? You don't say.'

Wes doesn't know the half of it, but now is not the time. 'The police are looking for you,' she says. 'For both of us. They could be watching right now.'

'I know. We have to go.'

'But –'

'If we both go to prison for what we did tonight, we'll never see each other again,' he says. 'Never.'

He's right. They would be like her parents, in prison and unable to contact each other.

Even when Wes wasn't there, he was *there*; she always had the option of seeing him. But now she thinks about not having that. For years. Maybe forever.

The idea makes her heart hurt in a way she didn't know was possible. For once, Ivy does not feel the urge to argue with him.

'Okay,' she says.

'Pack light. No phone, no electronics,' he says. 'Bring your bank card.'

Ivy goes to her bedroom and stands in front of her closet, frozen. She doesn't know where to start. For the first time ever, she wishes she had listened to the doomsday preppers and made a bug-out bag.

No time for regret. No time for anything. Ivy grabs her backpack and shoves some clothes in it. Underwear, T-shirts, leggings. A sweater and a down vest, because she has no idea where they'll end up. For toiletries, the barest of essentials. Only the things she truly can't live without.

It takes her less than five minutes to gather it all up. The rest will have to stay, including things that are sentimental. Framed photos, notes, and gifts that Wes has given her over the years. She can't fit any of it.

'Come on,' Wes says.

She walks out of the bedroom, leaving it all behind. Wes is waiting for her, wearing a baseball cap, a fresh shirt, and a backpack slung over his good arm. He still hasn't shaved. Wes barely resembles the photograph they keep showing on the news.

'I hope you have a plan,' she says.

He leans over to kiss her, slow and deep enough to make her head spin.

'I always have a plan,' he says. 'First, I need a screwdriver.'

77

Twenty minutes. That was all Wes needed.

Heath's car was not an option. It's a Tesla, brand-new and easily trackable. Heath was probably staring at his phone, watching everywhere it went.

They had to use Abigail's Toyota. Wes took a license plate off an old Honda parked behind Ivy's apartment building and switched it out to buy a little extra time. Enough to stop at an ATM, where Ivy withdrew as much money as she could.

The police would find out – they would see the transaction and they would see Ivy on the security camera – but by then they would be long gone. He hoped.

'Now throw the card out,' he told her.

She looked confused for a second, then understood. She can't use her bank card again. Ever. Ivy threw it into the trash can on the sidewalk.

From the bank, he drove straight to the mall parking lot. But instead of pulling in, he went around the block to leave Abigail's car somewhere else. Not where they would actually be. A calculated risk, because it meant walking a couple of blocks, but he didn't want to risk the police figuring out how they left town. At least, not right away.

His mind continued to spin, searching for anything he might have forgotten. Like that parking sticker. There's always something, a tiny thing that could lead police right to them. Luckily, they have no idea where they're going.

Wes told her they need to start using fake names. 'The guy we're riding with doesn't know who I am. We can't tell him.'

'Adam and Eve,' she said.

'No.'

'Romeo and Juliet?'

'They committed suicide.'

'John and Yoko,' she said.

'Stop. I had to make a fake profile for the app. This guy already thinks my name is Mark.'

'Mark? Of all the names in the world, you picked *Mark*?'

He shrugged.

'Then I have to be Cleo,' she said.

'Why do you –'

'Mark Antony and Cleopatra.'

He didn't tell her that they also committed suicide.

They walked around a corner, dodging to avoid street-lights. The empty shell of Rolling Hills Mall loomed in front of them. Before heading into the parking lot, he stopped her.

'Are you sure about this?'

'I'm sure,' she said.

'Because this isn't a game. We'll be on the run for the rest of our lives.'

'Are you always going to be annoying and frustrating?' she asked.

'Of course. So will you.'

She touched him on the nose with the tip of her finger. 'I love you.'

'I love you more.' He kissed her on the forehead. 'Just don't hit me with a car.'

Their ride was waiting for them in the parking lot. The van was painted on the outside to look like a house. Clever. A little conspicuous, but still clever. The driver looked exactly like the picture on his profile: young, a little scruffy, a little stoned.

Now Wes is in the back of the van, nestled within the small living space, while Ivy sits in the front with their driver. He has traveled all over the world and speaks a little bit of everything. So does Ivy. They talk in broken words and sentences in a variety of languages.

Wes doesn't understand any of it. He watches the road as they drive due east, straight out of California.

Who knows how long they'll last out here, on the run. No real names, no Social Security numbers, nothing except a bit of money and whatever is in their backpacks. A couple of weeks, maybe a month. If they can make it that long, everything will start to settle down and the police will move on to other crimes. Maybe then he'll be able to contact his sister. Stella may hate Ivy, but she loves her brother.

But that won't even be an option unless they get very, very lucky. A long road between now and then.

Wes forces himself to stay awake, fighting the urge to close his eyes. Eventually, Ivy exhausts herself and her knowledge of foreign languages. She crawls into the back of the van and curls up next to him on the couch-slash-bed.

'How's your arm?' she says. 'Are you in pain?'

'This whole van smells like weed. I don't feel much of anything.'

She sighs. 'We're going to make it. I can feel it.'

Make it where? He doesn't ask, doesn't know. He's too busy thinking of all the other ways this could have gone.

Wes leans in close and whispers in her ear. 'I wish you hadn't done it.'

'Done what?'

'Called the police.'

'I wish you hadn't stalked me,' she whispers.

He sits up a little, jostling her with the sudden movement. 'What did you say?'

'You shouldn't have stalked me,' she says, still keeping her voice low. 'Sent me those photos and the truffles. Jesus, those damn truffles.'

'But I didn't.'

She frowns. 'You did. That's how I knew it was you.'

'Ivy,' he says, 'I never stalked you. I never sent you any of those things.'

'Of course you did.'

'I thought you had done it. Faked it.'

She shakes her head. 'No.'

'Then who?' he says.

Even as he asks, he knows the answer.

Epilogue

Six Months Later

MILO: Welcome to episode 127 of the *Broken Men* podcast. I'm Milo, and I'm here with my cohosts and two of the best guys ever, Brock and Diego. We have a very special guest with us today. But before we get to him, let's talk about Wes Harmon and Ivy Banks. I know everybody remembers them.

BROCK: Hard to forget. How many people died? Was it two or three?

DIEGO: Two. Joey Fisher and that woman from Siphon. Abigail. Plus the detective who ended up in the hospital.

MILO: Karen. She lived, though. That was right before they disappeared.

BROCK: Wes and Ivy are like our own Bonnie and Clyde.

DIEGO: Except they didn't rob banks or gas stations.

BROCK: That we know of.

MILO: Indeed. I suspect there's a lot we don't know about Wes and Ivy. Which brings us to our guest. Heath, welcome to the show.

HEATH: Thanks for having me.

MILO: I first saw Heath interviewed on a local news show after everything went down. Heath was a friend of Ivy's, so I reached out and eventually convinced him to join us on the podcast. Heath, thanks so much for doing this.

HEATH: No problem.

MILO: Full disclosure here. A while back, I met Ivy Banks in a bar and we had a drink together. Let's just say I wasn't too happy when she posted a picture of us online. It caused a huge problem with my fiancée.

BROCK: You mean your ex-fiancée.

HEATH: I actually remember that night, when Ivy met you at the bar. That's the kind of thing Wes and Ivy did all the time. Always trying to provoke each other.

MILO: Believe me, I know that better than anyone. But we're not here to talk about me, at least not today. Now, you've known Ivy since you were kids. Is that right?

HEATH: Yes, we were neighbors and grew up together.

MILO: Since you knew her so well, do you have any idea where they are?

HEATH: No, not at all. The police asked me the same question, but I really don't know. She and I are both from Humboldt County and Wes is from Michigan, but I can't imagine they went to either of those places. They would've been found by now.

BROCK: And you haven't heard from her at all?

HEATH: Not a word.

MILO: She came to you that night, didn't she? When she ran her car into the detective?

HEATH: She did, and she was a mess. Seriously out of her mind. I told her she had to go to the police, even loaned her my car. I had no idea she was going to disappear. But I probably should've guessed, because she didn't want me to go with her to the police station. I trusted she would do the right thing.

MILO: At least she left your car behind, right?

HEATH: Yes, I got my car back.

MILO: Let's go back to your relationship with her. What was it like growing up with Ivy?

HEATH: She was definitely the closest friend I had, but everything changed when she met Wes.

DIEGO: When was that?

HEATH: In college, when she was at UC Davis. I met him when she brought Wes home for Thanksgiving. They were seniors, if I remember correctly. He came with Ivy for the holiday because he was too broke to fly home to Michigan.

Anyway, they were pretty nauseating at that point. All smiles all the time. Wes was polite to her parents, even offered to help wash the dishes or take out the trash. He seemed nice, but appearances can be deceiving, can't they?

MILO: They sure can. Ivy definitely had me fooled.

HEATH: That's the thing. The truth is, I didn't even know Wes. I knew Ivy, and I knew she didn't act the same when she was around Wes. On the Friday after Thanksgiving, I joined her family for dinner. What I saw stunned me.

DIEGO: You have to elaborate on that.

HEATH: It was the way Ivy tried to take care of Wes. Making sure his glass was filled or asking if he needed another roll or whatever . . . It disturbed me. I was sitting there thinking, 'Really?' She would sooner punch me in the arm than refill any glass I ever had. Wes showed up, and all of a sudden, she became June Cleaver.

MILO: That doesn't sound good.

BROCK: I can't lie. A girl who acts like June Cleaver isn't entirely bad.

HEATH: It wasn't good for Ivy. I didn't know what he was doing to her, but she wasn't the person I had grown up with. She wasn't *my* Ivy.

BROCK: Sounds like you were kind of into her.

HEATH: Not at all. She was like a sister to me.

DIEGO: Sure she was.

MILO: So did you do anything? Did you talk to her about it?

HEATH: Not during Thanksgiving, I didn't talk to her. But, yeah, I did accidentally spill a glass of red wine in Wes's lap. And I took his phone for an hour or so, making him search all over until I dropped it behind a cushion on the couch. But I didn't interfere in their relationship or anything. Because at that point, Ivy was still in college. I figured, how long could it possibly last? Another month? Nope. Ten years.

BROCK: *Long* time, bro.

MILO: So is it safe to say you were never a Wes fan?

HEATH: We were never friends. Probably because I kept trying to get her away from him.

MILO: Tell us about that. What kinds of things did you do?

HEATH: I tried to get her into therapy. I thought maybe she needed to hear it from someone else. A professional. Someone who could tell her she deserved better and this thing she had with Wes was not love. It was everything love shouldn't be. I believed that. I really did.

BROCK: That's it? Therapy?

DIEGO: I feel like we aren't getting the whole story here.

HEATH: Um . . . I definitely did some things I shouldn't have. Like, not too long ago I was supposed to be out of town, but I came back and sent some things to . . . Well, the details don't really matter, but I did some things that were a little crazy. She wanted to get back together with him, and I just . . . I couldn't believe it. After everything, she still wanted him.

I guess what I'm trying to say is that I interfered in their relationship far more than I had a right to. But it was coming from a good place, because I cared about Ivy. I didn't want to see her in a relationship like that.

DIEGO: But it didn't work.

HEATH: Not at all.

MILO: I'm not sure I'm buying that brother-sister thing. Sounds like you were a little bit in love with her.

HEATH: I don't know. Maybe I had a crush on her.

DIEGO: Just a crush?

HEATH: I genuinely believed she was in a bad situation. And I wanted to get her out of it. To me, everything about their relationship was wrong. It was obsession, lust, addiction . . . whatever you want to call it. But not love. Wes and Ivy were like a human tornado that destroyed everything in its path.

BROCK: That's actually pretty deep.

HEATH: The thing is, I was the one who was wrong. I actually understand them a lot better now.

MILO: Why is that?

HEATH: I met someone.

DIEGO: Uh-oh.

HEATH: Yeah. And it made me realize a few things.

MILO: Such as?

HEATH: Whatever I might've felt for Ivy, I know it wasn't love. Not *real* love, because I had no idea what that was. Now I do.

MILO: Wow, that's huge. Tell us about her.

HEATH: Her name is Bianca, and she's like . . . Okay, wait. First, I never would've met Bianca if it wasn't for Ivy and Wes. She saw the same interview you did, the one on the local news, and she contacted me on social media to ask a question.

BROCK: What do girls call that? Serendipity or something?

DIEGO: Luck. It's called luck.

MILO: So what happened? You started seeing her and fell in love?

HEATH: Basically, yeah. Bianca knew Wes, I knew Ivy, and it turned out we had a lot to talk about. Given everything that happened, neither of us were in a good place and we had a natural bond or something. I know this sounds weird, but my life has been a lot better without Ivy in it.

MILO: Funny how that happens.

HEATH: I know, right? It's impossible to describe how it feels, like words just aren't enough. Ivy used to say that all the time about Wes.

DIEGO: You're comparing your relationship to Wes and Ivy's?

HEATH: To be clear, Bianca and I aren't anything like Wes and Ivy. Neither one of us is that dramatic. Our relationship is based on respect and trust, which Wes and Ivy never really had. At the same time, I've realized it wasn't my place to judge. Everybody has to choose what's right for them.

MILO: So you've changed your opinion about Wes and Ivy?

HEATH: They were, and probably still are, one hundred percent in love. I have no doubt that they're somewhere out there, breaking up and getting back together ten times a day. And I bet if you could talk to them, they'd say they're happy.

MILO: But is that healthy? Or is it toxic?

HEATH: I don't know. I don't even know what *toxic* means at this point, that word is so overused. But who does know? And who can judge something like that, because who's really in a 'functional' relationship? Honestly, do you know anyone who is?

MILO: No.

BROCK: Definitely no.

DIEGO: Not a hundred percent functional, no.

HEATH: Exactly.

MILO: So is that what you've learned? That no one is in a functional relationship, and we're all just screwed up and screwing everyone else up?

HEATH: It's bigger than that. You know how they say love makes the world go round? That's not quite right. Love *runs* the world.

MILO: It doesn't care who you are, either. When love comes for you, you're done.

BROCK: Like the grim reaper?

DIEGO: More like a psychopath.

HEATH: Doesn't matter what you call it, the result is the same: Love always wins.

Acknowledgments

So many people to thank for making this book happen, starting with my agent, Barbara Poelle, and my editor, Jen Monroe. They let me throw out the terrible book I wrote during the early days of the pandemic and I wrote this one instead (which hopefully is not terrible).

Many thanks to the whole team at Berkley, including Lauren Burnstein, Dache' Rogers, Jessica Mangicaro, Jin Yu, Jeanne-Marie Hudson, Craig Burke, Candice Coote, Tawanna Sullivan, Emily Osborne, and so many more. I appreciate everything that you do.

A special thanks to my incredible copyeditor, Elizabeth Johnson, who keeps me on point.

Much gratitude to my UK publishing team at Michael Joseph, including Joel Richardson, Grace Long, and the whole team across the pond for doing such a wonderful job.

To Sean Berard, my film and TV manager out in Hollywood, thank you for all you've done.

I am eternally grateful to so many booksellers and indie bookstores. Thank you for all of your amazing support, with a special mention to Pamela Klinger-Horn, Mary O'Malley, Elizabeth Ahlquist of Blue Cypress Books; Barbara Peters of The Poisoned Pen Bookstore, Maxwell Gregory, and McKenna Jordan of Murder By The Book, along with The Novel Neighbor, An Unlikely Story, Mystery Lovers Bookshop, Magic City Books, and so many more.

Two very special people have to be mentioned here. They had the winning bids at two separate auctions benefiting nonprofit organizations, and they won the chance to name a character in this book. I won't name them here to protect their privacy. The names they gave me appear in *A Twisted Love Story*, though the characters do not represent anyone real and are completely fictional. Thank you both for bidding in these auctions!

Many, many people contribute to promoting a book, including the bloggers, Bookstagrammers, TikTokkers, and all the readers who recommend books to others. You are simply the best. A lot of authors, including myself, need you. Never forget it; I certainly don't!

I have had the pleasure of attending many book club meetings over the past few years. The list is long and I can't name them all here, but I am grateful you chose one of my books to read and it was a pleasure to meet you all!

Many authors are so gracious with their time and read an early copy of this book, including Christina Lauren, Sylvia Day, Jeneva Rose, Jaime Lynn Hendricks, Hannah Mary McKinnon, and Hank Phillippi Ryan. Hope to meet all of you in person one day! And a huge thanks to all the authors who help make the thriller community so supportive.

To my friends, family, and critique partners . . . thank you for putting up with me when I'm in the middle of writing a book. And when I'm not.

Last but never least, thank you to everyone who has read any of my books. I appreciate it more than you could ever know.